TRISTA ANN MICHAELS

ELLORA'S CAVE
ROMANTICA PUBLISHING

Star Crossed

When a sudden twist of fate has Krista on the run with the arrogant and insufferable Galactic Senator Stefan Marcone, she'll need all her willpower to not give in to the seduction of the charming rake. She's had enough of men like him. But sometimes you have to just forget the past and take advantage of what's right in front of you, right now.

Stefan hasn't stopped thinking about Krista since the day she dumped a bowl of punch over his head. Okay, maybe the kiss had been a little forward, but he hadn't been able to stop himself. Just like he knew he wouldn't be able to keep his promise to his sister-in-law and not seduce the beautiful blonde. Especially when they are forced to go into hiding together.

The two will travel the galaxy, staying one step ahead of the man determined to see Stefan pay for his involvement with the rebel forces that brought down the previous dictator. Until the day Stefan decides he's had enough. He'll use himself as bait to catch the assassin. But it's not Stefan the assassin's after anymore. It's Krista.

Crossing the Line

Alyssa came to Veenori in search of the man who killed her brother. It was the perfect plan—or so she thought. Then she finds herself being sold as a slinoy, a sex slave, and bought by one very gorgeous overseer to the very mine she'd been trying to infiltrate.

Taron didn't want the undercover assignment, nor did he want a slinoy. But the second he saw those gray eyes, he knew he didn't have a choice. The woman his brothers had been searching for had slipped through their fingers and fallen right into his lap. He'd promised her brother he'd find her and keep her safe, but resisting the temptation of her passionate nature would be damn difficult—and not losing his heart even more so.

Unfortunately, before they can find a future together, they will first have to survive the present and the man bent on seeing both of them dead.

An Ellora's Cave Romantica Publication

www.ellorascave.com

Entwined Fates

ISBN 9781419957376

Edited by Ann Leveille.
Cover art by Syneca.

This book printed in the U.S.A. by Jasmine-Jade Enterprises, LLC.

Trade paperback Publication March 2008

Also by Trista Ann Michaels

Callie's Sexy Surprise
Fantasy Bar
Fantasy Resort
Holiday Love Lessons

About the Author

ᘎ

Trista penned her first ghost story at the age of eight. She still has a love of ghosts, but her taste and writing style have leaned more to the sultry side. She started writing erotic romance two years ago, and with the help of her critique partners was soon published. She's been running full steam ever since.

Raised an Air Force brat, Trista surprised her family by marrying a Navy man. But just as she knew he would, her husband won them over despite his military choice. Together they've had three children, and she attributes their successful marriage to the fact he's away flying a lot. Separation does make the heart grow fonder. After all, if he's not here, she can't kill him.

All joking aside, her family and writing partners are her biggest form of support and encouragement. Trista's a big believer in happily ever after and although she may put her characters through hell getting there, they will always achieve that goal.

Trista welcomes comments from readers. You can find her website and email address on her author bio page at www.ellorascave.com.

Tell Us What You Think

We appreciate hearing reader opinions about our books. You can email us at Comments@EllorasCave.com.

ENTWINED FATES

Trista Ann Michaels

༄

STAR CROSSED

Prologue

Daego, Legana Sector of the galaxy
Present Day

ꙮ

"I now pronounce you man and wife, Lord and Lady Marcone."

Stefan stood back, admiring the newlyweds. His brother Sidious had married the love of his life, Mikayla. They were perfect for each other, and he was thrilled Sidious had found the same kind of love their parents shared—the kind of love that lasted forever.

He'd given up on finding that kind of love. For one, he didn't have the time to put into the search, and two, women were usually only after his money and status anyway. So he just had fun—no-strings sex and lots of it.

Letting his gaze wander around the onslaught of well-wishing family and friends, he locked eyes with Mikayla's maid of honor, Krista. They hadn't been introduced, but his mother had pointed her out to him earlier. He'd barely made the ceremony, and his mother made sure he knew she was aware of it. So sneaking in through the side entrance to the garden hadn't been all that great of an idea after all.

Mothers. Always on your ass about something.

Throughout the wedding, he couldn't stop sneaking glances at Krista. She was beautiful, with eyes the color of a spring sky—so striking and intense. When he smiled at her a blush covered her cheeks before she looked away. The sunlight beamed down and highlighted the gold streaks in her long honey-blonde hair. The strands teased him with soft curls he could easily see wrapping around his fingers, and he had no doubt they would be soft as silk.

She strolled across the garden to the refreshment table and he swallowed, his eyes mesmerized by the soft swaying of her hips. Her blue dress mirrored her eyes and draped over every last luscious curve of her hourglass figure. Curves his hands craved to touch and explore.

She's your sister-in-law's best friend, you idiot, the voice of reason screamed at him. *Mikayla considers her a member of the family.* Yet his feet and hardening cock urged him forward. It had been a long time since a woman had affected him this quickly and this strongly. He'd be a *vigic* if he didn't at least explore the possibility.

Standing behind her right shoulder, he leaned forward slightly and whispered, "I don't believe we've been formally introduced."

She jumped and spun from her perusal of the refreshment table to face him. Her blue eyes narrowed and darkened like impending storm clouds. "I know who you are."

He raised an eyebrow in amusement. "You say that like it's a bad thing."

"Let's just say your reputation precedes you."

"I have a reputation?" A grin tugged at the corner of his lips.

"Several."

"Such as?"

"Your reputation as a leader and fighter is flawless. We've all heard the stories concerning your organization of the rebels. Your reputation with the ladies, however, leaves much to be desired."

"Wow." He sighed in mock distress. "I don't recall ever hearing any complaints."

He wiggled his eyebrows, but frowned when she turned away from him. Her animosity surprised him, and he wondered what was behind it. He knew he had a reputation as a lady's man, but was that a reason for her to hate him?

Reaching out, he brushed her hair from her shoulder. "How about we start over? I'm Stefan—"

"Yes, I know. Count Stefan Marcone, recently appointed Senator for Tilarus in the newly formed Senatorial Government. And of course let's not forget, all-around playboy and womanizer."

"Ouch." He winced.

Setting a sweetball on her plate, she turned to face him. Her gaze met his as she placed her finger in her mouth to suck off a bit of powdered sugar from the confection. The action, seemingly innocent, shocked him. Damn, he wanted to kiss those lips, to slide his tongue into her mouth and taste the sugar she'd just licked off her finger. Without thinking, he took a step toward her.

A scowl crossed her china-doll features as she retreated.

"I think I'm being judged a little unfairly." He moved even closer. "After all, we've never met before. Don't you think you're making a lot of assumptions?"

For some reason he couldn't stop himself from invading her space, from pushing buttons he had no business pushing. There was something about her that drew him in, made him think with his crotch instead of his head. That was a first for him. He loved seducing women and he was good at it, but one thing he never did was lose control of his common sense. He'd never met a woman that made him addle-brained. Until now.

She swallowed, placing her hand against his chest to stop him from getting any closer. The warmth of her palm seeped through his shirt and sent jolts of electrical sensation throughout his limbs.

"I'm not judging you. I'm just stating a fact."

Her voice came out like a croak, and he had to bite back a grin.

"Then shouldn't I be entitled to an opportunity to prove those facts false?"

"At the moment, you're proving them true."

This time he did smile. "Then you won't be surprised when I do this."

Before she could utter a word, he dipped his head and captured her lips. They were soft and warm against his, sending liquid heat straight to his cock. Framing her face with his hands, he ran his tongue along her bottom lip and she stiffened. He tasted powdered sugar and fruit punch, but it wasn't enough. He wanted to feel her silken tongue gliding against his, to feast on the essence of her mouth. He silently encouraged her to open for him.

With a soft moan, she melted against his chest and opened her lips in silent invitation. He slid his tongue inside and stroked hers. He was lost. Audience or not, he couldn't stop kissing her—couldn't stop feeding from the sweetness of her mouth. Sliding a hand into her hair, he pulled her closer, deepening the kiss. With his lips and tongue, he let her know exactly what he wanted to do with her.

He completely forgot about the other guests. He could only feel her lips molded against his, her dainty hands gripping his shoulders. At least until he heard Sidious clearing his throat behind him. Reluctantly, he broke the kiss and growled, "What?"

"What the hell are you doing?" Mikayla hissed.

Stefan glanced over his shoulder and caught his new sister-in-law shooting daggers in his direction. For someone so little, she had a temper to rival his younger brother's, or his own.

"I was just acquainting myself with the newest member of the family."

Mikayla crossed her arms and glared at him while Sidious tried his best to hide a grin. Okay, so maybe the kiss had been a little forward, but for some reason he'd just had to. He couldn't have left without kissing her at least once. Other family members stood around watching, the smiles on their faces evidence of the fact they found the whole thing amusing. A few scowls sent their way quickly dispersed the crowd.

"Stefan," Krista's soft, sultry voice purred behind him.

He turned around to face her and was greeted with a punch bowl being dumped on his head. Lavender punch fell over his shoulders and down the front of his shirt. He gasped as the ice-cold punch hit his skin. In shock, he watched Krista stomp away as laughter rang around him.

"Oh dear," his mother sighed in annoyance, and he cringed at what he knew she would have to say to him later.

"She's my best friend, Stefan, not one of your playthings." Mikayla pointed her finger at his chest. "If you run her off with your antics, I'll have your head."

He stared after Mikayla as she joined Krista by the fountain. His brother chuckled, and Stefan clenched his teeth in aggravation. Turning, he glared at him. "It's not funny, Sidious."

"Considering your platinum blond hair is now purple, it's hilarious."

"Nice of you to stand up for me, little brother."

Sidious snorted. "You're well capable of taking care of yourself. Isn't that what you continually insist, anyway? Besides, I have to agree with Mikayla on this one. What the hell were you thinking? You can't treat Krista like a challenge."

Stefan winced. "You're right. But damn, the woman is gorgeous."

His brother shook his head and patted him on the shoulder. "You'll never change."

He made a face at Sidious' retreating back before casting his gaze back to Krista. She caught him looking at her and scowled. Even when she was ready to kill him, she was adorable. His mischievous side couldn't resist, and he winked at her before heading to the house.

So she wasn't interested. There were plenty out there who would be, lavender hair and all, but as he walked up the steps to the veranda a slight pang of disappointment hit him. At the top, he came to a stop and turned toward the garden to study her. She stood beneath the rose trellis, talking to Mikayla, a smile lighting up her face.

What was it about her? He could still feel her lips against his, could still smell her flowery scent.

"I'll be damned if that's not a first," Taron's amused voice sounded behind him.

Great. Just what I need. The adopted brother's smart-ass humor. "What are you talking about?"

"A beautiful woman not succumbing to your charms."

Stefan rolled his eyes. He would never hear the end of this one. "It's for the best. Mikayla considers her a sister. She would have a fit if I seduced her then dumped her."

"True." Taron's dark brown eyes raked over Krista in interest. "She is definitely a beautiful woman."

Stefan frowned. "Mikayla is not going to let you do it, either."

"Who said I was going to?" The amusement in Taron's eyes made Stefan grit his teeth.

"I'm going to take a shower."

"Might want to make it a cold one."

Laughter laced Taron's voice, and Stefan clenched his hands in frustration. He was tempted to knock the hell out of him, brother or not.

"Go to Venok, Taron."

Stefan stepped through the double doors into the house. He didn't have time for this. He had a Senate to rebuild. The last thing he needed was a stubborn, opinionated, sassy woman to distract him.

But damn. The woman would be one hell of a distraction.

* * * * *

"Are you okay?"

Krista turned to look at her best friend. Mikayla's green eyes narrowed slightly in concern as she studied her. She hated it when Mikayla watched her like that—as though she could read every thought running through her mind.

"I'm fine," she answered with a hesitant smile.

"Fine, my ass. I still can't believe he did that."

Krista couldn't believe he'd done it either. Especially in front of all these people, but then, it fit what she'd heard about him. Stefan was the last type of man she wanted in her life. Her friend's lips lifted slightly and Krista squirmed uncomfortably. "What?"

"I can't believe you kissed him back."

She closed her eyes and sighed. "Neither can I. I can't figure out what the hell got into me."

Mikayla grinned in amusement. "You want me to tell you what I think?"

"Not really."

"Don't let what Stefan did unsettle you." Mikayla reached out and rubbed her hand down Krista's arm in a soothing motion. "He's harmless, I assure you."

"All I've heard about him is how much a playboy he is."

"You can't always believe what the news media on Earth have to say. They were only going on what people knew of him, and most of what he did was for show."

She frowned. "Show for what?"

"Stefan played the philandering, partying womanizer to take the focus off what he was really doing."

Out of the corner of her eye Krista caught sight of Stefan on the veranda steps, talking with Taron. Both of them were incredibly handsome. Taron was dark and brooding with brown eyes and a bald head. Very hard and unyielding. Stefan was light and playful with long platinum hair and light gray eyes. A breeze blew, whipping Stefan's hair into his face, and he brushed it back with one strong hand.

She still felt the touch of those fingers against her cheek. And damn, the man could kiss. Just thinking about it made her nipples tingle. She crossed her arms over her chest to hide the evidence of her arousal. When Stefan headed into the house, she turned back to Mikayla.

"Let's talk about something else," she mumbled.

"Okay. Are you sure you don't want to stay on here?"

"And feel like a third wheel?" Krista grinned. "No way. Besides, I want to start my life over, and I think the job Sidious set up for me back on Earth will be the perfect opportunity. It'll be the first time in my life I've been on my own, and I'm looking forward to it."

"I'll miss you, though. You'll be so far away."

"We have the communicators. We'll keep in touch, and I promise to come back for visits as often as I can."

Mikayla pointed a finger at her. "I'm going to hold you to that."

"Krista." Taron's deep voice boomed from the veranda, and she spun to face him.

Raising her hand, she shielded her eyes from the late afternoon sun. "Yes?"

"We need to get going."

She nodded and faced her best friend. "Taron's giving me a ride back to Earth so I don't have to take the public transport. He thought it would be quicker."

Mikayla nodded, her eyes filling with unshed tears. "It'll definitely be quicker."

They embraced in a quick hug. "I'll send you a communique to let you know I've made it back safely."

Wiping at the burn that signaled oncoming tears, Krista headed into the massive stone house that resembled a French château to grab her bags. She hated space travel, but at least they would be in Taron's ship. The *Vultair* was huge, and she could stay in a room toward the center. With no windows there would be no evidence that they were moving, which was perfect with her. She could pretend they weren't flying through deep space at twice the speed of light.

With a bag in each hand, she rounded the corner of the second-floor landing and almost ran smack into Stefan. Her gaze took in his open shirt, showing off a smooth tan chest and washboard abs. His feet were bare and his pants clung to his thick thighs and outlined the impressive bulge between his legs. Her fingers clenched the suitcase handle tighter as she realized just how long it had been since she'd been with a man.

Way too long.

"Leaving us already?"

Her gaze locked with his and the heat of a blush moved up her cheeks. She could tell by the mischievous glint in his eyes he knew exactly what she'd been staring at. He watched her in silence while he rubbed at his wet hair with a towel.

She swallowed. "I need to get back to Earth. Taron's giving me a ride."

"Taron's an excellent pilot. You'll be in good hands."

She nodded and licked at her lips. All she could seem to think about was how his mouth had felt on hers.

"I'm sorry about earlier," he said softly.

"No you're not."

A tiny smile lifted the corner of his lips and her breath caught in her throat. How could any one man be so gorgeous? Normally she wasn't attracted to men with long hair, but his gave him a sexy look and his storm cloud gray eyes held her mesmerized, making her wish for things she never even knew she wanted. Like this man having his way with her.

That would be such a stupid thing to do. What if things went badly? She would feel too uncomfortable to come back and see her friend for fear of running into Stefan again.

Mikayla was all she had left and much more important than a fling.

"You're right. I'm not." He lowered the towel and stepped closer. She smelled the slight scent of musk and the soap he'd used. With determination, she resisted the urge to inhale deeper. "Come on, Kris. Admit it. You enjoyed it just as much as I did."

She tilted her head and scowled up at him. "You're an arrogant ass, do you know that? And my name is Krista."

"What's wrong with Kris?"

Only her mother had called her Kris. "I don't like it."

"All the more reason to use it. I like it when you're angry. Your eyes get darker and flash fire." He smiled, the gray in his eyes darkening. "It makes for quite a picture."

Krista rolled her eyes at his gall. "Why don't we both do ourselves a favor and steer clear of each other."

"But sweetheart, we're family," Stefan reasoned, the playful glint still evident in his gaze. The man was going to drive her crazy. She would do well to avoid him.

"You don't kiss family in front of over eighty guests."

"Would you prefer I kiss you in private?"

"I would prefer you not kiss me at all."

"Now who's lying?"

She opened her mouth to tell him exactly where he could go, when Taron's voice interrupted them. "There you are. Ready?" His deep brown stare traveled between her and Stefan before a knowing grin spread his lips. "Am I interrupting something?"

"No," Krista snapped.

"Yes," Stefan drawled.

"I see," Taron replied, his shoulders shaking in quiet laughter. "I can come back—"

"No." Krista quickly stepped forward and handed Taron her heaviest bag. "The sooner I get home the better."

More like the sooner she got away from Stefan the better.

Chapter One

Senate Building, capital city of Rhenari, Rineah System, One year later

ഇ

Senator Stefan Marcone turned his attention from the list of expected senators for the planetary vote scheduled later that week and gazed toward the window that ran along the far wall. The incredible view was one of the reasons he chose this particular space. He could see all the way to the desert wasteland that bordered the capital city of Rhenari.

It had been over a year since the battle that had freed the galaxy from Prime Minister Rigora and his dictatorship. Winning the battle had only been the beginning. Their most difficult challenge—reconstructing the Senatorial Government—came after.

Stefan released a tired breath and rubbed at his dry, overworked eyes. He couldn't remember when he'd last had a day off, and the constant demands of his job had caught up to him. As he stood, he closed the file and set it on his desk. Walking over to the window, he gazed out at the city spread below him.

He loved the view at night. Most every evening he watched the setting sun turn the sands of the wasteland red as it slipped below the horizon. But at the moment all he could see was the never-ending pile of work he needed to finish, the constant demands on his time and his ever-shortening temper.

He knew he'd spread himself too thin, but every time he turned around another problem needed to be solved. Now they had a new problem. Someone was killing the senators.

"Stefan." Taron's deep voice brought him back to the meeting at hand.

"Damn it, what?" Stefan sighed and dragged a hand over his face. "I'm sorry." Taron didn't deserve his temper, no matter how tired and irritable he felt.

"Do yourself and everyone else a favor. Take a vacation and get some rest before I wring your neck. You've been snapping at way too many people lately."

Stefan turned to face the man he considered his best friend. "I have too much to do. And now, with this assassin picking off senators, I need to be here."

"What you need is to learn how to let other people take care of things. I can handle the investigation. If for any reason I need you, I know where to find you." Taron pinned him with a glare. "I mean it, Stefan."

"All right," Stefan said with a sigh, pretending to give in for the time being. "I promised Mikayla I would deliver Krista to Daego for a visit after I meet with Senator Blake, so I'll stay there for a while myself. Happy?"

"Immensely." A small grin tugged at Taron's lips and Stefan braced himself for the ribbing he knew was forthcoming. "Speaking of Krista, have you seen her since the wedding?"

And it starts. "No."

"It's probably a good thing. Surely a year is plenty of time to cool off. Maybe you should make sure there are no punch bowls around for her to dump on you."

Stefan sent him a tight-lipped smile. "Maybe you should kiss my ass."

"Not my type, sorry," Taron remarked with humor as he lifted his coffee cup to take a sip. "I can't believe Krista actually agreed to your escort."

"I'm not sure she knows."

Taron choked on his coffee and Stefan grinned.

"Damn, what I wouldn't give to be a fly on the wall when you pick her up."

Stefan shrugged. "It's been a year, maybe she's forgotten all about the incident." He certainly wished he could. The woman invaded his dreams day and night. He hadn't been able to get her out of his mind.

"Somehow I doubt it. She was pretty pissed." Taron's brown eyes suddenly turned serious. "I want you to take an escort with you."

A grimace scrunched up his face and he scowled. "Hell no." With a shake of his head, he moved back to the desk. "You know I hate having people tail me like that. I can handle myself."

"Stefan, as your security advisor, I'd feel a lot better if you took an escort."

"Why?" he demanded with a frown. Why was Taron so concerned about his safety all of a sudden? Needles of apprehension snaked down Stefan's spine. Something must be up if Taron was worried.

"Let's just say it's a bad time to be gallivanting around the galaxy alone."

"Unless you can give me a better reason than that, alone is exactly how I'm going."

"What about all the assassinations? How do you know you're not next?"

Stefan narrowed his eyes and watched Taron fidget with the file on his lap. "What are you not telling me?"

Taron sighed and stood, slapping the file against his leg as he paced. "I have reason to believe the assassin is ultimately after you."

"Care to elaborate?"

Taron met his gaze head-on. "Not at the moment."

"So that's what all this vacation talk is really about?"

Taron nodded his bald head in acknowledgment.

"You know damn good and well I don't hide, Taron."

"I'm not suggesting you hide. I'm suggesting you take a much-needed break while I try to find the man responsible."

"And what if you don't find this man? Am I supposed to continue on this break indefinitely?"

Taron snorted. "When have you ever known me to fail?"

One side of Stefan's lip lifted in a grin. "Point taken."

"Good. Now go get Krista, and try not to kiss her this time."

* * * * *

Krista Sinclair placed her favorite blue blouse in the suitcase as she prepared for her first vacation since returning to Earth. She looked forward to seeing Mikayla and Sidious again. The last time she had seen them—other than by video communicator—was at their wedding on Daego.

Leaving them behind to come back home had been one of the hardest things she'd ever done, but had also been one of the smartest. Returning to Earth to help with the rebuilding process was the best thing she could have done for herself.

Besides, Earth could use all the help they could get. The war with the Imperial Militia only lasted a few months, but the devastation had been worldwide and unlike anything they'd ever experienced.

Cities like Atlanta and New York no longer existed. The smaller towns now served as the new capitals and the midwest region of the United States, once sparsely populated, soon became overpopulated. Cleanup would take years, but the process provided much-needed employment for millions of people.

Sidious had done her a huge favor and pulled some strings to get her a job. It was a management position for one of the charities responsible for finding and building housing for displaced families. She loved her work and would forever be grateful. For the first time in her life, she'd found something she excelled in.

But it was time she took a break. She'd worked herself ragged trying to put her past hurts behind her. Mikayla had offered to send someone to pick her up, and she'd jumped at the opportunity. One month of relaxation and visiting her friend was just what she needed. And there was no better place to relax than Daego. The planet was a paradise.

A loud knock sounded at the front door and she jumped in surprise then glanced at her watch with a frown. She'd assumed Mikayla had sent Taron to play chauffeur, but was relieved of that notion the second she opened the door.

Stefan stood with one hand resting on the doorframe, the other on his hip. Her eyes widened in surprise and her heart pounded in her chest at the sight of his sexy body before her. She'd seen him on the news being hounded by reporters numerous times but nothing compared to his masculine presence.

His thick platinum hair hung just past his collarbone and with it worn loose he looked more like a sexy calendar stud than a galactic leader. His eyes were soft gray now, but she knew from experience they would darken to black when aroused or angry. Her gaze moved over his full lips and she remembered how they had felt against hers, how his erotic kisses had made her weak in the knees. Aggravated with herself for letting her thoughts trail in that direction, she snapped, "What the hell are you doing here?"

"Is that any way to talk to your ride?" he asked in amusement.

Sighing, she stepped aside. "No, of course not. I thought Mikayla was sending Taron."

"Actually she was going to, but I volunteered instead."

Krista stared at him in surprise.

A tiny grin touched his lips. "What's that look for?"

"What look?"

"The look that says you can't believe I said such a thing."

"Sorry, it's just with our history..." Her voice trailed off as he walked by.

With an inward groan, she couldn't help but admire how nice he looked. He wore a white denim shirt unbuttoned at the neck. The sleeves were rolled up and showed off tanned, muscular forearms. The lack of hair made his skin look smooth and her fingers itched to skim over that softness, to feel the warm texture of his flesh beneath their tips. The jeans hugged his hips and thighs and she had to bite back the sigh that threatened to slip out.

With the clearing of his throat, her eyes snapped back to his and she tried to control her thundering heart. He raised an eyebrow and his mouth spread in a suggestive grin. He looked devilish and seductive and oh so dangerous. "We do have quite a history, don't we?"

She frowned.

Clearly amused, his eyes roamed over her in a way that made her feel exposed. Shaking off her increasing desire, she moved aside.

"I'll be ready in a second. I just need to pack my laptop so I can get some paperwork done while I'm away."

"I'm in no hurry, take your time."

The rushing of her blood sounded loudly in her ears. Trying her best to block it out, she quickly packed her computer. She glanced over and noticed him studying her bare apartment and felt the need to explain the lack of décor. "This place is only temporary, so I didn't spend a lot of money fixing it up. I wanted to save as much as possible to buy my own place."

He nodded. "That's a good idea. I haven't seen my home in so long I'm not sure I even remember what it looks like."

"Don't you have a place on Rhenari?" Since he worked there, she assumed he lived there as well.

"I have a small apartment next to my office, but I don't consider it home."

"Well," she said as she took one last look around, "I think that's everything."

He picked up her suitcase and held the door open. "After you."

She stepped outside and waited for him to shut the door. Her hand shook as she slid the key into the lock and she scowled at it, hoping to make it stop. Taking a deep breath, she tried to get herself more under control. With determination, she steeled her spine against him and the things he made her feel. She refused to be another one of his many forgotten conquests.

Turning around, she found herself staring straight into his wide chest. With a gasp, she pressed her back against the door. Her gaze moved up to his, over his wide shoulders and strong neck. She swallowed a lump as desire screamed through her body. His eyes darkened to charcoal as he stared at her, his hand resting on the door by her head.

For the life of her she couldn't utter a word as they continued to watch each other.

"I suppose I should apologize for what happened at the wedding," he whispered.

Her heart fluttered so hard she couldn't breathe. "We should just forget it happened."

"There's just one problem with that." His head dipped even closer and his musky scent surrounded her, seeped into her bones. "I can't."

Chapter Two

ᢒ

Krista jerked her head back, knocking it against the door. His amused gaze locked with hers and he grinned.

"Don't start, Stefan."

"It's already started, Kris. It started at the wedding."

God, the man was unbelievable. "Well, I'm stopping it now. You know damn good and well this is not a good idea."

"We're adults. We can make this work," he reasoned.

She placed her hand against his chest and pushed him away. Taking a deep breath of air, she tried to rid herself of his heady scent. "Maybe you can, but when it comes to sex and relationships I can be very childish. I refuse to let you come between me and Mikayla." When he opened his mouth to argue, she snapped, "End of discussion."

"End of discussion for now."

Grumbling to herself, she kept her eyes on her purse as she put her keys away. "So, how are we getting to the *Vultair*?" At least on the large ship, she could find somewhere to get away from him.

"We're not going in the *Vultair*."

Krista snapped her head up in surprise. "We're not?"

"No." He pointed to the small ship in the field across the street from her apartment. It didn't look much bigger than a single-engine prop plane from the mid 1900s.

"We're going in that?"

Stefan chuckled. "It's safe, I promise."

She should have been used to this by now. Since Earth's induction into the Galactic Senate, small ships parked in odd places were the norm. They had the same leeway as helicopters—they could land wherever there was an empty spot big enough. But it wasn't its safety she was worried about. It was her and Stefan's close proximity to each other for the duration of the trip.

Krista warily studied the ship as they made their way to the field. Wings curved forward from the long narrow center section and ended in a point about two feet in front of the cockpit. The solid black color made it appear even more menacing, if that were possible. Three windows surrounded the center section, one big one across the front and one on each side.

Stefan patted the side of the ship and smiled. "You'll be traveling in style to Daego, my dear. Top-of-the-line Litarian Cruiser. It was a gift to Taron when the rebellion ended."

"And he actually let you borrow it?" She knew how possessive Taron was of his toys, as well as how much Mikayla enjoyed teasing him over it.

"Well." Stefan glanced at the ship and grinned. "Forced me to take it is more accurate. A military escort would only draw unwanted attention. Since I refused the hounds, as I call them, Taron thought the cruiser's cloaking capabilities might be useful."

"Sounds like your security advisor is doing his job." She stood back and allowed him to open the side hatch.

"More like my little brother is being an overprotective, overbearing pain in the ass."

Krista laughed until she saw the way he looked at her. His seductive gaze locked with hers and for a moment she swore he could see right into her soul.

Did he do that on purpose? Did he have any idea how her heart raced when he looked at her like that? Resisting a slight shiver, she turned her gaze away and climbed into the ship. With a sigh, she tried her best to make herself comfortable in a seat she considered to be way too close to his.

Oh, lord, this is going to be a long trip.

He climbed in, tossed her overstuffed suitcase behind the seat and settled beside her. The engines roared to life but he kept the ship on the ground while he made a few adjustments to the wings.

Krista noticed him glance in her direction, and she turned her head to stare out the side window.

"You seem a little nervous. You've made this trip before, this time should be a breeze."

Krista faced him. "Both times were in the *Vultair*. At least in that ship I could stay in the kitchen. No windows."

"You could always just close your eyes. Lay your head on my shoulder, perhaps. Once the autopilot kicks in you wouldn't believe all the things we could do in here to help you relax."

"Perhaps not," she countered dryly.

"Come on, beautiful. We should at least try to make this trip a pleasant one. And nothing would be more pleasant than your body molded to mine."

"I don't believe pleasant is a word that can be used to describe this trip. Especially with you making crude comments the whole way."

"You could always just give in to our attraction." She opened her mouth to reply, but he continued, "And don't try to tell me you're not attracted to me. I may not be a Legana mind reader, but I know desire when I see it."

Krista's mouth almost dropped to the floor. "I can't believe how arrogant you are."

"I'm not arrogant. I'm observant," he said with a grin.

"You're impossible," she growled. "Can you just please get me to Daego, without the seduction."

"But where's the fun in that?" he asked, his gray eyes dancing with mischief.

"How much fun do you think a slap upside the head would be?"

Stefan chuckled as he turned back to the controls. He lifted the ship then punched it out of Earth's atmosphere. The force of the unexpected acceleration threw her back against the seat and she gripped the armrests. She could only anxiously stare as they zipped through the clouds, passing birds and even planes so fast the objects were nothing but a blur. Once in space the pressure eased and she was able to move again.

"Was that necessary?" she growled through clenched teeth.

"I'm sorry. I probably should have warned you about that." He gave her a sheepish grin, and she didn't believe for a minute he was sorry. "In order to get through Earth's atmosphere we need a lot of speed. It's either fly low and slowly build or just gun it."

"You could have warned me you were going to gun it."

"True." He grinned mischievously. "But then you wouldn't be staring at me as though you wanted to kill me. Which makes you look absolutely gorgeous, by the way."

She rolled her eyes and looked out the side window. The man was impossible. He'd done that just to piss her off. So much for trying to make the trip pleasant.

His arm brushed hers, and she stiffened. Looking down, she noticed the offending appendage as it rested on the small ledge between their seats, scant inches from her own. The heat emanating from his muscular arm seeped into her pores and settled with alarming swiftness in the pit of her stomach. She shifted and crossed her arms.

Forcing herself to relax, she studied the field of stars spread out before them. They seemed so much brighter up here than they did from Earth—more touchable. She wanted to test that theory and try to grab one.

Glancing to her left, she noticed Stefan entering information into the navigational computer. *Oh God,* she thought. She'd forgotten all about the transport gate. "How long would it take us to get there if we didn't go through the gate?"

"We couldn't do it in this. Even in the *Vultair* it would take years. Not nervous about flying through it, are you?"

"No," she said, then inwardly cringed at the slight squeak to her voice.

Stefan smiled slightly and pointed out the window. "Take a look at that."

Turning, she caught sight of the moon and sucked in a breath from surprise. She'd never seen it this close before. It was beautiful. What looked like small lakes from Earth were in fact huge craters created by long-ago asteroids. The mountains wove shadows across the floor of the valleys, creating stark black and white images. There was no gray. Only white where the sun hit and black where it didn't.

Earth had been toying with the idea of colonizing the moon for the last six months. Krista didn't understand what the point would be. They had the whole galaxy at their disposal, what did they want with the moon? Stefan slowed the ship to allow her a better view. "That is amazing," she sighed.

He chuckled. "See what you missed by staying in the kitchen?"

* * * * *

Stefan loaded the last of the coordinates into the flight computer to open the transport gate, a manmade wormhole that allowed ships to pass from one galaxy to another. They had to be opened in specific locations based on where you wanted to exit. Sometimes navigation took a while, depending on how far you were going.

Out of the corner of his eye, he watched Krista. She fidgeted with her hands, twisting her fingers around each other. Was she nervous? He wondered if it was from being this close to him or traveling through space in a small ship.

She was just as beautiful as he remembered, with her long honey-blonde hair and sky blue eyes. *Lord, I could get lost in those eyes.* Her figure was slim but curvy, and she had an adorable pert nose. Although tall for someone from Earth, she still only came to his shoulder.

She bit her lower lip and he almost groaned, then looked back at the controls with a frown. He needed to keep his mind on flying and not those lips. He had to keep reminding himself what happened the last time he couldn't keep from kissing her.

"How long will it take us to go through the gate?"

Her voice startled him from his thoughts and he looked at her. "Not long. Twenty minutes, give or take."

"The thought of traveling through a wormhole..." She shuddered. "Are they stable?"

"The manmade ones are much more stable than the ones that occur naturally. We only have problems about once a month or so. Actually, we're overdue for one. It's been over two months since the last collapse."

He laughed at her pale face and wide-eyed expression. That comment had been a little mean, but he couldn't help teasing her. Besides, he owed her one.

"That's not funny," she said with narrowed eyes.

"You've done this before."

"I know, but I didn't see it. I never even knew we were going through the thing. Here," she waved her hand, indicating the massive front window, "I have a bird's eye view."

He smiled at her comment. "Would you feel better if you knew how the gate worked?"

With a shake of her head, she scrunched up her nose. "No. I wouldn't understand. When it comes to anything scientific, despite my best efforts, I'll end up tuning you out."

"Just think of it as a shortcut."

"A shortcut." She took a deep breath and let it out with a whoosh, then grumbled, "A shortcut that folds space."

"I thought you didn't know how it worked?"

"I know the basics, but I don't really understand the specifics. I'm not sure that I want to. I may refuse to go through it at all."

He reached out and flipped a couple of switches. His hand brushed the side of her thigh and the contact sent an electrical jolt through his forearm. She shifted in her seat, putting a little more space between them. He couldn't blame her, if she'd felt the same current he had. It would be a smart thing to think about something else.

"You sound like Mikayla." Raising his voice a couple of pitches, he mimicked her. "I didn't ask for a science lesson, just tell me which button to push to turn the damn thing on."

She laughed and the sound vibrated through the cockpit like bells. It floated around him, over him, even through him, to settle in his cock. *My ever-tightening cock,* he thought with a groan. Despite their last encounter, the woman still had the power to send him into an immediate state of arousal.

And all the hell she did was laugh.

He punched in the last coordinate, hitting the enter key a little harder than necessary. Immediately, the space in front of them was awash with blue light.

* * * * *

Krista watched with dread as the blue circle was engulfed in black.

God, I hate dark places.

She took a deep breath as Stefan piloted the ship right through the center. It made her feel so claustrophobic. There was nothing here. No stars, no light, not even sound—it was like they floated through nothing.

She hugged herself as the ship suddenly became several degrees cooler. She wondered if it wasn't all in her head.

Trying to direct her thoughts elsewhere, she studied the dashboard of the ship. Nothing there looked familiar. Everything was foreign, even the symbols. They looked similar to what she'd expect to see on the side of an Egyptian pyramid.

"Is that Litarian?" She pointed at the symbols across the dash.

"Yes." Indicating each symbol, he told her what they were. "These are our speed, location and engine readings." He brought her attention to the ones above them. "This is the cloak and that one is environmental control."

She glanced at the black void that spread before them. The only lights were the ones from the dash casting an eerie glow over everything. It gave her the creeps, and she couldn't stop the shiver that ran through her.

"You okay?" He placed his hand on her knee and gently squeezed it.

For a second, she closed her eyes. His touch sent a wave of sensation up her leg that she wasn't entirely comfortable with—or wanted.

He'll just use you and break your heart, remember that, Krista.

But that didn't stop her from wondering what he'd be like in bed. It had been over two years since she'd been with anyone. For a second she wondered what she was fighting this for. He was gorgeous and he could certainly kiss. She had no doubt sex with him would be incredible, but also not a good idea. He was Mikayla's brother-in-law and Mikayla was her best friend. She considered Mikayla family, the only family she had left. And that made Stefan off-limits.

"Hey," he said as he gave her knee a slight shake. "You still with me over there?"

"Yeah." She let out an anxious breath.

"You'll get used to it after a while." He gave her a reassuring smile and put his hand back on the controls.

She wanted him to put his hand back on her knee. With a frown, she brushed that thought aside. "Get used to what? The feeling that you're falling into nothingness?"

"For me it was the feeling of space closing in on me."

Krista snorted. "That too."

"Let's talk about something. It'll take your mind off of the claustrophobia."

"People are speculating that we originally came from your end of the galaxy, thousands of years ago. There are all sorts of theories floating around."

"When the Prime Minister first found Earth, he was surprised you spoke our mother tongue, English. I did some checking and found in the archives a story about a group of people who left Rhenari to find a much quieter life. They no longer wanted technology. They boarded a ship and no one ever heard from them again."

"Do you think they came to Earth?"

Stefan shrugged. "Anything's possible. It would certainly explain the language similarities."

A brilliant blue flash and suddenly they were among the stars again. Inwardly, she gave a sigh of relief.

"Now that wasn't so bad, was it?"

She raised her eyebrow. "Wanna bet?"

* * * * *

"Krista!" Mikayla yelled with a smile as she ran out the front door and engulfed her in a hug.

"I've missed you guys." Returning the embrace, Krista gave a sigh of relief that they were finally on Daego.

Krista pulled away and smiled at her friend. She hadn't changed much in the last year. Still as beautiful as ever, with dark brown hair and emerald green eyes. Mikayla chose to keep her hair shoulder-length. The layered cut with curls framing her cheeks suited her face, as well as her sassy personality.

"I'm so glad you're here," Mikayla said. "I can't wait for you to see Hayden. He's grown so much."

"Hello, beautiful." Stefan leaned over and kissed Mikayla on the cheek. "Where's that no-good brother of mine?"

"Where else but in his study." Mikayla waved her hand toward the house.

Krista's eyes followed Stefan in an admiring fashion as he strolled through the front door. Someone could flip a coin on that man's ass.

"It is nice, isn't it?" Mikayla whispered.

"I was admiring the door."

"I could see that. The mahogany door always inspires looks of admiration and lust."

"Would you stop?" Krista tried to sound exasperated but she couldn't hide her grin as she followed Mikayla through the entrance.

Walking into the beautiful home was like stepping back in time. Built of stone, the massive structure stood three stories high, with English Tudor-style windows and turquoise vines covering the front.

Mikayla had spent months looking through magazines and drawing sketches of antiques from memory. The woodworkers had done an excellent job reproducing Earth's furniture.

To keep the Old World charm intact, anything high-tech was well hidden. The kitchen and Sidious' study were the only exceptions.

Mikayla grabbed Krista's bag and started up the large sweeping staircase that led to the second floor. "Let's get your things unpacked and we can talk about what you'd like to do while you're here."

"If I know you, you've already got my schedule booked solid."

Mikayla chuckled. "Well, maybe a couple of things."

*****

Stefan knocked once before stepping into his brother's study. He loved this room. A massive fireplace took up one wall beside the desk and floor-to-ceiling bookshelves covered the other wall and included artifacts from various places in the galaxy. Behind the desk a huge set of windows overlooked the grounds and the lake beyond—Stefan's favorite view.

Sidious looked up from the computer and smiled. "You're early. Did you have any problems?"

"Not a one." Stefan shut the door behind him. "Have you spoken with Taron?"

"Earlier this morning." Sidious studied Stefan before adding, "He gave me strict instructions that I'm to sit on you, if necessary, to keep you here."

Stefan rolled his eyes and walked over to the fireplace. He rested his forearm on the mantel and stared down at the fire burning within the grate. The warmth coming from those flames felt good, but all he could think about were all the things he needed to be doing, all the responsibilities he felt as though he was turning his back on. And all because they thought his life was at stake. When in the last twelve years had his life *not* been at stake?

Rebuilding the Senate had been a breeze compared to organizing the rebels and bringing down their previous dictator. He'd received more death threats from sympathizers that wanted a dictator back in control than any he'd gotten as a rebel leader. What was it about these incidents that made things different? What were his brother and Taron not telling him?

"You want to talk about it?" Sidious asked.

"Talk about what?"

"Whatever it is that's bothering you."

Stefan ran his hand through his hair, then turned to his brother with a sigh. He didn't want to get into an argument with Sidious right now about keeping secrets, so he lied. "I'm just aggravated that we can't seem to get a break in this investigation into the assassin."

Sidious gave him a look that said he didn't believe him, but Stefan knew he wouldn't push. "You've been at it long enough. Let Taron handle things for a while. Besides, I think you'll find that once you step away from it, you can go back much clearer. You might even find something you overlooked."

"Did Taron tell you he thinks I'm a target?"

"Yes." Sidious nodded.

"And you agree with him?"

"There have been three senators assassinated. All three were involved in the rebellion, just like you. That's a little too much of a coincidence for me. Taron was right to insist you come here."

"He's overstepping his bounds," Stefan grumbled.

"He's doing his job. A job you insisted he take, if I recall."

"Taron is the only man I trust, other than you."

"Then let the man continue to do what he does best—keep your ass out of trouble."

Stefan scrunched his face at Sidious and began to pace the room. If what they thought was true, he'd placed everyone here in danger. The mere idea that anything could happen to his family scared the hell out of him.

"Out with it, Stefan," Sidious said with exasperation.

"I shouldn't be here. You know it as well as I do."

Sidious' eyes narrowed. "Don't be ridiculous."

"If I am a target, I'm only endangering everyone here. I think it would be best if I went somewhere else."

Sidious threw the pen down on his desk and sighed. "We've always watched each other's backs. That hasn't changed, nor will it. No one knows of this estate so you'll be much safer here than you would be somewhere off by yourself."

Stefan opened his mouth but Sidious held up a hand and stopped him. "I'm not arguing with you about this. I have the house under surveillance. I'll have men following the women whenever they leave here without me. Everything is covered."

"So that's it then? Lord Marcone has put his foot down?" Stefan frowned as he turned back to the fireplace.

"If the situation were reversed you would do the same. And don't try to tell me otherwise."

Sidious was right. He would do exactly the same thing. But damn it! He didn't have to like it. He hated feeling as though his life were no longer his.

"Fine. You win this round."

Chapter Three

ᘓ

The satin sheets felt cool against her hot flesh as Stefan slowly pushed her back to lie on the bed. His hands gently skimmed up the inside of her thigh, sending shocks of hot current to her core. Her juices flowed, dampening the material beneath her. Trembling fingers gripped the sheets at her side as he placed gentle kisses along the sensitive flesh just below her pussy on her thigh. She squirmed, anxious for the feel of his hot mouth against her aching mound. If he didn't touch her soon, she'd die.

A candle flickered on the table, sending soft golden light across his flesh as he rose above her and removed his clothes. His muscles bulged with every movement and she couldn't take her gaze off his beautiful form. He was perfect. Slowly, her gaze worked lower to his massive cock, which stood proud and ready to invade her body. Her pussy clenched at his thick size, his long length. Bringing her gaze back to his, she licked her lips brazenly, making him smile.

"Do you want a little of this, sunshine?" he asked as his hand stroked his length.

"I want all of it," she whispered, amazed at her actions.

"All in due time," he purred, then spread her legs wide with his hands.

His mouth lowered between her legs and she gasped as his hot tongue slowly slid along her wet slit. It felt so good, so wild. She didn't want him to stop. Gently, his fingers spread her lips and blew against her engorged clit. Her hips bucked off the bed, trying to get closer to his touch.

With a moan, he tortured her clit with teasing circles, then moved lower to dip his tongue deep into her channel. Her head moved from side to side as he fucked her with his mouth, bringing her so close to release, then retreating only to begin again. He drove her crazy and ignored her cries for more, continuing to tease her relentlessly as he licked his fill of her juices.

Just when she thought she couldn't take any more, he sucked at her clit. Instantly, her body spasmed out of control as her orgasm raced through her extremities. She smiled in complete contentment as he rose above her and settled between her splayed thighs. Pushing them even wider, he invaded her sopping pussy with his massive cock. She screamed, lifting her hips to meet every breathtaking thrust.

"Oh, god. It feels so good," she moaned, thrusting her breasts in the air. His palm cupped one and squeezed, then pinched her nipple with his fingers. The slight pain only intensified her pleasure – made her want more.

He pounded into her harder, each thrust going deeper. The tip of his shaft hit her womb and she shuddered as sharp tingles of intense pleasure ripped through her. Every muscle in her body tensed as her release began to work its way along her flesh. With a shrill scream her body erupted into a blinding ball of sensation unlike anything she'd felt before. Her pussy pulsed around his shaft as she ground her hips against him, trying to take his cock even deeper.

Krista awoke with a start and glanced at the curtains blowing in the light breeze, her body still reeling from the massive orgasm she'd experienced. It wasn't the first time she'd dreamed of Stefan, but this dream had certainly been more intense. Her whole body tingled with sensation as her mind replayed the things he'd done. The way his hands had roamed her body with deliberate slowness and the feel of his tongue circling her clit made her whole body tense in need.

He'd not only brought her to orgasm with his mouth, but he'd fucked her to the point she'd screamed in pleasure. She could still feel him thrusting in and out of her.

If the man was half as good in real life as he was in her dream, she was in deep trouble. With a sigh, she brushed her hair back from her forehead. She needed a walk and a good strong drink.

Grabbing her blue satin robe and matching slippers, she headed to the massive garden toward the back of the house. It was a beautiful night. The jasmine was in bloom, filling the air with its musky scent. The rings of Metalon were bright blue and shone down on the small planet, lighting the garden path. Daego's sky was so different from Earth's. Instead of just stars, numerous planets could be seen filling the night sky.

She loved the view and could spend hours looking at it, but then most anything was preferable to the dreams she'd been having about Stefan. His hands and lips all over her body, his thick cock thrusting into her over and over. She closed her eyes against the throbbing between her legs and continued around the path. She had to stop thinking about him.

All through dinner they'd bantered back and forth. More than once Sidious stepped in and chided, "Children, please." Twice Krista had caught Mikayla watching them in interest. Krista had no doubt what was going through her friend's mind. She was thinking of ways to get them together. Even Krista could feel the sexual tension between the two of them. She might not want to acknowledge it, but she could certainly feel it.

Rounding the corner toward the center fountain, she stopped dead in her tracks. Standing with his back to her was Stefan. His hands were clasped behind his lower back, his legs spread wide like a captain at sea standing watch over his ship. The wind coming off the lake blew through his hair and sent his sensuous scent in her direction.

Maybe if she left quietly he would never even know she was there. Slowly, she spun around and started to head back toward the house.

"You don't have to leave."

His soft, deep voice shimmered along her flesh, and she turned to find him staring at her. His gray eyes darkened with the same passion that slammed through her body.

"I'm sorry. I didn't mean to disturb you." She tightened the belt around her robe and crossed her arms over her hardening nipples. *It's just the cool air that's all, certainly not his presence.*

"You didn't. What are you doing out here so late?"

"I could ask you the same thing."

His eyes crinkled slightly when he grinned. Chewing on her lower lip, she watched as he moved closer.

"I couldn't sleep," he said.

"Neither could I."

The soft touch of his fingers against her cheek sent her senses into an immediate tailspin. "It seems you antagonize me even in my dreams," he whispered.

Putting on an indignant expression, she stepped away from his touch. "I don't antagonize you."

"Maybe antagonize is the wrong word. How about arouse me, turn me on?" He brought his body so close to hers she could feel the heat emanating off his skin. The wind blew, parting his blue shirt and exposing his muscled chest and abs. God, the man was a dream. A very dangerous, sensuous, untouchable dream.

"I can't sta…stay here if you're going to keep this up," she stammered.

She continued walking backward until the back of her legs hit a smaller fountain. The contact startled her, causing her to almost lose her balance. In reflex, she grabbed Stefan's arm just as it snaked around her waist to steady her, pulling her against him. Her breasts pressed into his chest and she sucked in a gulp of air in shock.

Her gaze flew to his and it took everything she had not to capture his mouth with hers. The remembered feel of his lips against hers had haunted her for months. Slowly his head lowered, and she was powerless to stop him. Deep down she wanted him to kiss her. This time there would be no audience, no one to interrupt them.

At first his kiss was gentle, questioning, as he nipped at her lips. She realized he was giving her the opportunity to back away if she wanted to, but she didn't. She wanted to feel the silkiness of his tongue against hers, needed to feel it just like she needed the air she breathed.

Parting her lips, she allowed him access to deepen the kiss. He moaned deep in his throat and tightened his arms around her lower back. His palms slid up along her spine and into her hair, making her insides burn with liquid fire. Her arms wrapped around his neck and she moved her body closer. Their thighs pressed together and she could feel the rock-hard length of him poking her stomach. Even through their clothes she could tell he was huge.

"Oh! I'm so terribly sorry."

The soft female voice startled them both and they broke apart quickly. Standing not three feet from them was Stefan's mother, Kaylar. The fiery heat of a blush moved up Krista's cheeks at the knowing grin on Kaylar's face.

"Mother, what the hell are you doing here?" Stefan snapped.

Kaylar frowned at Stefan. "I was invited here by Mikayla, if I recall. I was too wound up from your father's flying here to sleep, so I thought I would take a walk." She smiled faintly at Krista. "I swear, I think Damon deliberately flies like a bat out of hell to aggravate me."

Krista bit back a grin and turned a pointed look toward Stefan. "I know what you mean. Damon isn't the only one who flies as though the demons of hell are on his tail."

"What can I say," Stefan said with a shrug. "I like the rush. I think that's probably the only thing I inherited from my father, other than looks."

"That's not the only thing, Stefan," Kaylar replied dryly, but didn't elaborate. "I'll leave you two alone and head back to the house. Damon should be finished securing the ship. Good night."

"Good night, Mother."

"Wait, Kaylar, I'll head back with you." Krista quickly took off after her, desperate to get away from Stefan before she let him kiss her again and they ended up going at it on the lawn.

"Krista," Stefan hissed.

"Good night, Stefan," she threw over her shoulder.

Stefan watched her go in aggravation. His throbbing cock demanded he take off after her, but his common sense overrode it. He would never force himself on her, but *shetah,* he wanted her. The feel of her in his arms was the closest to perfection he'd ever felt, and he wanted to feel it again. Over and over.

Damn his mother and her untimely interruption.

* * * * *

Krista stared at herself in the dressing room mirror. She'd hoped the afternoon of shopping with Mikayla would take her mind off the sexy senator. Unfortunately it hadn't happened yet.

Pursing her lips, she contemplated her reflection. The blue of the outfit really brought out her eyes, but it was so different from what she usually wore. The pants were silk, loose at the waist and tapered at the ankle. The top had long sleeves that flared out above the wrist. It had straps that wrapped around and tied in a knot just below her rib cage, showing off a good portion of her stomach. She had a nice figure and the belly button ring she'd gotten years ago went perfectly with the outfit, but she wasn't used to showing so much skin.

"That's gorgeous," Mikayla said from her position behind her.

"You don't think it's too…"

"Too what?"

"Slutty?"

"Slutty? Absolutely not. You look great." She grinned at her through the mirror. "Stefan will keel over when he sees you in this."

"That's a good thing only if he doesn't get back up."

"What?" Mikayla asked with a chuckle.

"The man is driving me nuts."

"I can tell," Mikayla snickered.

"I know that Stefan is a great guy. He's always there for the people of Tilarus. He's a great senator and has done wonders with the new government."

"But?"

Krista turned and looked at Mikayla with a sigh. "But you and I both know he's only interested in one thing."

Mikayla shrugged. "Give it to him."

Krista's mouth dropped open in shock.

"Krista, how long has it been since you've been with anyone?"

"A while." She stared at Mikayla's raised eyebrow and scowled. "You know I can't have sex and not get emotionally involved. Stefan would rip my heart to shreds. You know it as well as I do."

"I know no such thing."

Krista sighed and went back into the changing room to take off the outfit.

"I've seen the two of you together, Krista. I've seen the way he looks at you when he thinks no one is paying attention. Deep down he wants a family. You've seen how he is with Hayden. He wants a child of his own so bad he can't stand it."

Handing the outfit over the door to Mikayla, she grabbed her own clothes and began to put them back on. "So what do you want me to do, get pregnant?"

"No, of course not. I just want you to give him a chance. Who knows, the two of you may just hit it off."

"And we may not. Have you thought about what would happen if it doesn't work out? He's your family, Mikayla."

"And so are you," Mikayla chided. "Even if it didn't work out you would still be welcome here. But what if it did work out?"

"What about the whole monarchy thing?"

"What about it?"

"He's a count. Can you imagine me as a countess? Come on, Mikayla."

"Yes, I can. Stefan doesn't care about any of that monarchy nonsense. He wants a woman to love him for him, not his title."

Krista opened the door to the changing room and frowned. "If I say I'll think about it, will you let it go?"

Mikayla grinned. "For now."

Krista rolled her eyes at Mikayla's comment. How many times had she heard Stefan say the same thing in the last couple of days? "Now I know where Stefan gets it."

Chapter Four

ꙮ

Krista admired the small town of Daego as she and Mikayla made their way down the cobblestone street. Daego was so much like Earth's Europe. It had an Old World style that seemed so charming and slow paced. Nothing was hurried here. Not for the first time, she wondered how a planet so far from Earth could look so much like it.

There were fountains everywhere, surrounded by flowers of all colors and sizes. Their scents filled the air, mixing with the smell of coffee. She could live here forever amongst the stucco buildings and shops, stone walkways and flower-lined streets. Life was slow here, peaceful.

"Well, well. Speak of the devil." Mikayla tapped Krista on the shoulder and pointed across the street.

Krista turned to see what she was talking about and immediately noticed Stefan walking toward them. Devil was right. Her whole body came alive, and she stamped down a wave of lust and yearning for something that could never be.

He looked incredible with his hair parted on the side and hanging down around his shoulders. The black slacks contoured to his slim waist and hips, but the black turtleneck, the way it stretched across his wide chest, outlining his hard pecs, brought new meaning to the words "sex appeal".

As Stefan stopped in front of them, his gaze roamed over her in a way that made her feel naked despite her clothes. She licked her dry lips and fought the string of goose bumps that shot down her spine.

Geez, Krista, get a grip. What are you going to do, attack the man here in the street?

"What are you doing out and about?" Mikayla asked.

He puckered his lips as though he had just taken a bite of something sour, then shuddered. "I had to get out for a while. My father and Sidious are going to drive me to drink."

Krista couldn't stop the chuckle at the face he made, but her smile faded somewhat when she spotted Mikayla studying the two of them. Unfortunately, her friend had a way of reading between the lines—or in this case between the looks—that made her a little uncomfortable.

"Your timing is perfect," Mikayla said as she moved all her bags to one hand. "These bags are getting heavy, so why don't you take Krista down to the pastry shop while I load them in the hovercraft? I'll meet you there in a few minutes."

"Mikayla," Krista hissed. Sudden alarm made her voice sound harsh.

"I'll only be a few minutes." She grabbed Krista's bags as well and headed down the sidewalk, leaving the two of them alone.

"She could be a little less obvious." Krista frowned at her retreating back. She couldn't believe Mikayla was doing this. She knew how uncomfortable she was being alone with Stefan.

Stefan laughed. "Subtlety is not in her vocabulary." Turning to look at her, he smiled. "I don't bite, Kris. I promise."

"What a shame," she mumbled as she turned away to walk toward the pastry shop a half block away. When she heard Stefan chuckle the heat of embarrassment scorched her cheeks.

What on Earth made me say that?

Stefan fell into step beside her. "Did you enjoy your shopping?"

"Yes." She turned her head in his direction, desperately wishing he would go antagonize someone else. The man had a formidable presence and an obvious sex appeal that made her uncomfortable. "You know, you really don't have to keep me company. I can wait for Mikayla by myself."

"Trying to get rid of me?"

She came to a stop and faced him with a smirk. "Boy, you're quick."

He took a small step, bringing himself closer. "If you keep this up you're going to make me think you don't like me."

He was so tall she had to tilt her head back to look at him. She crossed her arms. "You mean the punch bowl over your head didn't tip you off?"

Stefan narrowed his eyes and Krista drew in a nervous breath. Whoever thought eyes the color of gunmetal could be so sexy?

"Look, Kris, I'm not going to get into another argument with you. So let's just make the best of this. Okay?"

She raised an eyebrow. "The best would be if you—"

Stefan put his hands on his hips, bringing his face even closer to hers. So close she could smell the hint of coffee on his breath. His lips were full, and she knew they were soft. She swallowed as she remembered the way he kissed. The cologne he wore drifted through the air and she had to stop herself from inhaling deeper.

"I mean it," he growled. "Or would you rather I kiss you right here?"

Her heart nearly jumped from her chest. God, she would love for him to kiss her, but she wasn't about to give him the satisfaction. "You wouldn't dare."

"Oh, but I would dare. That and a whole lot more."

"Why do you do that?"

"Why? Because it drives you crazy. Admit it," he purred, a sensual smile spreading his lips and making her heart flutter, "Deep down you want me to kiss you."

"You're unbelievable. What makes you think I even want you near me, much less kissing me?" she demanded.

"Why are you so flushed, Kris?" His eyes traveled down to her breasts then back to her face. "Why is your breathing so erratic?"

"Maybe because I'm angry?"

"Maybe you're aroused."

"Maybe you need to go to hell!" she snapped.

"Such anger." His smooth, deep voice poured over her like honey and she trembled. "All that passion shouldn't be wasted. It should be used for more…pleasant things."

"Pleasant would be my hands wrapped around your neck," she snarled as she walked past him into the pastry shop. His laughter followed close behind and she inwardly chided herself for letting him get to her.

She didn't strive to be mean. She just immediately switched to bitch mode whenever he was around. It was terrible of her, she knew, but she couldn't help it. Was it right for her to lump him in with every other rich guy, every other man that had broken her heart?

Krista sighed as she glanced around the small shop. Moving to the other side of the room, she looked through the display case and pointed out her selection, leaving Stefan at the door. Someone had recognized him and trapped him in a conversation. Thankful for the slight reprieve, she paid for her selection and headed outside.

With a contented smile, she looked around at all the unusual colors. It always seemed as though her eyes played tricks on her here. The trees and grass were more turquoise than green. The flowers had colors so bright and vivid they appeared almost neon. Sidious said it had something to do with the atmosphere.

Looking up, she noticed Stefan exit the shop and silently wished for invisibility. They made eye contact and he headed in her direction.

Damn, so much for being invisible.

Although he appeared relaxed as he strolled over, there was a tenseness about him as he constantly scanned the streets around them. His eyes never seemed to stay in one place too long. It was as though he were watching for something—or someone.

"Looking for anyone in particular?"

Stefan whipped his gaze back to her and took a seat across the table. "What?"

"You keep looking around." Krista smiled and waved her hand in the direction of the center of town.

"Old habits." Stefan picked up his cup of coffee then shrugged.

"Ah. And here I thought you were plotting an escape route."

He grinned. "Why? I have much more fun sitting here antagonizing you." He set his cup back down, leaned back in his chair and spread his arms, palms up. "So, what do you think of Daego?"

"It's like being home." She put her elbows on the wooden table and leaned forward. "Why is that?"

Stefan added more sugar to his coffee and stirred it with a spoon. "A long time ago, probably about one hundred and fifty years or so, a man from Rhenari disappeared. No one knew where he went or why. A few years later he returned with the idea to build an exclusive resort town with unusual architecture, food and drink, in particular, Earth's coffee." He raised his cup and with a smile, continued, "He proposed the idea to several people. They all liked it and agreed to back him financially. This place was that dream."

"So you think he disappeared to Earth?"

"He must have. This place is too much like your Europe to be a coincidence."

"That makes sense, I suppose." She watched him run the tip of his finger along the edge of his cup, wiping away a drop of coffee. An image of him running that same finger along her skin made her breath catch in her chest, and she turned away.

"Have dinner with me tonight. Just the two of us," he said.

Her startled gaze met his. Dinner. With him. Alone.

She shook her head slowly. "I don't think it'd be a good idea."

He leaned forward, his elbows resting on the table. "Haven't you ever done anything that you shouldn't have?"

"Sure. Lots of times," she whispered, her eyes locked with his deep gray ones.

A tiny smile touched his lips and he ran his finger along the back of her hand. Tingling sensations spread along her arm, and she tried desperately to ignore them.

"Then do it again and have dinner with me."

She gazed down at his fingers as he gently brushed her skin. Such long, strong fingers. She wondered what they would feel like against her flesh, between her legs. Swallowing down a huge rise of lust, she once again met his gaze.

"It's against my better judgment, but all right."

He smiled a sexy smile and she almost backed out, realizing instantly what she was in for.

"Good."

"I'm amazed." The sound of Mikayla's amused voice made Krista sit up straight and remove her hand from under Stefan's. She looked up into her friend's grinning eyes. "It's about time the two of you had a civil conversation without biting at each other."

"Biting at each other," Stefan began with a sultry purr that sent shivers down her back, "Now there's an image. But don't worry, Mikayla, the day isn't over yet."

* * * * *

Stefan sat behind the desk and read the letter his brother had handed him. The more of it he read the more furious he became. He couldn't believe Taron would have kept this from him.

The letter left no doubt that whoever was behind the assassinations was ultimately after him. The previous murders had just been the assassin playing a game, flaunting it in Stefan's face that he could get close enough to kill him any time he wanted to. And he made it clear that killing him was exactly what he had in mind.

Sidious entered the study, several files in his hand. He studied the one on top with a frown before snapping it closed.

"Why didn't Taron show this to me?" Stefan demanded as he held the letter up.

Sidious placed the files in a hidden drawer in the bookcase. "You've been under a lot of stress lately. He didn't want you to worry about it."

"I hate this." Stefan tossed the letter back onto the desk. "I should be on Veenori helping Taron, not sitting here hiding out."

"You're not hiding out, you're taking a well-earned vacation," Sidious replied sternly, the creases between his eyes made more prominent by the frown he was giving Stefan. "You needed this break, Stefan. You've been running yourself ragged for the last several months. What good are you to Taron when you're so overworked you can't think straight?"

"Point taken." Stefan sat back in the chair and crossed his arms over his chest.

Sidious slammed the drawer shut. "Just remember this one simple rule and you'll be fine."

Stefan frowned. "What rule?"

"Little brother is always right."

Stefan snorted. "Little brother needs to be knocked down a peg or two."

Sidious sat in one of the chairs facing the desk. With a taunting smile, he propped his feet on the surface of the desk and crossed his ankles. "And I suppose you believe you're the one who's going to do that?"

Stefan narrowed his eyes. As black as his mood was at the moment, he would just as soon hit Sidious as talk to him. "Do you really want to rehash that old debate…again?" He raised an eyebrow.

Sidious chuckled as he rubbed his jaw. Stefan was sure Sidious remembered the last time this same argument came up. Stefan had proved that his skill as a fighter was just as good as his brother's.

"Passing on the opportunity to put me in my place? Wow, two years behind a desk has turned you into a wimp."

Stefan slowly rose to his feet, his already foul mood worsening by the second. The scowl he sent his brother would send most men running, but not Sidious.

"Damn it, Stefan, sit down. Where the hell is your sense of humor?"

He slumped back down in the chair and drummed his fingers on the desk. "I'm not in the mood to be joking around."

"Since when?"

He slapped the desk with his palm. "Since you and that pain in my ass, Taron, decided to play Lord Protector and keep things from me you had no business keeping."

Sidious dropped his feet on the floor. He pinned Stefan with a glare as he leaned forward and placed his elbows on the desk. "So we're just supposed to sit back, knowing there's a threat hanging over your head, and let you do whatever the hell you want to?"

The two of them glared at each other in silent combat, neither willing to back down. Sidious was younger by two years, but he had always been the sensible one, the protector. In Stefan's mind, Sidious should have been the older brother.

He couldn't count the number of scrapes Sidious had pulled him out of.

It's supposed to be the other way around, damn it.

Although it galled him to give in, he tore his gaze away. "This is pointless. Change the subject."

"All right." Sidious sat back in the chair. He didn't say anything else but watched him with an expectant expression. Stefan got the impression he wanted him to start. So be it, he thought with a sigh. "Does Mikayla know what's going on?"

"Are you kidding? Absolutely not." Sidious shook his head, his lips set in a firm line.

"If you want to keep it that way you might want to tell the men you have following her to be more careful. She saw one of them yesterday when she and Krista were shopping. She's a smart woman. If she keeps seeing them she'll figure something's up."

Sidious sighed. "I'll talk to them." A knock at the door sounded and he turned. "Come in."

Count Damon Marcone marched in and took a seat next to Sidious. Even in his late fifties, his father had a formidable presence. He was an older version of Stefan and Sidious, in looks as well as temperament. "Has Taron found anything out yet?"

"He believes he's found where the bomb came from that destroyed Senator Lengosa's ship. He's on his way to Veenori to investigate. Devlin still owns the largest bar on Veenori, and Taron is convinced he can help. He'll contact us as soon as he knows anything more," Stefan replied.

"Good. I've met Devlin. He's a good man once you get past the gruff exterior." His father nodded.

"Gruff is putting it mildly," Stefan said with amusement.

"Do either of you have any guesses as to who this is?" Damon asked.

"Sidious thinks it's someone we know from the militia, and after reading this letter, I would have to agree with him." Stefan reached over and tossed the letter to the edge of the desk. His father picked up the paper and read it.

Raising his eyes, he looked at Sidious with alarm. "You don't suppose the prime minister escaped the *Destroyer* during the rebellion, do you?"

"If you had asked me that two months ago I would have said no," Sidious replied.

"But now you're not so sure?"

"Now I'm not sure of anything."

Chapter Five

ﬢ

Dinner with Stefan had been much more pleasant than Krista expected. He acted the perfect gentlemen throughout the whole meal, not once making a veiled sexual remark. Even the restaurant was more casual than romantic, with brightly lit tables and a noisy atmosphere.

With a smile, he stood and offered her his hand. "Come on, blue eyes. Let's go for a walk."

She placed her hand in his and let him lead her outside to the lantern-lit streets of Daego. His fingers were warm, surrounding hers possessively, and the tremor that moved up her arm took her by surprise. What was it about him that made her melt into a puddle whenever he touched her?

Once outside she pulled her hand from his. *Think about something else – anything else.*

As they made their way around the corner, Krista jumped at the sound of a woman's squeal. "Stefan!"

Turning to see who yelled, she watched in shock as a beautiful young woman threw herself at Stefan… Wrapping her arms around his neck, she kissed him soundly. At first Krista thought the whole thing was funny, but the longer she stood there the more she didn't like it.

What on Earth do I have to be jealous of? We're not a couple. But for some reason the sight of another woman touching him bothered her. When she noticed Stefan look at her over the woman's shoulder and mouth the words "help me", her notorious mean streak reared its head.

Raising one eyebrow at him, she pretended to not understand what he wanted, then smiled. It was obvious he was uncomfortable with the whole situation, and Krista was in just the type of mood to let him remain that way.

"Stefan, where in the world have you been? You haven't been on Tilarus in months! Daddy is giving this huge party tonight—you have to come by."

"I'm afraid tonight is out of the question. I already have plans. I'm sorry." Stefan tried to extradite himself from the woman's hands but wasn't having much luck. Once again he looked to Krista and silently pleaded with her to do something.

"Oh, that's a shame," she pouted prettily. "I was really looking forward to spending some time alone with you."

"Well," Stefan started.

Finally Krista took pity on him and walked over. Placing her arm possessively around his elbow, she leaned close to him. "Stefan darling, are you going to introduce me?"

Almost sighing in relief, Stefan placed his free hand over her arm. "Sweetheart, this is Ardra Morticio, daughter of Lord Morticio of the Northern Perimeter of Tilarus. Ardra this is Krista Sinclair."

"It's nice to meet you, Ardra." Krista kept her voice cordial but her eyes left no doubt she didn't like the woman encroaching on her territory.

"I didn't realize that you were..." Ardra looked to Stefan for him to clarify who the woman was.

"If we're going to get those errands done before we have to meet my parents for dinner, we should probably get going," Krista said as she looked up at Stefan. She didn't give him an opportunity to answer Ardra. *Let the woman wonder,* Krista thought smugly.

"Of course." Stefan smiled at her, then turned back to Ardra. "It was good seeing you again, and tell your father hello for me." He and Krista continued down the street.

"Took you long enough," Stefan grumbled, still holding her hand in the crook of his elbow. She liked it there and made no effort to move it.

Krista chuckled. "I was kind of enjoying watching you squirm. Old girlfriend?"

"No. Just a young girl who thinks I would make an excellent son-in-law for her father."

"Why haven't you married?" He was gorgeous, and she was sure he could get most any girl he wanted. Even her, if he were to try.

"I've been so busy I haven't had much of a chance to even think about it, much less find someone," he replied quietly.

"I don't know. Looks like Ardra there would be a pretty good catch. You wouldn't even need to put forth any effort, just a snap of your finger." She snapped her finger and gave him a teasing smile. "Instant wife."

"What about you? I think you would make a pretty good catch." Coming to a stop in the middle of the sidewalk, he turned to face her.

Not wanting him to see how much that idea appealed to her, she teased him back. "I would require too much effort on your part."

"Are you saying you would be a challenge?" He looked as though the very thought was intriguing.

"Of course. But a challenge you would find difficult to win."

Giving her his best seductive smile, he brought her hand up to his lips and kissed the back of her fingers.

"One thing you will learn about me, Kris," he looked at her through his lashes, "I never back down from a challenge."

Trying to get her furiously beating heart a little more under control, she pulled her hand from his grasp. It felt as though his lips had burned her flesh where they'd touched.

She turned and began to walk slowly down the street. Trying to take her mind off the very seductive look in his eyes and the way his gaze followed her every move, she tried to pay closer attention to her surroundings.

The thought of Stefan actually being interested enough to try and win her over excited her, but then reality sank in. *He's only teasing. Stefan needs a woman who is just as powerful and aggressive as he is.* He certainly wouldn't want her, at least for anything serious. The rich and powerful ones never did.

He fell into step beside her, his hand resting at the small of her back. For a few moments they remained silent, each lost in their own thoughts.

"Other than challenging," she looked at him out of the corner of her eye, "what are you looking for in a woman?" She was curious if she was correct about what kind of woman he would like.

"Do you think you know someone who would be perfect for me?" Up went that adorable eyebrow, she noticed.

"Maybe," she replied. "But you're evading the question."

Stefan smiled as he looked straight ahead. "You know, I haven't really thought about it."

"You don't know what kind of woman you want to spend the rest of your life with?" That certainly surprised her.

"I keep hoping the woman of my dreams will come running around the corner and barrel into me." He shrugged.

Krista laughed, for she knew that was how Sidious had met Mikayla. "I doubt miracles like that happen twice."

"Maybe the woman of my dreams is right under my nose." Turning back to her, he gave her a charming smile.

"Maybe the woman of your dreams is Ardra."

Stefan made a face and shuddered, making Krista laugh.

"What about you?" Stefan asked, turning the tables. "What are you looking for in a man?"

Krista sighed. "The same thing all women are looking for. The perfect man that doesn't exist."

Stefan laughed. "What is this perfect man like?"

"Well, he's sweet, funny, patient, romantic..."

"There you go." He stopped in the middle of the sidewalk and spread his arms. "You've described me to a T. See? The perfect man does exist."

She rolled her eyes. "I don't recall saying anything about him being arrogant, condescending, overbearing..."

"I am not arrogant." He put his hands on his hips, his expression the perfect picture of indignation.

"Of course you're not," she replied dryly. With a smile, she listened to Stefan halfheartedly grumble about how he didn't understand why everyone thought he was arrogant.

* * * * *

Standing on the far side of the street, the man who was once Commander Carlone quietly watched Stefan with the pretty young blonde woman. His plan had worked. The fortune he'd paid the informant had been well worth it.

He raised his hand and rubbed at the new skin mask that covered his face. It served two purposes. One was to hide the burn scars he'd received during the rebel attack, the other was to keep his identity hidden. Everyone thought he was dead, and he wanted to keep it that way. At least for a while longer.

He studied Stefan and the woman with interest. Could this be a girlfriend? It didn't matter. If she got in the way, that would be her problem.

Stefan would pay for what he did to him and forever regret getting involved with the rebels.

* * * * *

Stefan couldn't remember the last time he'd had so much fun. Krista was intelligent and funny—most certainly beautiful, but there was something about her that made him feel alive. When he was with her he laughed and looked at things in ways he never had before.

Staring down at her, he noticed her slightly pink cheeks and full lips. She had her arms crossed over her chest, studying the horizon. A cool breeze blew and she shivered slightly. He frowned and wished he'd thought to bring a jacket for her. The temperature had dropped, meaning a storm wasn't far behind.

Walking up behind her, he rubbed his palms up and down her arms. He had a strong desire to wrap his arms around her and pull her close. That thought made him smile. He knew without a doubt that if he did she would deck him. One thing about Kris, she would never be dull. "Do you want to head back to the house?" he asked.

"What?" She turned and brought her gaze from the planet above them to his eyes. "I'm sorry, I was fascinated with the rings. They're beautiful."

Stefan smiled as an idea came to mind. "Would you like to see them up close?"

"Up close?"

He nodded. "We can take the *Negash* and actually fly through them."

A slow smile spread across her face and his heart leapt in his chest. *Good Lord, I feel like some kid on his first date*!

"That actually sounds like fun."

He returned her smile. "Then let's go. I have the *Negash* secured in the general dock at the other side of town."

Putting his hand at the small of her back, he escorted her down the sidewalk.

* * * * *

Krista sat in the passenger seat of the *Negash* and watched the little moon of Daego disappear beneath them and the planet of Metalon loom larger. The planet was huge, with four rings in all—each one a different color, from red to purple.

Thinking back on the evening, she realized how much fun she'd had. When they weren't bickering with each other they got along very well. They had the same interests, laughed at the same things. Stefan could be adorable when he wanted to be, but he could also be a total arrogant jerk.

Denying her physical attraction was becoming harder and harder. Sometimes she wondered why she even tried. Why shouldn't she have a fling with him? She sighed as she tried to remind herself of the reasons why. Because he was her best friend's brother-in-law and if things didn't work out or it ended badly, coming back here to visit would be out of the question. It would be too uncomfortable. Mikayla meant more to her than a few weeks of sex. No matter how good it would probably be. Now, if she could only convince her body of that and resist him whenever he kissed her.

Yeah, right, she thought.

As they flew closer she noticed the rings were actually rocks and dust particles. Zigzagging through the debris to the third ring, Stefan parked the ship on a rock with a beautiful view of the planet below.

"Is Metalon inhabited?" she asked as she watched the sun set behind the curve of the planet.

"No. It's uninhabitable, mostly swampland."

Stefan's breath brushed against her cheek, and she turned to find herself nose to nose with him. His gray eyes mirrored the storm going on within her, and she swallowed nervously. His hungry gaze moved from her eyes to her lips, making her chest tighten.

The evening had gone so well. She couldn't let him do this. She knew the second his lips touched hers she would melt. She always did. There was nowhere for her to run this time. No place for her to get away.

Slowly he lowered his head toward hers, and she drew in a shaking breath. He rubbed his nose against the tip of hers, the contact causing her to almost jump out of her skin. The electricity in that one simple touch sent tingles throughout her entire body.

He didn't kiss her, he just watched her, his face hovering inches above hers. Waiting. Each second that passed made it harder for her to remember the reasons why she shouldn't do this. She had to say something, now. She opened her mouth to draw in a shaky breath and tell him to stop but his lips covered hers in a soft kiss, preventing her from saying anything.

She tried to resist at first, not responding, but he continued to nibble and tease. His patience and lack of urgency were erotic in themselves, and she opened her lips beneath his despite herself.

He ran his tongue along her bottom lip before sliding it against her teeth, slowly exploring as if he had all the time in the world. Running his tongue along her teeth, he barely touched his tongue to hers before retreating.

Krista moaned and leaned closer. She wanted to taste more of him. A hint of chocolate truffle and the hot cinnamon drink *korniga,* still lingered on his breath. His musky scent enveloped her, making her want to drown in it.

Gently he cupped her face in his hands and deepened the kiss further. Wrapping her arms around his neck, she met his hungry mouth with her own craving need.

One kiss led to another and she couldn't seem to stop. With a groan, she admitted she didn't want to. Her body burned with fire, his fingers scorching every place he touched, and he touched everywhere.

"Kris," he sighed against her mouth. Grabbing her at the waist, he pulled her onto his lap, her legs straddling his hips. Her knees rested on either side of him, causing her skirt to ride up her thighs, exposing them. She didn't care. She couldn't believe how badly she wanted him, how much she wanted to feel him inside her.

Stefan groaned and slanted his lips across hers. She delighted at the sound. She loved the fact she had just as strong an effect on him as he had on her. Reaching up, he undid the buttons of her shirt as his lips trailed a path down her neck. She sighed as his thumbs brushed across her hardened nipples through the lace of her bra.

Gently his fingers traced the edging before sliding it aside, freeing her breast. He captured the hard peak in his mouth, his tongue stroking and teasing. Krista buried her hands in his hair and tugged him closer, encouraging him to take more of her. With a gasp, she ground her aching pussy against his hard shaft, the material of his slacks creating a friction that drove her crazy.

She wanted to touch all of him with an urgency that defied understanding. Pulling at the buttons of his shirt, she opened it and slipped her hands inside, running her fingers along the smooth expanse of warm skin and hard muscle. She marveled at his strength and smiled when she felt the muscles twitch beneath her exploring fingers.

Stefan hit a switch on the side of the seat and it reclined slightly. With a soft squeal she lost her balance and fell onto his chest, causing them both to laugh. Framing her face with his hands, he brought her mouth back to his for a deep kiss, silencing her giggles.

He slid his palms up the outside her thighs, pushing her skirt even higher. She shivered at the feel of his fingers against her heated skin.

Stefan whispered against her lips, "Cold?"

"No," she sighed.

He smiled slightly as he sucked her bottom lip into his mouth. "If you are, I can warm you." His hands cupped her bottom and brought her more firmly against his thick cock.

She could hardly breathe. Never in her life had she been so caught up in something like this, so completely out of control. She moaned as his mouth devoured hers and his hands kneaded her behind, moving her in a slow rhythm against him that drove her crazy.

Sliding one hand between them to her stomach, he let his fingers trail along the top edge of her panties. Krista held her breath as he moved lower and traced the edge along the inside of her thigh. She wanted to groan in frustration, for he hadn't touched her yet. He seemed content to just tease.

His teeth nibbled her neck while he slid the crotch of her underwear aside and separated the lips of her wet sex with his finger. Gently he sucked on the spot where he could feel her pulse pounding.

Stefan wanted to rip her panties off and lose himself in her, bury every inch of his throbbing cock inside her, but he also didn't want it over yet. He was enjoying himself way too much.

Bringing his mouth back to hers, his tongue traced her lips at the same time his finger traced her clit. He smiled as she arched against his hand, her head thrown back, her eyes closed. She was so beautiful she took his breath away. "Like that, baby?"

At her deep groan, he had to swallow hard to keep from driving into her with the force of a madman. Sliding one finger into her depths, he sighed against her lips. She was so tight and wet, so ready for him. "Oh God, you're going to feel good."

"Stefan." She closed her eyes and moaned as he leaned forward and captured her nipple in his mouth—his tongue stroking, his teeth softly biting. She moved her hips against his hand and he groaned, taking more of her breast into his mouth.

He slowly slid his finger in and out, stretching her as he went. His thumb circled her nub, prolonging her torture on purpose. He smiled against her lips, enjoying what he was doing to her—what she was doing to him.

A second finger slid into her and she sighed as the first ripples of her climax fluttered through her. God, she wanted him, but she also didn't want him to stop. She was so close she could taste it, could feel her muscles tighten and grip around his fingers. His thumb brushed across her swollen wet nub and her whole body jerked. Rippling sensations shot through her limbs as he did it again, lingering a little longer this time, using a little more pressure on just the right spot. Suddenly her release gripped her and she screamed, her nails digging into his shoulder leaving half-moons on his skin.

"Oh, God," she sighed as her head fell forward onto his chest.

Her hands fumbled with his zipper until he brushed them aside with his own. "I want you, Kris," he hissed against her lips.

His cock sprang free from his pants and she swallowed a gasp at his size. He was perfect and her pussy clenched at the thought of him being buried deep inside her. She didn't have the opportunity to play as she'd wished. Stefan grabbed her hips and lifted her onto his thick shaft. The head of his cock teased her opening before slowly thrusting deeper. Her eyes closed as he stretched and filled her and she braced her hands on his shoulders. With a pleasure-filled groan she pushed down, taking his cock deeper, sheathing him balls-deep.

"Fuck," Stefan growled as he grabbed her hips, holding her still. "God, Kris. You're tight."

"It's been a while." She moaned against his neck, her tongue flicking out to lick his skin.

Slowly they began to move, her sighs becoming lost in his kisses. It felt as though his cock was splitting her in two, but at the same time it felt so good. Lifting her hips until just the head of his shaft remained, she slowly slid back down his length.

Stefan growled and settled his palms against her ribs, lifting her. "Again," he said and she obliged.

Shots of liquid fire passed through Stefan. Damn, she felt good. Hot and tight, like liquid lava encasing his cock. They fit together so perfectly. She was meant for him. He knew it deep in his soul. Leaning forward, he pressed her perfect breasts together and suckled both of them. Anything to keep his mind off losing control. He wanted her to come again. He wanted to feel her pussy clench his cock like it had his fingers. Sliding his palm up the inside of her thigh, he found her swollen clit and brushed his thumb across it. She shuddered in his arms just as the walls of her pussy shuddered along his cock.

"Mmmm," he moaned. "I like that."

He brushed his thumb across her again, applying just a little more pressure, and captured her gasp with his kiss. The muscles on the inside of her thighs began to tremble as he continued with his teasing strokes against her clit.

"Stefan," she groaned against his lips, the movement of her hips becoming more frantic.

"Come for me, baby." He applied stronger pressure to her clit, massaged it in tiny circles, honing in on the one spot he knew would send over the edge. She gasped and threw her head back. Her breasts thrust forward and he licked at one engorged nipple, reveling in the shudder that passed through her. "That's it, baby. Squeeze my cock with your pussy."

She screamed as her release slammed through her and Stefan grit his teeth, trying to hold his at bay. Her walls pulsed around him, milking his climax from him, and he lost it, spilling his seed deep inside her. She collapsed against him and he held her tight.

"Oh, God. What the hell did we just do?" she sighed.

"Something we should have done a year ago."

Suddenly the warning bell on the panel went off and she jumped, her eyes widening in surprise. They both stared at the computer screen on the dash. The shrill beep had stopped but the warning light still flashed. The sound of their harsh breaths echoed through the quiet of the cockpit.

"What the hell?" Stefan scowled.

"What is it?" she asked, trying to fix her clothes and pull herself together. She couldn't believe she'd let it get that far.

Stefan put his hands at her waist and settled her back into her seat. "Put on the harness."

With shaky hands, she snapped the harness together and then frowned at him. "Are you going to tell me what's wrong?"

"We've got company," he said as he fastened his pants back and scanned the controls.

"Is that bad?"

Suddenly the ship shook and sparks flew from the side console, making Krista squeal in surprise.

"It's bad."

Krista scowled at him. "Care to explain why?"

"Not at the moment."

The ship lifted from where they'd parked and Stefan began to make his way through the multitude of rocks surrounding the planet. Once again the ship was hit with fire, causing it to shake uncontrollably.

"Stefan, what's going on?"

He kept his eyes straight ahead. "I'll explain later. Right now I've got to get us out of this. Computer, engage cloak."

The computer's voice loomed through the small ship. "Cloak inactive, shields at forty-five percent."

"Damn it." Stefan spun the ship and missed colliding with a rock by what seemed like inches, only to be hit by yet another blast. The ship lurched, and Krista grabbed hold of the dash in front of her. Even with the harness on she felt as though she was being thrown from her chair.

"Can't you fire back at him?" she asked.

"This ship isn't equipped with weapons," he snapped.

She kept her mouth shut as Stefan flew clear of the rings' debris and headed out into open space, the ship attacking them directly on their heels. Her heart raced as they dodged one blast after another. The knuckles of her fingers began to ache from gripping the arm of the seat. She tried her best to remain silent, at least until she noticed Stefan hit a button to open the transport gate. "What are you doing?"

"We can't outrun him, so we're going to have to hide from him."

"We're going through the gate?"

"I can enter the gate and then close it. He'll have no way of knowing where we went."

"But what if he enters with us?" she asked, panic quickly rising in her chest.

"He can't, not unless I program it that way."

She swallowed her nervousness as the gate opened with a flash of blue light and they entered into the dark, dead silence of the wormhole. Turning toward Stefan, she scowled. "Want to explain to me what that was all about?"

He sighed, his brow drawn together in thought.

"Well?" she snapped.

"There's an assassin after me."

Her mouth dropped open and she stared at him in disbelief. "Oh, you've got to be kidding me."

"No, afraid not."

"You took me up in space knowing there was someone out there trying to kill you?" Her hands fisted against the desire to wring his neck. He should have told her. He should never have taken her up there.

"Damn it, Krista. I didn't know he would be up there waiting for us." He scowled back at her, his eyes a deep black, but his temper didn't scare her.

"So now what?"

"Well, we can't go back to Daego," he sighed.

"What?" Surely she hadn't heard him correctly. "Maybe you can't but I certainly can."

"No."

"What the hell do you mean, no? It's you he's after, not me."

"And what if he catches us again when I try to take you back?" he yelled. "I refuse to endanger Sidious and Mikayla and I really don't think you want to either."

That thought hadn't crossed her mind. She sat back in the chair and stared out at the empty space before them. They still hadn't exited the gate, and she wondered where he was taking them. "Where are we going?"

"The old rebel camp. It should still be intact, although it might be a little messy."

A blue flash of light preceded the exit and she sighed in relief. She hated going through that gate. A thought suddenly occurred to her, and she turned toward him. "All my stuff is still back on Daego."

"We'll swing by the Klindorah Space Station and pick up some things. I don't have anything, either." He turned troubled eyes on her and she felt bad for yelling at him. He'd just saved both of them, after all. "I'm sorry, Kris. Looks like you and I will be on our own for a while."

She swallowed the lump that rose in her throat at the thought of being alone with him. Especially after what just happened.

*****

Carlone growled loudly as he watched the small runner enter the transport gate. He had no way of knowing where Stefan went. He'd forgotten how good a pilot Stefan was. Next time, he'd try something else.

As soon as Stefan emerged from the gate, the tracer he had hidden in Stefan's ship would send a signal. How quickly he would get the signal would depend on how far away he was. Sooner or later the senator's whereabouts would be known and he'd get the chance to get even—to finally get his revenge on the meddling count.

Chapter Six

ℵ

Mikayla stood inside her husband's study door and watched the worry lines deepen around his eyes. Something was going on, something he wasn't telling her, and it was high time he spilled the beans.

"Sidious," she said. His eyes left the computer screen and locked with hers in surprise.

"Hey, baby. I didn't see you standing there."

"Obviously." She took a few steps closer, coming to a stop next to his chair. "Is there something that you want to tell me?"

"Why do you ask?"

Reaching out, he took her hand in his and pulled her onto his lap. Her arms wrapped around his neck, her fingers sliding through his thick platinum hair. She'd always loved his hair. "You looked as though something was bothering you. Not to mention the fact that Taron has been in and out of here more in the last couple of weeks than the last year, and of course there's Damon, who won't let any of us out of his sight."

"Okay," Sidious sighed. With a slight smile, he kissed her forehead. "Sometimes I think you know me too well."

"Well, are you going to tell me?"

Whatever he was about to say was cut off when Taron burst into his office. "I need to talk to you."

"Now?" Sidious asked.

"Now."

Sidious turned to look at Mikayla, and she shook her head. "No. I'm tired of being left in the dark. I'll hear it as well."

Sidious nodded as she stood from his lap. "What is it, Taron?" he asked.

"I was on my way back from Veenori when the alarm went off for the *Negash*. It's gone, and so are Stefan and Krista. The hanger bay personnel said they left in it earlier this evening."

Mikayla shrugged. "Maybe they just went for a short trip."

"If they did, something happened. The alarm was deliberately engaged with Stefan's code. Stefan must have turned it on to send a signal to the tracker on the *Vultair*. According to the tracker, he activated the gate and is docked at the Klindorah Space Station." Taron took a deep breath and continued. "Daego Security said there was a skirmish within the rings earlier. One of the ships was the *Negash*. The other was unknown."

"A skirmish?" Mikayla asked, her heart racing. Why would Stefan be involved in a skirmish, especially if he had Krista with him?

Sidious mumbled a few Tilarian curses and stood. "Can you contact Stefan?"

"I tried." Taron's eyes shot to Mikayla then back to Sidious. "Apparently communications are out on the *Negash*, and without the ship's booster I can't raise Stefan on his communicator. He's too far away. Should I head that way?"

"No. He'll contact us. If the ship is docked at the station we at least know he's made it that far. If what I think happened, Stefan will ditch the *Negash* and get another ship. Coming back here will be out of the question."

"I agree. We also have another problem." Taron handed Sidious a photo.

Sidious raised an eyebrow and took what Taron handed him. After a long silence, he sighed and tossed the photo on the table.

"Devlin was able to retrieve that from a security camera. The former dictator's right-hand man seems to have survived the destruction of the *Destroyer*. My guess is he's our assassin."

Sidious nodded, his brows drawn together in a frown. "He must have attacked Stefan in the rings. But the question is was he trying to kill him or just playing with him?"

"Okay, now you want to tell me what's going on?" Mikayla snapped. With her hands on her hips, she gave her husband what she hoped was her most forceful scowl. "Especially since my best friend is apparently involved?"

Taron grimaced and turned to leave the room. "I think I'll leave the two of you to your chat."

"Chicken," Sidious growled.

*****

"What are we doing here?" Krista asked as Stefan docked the *Negash* on the Klindorah Space Station and helped her to exit the ship.

The station was several miles long, with horizontal shoots that wove through the center like a subway. People of all races bustled throughout the busy docking bay, and she stayed as close to Stefan as she could. At one point he turned and took her hand in his, making sure they remained together.

"I want to ditch the *Negash*," he said while they stood waiting for the next shoot to come by. "There's always someone here selling runners, we'll just buy another one. There are also some clothing shops up on the promenade. Might be a little different than what you're used to though."

"I'll adapt."

Stefan grinned and gave her hand a squeeze. "I know you will."

Krista bit her lower lip as they climbed onboard the shoot and took their seats. The force of the start threw her back and she grabbed Stefan's leg in reflex. His hand covered hers and warmth seeped into her skin, making her whole arm tingle. Looking down at his long thick fingers, she remembered what he'd done earlier and the heat of a blush crept up her cheeks.

Turning to the side, she watched outside the glass walls as the shoot sped by, and closed her eyes against the nausea that threatened. She had to get her mind off her upset stomach and the movement of the shoot before she actually lost her dinner.

"Stefan?" she asked and opened her eyes to look at him.

"Yes?" He turned to look at her, his gray eyes seeming to devour every facet of her face.

She cleared her throat before continuing. "Do you know who this guy is that's after you?"

"No. But I believe he's the same man that killed the other senators."

"How long do you think we'll have to stay hidden?" The shoot came to a stop and she looked to see where they were. "Do we get off here?" she asked. It looked like another docking bay.

"No. We need the third stop. There are two docking bays on each side. The promenade is in the center. And as for hiding, I'm not sure. I'll let Taron know where we're going and he'll meet us there. We'll decide what to do then. But I don't want to go back to Daego yet and risk everyone else. It's bad enough you're in this." He smiled down at her, his eyes dancing with mischief. "Not afraid to be alone with me, are you?"

"Of course not," she lied. Oh boy, did she lie. She was terrified to be alone with him, for she knew exactly what would happen.

They finally reached their stop and stepped off, heading toward the flights of stairs that would take them to the promenade. As they topped the second flight, she stared in awe at her surroundings. It was like a tiny city. Restaurants, shops and bars lined both sides of the station. The ceiling was glass, giving the patrons a perfect view of the stars and two blue moons right outside.

Dim streetlights lit the walkways and the aroma of spicy food filled the air. She inhaled a deep breath and her stomach growled in response.

Stefan grinned. "Are you hungry? We just had dinner."

"A little," she said with a blush. "And dinner was several hours ago."

He chuckled. "True. We can get something." He looked around until he spotted what he was looking for, and pointed to a small place just down the corridor. "They have good food, we'll go there."

With a nod, she followed him.

* * * * *

Buy whatever you want.

Krista scrunched up her face as his words echoed in her ears. Dinner had been great—the food here was incredible. The clothes were another matter. With a sigh, she slowly looked through the selection of monk-like dresses and baggy harem pants. She didn't see a thing here that fit Stefan's description of comfortable outdoor clothing.

He'd remained outside to talk with a man about buying his runner and sent her in the shop alone with his currency chip. *Big mistake, rich boy.* She considered a pair of leather pants with a grin. Shaking her head, she replaced them on the rack. She wanted comfortable, not a chafed behind.

After going through what seemed like hundreds of outfits, she finally found something she thought might work. The pants were cut similar to jeans, but were made out of a heavier material. She lifted them and ran her hand across the soft, suede-like material. He did say it would be cool where they were going, so this should work perfectly.

She grabbed three pairs and four shirts, as well as shoes. As she made her way to the counter a satin tunic caught her eye. It was beautiful. On impulse, she decided to try it on and quickly headed to the dressing rooms.

Stepping out of the stall, she studied herself in the three-way mirror. The tunic was perfect. The way it felt against her skin and clung to every curve of her body. Even she had to admit she looked good in it. With a naughty grin, she wondered what Stefan would think if he saw it.

The lace hem rested about mid-thigh while the slit went all the way to her waist on both sides. Underwires pulled her breasts together, making it appear she had much more cleavage than she really did. It was definitely an outfit to tempt.

A movement in the mirror caught her attention and she looked up. Her eyes locked with those of a grinning Stefan, walking up behind her.

"What are you doing in here?" she asked, her voice a little more breathless than she would have liked.

"I was looking for you." His eyes traveled down her legs and then moved back up, locking with hers in the reflection.

They had darkened to a deep gray, and she licked her lips nervously. She knew that look. He'd had the same expression, the same passionate hungry gaze, when they were in the ship earlier. His fingers lightly touched her shoulder then slid down her arm. Goose bumps rose along her flesh, making her shiver despite the heat of the shop.

"If you don't buy this, I will," he whispered.

"You shouldn't be in here." She struggled to keep her composure. All she could think about was earlier. How wild and incredible it had been. How much she wanted him. Again.

"Afraid we'll get caught?" His hand parted the side slit and moved to her stomach.

The messaging motion of his fingers as they worked their way lower made her breath catch. He could take her right here without a word of protest. The man hadn't even really touched her yet and already she could feel the wetness forming between her thighs. Her heart pounded and for a second she forgot to breathe as his lips softly kissed the side of her neck. Finally she came to her senses and moved away from him.

"Stop. I have to change." She stormed past him into the dressing stall. She had to get away from him before she was all over him again.

"Need any help?" he asked, his voice full of amusement.

"No," she snapped. *Do I need any help? Of all the arrogant, conceited...* With a sigh, she tossed the tunic onto the bench. She could hear his chuckle as he walked away and she ground her teeth in frustration. The man was going to drive her to violence.

"Hurry up, Kris. I want to get out of here." His words reminded her they were running and the sooner they left the better.

"I'll be right there." Without another thought, she quickly dressed and met Stefan at the counter.

* * * * *

Krista awoke to the feel of Stefan's fingers on her cheek, his voice next to her ear. She sighed and leaned closer as he placed a kiss on her temple. Butterflies immediately came alive in her stomach, dancing and jumping like mad.

"Wake up, sweetheart. We're here."

Opening her eyes, she took a look out the window of the ship. She sat up straighter in surprise at the enormous rock wall directly in front of them. Turning her gaze out the side window, she saw nothing but rock there as well.

"We're in a cave?"

The cavern was huge. Or maybe it just looked huge because the ship they'd purchased was the only one in it. He opened the door and reached in, offering a hand to help her out.

"Where are we?" she asked as her eyes traveled around them in wonder.

"We used to call it Shlintori."

"Used to?" Krista stopped studying the cavern and eyed him.

Stefan grinned. "Well. Actually still do. Its official name is Glindogah, but when the rebels used it as a hideout we renamed it Shlintori. That way, no one but us would know what we were talking about."

"I take it we're inside it?" she asked as she began to once again look around.

"Yes. This cavern was here originally, we just improved upon it."

"I'll say."

In the ceiling of the cavern she noticed the huge opening in the rock, enabling her to see a large portion of the night sky beyond it. Apparently that's how the ships got in and out. "How do they keep from seeing in here?"

"You can't see in from the outside. There's a holographic image that simulates the rockface." Stefan shrugged. "Just looks like a regular mountain."

He looked up at the entrance. "You can tell it's on because the stars look blurred."

"That's amazing." She looked at him and smiled. "So what else is here?"

He pointed toward a long hallway beginning at the far end of the hangar. "Down that hall are quarters, each with their own bath, as well as what we called a great room and a training facility. Kept the guys from getting too bored when they were here."

She began to make her way toward the hall while Stefan pulled their bags from the ship. "What's in the great room?"

"It's sort of like a rec room. There are games, replicators for meals, that sort of thing."

She turned to face him, wrapping her arms around her more tightly. The cavern was chilly. She hoped the rest of the place wasn't this bad. If it were she would freeze. The clothes she'd bought wouldn't be near warm enough.

"So we can't actually cook?"

Stefan walked up next to her and grinned. "Don't like the idea of eating replicated food?"

Krista scrunched up her face. "Not particularly."

"Well then, I guess I'll have to scrounge up some real food." He smiled as he tapped her nose with the tip of his finger. "Just for you."

Krista smiled as she watched him go around her and continue down the hall. "You're too kind."

She fell into step behind him, studying the rock walls and solid earthen floors. Lights hung from the ceiling, the connecting wires exposed. She could feel the slight slope to the ground and vaguely wondered how deep they were.

He eyed her over his shoulder. "Kind, huh? Can't say too many people have accused me of that one."

She waved a hand and rolled her eyes. "You were the driving force behind the men and women who freed the galaxy of an abusive and sick tyrant. You can't get any kinder than that."

Stefan came to an abrupt halt and spun to face her with a thoughtful expression.

She frowned. "What?"

An eyebrow arched adorably and she fought the desire to smile. "A compliment? Coming from you?"

"Yeah, well. Don't get too used to it."

One corner of his mouth tipped up in a smile. "Most people would say I had an ulterior motive."

She tilted her head and studied him. "Did you?"

"No."

She shrugged. "Then what do you care what other people think?"

"I don't." His expression sobered as he gazed at her. It made her uncomfortable, and she shifted her stance, trying to find a way around him. "I only care what you think."

She jerked her eyes back to his in surprise. "Why?"

His only response was to smile before turning away again. She frowned at his retreating back. He never failed to completely throw her for a loop. With a sigh, she followed him further into the cave.

*****

Krista surveyed the massive great room. It had three fireplaces, one in the center that she was sure someone could easily stand in, and two not quite as large on each end. They appeared to be made of the same stone as the cave, blending into the wall almost perfectly.

The center fireplace divided the room into two sections, a kitchen and eating area on one side and a living room-type area on the other.

Large overstuffed chairs and sofas in shades of burgundy and green filled the living room, while the kitchen offered numerous tables and chairs as well as cabinets filled with dishes and pots. Four replicators took up the opposite wall.

"How many people were usually here at one time?" she asked as she continued to scan the room.

Stefan set the bags down and turned on a replicator. "Two coffees. Black." While he waited, he leaned his back against the counter. "The most, I think, was about one hundred and fifty."

Walking over, she looked into the center fireplace. It was open on both ends, which allowed the heat to spread to both sides of the room. There were logs at the bottom but no burnt-wood scent. It just smelled damp.

"If you're cold I can turn that on."

She looked over at him and smiled slightly. "Please."

Stefan chuckled and grabbed their cups of steaming coffee. "Here, this will help." He handed her a cup before opening a panel to the side of the chimney.

She eyed the drink warily before taking a sip. *Hmmm…not too bad.* She really couldn't tell a difference. Wrapping both hands around the warm cup, she took another sip.

Suddenly there was a loud pop, and she startled as the logs came to life in bright orange and yellow flames. With a sigh, she moved closer to the heat.

Looking around, she noticed the other fireplaces had come to life as well.

Stefan smiled. "They're all interconnected and attached to gas lines running down through the ground. I can also turn on the ones in each individual guest room with this panel as well."

She raised an eyebrow. "The bedrooms have fireplaces too?"

He nodded as he closed the panel.

"How long did it take you to do that?"

"Not long." He came to stand next to her, putting his back to the heat.

Bringing her cup to her lips, she took another sip as she eyed him over the rim. "What was this place used for?"

"This was where we made the *Vultair*. We built her in pieces and then assembled her in orbit, cloaked. She's too big for the cavern." Stefan swallowed a sip of coffee. "After that, we used it as a place to gather in relative safety. A few fugitives, running from the prime minister, hid out here, as well."

"Now we're hiding here."

"So it would seem."

Krista watched him study the flames, a faraway look in his eyes. She wondered what he was thinking.

"If it wasn't for me...would you still hide out here?"

Stefan brought his gaze to hers and for a second she wondered if he was even going to answer her. He shook his head and whispered, "No."

She spun away from him and walked toward one of the many tables in the eating area. Pulling out a chair, she sat down, setting the cup on the table in front of her. The idea of him getting hurt didn't sit well with her, but she refused to analyze it—refused to even think about it. Acknowledging any feelings she had for him was too dangerous.

"Krista."

She looked up to see Stefan take the seat next to her. He reached out and placed his hand over hers. His fingers were so warm, his eyes so full of concern and compassion. Taking a deep breath, she pulled her hand out from under his and shook her head. "I feel terrible..."

"This whole mess is my fault, Kris. Not yours. I should have listened to Taron when he tried to warn me about this." Putting his finger under her chin, he turned her toward him. His dark gray eyes held hers as he rubbed his thumb along her cheek. "I promise I won't let anything happen to you."

How is it he can always do this to me? Why is it when he touches me all I want to do is drown in him?

She closed her eyes against the desire to make love to him again. They hadn't talked about it, but they probably should. Unfortunately, at the moment she was so tired she couldn't think straight, much less talk about what happened. She wasn't even sure what she would say anyway.

"It's going to be okay," he whispered and placed a soft kiss against her brow.

Krista wasn't as confident.

Chapter Seven

ꕤ

Stefan came down the hall late the next morning to the smell of bacon and coffee. With a slight smile, he followed his nose to the great room. He stopped at the entrance and searched for Krista. He found her standing by the counter, softly humming along with the music playing in the background. She must have found Taron's old disk player.

For a second, he leaned against the rock wall and watched her hips softly sway back and forth. The images her movements created in his mind made his cock thicken. The woman could drive him to distraction without even trying.

Keeping his steps whisper soft, he came farther into the room. She had her back to him, her hair hanging in soft curls. His fingers itched to run through its honey-blonde softness like they had on the ship.

With an inward groan, he grimaced. Just thinking about that night made him hard all over again. He shifted his gaze from her hair to her perfectly rounded behind. He remembered the feel of those tight mounds in his hands and his blood quickened.

Good going, idiot. Make it worse.

Coming up behind her, he placed his hands on her shoulders. The material of her sweater was soft beneath his fingers. Her singing stopped and she stiffened.

Leaning down, he whispered in her ear, "It's just me."

Her hair smelled like lavender and he inhaled the scent. She always smelled of lavender. He wondered if she bathed in it.

"I'm making breakfast, would you like some?"

He grinned at the breathless quality in her voice. "I'll take a side of you with that bacon." He placed a soft kiss just under her ear and smiled to himself when he felt the tremor run through her.

"Knock it off." She nudged him in the stomach with her elbow.

He grunted. "Yes ma'am," he mumbled with a grin.

Moving away from her, he ordered coffee from the replicator. "Do you need some help or have you figured it all out?"

"I think I've figured it out." She smiled and proudly held up a plate. Grabbing a piece of bacon off it, she set it in the center of the table with the rest of the food she'd prepared.

"Hungry this morning?" Stefan raised an eyebrow at the amount. There was bacon, eggs, potatoes, toast and fruit.

"Actually I am. In case you haven't noticed it's almost lunchtime and we missed breakfast." Krista grabbed her own coffee and sat down.

He smiled as he sat across from her. He liked this. Waking to find her in his kitchen, cooking breakfast, grinning at him over her morning coffee. He liked her smile much more than her surly attitude. Although he had to admit her smart mouth could certainly be entertaining.

"What's it like outside?"

Her question snapped his mind back to the present.

"That's right. You were asleep when we landed." He scooped some eggs onto his plate. "It's mostly wooded. There are a couple of clearings, one with a large lake. Some of the men used to fish there. This time of the year it's a little too chilly for that, though."

"Not too chilly to go out, I hope." She offered him the plate with toast on it.

"Thank you, sweetheart."

He grabbed the plate and their fingers touched. For a second he didn't move, just let them rest over hers. "You look gorgeous when you blush."

Krista jerked her hand away so fast he almost dropped the plate. She narrowed her eyes. Picking up her fork, she stabbed a few potatoes. Stefan got the distinct impression she wished they were his head.

"You never answered my question," she said.

"Oh, yes." He nodded. "Back to the weather." He put his coffee cup to his mouth to hide his grin. "It's cold right now, but not too terribly bad. Were you warm enough last night?"

"Yes. I found some extra blankets in a trunk at the foot of the bed. The fireplace really kept the chill off."

"If the cold ever gets to be too much for you, you're always welcome in my bed."

Krista snorted. She couldn't believe the gall of this man. "Only if I could hogtie you first."

"Hmmm." Stefan took a bite of bacon and chewed thoughtfully.

Krista could just imagine what was going through his mind. *Probably the same thing that's going through mine*. The image of Stefan tied up in a bed was definitely interesting.

"If you hogtie me will you have your way with me? Or better yet…"

Her fork stopped halfway to her mouth and she scowled at him.

"Why don't I tie you up and have my way with you?"

"Okay, look…" Krista dropped her fork onto her plate with a loud clang.

Stefan raised an eyebrow in amusement. "You brought it up." One corner of his mouth twitched up as he fought a smile.

"Yeah, well, I'm sorry I did." She picked up her plate and took it to the counter.

The hairs on the back of her neck stood on end and she knew Stefan was behind her. She fought the wave of desire that surged through her like a runaway train as he placed his hands on her shoulders and gently squeezed.

He'll just use me and I refuse to be used.

"I'll take care of these. You go find some warm clothes and we'll head outside for a while." She turned to look at him and he shrugged. "If we don't see sunshine occasionally, we'll become claustrophobic."

She eyed him warily, unable to bring herself to relax after his latest comment.

"I promise to behave myself." He put his hand over his heart, his expression turning somber.

"Where have a heard that before?" she mumbled as she headed toward her room.

Stefan chuckled. "Yeah, but that time I had my fingers crossed."

Krista smiled despite herself.

* * * * *

Krista turned her face up toward the sky and sighed. The trees were so tall and thick she barely saw the lavender sky peeking out between the tips of the branches, which made the valley floor dark and cold.

Just being outside made her feel ten times better. The cool wind against her cheeks, the smell of damp dirt and dead leaves mingled in the breeze, tickling her nose. She could hear a stream in the distance, but the further up the mountain they went the further away the stream sounded.

Coming to a stop, she put her hand against the side of a tree. She ran her fingers over the smooth blue skin of the trunk. No grayish bark here. It almost felt like the leathery skin of a frog. Holding back a shudder, she let go of the tree and put her hands back in the pockets of the jacket Stefan had loaned her.

"You doing okay?"

She brought her gaze to Stefan's and smiled slightly. He was standing sideways, one foot resting on the log beside him, his hands on his hips. He didn't look the least bit winded, whereas she was almost breathless.

"I'm fine. Just taking a breather."

He studied her with a frown. "I keep forgetting you're not used to the atmosphere on this planet. I shouldn't have brought you up this far."

She shook her head and went to sit on the log next to where his foot rested. "It's not that. I just haven't hiked like this in ages. I didn't realize how out of shape I was."

One side of Stefan's mouth twitched as he let his eyes roam over her from head to toe. Her body immediately responded and heated up several degrees, her heart racing out of control.

"You look pretty in shape to me."

Krista scowled and reached out, slapping the side of his leg with her hand. Stefan laughed and the sound echoed in the trees.

"We can head back if you want," he said, sitting on the log beside her. The heat coming off his thigh seeped into hers and she ran her sweaty palms down her jeans.

She shook her head. "No. I'm not ready to go back yet. I like it out here. Is the whole planet like this?"

"Pretty much."

It suddenly became darker, and he looked up at the sky with a frown.

"What is it?" she asked as she raised her eyes as well. The blue had been replaced by dark gray clouds that obscured the tips of the trees. She pulled the edges of Stefan's jacket more firmly around her as the wind began to pick up. "Is it a storm?"

"Looks like it." He stood and pulled her to her feet. "We better get back."

She had no idea how far they were from the entrance to the cave, but she knew they had been outside for a while. Stefan came to a stop and she grabbed his elbow to steady herself on the slope. Following his gaze, she gasped.

Directly in front of them was nothing—everything was obscured by white. At first she thought it was fog but it appeared to move. "What is that?"

"It's snow."

She sucked in a breath as she watched it slowly approach them. "Oh my God, a whiteout? How are we going to find our way back?"

He squeezed her hand and gave her a firm look. "You hold onto my hand and don't let go, no matter what. Do you understand?"

She nodded her head and swallowed nervously. She could feel the biting cold of the wind as the storm moved closer. Never in her life had she seen anything like it. Holding tight to his hand, she followed him into the blinding white of the storm.

*****

Stefan stopped and tried to get his bearings. As a child he'd had a strong sense of direction and had been taught to use it. He just hoped he still could. It had been years since he actually had to rely on it.

Taking a deep breath, he closed his eyes for a second, trying once again to get a feel for the direction he needed. The mountain was to the right, he just knew it. Slowly, he began to make his way toward what he hoped to be south.

He could still feel Krista's hand in his, although he really couldn't see her that well. The snow was coming down too hard. He knew she had to be cold, he was freezing.

The wind had picked up and more than once almost knocked them off their feet. The cold felt like knives slicing through his skin. The snow coated their clothes, making them wet and only adding to their misery.

He turned sharply when he heard her squeal then felt the tug on his hand as she fell to the ground. Immediately he was down on his knee next to her. With one hand on her back, he leaned down next to her ear. "You okay?"

"Yeah." She nodded her head, her lips quivering and blue from the cold. Her nose was bright red, her cheeks already chapped. They had to find the cave soon or they were both in trouble.

"We're almost there. Hang onto me." He put her hand firmly back into his and helped her stand before starting off again.

After what seemed like an eternity, the white in front of him began to grow darker. Putting his hand out, he touched cold rock and let out a sigh of relief.

The entrance has to be here somewhere.

Moving to the left, he quickly found it and helped Krista inside. She let go of his hand and ran farther into the cave ahead of him. She wrapped her arms around her, shaking from head to toe. "Oh God. I am so cold."

He came up behind her and pushed her toward the hall, heading straight for her quarters. Once in the door he stood her before the fireplace and then headed to the bathroom.

"What are you doing?"

"I'm running you some water. I want you in a warm bath. While you're doing that I'm going to go fix us something hot to eat."

"What about you?"

"I'll be fine. You get in the tub."

She raised an eyebrow. "Yes, sir, bossy."

From his position sitting by the tub, he turned to look at her and almost laughed. She tried to scowl but her quivering lips only made her look comical. The idea of getting into the tub with her flashed through his mind, but he quickly pushed it aside.

Neither one of them had eaten since their brunch earlier and that had been several hours ago. He hadn't meant to keep her out that long. Reaching down, he swirled his hand through the water, checking the temperature.

"I can run my own water, you know."

He eyed her over his shoulder. She had come into the bathroom and was leaning her shoulder against the doorjamb.

Lord, she was tempting. Her hair was damp from the snow, her cheeks still kissed pink from the cold, her nose red. Her lips continued to quiver, and he was tempted beyond reason to cover them with his, to warm them until they stopped and melted against his own. Just thinking about it made him shift uncomfortably before standing.

"By all means."

He walked over, never taking his eyes off her nervous ones. Reaching out, he tugged at one of the buttons of her shirt. She swatted his hand away and he grinned.

"I guess that means you don't need any help disrobing, either?"

"Nope." She frowned and stepped aside, allowing him room to slip through the door.

"Okay, I get the hint." Before going completely out, he stopped. Putting his hand on the frame, he turned to look at her. "Would you like anything special for dinner?"

"Anything warm is fine."

"Warm it is." He winked at her before heading to the replicators.

*****

Krista sank deeper into the tub and let the warm water cover her shoulders. With a sigh, she looked around the unusual bathtub. People of Earth would pay a fortune for this look—the rock walls and floor. It was like sitting in a pool.

Reaching out, she touched the wall with the tip of her finger. A tiny waterfall cascaded along the rock and into the bath water. The trickling sound relaxed her and she leaned her head back, closing her eyes.

She tried not to think about Stefan, but her mind kept recalling the way he looked at her. The concern in his eyes when he thought she had overdone it, the seductive way he gazed at her, making her skin heat up. The way his lips felt on hers… God, just thinking about it sent a shiver of awareness through her body.

Watching the water ripple with her movements, she wondered if she could have a physical relationship with him and not let her heart get involved. But then what would she do if it did get involved? She didn't want to spend night after night crying herself to sleep, hating herself for once again losing her heart to someone she shouldn't.

She was almost thirty years old. She should know not to believe in fantasies. Stefan was one of the richest, most powerful men in the galaxy. He would never want her for anything other than a fling. And she couldn't forget that for even a second.

"Dinner's ready."

She jerked in surprise and swung her head toward Stefan's voice. He stood just inside the door, one hand on his hip, the other on the doorframe. He had changed into a pair of dry beige pants and what looked like a blue wool tunic. Slipping further into the water, she frowned at him. "Do you mind?"

"Not at all."

He grinned and leaned his back against the corner of the jamb. He tilted his head to the side, studying her as he crossed his arms over his chest.

She growled and splashed water at him, hitting the floor by his feet.

"You missed."

"You know, it just amazes me that some woman hasn't had you shot yet."

Stefan chuckled. "You may very well be the first." Reaching into a drawer, he pulled out a towel and laid it on the side of the tub.

She warily watched him as he stepped back into the bedroom, giving her some much-needed privacy. Standing, she quickly grabbed the towel—keeping her eye on the door the whole time—and dried herself. She realized she didn't have any clothes and groaned.

Wrapping the towel around herself, she called out, "Stefan."

"Yes?" He came to the door but kept his back to her. Silently, she commended him.

"I need a robe. Is there anything out there that would work?"

"How about this?" He held his hand up, a black robe dangling from his finger. "I must have left it the last time I stayed here."

"That will work." She snatched the robe from his hand and stepped back into the bathroom. She slipped her arms through the sleeves, then tied it tightly around her waist. Looking at herself in the mirror, she wasn't at all comfortable with the thin, revealing robe.

Krista could see her distended nipples through the silk and with her hair piled on her head, a few damp tendrils hanging down, it made her look sultry. Which was most definitely not what she had in mind. Maybe clothes would be a good idea.

"You better hurry or dinner's going to get cold."

The amusement in his tone was obvious, and she scowled in the direction of his voice. When she heard her stomach growl from hunger she decided to just forget it and go eat.

She stepped into the bedroom and was struck speechless by the scene. He had moved the small table to the center of the room and covered it in food that smelled heavenly. Her stomach growled so loudly she was sure he could hear it.

There were candles everywhere. On the dresser, on the table and even scattered along the walls on little ledges created by the uneven rock. The candlelight reflected off the damp walls of the cave, creating a shimmering effect she found beautiful—and very romantic. She stared back at him, an uneasy feeling in the pit of her stomach.

"I wasn't in there that long. How did you do all this?"

"You were in there longer than you think." He grinned as he pulled her chair out for her.

"I fell asleep?"

She wasn't sure she believed that, but now that she thought about it, maybe she had.

"You were snoring."

Krista frowned. "I do not snore."

Stefan just smiled in response.

"What's for dinner?" she asked as she sat in the chair, changing the subject.

"It's a Tilarian soup called mishowie." He ladled the food into a bowl and handed it to her.

"It smells wonderful." She lifted her spoon and took a small bite, then smiled. "It tastes similar to chicken soup."

"There's also fruit and bread," he said as he lifted the cloth cover. "As well as chocolate cake."

"Lord, if I eat all this I'll gain twenty pounds."

He shrugged as his eyes roamed over her. "You could afford a couple of pounds here or there."

She set her spoon down and eyed him. "Like your women a little chunky, do you?"

He chuckled as he reached for a piece of bread. "I wouldn't say chunky, since I don't have a clue what that is. But I definitely don't like overly skinny."

"So you think I'm overly skinny?"

She tried her best to look offended without grinning but it was hard. Especially when she saw him redden slightly before tripping over himself trying to explain.

"You're by no means overly skinny."

"So you think I'm fat?" She crossed her arms over her chest and tapped a finger.

Leaning his forearms against the table, he leered. "I don't know. Perhaps you should take off the robe and let me check for myself."

She rolled her eyes. Uncrossing her arms, she reached for a roll.

"Stefan one, Kris zip," he said.

He was rewarded with a roll in the face, which caused them both to laugh.

"See, you're laughing. And to think, earlier you wanted to shoot me. Now what would your life be like without me?" he asked.

"Peaceful?" She raised her eyebrow.

"Boring."

"Maybe I like boring." She took another spoonful of her soup.

Stefan snorted. "Yeah and maybe I like men."

"Really? I would have never guessed," she replied seriously and then giggled at the expression on his face.

Pointing his finger at her, he started to say something but shook his head with a grin. "You are something else."

"And you are a very good cook." She smiled as she took another sip.

"It doesn't take a whole lot of talent to push a button."

"Have you ever cooked real food?"

"I cook whenever I'm at my home on Tilarus. When I'm on Rhenari I usually don't have the time and just use a replicator. I enjoy cooking. Does that surprise you?"

"Actually, yes."

"Why?"

Krista shrugged. "Things are so advanced in your world it's just hard to imagine anyone doing something as mundane as cooking."

"My mother was from a farming community called Ricktoric. They had never even heard of replicators until she married my father. She was the one who taught me."

For a second she stared at him. "Your mother wasn't a monarch like your father?"

Stefan shook his head. "You didn't know that?"

"No, I just assumed... I thought your royalty system worked like ours, royalty marries royalty."

"In most cases, yes. But leave it to my father to do the unusual."

She watched him dip his bread in the soup. "You don't approve of what your father did?"

Stefan drank some of his wine and gazed at her over the rim. Shaking his head, he set his glass back down on the table. "I don't agree with arranged marriages—never have." Lifting the bottle, he filled her glass. "I think you should marry who you love, not who will enrich the family name."

"That's an unusual sentiment."

"True, and I might have felt differently had my father not married a farmer's daughter. I think the way you see things has to do with the way you were raised. I come from a very close family and I grew up seeing how happy and in love my parents were. I want the same thing they have." Krista couldn't seem to move her gaze from his as he stared into her eyes. "I want my wife to love me for me, not what I can do for her."

Clearing her throat, she studied the bowl in front of her. They were alone in this incredible place, they were attracted to each other. It would be very easy for one thing to lead to another. Again.

"How did your father meet your mother?" Krista asked as she scooped some pineapple onto a small plate.

"He crashed his ship on their planet. On my grandfather's property actually. My mother found him and they took care of him. When he regained consciousness he didn't remember who he was. In time he regained his memory, but by then he had fallen in love with my mother."

"What did your grandfather have to say about that?"

"Which one?" Stefan asked with a grin.

"Both."

"They were furious, but for different reasons. My mother's father thought he had used her, because she was pregnant with me at the time." He leaned across the table and whispered, "But don't tell my mother I know that."

She chuckled and whispered back, "Okay."

"My father's dad was angry because his son refused to come back to Tilarus and marry the girl they had picked out for him. Eventually everything worked out. But not before my father had some serious amends to make with my mother. She had found out he had regained his memory but didn't tell her."

"Sounds like quite a mess." Krista grinned and popped a grape into her mouth.

"Yeah." Stefan reached for a piece of chocolate cake. "But love like that is worth fighting for, no matter the mess it's in." He smiled seductively. "Wouldn't you agree?"

"I suppose." She looked down and twirled her spoon in the soup. "But how will you know that she really loves you and isn't just after your money?"

"She'll look at me the way my mother looks at my father."

At that, she brought her gaze back to his. The color of his eyes had deepened somewhat and he searched hers as though trying to read her innermost thoughts. She quickly averted her gaze. "You can fake that."

"No." He shook his head. "You can fake many things, but not that."

He stood and walked to her side of the table. Taking her hand in his, he brought her to her feet. She followed in a daze as he led her to a clear spot in the floor and pulled her into his arms. Slowly they began to dance. What was he doing?

"You do realize there's no music?" she asked.

He grinned and pulled her closer. "We don't need any."

His hand rested at the small of her back, sending jolts of tingling warmth up her spine. He grazed his lips against her cheek, stopping just short of her mouth, and waves of desire swirled in her stomach.

Clearing her throat, she moved her head to the side, pulling away from him. "So back to this idea that you can't fake it."

One corner of his mouth twitched as though fighting a grin. "Someone who is very good might fool some people, but I've spent most of my adult life learning how to read reactions. The eyes are the easiest to read, I think."

"For you, maybe. For me I don't think it would be that easy."

"Sure it would. You just have to pay attention. For example..."

She brought her gaze up to his and the corner of his lips lifted in a smile. "Your body tenses when it's this close to mine." He trailed the tip of his finger down the side of her neck, pausing to rest over her pulse point. "Your heart rate speeds up, I can feel it here."

Krista's face burned. Her skin tingled under his finger. Was she so easy to read?

He leaned down to kiss the throbbing spot with his lips and her mouth went dry. When his teeth found the sensitive spot below her ear she closed her eyes and tried to swallow the mewling sound deep in her throat.

"I can hear your sighs."

He ran his hand through her hair and removed the clip holding it on top of her head. As her hair cascaded down, he grabbed a handful and tugged her head back, exposing her throat.

He nibbled along her neck as he untied her sash. She gripped his shoulders, praying her knees didn't give out. His hands slipped inside her robe, and she shuddered as his featherlight touches ran up her ribs and grazed along the sides of her breasts.

Taking her hand in his, he placed it over his heart. The pounding rhythm matched her own and she looked up into his eyes.

"You can't fake this," he whispered as he lowered his lips to hers.

Chapter Eight

ꙮ

Krista groaned as his lips covered hers. He kept them light and teasing, nibbling on her lower lip before pulling it into his mouth and sucking on it.

She opened her mouth, but he didn't deepen the kiss. Instead he softly brushed his lips along hers—perfectly content to tease. With one hand at the small of her back, he raised his other and ran the back of his fingers along her cheek.

Her limbs felt heavy and her eyes drifted closed as she leaned into his hand. He planted soft butterfly kisses along her jaw.

She wanted him to kiss her, really kiss like he had the other night. He was so unhurried, so slow and deliberate. His hand roamed along her spine, making her tremble.

She slid her hands into his hair. It was thick and soft, like silk between her fingers.

"Don't ever cut your hair," she whispered as her hand continued to weave through its softness.

"Is that an order, blue eyes?"

She could hear the amusement in his soft husky voice as they continued to sway to an imaginary tune.

"No," she whispered. "Just a request."

He opened his eyes and gazed into hers. "What do I get in return?"

"What do you want?" Oh God, that was a bad choice of questions. She knew it the second she saw his grin.

"I want you."

Those three little words made her heart trip. "You want me? Whatever for?"

He chuckled seductively. "For starters," he leaned down and lightly kissed her, "I want to kiss you." He placed another kiss on the corner of her lips. "And I want to touch every inch of you."

She sighed as he nibbled his way to her neck.

"Kiss every inch of you."

The way he seductively whispered those words sent tingles along her skin. His light kisses continued across her shoulder as he pushed her robe down her arms, leaving her completely naked. The cool air of the room hit her feverish flesh and she shivered. His thumb circled one taut nipple and she swallowed down a groan.

"I want to kiss you here," he whispered against her lips.

She moaned into his kiss as he cupped her breast and gently squeezed before moving down her stomach and teasing her navel. "And here," he murmured. "Around this adorable navel ring."

His fingers moved further down and sifted through the hair at the juncture of her thighs. She sucked in a breath and held it, helpless against the sensations coursing through her.

"And here. I want to taste your cream as you come."

He was driving her crazy, she thought as she licked her suddenly dry lips. Why should she fight it anymore?

He watched with heavy-lidded eyes as she grabbed the bottom of his tunic and yanked it over his head. Her breath caught as she stared at him in wonder. She softly trailed her fingertips along his hard chest and swallowed. She recalled the day of the wedding, when she'd seen him without a shirt for the first time, and how much his muscular build had surprised her. He was hard and toned and oh so gorgeous.

Her fingers continued along his washboard stomach and he sucked in a breath, the muscles along his rib cage twitching. She swiped her thumb across his nipple and felt it harden beneath her touch. She peered up at him through her lashes and leaned forward to flick her tongue across the hard peak. A groan rumbled through his chest as he grabbed her face in his hands, pulling it back to his.

"No," he growled, nipping at her lower lip. "I barely have any control as it is. You start that and I won't have any at all."

Burying his hands in her hair, he captured her mouth with his. She moaned as his tongue slid past her parted lips to do battle with hers. It was a demanding kiss, one that stole her breath and left her weak. He pulled back and gazed at her, his finger running along her bottom lip.

"You are so beautiful," he sighed.

He made her feel beautiful with the way he looked at her, the way he touched her. He made her feel cherished and special. She could hardly breathe as he bent down and picked her up in his arms.

Putting one knee on the bed, he leaned over and placed her in the center of the mattress. The coolness of the sheets felt good against her hot flesh. She watched as Stefan stood and removed his pants, slowly revealing every inch of his glorious limbs, his skin glowing gold in the candlelight. Her eyes found his erection and her heart raced. It stood straight and thick, coming almost to his navel, and she remembered how good it had felt buried in her pussy.

The warmth of his hard body coming in contact with hers as he settled over her made her sigh. His lips took hers in hot urgency while his hands expertly explored every inch of her sensitive skin.

With featherlight touches they slowly moved down her stomach, then across her hip. She shifted as his fingers ran down the outside of her thigh, then slowly back up to tangle in the curls between her legs.

He drove her mad. Never in her life did she think sex could be like this. His touch was gentle yet passionate, soft yet demanding. She was completely out of control. She wanted him, but he was in no hurry as he continued with his slow seduction.

Sliding his hand between her thighs, Stefan moaned at how wet and hot she was. Pushing a finger inside her, he almost lost his willpower to take it slow. She was so passionate. It took everything in him to not bury himself inside her—to lose himself in her velvety softness.

"Like this?" he whispered against her lips as he moved his finger in a slow, gentle rhythm.

"Mmmm…yes."

His thumb lightly circled her sensitive clit, spreading her juices all around, teasing but never completely touching. He lowered his head and captured a nipple between his teeth, softly biting and then gently sucking.

"Stefan, please." She buried her hands in his hair as she arched toward his mouth.

He left her breast and moved lower along her stomach. Heedless of her pleas, his tongue teased her navel and his teeth tugged at the belly button ring. "This thing is sexy as hell, whatever possessed you to get one?"

"It was an impulse thing," she murmured.

"Good impulse." Moving even lower, his lips brushed the hair between her thighs. She gasped and spread her legs wider. Keeping his finger deep inside her, his tongue gently circled her swollen nub. He licked, nibbled and sucked, inhaling her sweet fragrance. "*Shetah*, you taste good, Kris."

The tip of his tongue grazed across her swollen clit and her hands gripped the sheets as sensation raced through her body like a speeding freight train. She wanted him inside her.

"Stefan," she gasped.

He kept teasing her, kept pushing her ever closer to that elusive pinnacle.

"What, *kisary*?"

She moaned, unable to form words as his tongue and fingers continued to turn her to mush.

"This?" The tip of his tongue flicked across the right spot. Lifting her hips off the bed, she screamed as her release hit her full force. He continued until every last aftershock had passed before lifting his body above her and settling between her thighs.

His eyes were a deep black, his jaw clenched tight. He looked as though he held onto his control by a thin thread as his gaze locked with hers. Something passed across his expression, but just as quickly it was gone. Like a ghost. Had she only thought she'd seen it? Was it wishful thinking on her part?

Her questions were soon forgotten as he spread her thighs with his and thrust himself inside her. "Damn, Kris."

In answer, she lifted her hips against his. He pulled back slightly then pushed further in, burying all of himself deeply. She closed her eyes and tilted her head back, lost in the sensations of him filling her, the perfection of how they fit together. A moan escaped her lips and he covered them with his. Her taste lingered on his lips and she swiped at her juices with her tongue, intrigued.

He made love to her with slow, deep strokes that fulfilled her like no one else ever had. His expert moves and thrusts once again ignited her passion, making her hunger for that release she knew instinctively only he could give her.

She felt so close, her body tense, her nerve endings screaming as she clung to him. The more he gave, the more she wanted. She couldn't get enough of him.

"Stefan. Ahhh…"

"I know, *kisary*."

He gripped the back of her thigh, pulling it up around his hip. "Let it go. Come for me," he whispered against her lips.

She gasped as he slid deeper, his thrusts becoming harder, more demanding. She closed her eyes as the sensations within her body built to a fever pitch.

Suddenly everything shattered as a release unlike anything she'd ever felt before took hold. She screamed his name, lifting her hips higher against his.

He moaned, slowing his thrusts, moving in a way that prolonged her pleasure. He could feel every contraction milking him, pulling at him, bringing him ever closer to his own release. Finally giving in, he buried himself deep inside her, his body trembling from the force of his own orgasm as he emptied his seed deep inside her.

Slowly their breathing returned to normal and he lifted himself up on his elbows. He gazed down at her and brushed the back of his fingers across her cheek. Her eyes drifted closed and he softly kissed her temple, his body still weak and trembling. He'd never experienced anything like it. Or anything like her.

My God, when did I fall in love with her?

She opened her eyes and stared up at him. She could still see the remnants of passion in his gaze, the tenderness she always associated with him.

He dropped his head and softly kissed her lips. "Kris, I…"

She held her breath. *Oh God, don't say it. Please don't say it.*

He closed his eyes and laid his forehead against hers. A shaky sigh escaped his parted lips. She let out the breath she'd been holding, relieved that he hadn't finished his thought. She knew if he said it, she would be lost.

She couldn't love him. No matter what, she had to remember that.

* * * * *

The beep of his communicator woke Stefan from a sound sleep and he inwardly groaned. He reached to the floor and quickly grabbed it before it woke Krista. Looking at the screen, he saw the code for the *Vultair*.

Damn.

He slipped out of bed and threw on his pants. Before leaving the room, he walked over to Krista's side of the bed and stared down at her. His heart ached to tell her how he felt, but she had tensed up last night when he almost told her he loved her. He knew she wasn't ready to hear it.

Leaning over, he pulled the cover up around her shoulders. He would wait until she was ready—or until she told him.

A sense of dread passed over him. Was she stubborn enough to keep it in and never tell him? He wouldn't let that happen. He would confront her first, make her admit how she felt. Whether she realized it or not, he could see it in her eyes.

He placed a kiss against her temple and then left the room, quietly shutting the door behind him.

Once in the rec room, he sat at the desk and hit the switch to bring the computer to life. He punched in his access code to signal the *Vultair* and waited impatiently while it searched for the ship.

His feet were cold against the stone floor and he realized he should have grabbed his shoes. The signal was finally found and Taron answered after the second beep, his tired face appearing on screen.

"Do you have any idea what time it is?" Stefan scowled.

"No." Taron raised an eyebrow and brought his hand up, pointing at a spot where his neck met his shoulder. "But I have a pretty good idea what you've been up to."

Stefan brought his hand up and touched the side of his neck with a frown. It quickly dawned on him what Taron indicated and he grinned. He remembered Krista had bitten him there, and he was sure he had a good-sized love bite to show for it.

"This better be good." He looked pointedly at the screen and Taron chuckled.

"I'll make it quick so you can get back to other things. I talked to the informant today and found out Carlone has a place on Shevalli. I'm heading there first thing in the morning."

"Shevalli? Isn't that a farming community?"

"Yes, apparently his grandfather owned a farm there and left it to him when he died."

"That's interesting." He sat back in the chair, crossing his arms over his bare chest. "How did Carlone end up in the militia coming from that background?"

"It's a long story."

Stefan nodded. "Keep me informed."

"Will do. As soon as we're done I'll head to the camp."

Stefan grinned. "Take your time."

"Lucky ass," Taron grumbled before signing off.

* * * * *

Krista heard the door open and waited quietly for Stefan to climb back into bed. Her eyes wandered his firm body appreciatively as he stripped his pants off and slipped under the covers. Earlier had been so incredible. He had been incredible. He met her gaze and smiled. "Did I wake you?"

"No. The beeper did."

"I'm sorry." He rested on his elbow and rubbed her cheek with the pad of his thumb.

She shrugged. "It's okay. Was it anything important?"

His fingers running along her neck and collarbone again inflamed her desire. Her skin heated, her heart raced, even the spot between her legs throbbed. *How can he do this to me so easily?*

"It was just Taron. He'll be here in a day or two."

She placed her palm against his bare chest and watched the slow rise and fall of his breathing. She felt the steady beat of his heart beneath her fingers, the warmth of his skin. Had she made a terrible mistake? Did she love him?

No. She briefly closed her eyes, hardening her resolve. *I don't love him. Lust after him, yes. But I don't love him. I can't love him.*

"Kris?"

The question in his voice caused her to open her eyes and look at him. They were soft and filled with concern and something else she wouldn't name. He opened his mouth to say something and she placed her hand over his lips, silencing him.

He grabbed her hand, his brows drawn together in a frown. "You can't keep avoiding this or changing the subject." She leaned over and placed a kiss on his shoulder. He smiled slightly. "Or trying to distract me."

She kissed his neck, then softly bit it. "Is it working?" she whispered against his skin.

He moaned softly. "What do you think?"

Her hand slowly skimmed along his hard stomach, her fingers teasing every valley. The muscles twitched beneath her exploring touch and his chest muscles trembled under her gentle kisses.

When her fingers wrapped around his rock-hard shaft, she grinned. "I think it is."

Stefan grabbed her shoulders and rolled to his back, pulling her up on top of him. He wrapped one arm around her waist, the other hand he used to brush the hair away from her face.

"What am I going to do with you?" he whispered.

Her breath caught in her throat at the intensity of his stare. Could he see in her eyes how she felt about him? Could he tell in the beating of her heart?

"Make love to me." The words left her mouth before she even realized it.

He smiled slightly as he brought her lips down to his. "Gladly, *kisary*."

It was far from slow this time. But wild and passionate. His kisses sent her falling out of control and she wiggled her pussy against his hardening cock. "Damn, woman," he growled and rolled her to her back. "You're killing me."

"And you're driving me crazy," she answered back. "I want you, Stefan. Now."

"Ah, fuck," he groaned. "Move to your knees."

She smiled, intrigued with the idea of him slamming into her from behind. With a devilish glance over her shoulder, she positioned herself in front of him and wiggled her behind. He grabbed her hips and held her still as he invaded her tight passage with his massive cock. She screamed and laid her forehead against the mattress. He felt so good inside her. He pulled out, then slowly pushed back in with a moan. "God, that feels so fucking good."

It did, but she wanted more. "Stefan, stop playing. I want you to fuck me."

Stefan closed his eyes with a smile. He loved how she talked dirty when she was desperate. Putting his hands along her ribs, he lifted her against his chest, making sure to keep his cock deeply seated. His palms squeezed her breasts, and she thrust them forward with a sigh.

"I like your breasts, Kris." He pinched her nipples, making them harden. "I like how you respond to my touch. How well we fit together." He thrust his cock deeper to prove his point and smiled as she wiggled her hips against him. "Feel how well we fit together, Kris."

Taking her hand, he moved it to her pussy. She could feel his cock slowly moving in and out, her juices making him slick and wet. Her thumb brushed her clit, making her gasp. He felt so good, so right. Never in her life had she been this wild with someone, this uninhibited. With his hand over hers, she moved to toy with her clit. The sensitive nub hardened and swelled beneath her touch. She moaned as Stefan's hand moved in conjunction with hers. The two of them moving as one.

"It feels good, doesn't it, baby?" he whispered. "Make yourself come for me."

She groaned as her fingers moved faster, applying just a little more pressure. "That's it, baby." Stefan's hips thrust faster, his cock filling her impossibly deep. "Stefan," she screamed as her body shuddered from pleasure.

Falling forward, she braced herself on her hands as Stefan continued to plunder her pussy. Over and over he plunged and her body responded with another more powerful orgasm. Every muscle quaked in pleasure and she screamed as her release skimmed through her body again and again. Stefan growled and hot jets of semen emptied into her spasming channel.

"Oh, God," she sighed, her forehead lying against the cold comforter.

With a sigh, he pulled from her body and tugged her against him as they settled beneath the sheets. His warmth seeped into her relaxed body and it wasn't long before she fell sound asleep nestled in the safe cocoon of his arms.

Chapter Nine

ꕥ

"Oh, my God."

Krista sighed as she gazed around at the winter wonderland spread before her. She and Stefan had just finished lunch and decided to head outside to check out what the storm had done.

It was absolutely beautiful. Wet snow clung to branches and rockfaces, turning everything within view white. The sunlight glittered off icicles hanging from tree limbs, causing them to sparkle like diamonds.

The air was still cool and crisp and smelled fresh. With a smile, she inhaled deeply. "Now if we just had a sled."

Stefan raised an eyebrow in question. "A sled?"

"You're kidding, right?" she asked with surprise.

He shook his head.

"You don't know what a sled is?"

"No."

She placed her hands on her hips and studied him. "What did you used to do as a kid when it snowed?"

"We used to take a scrap piece of ship, go to the top of a hill and slide down on it."

She raised an eyebrow and grinned. "Stefan, that's a sled."

He shrugged and walked toward her. "You call it a sled. I call it a *gleent*." He smiled seductively, coming closer. "Have you ever made love in the snow?"

Narrowing her eyes, she held her hand up in front of her. "Stop right there, Senator."

He stopped and raised an eyebrow.

"You wore me out this morning."

"Did I?" He grinned as he began to walk toward her again.

She took a step back, moving toward the rockface. "Yes, you did. I'm quite sore."

She tried to keep a straight face, but was having a difficult time of it. He looked gorgeous this morning in his jeans and wool tunic, the white turtleneck underneath a stark contrast to the deep blue of the wool.

His gray eyes sparkled with a devilish light. Occasionally that flash of something she couldn't identify shone in his eyes but as soon as it was there it was gone again. She wondered if he was trying to keep his feelings hidden from her. Or maybe it was something he himself didn't even know was there.

Her back hit the rock wall, and she stopped. His hands on either side of her head kept her pinned in place. He wiggled his eyebrows. "Maybe I should kiss it and make it better."

Her laughter echoed through the valley around them. "You are so bad."

He returned her smile, then bent down, tossing her over his shoulder.

"Hey," she gasped. "What are you doing?"

"We're going to find something to make a *gleent* with."

"What? You don't think I can walk on my own?"

"I'm sure you can." His hand slowly made its way up the inside of her thigh and she gasped. "But this is so much more fun."

"Stefan Marcone!" She tried to reach around and swat at his hand, but she couldn't reach it. His laughter made her scowl. "You're impossible."

* * * * *

Finally finding a piece of metal, they spent the next couple of hours sledding down hills and challenging each other to snowball fights. He couldn't remember the last time he'd laughed like this, the last time he'd felt this alive.

Whenever he looked at her he fell a little more in love. He knew it now, without a doubt. But she still kept that wall up, only allowing him so close. The snowball to the side of his head caught him by surprise. His eyes closed and he fell to the ground in a heap.

"Stefan?" Her laughter stopped and concern filled her voice. "Stefan?"

He heard the crunch of the snow as she made her way to his side. Just as she dropped to her knees next to him he grabbed her arm and pulled her down. Rolling over, he pinned her beneath him.

She squealed and looked up at him with shocked eyes that quickly narrowed. "You faker." She swatted at his shoulder and he chuckled. "You scared me to death."

He smiled down at her. His lips softly brushed her cheek. "Were you afraid you'd hurt me?"

"No." Her breathing sped up slightly as he nibbled her neck. "I don't know how to get out of here. If anything were to happen to you, I would be trapped."

He stopped what he was doing and looked down at her with a raised eyebrow. "That's it?" he asked incredulously.

One corner of her lips twitched. "Well, what did you expect?"

"I don't know." He shrugged. "Lie to me. Tell me you can't live without me."

"It's more like I can't live with you," she grumbled.

They looked at each other and laughed. It was on the tip of his tongue to tell her he loved her, but he was afraid it would push her away. Fear was something he didn't often feel and to feel it over a woman made it even more strange and unsettling.

Slowly he dropped his mouth to hers, trying to convey what he couldn't say out loud yet. Her lips were cold and trembled slightly, but they quickly warmed against his as they kissed, their tongues in slow battle.

He moved his hand to her hip and gently squeezed. The way her body perfectly molded to his never failed to amaze him. The way she responded to his touch never failed to take his breath away. He put his hand at the back of her leg and raised it as he slid his thigh between hers. The desire he felt for her, coursing through his veins, shocked him. It seemed the more he made love to her the more he wanted her. She made him feel whole, complete, and he couldn't get enough.

His fingers lifted the hem of her sweater and brushed along the skin of her stomach. It felt soft and hot to the touch. She sucked in a breath and shivered.

"My hands cold?"

"A little," she sighed as he placed soft kisses along her jaw. "I'm getting all wet."

He grinned against her neck. "In more ways than one, I would imagine."

She poked her finger in his side and he chuckled.

"You know what would really be incredible right now?" she asked.

"Besides this?"

His thumb brushed across her nipple, and Krista had to concentrate hard to remember what she was saying. Shivers ran down her spine that didn't have anything to do with the temperature. At the moment she didn't even feel the cold.

She watched as he reached over and popped a small bit of snow in his mouth. "Lying in it isn't enough?"

He grinned as he raised her sweater and moved the lace of her bra aside. Bending over, he captured the peak of her hard, hot breast in his cold, snow-filled mouth, and she almost screamed at the sensation.

Slowly the snow melted and his mouth warmed as his tongue continued to stroke and tease her sensitive nipple. She buried her hands in his hair, arching further into his touch.

Lifting his head, he pushed her sweater back down, then moved to place nibbling kisses along her lips.

"What were you saying?" he whispered against them.

"I...uh..." She swallowed as his tongue traced the edges of her lips. "I was thinking a warm bath would be great about now."

"Mmmm." He shifted his thigh, rubbing it between her legs.

She sucked in a breath and moved her hips against it.

"A warm bath does sound nice," he whispered.

He bit her lower lip and then sucked it into his mouth. He pressed his thigh tighter against her aching pussy and she moaned.

"Stefan, you have to stop this." His lips covered hers. His tongue traced her teeth then retreated. "We can't make love in the snow."

"Who says?"

She giggled. "Me. I'm freezing."

Stefan smiled and kissed the tip of her nose. "Come on, then. I'll take you up on that bath idea."

"What makes you think I wanted to take a bath with you?"

Stefan bent over and grabbed her hands, pulling her up in front of him. "Just for that, you little minx," he hissed, bringing them nose to nose, "I'm going to make you beg."

Her lips twitched at the corners, fighting a grin. "Beg for what? The bath?"

"No. Me."

He quickly bent at the waist and lifted her in his arms. She squealed, her laughter floating around them. She buried her face in his neck and placed soft kisses at the spot where she could feel his pulse racing.

"Maybe I'll make you beg," she whispered against his neck.

She felt the tremor run through him and smiled. He stepped into the cave and headed for her room.

"Do your worst, *kisary*. We'll see who makes who beg."

* * * * *

Okay, so I begged.

Krista grinned and snuggled deeper into his arms, her head on his chest, one leg across his. The man was certainly talented, but there should be more to a relationship than sex. The reality was they were from two different worlds. Not just literally, but figuratively as well.

Stefan was royalty and no matter what he tried to tell her about how he wanted to marry for love, the fact of the matter was she didn't belong in his world. A countess she was not. And never would be.

A thunderous noise echoed throughout the cavern, jolting her from her thoughts. Her eyes widened and she sat up.

Stefan grabbed his beeping communicator and flipped it open. "It's okay. It's Taron."

"Is that a ship?" she asked as her nervous gaze took in the glasses shaking on the table.

"Yeah, he's in the docking bay. Sound echoes through here pretty good." He tugged on a small strand of her hair. "Hey, *kisary*. Come back down here."

"Don't you need to meet him or something?"

He grinned. "Taron knows his way around. We'll greet him in the morning."

She lay back down next to him, his arms wrapped tightly around her. He kissed her forehead and she smiled, snuggling closer to his warmth.

She finally remembered to ask about what he had called her. "What does *kisary* mean?"

"It's a Tilarian endearment."

She rose up on her elbow and looked at him. "But what does it mean?"

"It means stubborn."

She grinned. "No, it doesn't."

He studied her hair as he softly ran his finger through it and pushed a curl behind her ear.

"Well." She lifted an eyebrow. "Are you going to tell me?"

He rolled over and propped himself on his elbow as well. Bringing his lips extremely close to hers, he studied her thoughtfully. "Hmmm. Why should I?"

She smiled seductively and trailed a finger along his chest. "Because you can't resist me."

A chuckle rumbled through his chest. He put his finger under her chin and tipped it up. His fathomless gray eyes bored into hers, and she felt as though she was branded, made his just by a look. "It means 'my love'."

What was he saying? Was he saying he loved her? Or was "my love" just something like "sweetheart" or "honey"?

She knew this was a mistake. They were from opposite ends of the spectrum. A middle-class country girl and a monarch whose level of royalty would be equivalent to that of Britain's king. How would she ever go back to see her friend? She would always be worried she would run into him, and God forbid he should marry someone. She would be heartbroken.

She opened her mouth to speak, to tell him how she felt, but before she could utter two words his lips captured hers in a kiss that stole her breath.

She tore her mouth from his. "Stefan, we need—"

He didn't let her finish. He once again sought her lips with his as he pushed her to her back and settled over her.

Against her mouth, he whispered, "Shh. Be quiet, Kris. Just let me make love to you."

She wrapped her arms around his neck and returned his hungry kisses. She'd take this while she could. Soon it would be time for her to return home to her job, her apartment…and a life without Stefan.

Chapter Ten

ꕥ

Early the next morning Stefan found Taron at a table in the rec room. His brother looked troubled as he stared into his coffee. "How did it go on Shevalli?" Stefan asked as he ordered coffee from the replicator.

Taron sighed. "The house blew up before I could give it a good once-over."

Stefan choked on his coffee. "It what?" He took a seat and set his cup on the table in front of him.

"Carlone apparently anticipated someone coming there and had the house rigged."

He frowned. "For what purpose?"

Taron pursed his lips as he studied the cup on the table. "My guess would be just for kicks. As far as I could tell there was nothing there."

"There had to be something there. Why would he blow up an empty house?"

"Maybe in the hopes he would get one of you in the process?"

Stefan whipped his gaze around to see Krista standing not ten feet away. She looked adorable in her tight pants and one of his oversized shirts. It swallowed her whole, but he loved seeing her in it. It looked right.

Suddenly he frowned. He didn't want her concerned about what was happening. "Would you like some coffee?" he asked as he stood and headed for the replicator.

"Yes. Thank you."

Stefan handed her a cup and their fingers brushed. The electricity in that touch made him stop short. His gaze locked with her blue one, and he winked. With a blush, she set her cup on the table.

"So, Taron. How's the investigation going?" she asked.

"I think we've stalled. It seems no—"

"Taron." Stefan pinned him with a glare as he pulled his chair out and sat down.

"What?" Taron shrugged.

"You better not be doing what I think you are," Krista snapped at Stefan. Krista hadn't missed the look Stefan gave Taron. He was trying to keep her in the dark, but why? She narrowed her eyes at him. "I'm not a child."

"I never said you were."

"Then why are you trying to keep me out of the loop?" She leaned her elbows on the table and raised an eyebrow, her coffee forgotten.

Stefan opened his mouth but stopped when Taron stood. "Maybe I should just let the two of you hash this out alone."

"Oh no." Stefan reached up and grabbed his arm. With a scowl, he pointed to the chair Taron had just vacated. "Sit. This is all your fault to begin with."

Taron frowned. "Mine? Where the hell did you come up with that nonsense?"

Krista held up a hand and snapped, "Enough."

She almost laughed at the men's expressions. Both looked shocked to say the least. "Taron, sit down."

The corners of Taron's lips twitched as he took his seat. Stefan leaned back in his chair and crossed his arms over his chest. His shirt was open down the front and she fought the desire to let her eyes roam over his muscles. She brought her gaze back to his eyes and noticed they were filled with laughter.

"Are we about to be put in our place?" Stefan asked with amusement.

"You are."

Taron chuckled but stopped when Stefan flashed him a glare. She watched the two of them and would have fought back laughter of her own if she hadn't been so mad. Stefan had a bad habit of babying her, and she'd had enough.

"At least Taron has the decency to treat me like an adult and not hide things from me. I'm in this just as deep as you are, remember?"

Stefan sighed. "You're right."

Wow, that was easy. Too easy.

She eyed him with suspicion as he stood and walked to her side of the table. Squatting down on his heels, he put one hand on her knee, the other on the back of her chair. Some of her anger began to melt away as he rubbed her thigh with his thumb. Tingles spread along her skin, and she placed her hand over his to keep it still.

"Why don't I fix us all some breakfast and we can talk about this later?" He smiled up at her. "How's that?"

She crossed her arms in front of her. "I have an even better idea. How about we fix breakfast and continue discussing the assassin."

Taron choked trying to hold back a chuckle and Stefan glared at him. "I'm so glad you find this amusing."

"Come on, Stefan. She's right."

"Why are you having such a hard time with this?" She touched his hair and let a lock of it fall between her fingers.

"I just don't want you involved."

He stood and walked over to the replicator, keeping his back to her. She faced Taron and he nodded his head in Stefan's direction, a ghost of a smile tugging at his lips.

"Stefan?" She stood and walked over next to him. She touched his arm and felt the muscles tense beneath her fingers, but he didn't pull away. Instead he turned to her with eyes full of guilt and remorse.

"I don't want anything to happen to you because of me. If I hadn't brought you up to the rings of Metalon you would still be on Daego shopping and sightseeing."

She tugged at his shirtsleeve and grinned. "Shopping and sightseeing sounds rather boring after a few days here with you."

Stefan didn't rise to the bait. Instead he frowned slightly.

With a sigh, she continued. "We can play the 'what if' game all day. In the end it's still the same. I don't blame you, and you shouldn't blame yourself. I'm actually glad I came with you." A cocky grin spread across her face. "Besides, I can take care of myself, you know."

The corner of his mouth lifted in a grin. Some of the tension eased out of him and his arm relaxed. "Is that so?"

"Yep. Do I need to prove it?"

He chuckled and touched the side of her face with the back of his fingers. "No, *kisary*. You don't need to prove it."

His eyes softened and he tipped her chin up with his finger. She held her breath, anticipating his kiss as he dipped his head, but Taron's loud cough stopped them. "I hate to interrupt..."

"Then don't," Stefan growled.

"But I'm starving."

She listened to Stefan's halfhearted grumbles about Taron being a pain in the ass and laughed.

"Okay," she sat at the table and took a sip of her coffee, "So back to what we were discussing."

Stefan sat a plate of Tilarian finger foods on the table and everyone dug in. Krista loved the small sweet cakes that were similar to donuts.

"Any sign of Carlone on Daego?" Stefan asked.

"Sidious has people looking, but so far nothing. I'm beginning to wonder if maybe he just happened to run across you in space."

Krista swallowed her bite and cleared her throat. "Could he be in some sort of disguise and that's why no one is seeing him?"

"That's a very real possibility." Stefan sat back in his seat and tapped his finger on the side of the coffee cup. "The question is what kind of disguise is he using?"

"What kinds are there?" She shrugged her shoulders.

"Unfortunately, numerous," Taron replied dryly. "But before we get off track, I received a transmission from Senator Woods yesterday. Several of the senators have decided to postpone their upcoming meetings for the time being, until this assassin can be caught."

Stefan nodded his head. "That's probably a good idea."

"They've decided not to postpone the upcoming vote, though."

"That doesn't make any sense. Why would they postpone meetings but not the vote?" Krista frowned.

Taron turned to her. "Meetings are expendable. They can always discuss what needs to be discussed later or conference through transmissions. They've been preparing for this vote for months. They weren't willing to put it off."

Her gaze went from one to the other. "When is the vote?"

"Three days," Stefan said.

She watched Stefan study his cup. What was he thinking? Did he want to attend the vote? More than likely he did. He hated being cooped up here. Even though he tried to make the best of things she could tell that he was fidgety and ready to finally have this problem at an end.

"What if you took me back to Daego? I should be safe enough at Sidious' estate. He isn't even after me, I was just in the way." She waved her hand toward Taron. "You said yourself you don't believe Carlone is there."

Stefan brow drew together in a frown. "What brought this on?"

"I just thought you might want to get back in the swing of things instead of being stuck here taking care of me."

"I like taking care of you."

The intensity in his eyes made her breath stop short. She averted her gaze and intently studied her cup.

"It's settled. We're staying," Stefan said.

Her head snapped up and she frowned. "It's not settled. Frankly, I'm tired of being cooped up here. I want to go back to Daego."

Taron coughed and raised an eyebrow at Stefan. "Go ahead and say it, Taron," Stefan sighed.

"I agree with Krista. I think she would be fine on Daego. I can put the *Vultair* in orbit cloaked and transport you straight to Sidious' study undetected. Maybe if we play our cards right, your going to Rhenari might just work in our favor."

"So you want to use me as bait?"

"What?" Krista snapped but neither man paid attention to her.

Taron nodded. "Your return might be the very thing that will lure him out. I think it's time we played this card. I'm tired of chasing the son of a bitch all over the galaxy."

"I agree." Stefan stood to get more coffee and Krista followed.

"Wait a minute."

Stefan turned to look at her and raised an eyebrow. "What is it, Kris?"

"When I suggested going back to Daego, I didn't think you would be putting a target on your back."

He glanced at Taron and he stood, setting his cup on the table. "I'll go prep the *Vultair* and get her ready for the trip."

Stefan nodded then turned back to Krista. He took her hand in his and kissed the backs of her fingers. Fear for him tightened her stomach but she refused to admit to herself the real reason she was scared.

"Everything will be fine."

She opened her mouth to argue but Stefan put his finger over her lips. "Trust me. You'll be fine with Sidious while Taron and I take care of this."

The question "what then" formed on the tip of her tongue, but she already knew the answer. She would return to Earth and Stefan to Rhenari. What they shared would be a fond memory and her life would return to normal, but she knew in her heart she would never love anyone like she loved him. She wasn't sure what hurt more—the thought of him being killed, or the thought of loving him but never being able to have him.

* * * * *

Stefan loaded the new runner onto the docking bay of the *Vultair* and they took off for Daego. Krista stood on the bridge and watched the stars shoot by like in the screen saver on her computer. She had no idea how fast they were going, but she was sure it was well beyond anything Earth was capable of.

She noticed Stefan approach in the reflection of the glass, the smile on his face making the corners of his eyes crinkle. As always, the sight made her heart beat faster. His arms gently wrapped around her and pulled her close. The warm heat from his chest seeped into her back, chasing away the slight chill of the bridge.

"You okay?" he asked. "You've been awfully quiet since we left the camp."

"I was just thinking how much I'm going to miss that cave."

"I'm going to miss what we shared at that cave. Now we'll be back in the middle of the usual Marcone three-ring circus. We'll have to get creative when it comes to privacy."

She had been thinking about that ever since they left the old rebel camp. It had been fun and absolutely incredible but maybe she should call an end to it. After all, they were back home now. The fantasy was over.

"Stefan," she began.

"If you're fixing to say what I think you are, I'm going to put you over my knee," he growled in her ear.

"You're going back to Rhenari in a few days and I'm going back home to Earth. Why prolong it? It was fun while it lasted."

"What?" He stepped back and ran a hand through his hair, then turned to Taron. "How long until we reach Daego?"

"About two hours. Why?"

"Can you handle it without me?"

Taron snorted. "Now that's a stupid question. It's my ship."

Stefan nodded and grabbed Krista's hand, pulling her behind him.

"Where are we going?"

"You and I are going to talk." He dragged her into the chute that would take them to the residential level.

"There's nothing to talk about," she said, her frustration rising quickly to the surface.

He turned to face her, his eyes ablaze with anger. "There is something to talk about and I'm not about to let you push it aside and ignore it."

The door opened and she followed him down the hall to his quarters. "I'm not ignoring it, I'm facing reality."

"Your perceived reality," he said as he stepped into his quarters.

She entered just after him and the door closed with a swoosh behind her. The elegant room drew her up short. Taking a second, she looked around. A huge window took up one wall, a massive bed sat against the other, a blue silk comforter draped over the top. It was a beautiful room, decorated with top-of-the-line furnishings and paintings. The scene only brought home the fact they didn't belong together.

"You're only forestalling the inevitable," she said with a sigh. "You know it as well as I do."

He stepped closer and glared down at her, his hands resting on his hips. "I know no such thing."

"Please don't make this any harder than it has to be. Mikayla is the only family that I have left."

He shook his head, his brow wrinkling with a look of confusion. "What does that have to do with us?"

"That has everything to do with us. If we make this hard, it'll be too difficult for me to ever come back. I don't want that to happen." With a shaking hand, she wiped away a tear as it slipped down her cheek. "You're a monarch for crying out loud!"

"And you're a commoner, is that it?"

"Exactly."

"That won't hold water with me and you know it." He took a step closer, his hand gently wiping away another tear. "My mother was a commoner, Mikayla is as well. You're making excuses, Krista."

"I'm trying to be realistic."

"This is realistic," he said as he dipped his head and lightly touched his lips to hers. "You and I are real. What's between us is real."

His breath whispered across her lips like a soft breeze, and she swallowed the desire to feel his lips against hers again. She couldn't let him do this. Shaking her head, she opened her mouth to argue, but Stefan interrupted.

"I'm not willing to walk away from this and I'm not going to let you either." His mouth captured hers in a kiss that robbed her of speech and breath.

All she could do was melt against him and surrender to the passion raging between them. His arms slipped around her waist, pulling her tightly against him. Her aching breasts pressed into his chest and she moaned, trying to bring them closer.

Tongues mated with a fierceness that made her weak and hungry for more. Stefan's hands moved between them to the front of her shirt. He jerked it apart and she gasped as buttons broke free and hit the metal walls of the ship with pings.

"I'll buy you a new one," he whispered against her lips as he pushed the shirt down her arms.

He was making love to her in anger, trying to prove a point. She knew it but couldn't bring herself to stop him. Her body wanted this too much.

Wrapping her arms around his neck, she groaned as his hands covered her breasts and squeezed. Slowly his kisses gentled, his touch becoming more tender, loving. This was the Stefan she knew, the Stefan she loved with all her heart.

He broke the kiss and laid his forehead against hers. The gentle touch of his hands against her cheeks sent tingling sensations to the pit of her stomach.

"I'm not letting you go," he whispered.

"Why?" Swallowing down a lump, she continued, "Why can't you just accept this is what I want?"

"If you can look me in the eye and tell me this is truly what you want I'll agree to let you go. Can you do that? Can you tell me you have no feelings for me at all?"

She shook her head as more tears slipped free. Of course she had feelings for him. She loved him. His lips kissed away her tears and that only made more fall.

"Don't cry, *kisary,*" he sighed against her cheeks. "I never thought I would ever love anyone. Until you. Your stubborn, opinionated, sarcastic attitude stole my heart."

She smiled and sniffed, trying to keep the tears at bay. "I'm not stubborn."

"Not stubborn, my ass." A chuckle rumbled through his chest as he held her tight. "I love you so much, Kris. Commoner or not, you're the woman I want to spend the rest of my life with. The woman I want to have my children."

She shook her head and looked up at him, her eyes pleading for him to understand. "I have no idea how to be a countess."

"I'll teach you." He kissed her forehead with a grin. "It's not that hard." Lifting her chin with his finger, he forced her to look at him. "Is that all that's bothering you?"

She took a deep breath before replying. "I'm afraid I'll disappoint you."

He shook his head, a tender smile spreading his lips. "Kris, you could never disappoint me. I have faith in you."

Relief tugged at her heart. Could they really make this work?

"I love you," he whispered just before his lips captured hers in a soul-stirring kiss. One full of promise and love.

Sliding her arms around his neck, she clung to him and kissed him back with everything she had in her. His lips left hers to nibble along her neck, sending goose bumps down her arms. The tip of his tongue touched her pulse point and she gasped. Heat spiraled down between her legs and she gripped his shirt in an effort to remain upright.

With deft hands, he removed his clothes as well as hers and turned her toward the bed. "Lie on your back."

She did as he demanded, then grinned devilishly. Spreading her legs, she locked her gaze with his and let her hand roam down her body. Her fingers pinched her nipples and his eyes darkened a shade. Moving lower still, her fingers settled between her legs, rubbing and circling her clit.

She could tell by his desire-filled expression he liked what she was doing. Moving closer, he grabbed her hand and brought her juice-coated fingers to his lips, licking off every last drop. The bed was so high his cock rested easily against her dripping pussy as he stood between her thighs. The head of his shaft teased her sensitive clit, gently rubbing against it.

She moaned and moved her hips in rhythm with his.

"Like that?" he asked, lifting her legs over his shoulders.

She nodded, her eyes closed tight against her oncoming orgasm.

"Do you want me to fuck you, Kris?"

Again, she nodded.

"Tell me how you feel."

Her eyes flew open. Slowly, he pushed the head of his cock into her tight channel before quickly withdrawing it and continuing his teasing massage.

"You know how I feel," she whispered.

"Then say it," he demanded, his shaft poised to enter her hungry flesh.

"I love you."

With a growl he penetrated so deep and hard she cried out in pleasure. With each thrust he took her higher, ever closer to that elusive height. Resting his hands by her shoulders, he leaned forward, pressing himself even deeper. His grinding hips against her swollen nub caused sensations to scream through her, making her body shake with the intensity of her release. Within a second Stefan tensed above her, his own growl drowning out hers.

With a shift of his arms he lowered her legs and laid his forehead against hers. His eyes closed as he tried to regain control of his breathing. Her hands feathered along his ribs and back, listening to the sound of their sighs mingling in the quiet room.

"You're mine, Kris."

She opened her eyes and caught his possessive gaze. The love she saw reflected in the depths of his gray eyes took her breath.

"I'll always be yours," she whispered.

"Don't ever forget it," he snarled playfully.

Chapter Eleven

ꟿ

After dinner that evening on Daego, everyone decided to take desert and coffee on the veranda. It was an unusually cool night and the men decided there would probably be a storm moving through later. Storms on Daego were scary. They made Earth storms look like spring showers.

Krista walked out and placed the cake platter on the table in front of Mikayla. With a glance toward Stefan, sitting on the wicker sofa, she began to pour coffee into cups. He looked so gorgeous she couldn't stop staring at him.

Picking up the knife, Mikayla looked around at everyone. "Okay, who wants cake?"

"I'll take a piece if you come with it," Sidious said as he wiggled his eyebrows at her.

Pointing the end of her knife at him, she smiled slightly. "Behave yourself."

"Never," he growled as he leaned down and kissed the side of her neck.

Laughing, Mikayla tried to wiggle away from him.

"Excuse me," Stefan drawled, teasing the two of them. "But some of us are still waiting for our cake."

Sidious looked at his brother and scowled. "I've got your cake." He picked up a small piece and started to throw it at him.

"Sidious, don't you dare!" Mikayla hissed as she grabbed the cake from him. "You're not about to start a food fight on my veranda."

With a raised eyebrow, he looked at her. "Since when did it become yours and not ours?"

"The minute you tried to start trouble," she said, making Sidious chuckle.

Smiling, Krista grabbed her cake and coffee then sat down on the wicker sofa next to Stefan. She loved being around these people. Growing up it had only been her and her mother so all this family interaction was new to her.

She loved the way they were with each other. They could tease without becoming angry and could even argue. It was obvious they were all very close. But what she loved the most was just sitting around and listening to them talk amongst themselves.

As she ate her cake Stefan slipped his arm around the back of the sofa and slid his hand under her hair at the base of her head. With a featherlight touch he ran his fingers along the back of her neck. Goose bumps rose along her arms and she shivered.

"You should save some of that cake for later," he whispered as he ran his fingers down the side of her neck.

"Why?" she asked, trying to ignore the goose bumps that his fingers were leaving along her skin.

Leaning down, he softly whispered in her ear what he planned to do with the cake, then chuckled when she almost choked on her coffee.

"You can't be serious," she said, wiping the coffee from her lower lip. The heat of a blush moved up her cheeks as she visualized what he'd just said.

"Stefan, what in the world are you saying to her?" Kaylar asked, which only made Krista blush even more.

Damon jumped in, a teasing glint in his eyes. "Probably nothing that I haven't said to you at one time or another." Leaning over, he nibbled the ticklish spot behind Kaylar's ear, making her giggle.

"Take it upstairs," Sidious said dryly. Damon shot him a glare while everyone else laughed.

"I don't know, Sidious," Stefan said with a snicker. "At their age a trip up a flight of stairs may just do them in."

"Speak for yourself," Kaylar replied as she looked down her nose at her son.

"Don't encourage them, Stefan," Sidious said with amusement.

"Sounds more like a challenge to me," Damon said with a slight smile.

"Maybe I'm just trying to get rid of you," Stefan countered.

"Am I going to have to ring the bell and send the three of you back to your corners?" Mikayla asked as she walked to stand beside Sidious' chair. Reaching up, Sidious grabbed her hand and pulled her down onto his lap.

"It wouldn't be dessert and coffee without the three of them going at it," Kaylar said with a grin.

"We do not go at it." Stefan looked at Sidious, then the two of them began to chuckle. "We have spirited discussions."

Mikayla smiled and scooted down on Sidious' lap slightly so that she could lay her head against his shoulder.

"Tired, baby?" he asked, kissing her forehead.

"A little."

"It is getting late," Kaylar said as she looked at her watch.

"Come on, old woman." Damon stood and held his hand out to his wife. "Let's see if we can help each other up these stairs and into bed."

Krista smiled as she watched the two of them walk into the house. It was so wonderful to see two people that had been married as long as they had still love each other like they did.

"I think I'm about ready for bed, too," Mikayla said sleepily from her position on Sid's lap.

"Come on, sweetheart. Let's go." Sidious helped Mikayla to stand and they headed into the house.

"Good night, you two," Mikayla said.

"Good night," Stefan and Krista offered in unison.

"It's about damn time they left," Stefan grumbled with a slight smile and leaned down to nibble below her ear. Hearing the low rumble of thunder in the distance, they both looked up at the darkening sky.

"Do you suppose it will be a bad one?" Krista asked. She'd always hated storms, even as a child.

"Probably." Stefan grabbed her chin turning her to look at him. "But we'll be fine." He leaned down and softly brushed his lips across hers. "Matter of fact, I can just about guarantee you won't even hear it."

"Is that a fact? Awfully sure of yourself, aren't you?"

"I know my strengths," he replied with a smile as he gently kissed the corner of her mouth, sending little jolts of awareness through her veins.

"And to think, you don't believe you're arrogant."

Slipping his arm under her knees, he lifted them and turned her so he could place them crossways over him. She didn't think she would ever get used to the way he made her feel. She had thought once she made love to him some of the attraction would wear off, but instead it only seemed to have made it worse. Before, she could only image what being with him would be like. Now she knew, and that seemed to be all she could think about.

He was gentle and attentive, always seeming to know what she wanted even before she did. Breaking off a piece of cake, she waved it in front of his face before popping it into her mouth. He grinned as he watched her, his finger softly tracing her jawline.

"Want a piece?" she asked before placing another one on her tongue.

"I would love some." He leaned forward and captured her lips in a passionate kiss, expertly taking the cake she had just put in her mouth. Breaking the kiss, he smiled mischievously at her.

"I don't believe you just did that."

Chuckling, he broke off another piece of the cake. "It's the best way I know of to eat cake," he said just before he placed another piece in her mouth and once again kissed her.

She giggled and pulled away from him with a blush. He could do some of the wildest things sometimes. His deep gray eyes roamed over her face as though trying to memorize every line.

I must be out of my mind to even be considering this, she thought as he put his finger under her chin and brought her lips to his. But the second he kissed her, she forgot all about her misgivings and lost herself in his touch.

Framing her face with his hands, he continued to place one gentle kiss after another against her lips. Long, slow kisses that made her body melt and her heart race furiously. She had completely forgotten about the approaching storm until a clap of thunder sounded so loudly it shook the cup on the table next to them.

Just as they pulled away from each other rain poured down in heavy sheets, drenching them in seconds. Krista squealed and laughed. The two of them quickly jumped up and took off toward the house, trying to get away from the deluge. Once inside they shut the door against the increasing wind.

"God, that rain is so cold," Krista said as she hugged her arms around her.

Grabbing her, Stefan pulled her wet body against his. "I'll warm you up."

I have no doubt about that, she thought as she opened her lips beneath his. She already felt as though she were on fire inside. He put his hands at her waist and walked her backward. "Where are we going?"

"The den," he whispered against her lips.

Once in the den, he shut the door behind them and started a fire in the fireplace. Helping her to remove her wet clothes, he set them on the chair next to the fire to dry. Throwing a couple of pillows and a blanket on the floor, he took Krista's hand and pulled her to the floor with him.

There they spent the rest of the night making love by the warm glow of the flames. And Stefan had been right—she didn't hear the storm at all.

* * * * *

Krista opened her eyes and looked around the bedroom decorated in shades of blue and burgundy. When had they come back to Stefan's room? She smiled sleepily at the sight of Stefan lying next to her. He was on his side facing her, his eyes closed in sleep. She couldn't resist lightly touching his lips with the tips of her fingers. They were so full and always gentle. With a sigh, she realized they also had way too much power over her.

Their time together had been incredible. She was completely in love with him, and she knew in her heart she would never feel this way about anyone else. As she watched him sleep she thought about the night before, and that brought a smile to her face.

The man was certainly insatiable, but then so was she. All it took was a look or a touch and he would have her wiggling and pleading for him to take her, fuck her until she screamed. He knew every trick and position in the book.

"What's that smile for?"

His sleepy voice broke her from the naughty thoughts running through her mind, and she glanced up at him. "I was just thinking about last night."

He took her hand and placed it over his rigid cock. Heat traveled up her arm to settle in the pit of her stomach. He was so large and always felt so good. "Apparently, so was I."

Her fingers gripped him, roaming over his silken length. "I like how you do that," he moaned.

"I like how you kiss."

He grinned cockily. "Would you like another demonstration?"

"Most definitely."

Wrapping her arms around his neck, she welcomed the onslaught of his warm tongue against hers. He was so slow, so unhurried, so seductive. His lips moved to the side of her neck and the entire length of her body trembled in response.

"They're waiting on us downstairs. It's time for breakfast." Her words were a whisper as he softly bit the sensitive spot behind her ear.

"Breakfast can wait."

She grinned and pulled away from him with a teasing giggle, turning to scoot off the other side of the bed. "But I'm starving."

"So am I," he growled as he grabbed her around the waist, pulling her back against him. "But not for food."

His free hand moved up to cup her breast and she arched into his hand with a moan.

"What exactly are you hungry for, then?" she asked, a grin tugging at her lips.

"For you." His lips continued to nibble along her shoulder as his hand moved downward, closer to that spot that ached for his touch.

Closing her eyes, she leaned her head back against his chest. The feel of his palms along her skin made her body burn. It was always quick like this—instant passion that never failed to amaze her.

"But if you would rather go eat…" he trailed off, waiting for her answer.

Panting breaths escaped her lungs as his fingers sifted through the hair at the juncture of her thighs. Her hips shifted, trying to get him closer to the spot that now throbbed with wanting him. "Like you said, breakfast can wait."

He chuckled against her neck, then gently sucked on her pulse point. The beat of her heart fluttered in her chest and she sighed, turning her head to give him better access. Bringing her hand up, she fisted it in his hair. His musky scent surrounded her, enveloped her, and she inhaled deeply, bringing his essence inside her.

His hard shaft pressed into her hip and she moved against it. A growl from deep in his throat rumbled through his chest, vibrating against her back. She liked it when she teased him to the point he lost control, but this morning he didn't. He kept his control and drove her to the point of losing hers.

Teasing fingers shifted lower, toying with the wet opening to her sex. "I like it when you're like this," he whispered against her ear. "Hot and wet."

"Stefan," she sighed, moving her hip against his erection.

She tried to turn but he held her still, his fingers continuing to work their magic, teasing, delving. If he didn't do something soon, she would scream. She wanted him inside her, filling her.

Lifting her leg, he slid his shaft between her thighs, rubbing the tip against her opening. "Arch your back."

She did as he said then groaned as he slid himself into her. Her thigh rested over his as he continued to make love to her slowly, his lips kissing her neck, his hand messaging her breast. Placing her hand over his, she pressed his palm against her, encouraging him to squeeze harder.

Slowly his fingers slid lower, coming to rest over her swollen nub. Biting her lower lip, she tried not to scream, tried to let him lead her, carry her over that edge she clung to so precariously. In her ear she heard his whispered words, but they were in Tilarian. For the first time she cursed not learning that language. Even though she didn't understand him, his voice was so deep and seductive it still made her insides burn like molten fire.

Her blood pounded through her ears. Her tense body hummed with pleasure as his middle finger applied gentle pressure to her sensitive clit. Suddenly her whole body erupted into a mass of sensations as a scream tore from her throat. From behind her she heard Stefan's groan as his own body tensed and his hot semen emptied into her spasming channel.

"I don't think I could walk downstairs, even if my life depended on it," he sighed in her ear.

Krista giggled as she relaxed against him, his arms tightening around her stomach, pulling her closer. The erratic beat of his heart thumped against her back as her own slowed. Eventually the two beat in time and she snuggled closer.

His hand rested possessively over her lower stomach and she placed her hand over it. For the first time, the realization that they hadn't even once used protection hit her like a slap in the face. She could be pregnant. Where on Earth had her mind been? How could she have been so careless?

"What are those wheels in your head turning over?" he asked.

She wasn't sure she wanted to talk about this yet. How would he feel if he thought she might be pregnant? Or had he been trying to get her pregnant all along? "What makes you think they're turning over anything?"

"Your body tensed. Something upset you."

Was she that easy to read? "I was just thinking that everyone in the house probably heard that."

She felt as well as heard his chuckle. "We're on the third floor. I'm sure they didn't hear a thing." He rose on his elbow and tugged her to her back. Grasping her chin, he turned her so she had to look at him. "But I don't think that's really what you were thinking about."

Unable to tell him the truth, she lied. "I was thinking about your return to Rhenari. I'm concerned about you."

The corner of his lips lifted in a slight smile, the back of his fingers sent goose bumps down her spine as they brushed along her cheek. "I'm too stubborn to get rid of that easily."

"I hope you're right. I don't know what I would do if anything happened to you."

"I'll be fine." His hand rested possessively over her stomach.

She cupped his cheek with her hand. "Just please be careful and come home."

He turned and kissed her palm. "I will. I promise. I've decided after the vote tomorrow I'm going to make the announcement that I'm retiring."

"Retiring?" Krista said, staring up at him in surprise. He had never said anything about this before. "Why?"

"I thought when I first started this that I could handle the senate as well as the responsibilities as count, but I can't. Maybe I did at first but now it's just getting to be too much. Dad has helped some, picking up the slack with Tilarus, but he wants to retire, that's why he went ahead and passed the title to me. I can't keep asking him to help. Besides, I want to settle down, marry and have children. Our children," he said as he rubbed his hand back and forth over her stomach. "I can't do it all. Something has to go and I think this is the best thing."

"Who will take your place?"

"Probably Count Britton. He has a lot of political experience behind him. I think he would make a good senator." He softly bit the tip of her finger and grinned. "Think you could tolerate me being around more often?"

"I don't know." She winced and blew out a long breath. "That's asking a lot, but I think I could handle it."

"Minx," he growled and quickly found her most ticklish spots.

*****

"So what did the two of you find out?" Damon asked as the men gathered in Sidious' study later that morning.

"Not a lot," Taron replied with a sigh. "We know that Carlone was on Shevalli not long after the destruction of the prime minister's ship. Unfortunately, anything that might have been useful was destroyed in the explosion."

"So where do we go from here?" Sidious asked, mostly to himself.

Stefan heard Taron call his name but he didn't reply. He sat on the corner of the desk watching the women and Hayden play in the yard just beyond the veranda. Krista's laughter floated across the distance and wrapped around his heart. He wanted to shout his love for her. Scream at the top of his lungs from the highest rooftop that she was the only woman for him. His soul mate.

"He's got it bad," Damon said with a chuckle.

"What?" Stefan frowned at everyone's laughter. "I hope you all are enjoying whatever joke I seem to be the butt of."

"Sorry, Stefan," Taron said as he chuckled. "You just seem to be a little distracted today."

"I heard you," he said, looking back out the window. "You said you didn't find anything on Shevalli. I already knew that."

"Any suggestions as to where we should go from here?" Taron asked as he took a seat in one of the chairs next to the fireplace.

Stefan turned to Taron. "I want you to make one more run to Veenori and talk with Devlin. See if he's found anything else out. We'll meet back here tomorrow and head back to Rhenari."

Taron nodded.

"Excuse me? Did I just hear you say you were headed back to Rhenari?" Damon demanded.

"I have to go back for the senate vote."

"The hell you do!" Damon's voice thundered through the room.

"Don't start with me, damn it, I'm not a child."

"No. What you are is daft."

"Should we run for the hills?" Taron mumbled to Sidious.

"No," Sidious said. "If it gets out of hand, you take Stefan, I'll take Dad."

"That's not funny!" Damon roared toward the two of them. "The two of you can't seriously be supporting this nonsense."

"Using Stefan as bait is not my first choice, but it's the best idea we've got. The galaxy's too big, Dad, he could stay hidden forever. We've got to get this guy."

"Bait?"

Stefan rolled his eyes. He'd thought Damon would have figured out that's what they were doing, but apparently not. "You didn't think I was going just for the vote, did you?"

Damon paced, Tilarian curses spewing from his mouth. "I'm against this."

"I kind of figured that," Stefan grumbled.

"Stefan," Sidious cautioned, shaking his head.

Turning, Damon pointed his finger at Sidious and Taron. "I'm holding the two of you responsible."

"Don't worry," Sidious snorted. "I have no desire to take over his title of count."

"I think I would almost prefer that to trailing him all over the galaxy," Taron snickered, trying to bring some humor back into the room. Three angry Marcone men were not something he liked being in the middle of.

"Well, Taron," Damon said with a grin that made Taron cringe. "As my *adopted* son who's older than Sidious, that makes you next in line."

"Ah, hell."

Stefan and Sidious laughed.

Chapter Twelve

ഇ

Taron stepped into Devlin's office on the top floor of the Veenori bar, Mirage. To his right, a one-way glass window looked out over the crowded bar area. Scantily clad women sauntered through the throng of men offering drinks or other, more personal wares.

Devlin sat behind his desk, a set of nude identical twins on either side of him. His black hair hung around his shoulders in unruly waves, his sapphire eyes shining bright with intelligence. They never missed a thing, no matter where he was or what he was doing. Devlin had uncanny reflexes—quick, and when necessary, deadly.

His broad frame, even in the chair, dwarfed the twins, one of whom had her hand in Devlin's shirt. The other nibbled along his neck. Taron cleared his throat. All three pairs of eyes turned in his direction. The women's twinkled in interest, Devlin's sparked amusement.

Taron grinned. "Ladies," he drawled. "May I have a moment alone with Devlin?"

The one on Devlin's left pouted and moved forward. With a wave of her hand she brushed her thick, flame-red hair back and he noticed the tattooing on her chest.

A Beganite?

One Beganite woman was quite a catch. Their powers in the bedroom were unmatched by any other female species, but to have twins was almost unheard of. The two of them together could probably paralyze a man.

Her gold eyes raked over him and she licked her full, sensuous lips, running her hand down to his cock. "My," she purred, "it feels very nice."

"It is nice, sweetheart."

"Would you like to join us?" Her twin came forward as well, her lips nipping at his ear. "We've always wanted two men at once."

"Something tells me the two of you have already done that, more than once." He stepped back from them, trying not to breathe their essence in too deeply. It was their scent that sent men into an immediate state of undeniable arousal. "I appreciate the offer, ladies. But Devlin and I need to talk."

"That's a shame," she pouted, giving his straining bulge one last squeeze. "He seemed so ready for the task."

She sauntered out of the room, her firm ass swaying in invitation.

"Damn," Taron murmured.

The other one left as well, her hand lingering on his backside as she walked by. Taron turned back to Devlin. "Where the hell did you get twins?"

"I won them," he answered with a grin.

"You weren't by any chance trying them out when I walked in?"

"You don't think I would unleash them on my customers without experiencing them firsthand, do you?"

"Of course not, lucky ass."

Devlin chuckled. "Whenever you want to try them out, they're yours for free."

Taron raised an eyebrow in amusement, stepping further into the room. "That's very generous of you."

Devlin shrugged. "I owe you one or two, if I recall."

Taron took a seat across from him. The huge mahogany desk took up most of the room, leaving little space for other pieces of furniture.

"Please tell me you have something," Taron said, suddenly all business.

Devlin nodded. "Yes and no. The *Negash* was docked here and a man was seen asking a lot of questions about it. He wanted to know who flew it in."

"It wasn't Stefan. He ditched the ship a while ago."

"The mechanic found a long-range tracer on it. I'm assuming that's how Carlone was able to track it here."

"You know for certain it was Carlone?"

"No. But my gut tells me it is. We searched through the docking bay security film until the mechanic recognized him." He tossed a picture toward Taron. "That's what he looks like."

Taron frowned down at the image. The body size was right, but it was the wrong face. Was Carlone working with someone?

"My guess is," Devlin folded his hands beneath his chin, "if it's Carlone. He's wearing a new skin mask."

Damn. "Hopefully, he only has the one."

"I'll get this, as well as the other image of him, out to all the planets and stations. Surely someone will recognize him."

"I hope you're right," Taron sighed. "At least with his face plastered everywhere he won't be as free to roam the galaxy as he was."

"There's a little more."

Taron raised an eyebrow in interest.

"He left here this morning in a ship."

"Any idea where he was headed?" Taron asked.

"Carlone, if that's who it is, covers his tracks well. The security cameras picked up no markings on the ship of any kind, nor was there any information given to the hangar crew prior to his leaving. The only thing we can determine is that the ship was of Litarian design."

Taron sighed and tossed the picture back onto the desk. "So basically we know he left here but we have no idea what he left here in or where he was headed."

Devlin sat back in the chair behind his desk and folded his hands in front of him before replying. "Apparently when he landed he didn't leave any instructions for the ship so the hangar crew pretty much ignored it. Unfortunately that's what the people here pay them to do, ignore things. "

Taron nodded. "If it's Litarian, that would mean it's fast."

"Yes," Devlin replied. "And more than likely also means it has cloaking capabilities."

Looking up at the ceiling, Taron replied, "Is there anything that's going to go right with this investigation?"

Devlin smiled slightly. "Do you really want an answer to that?"

"The only answer that I want to hear is yes. If you can't tell me that, don't tell me anything."

Devlin leaned forward, resting his elbows on his desk. "I can't tell you yes, but I think I can do one better."

"What?" Taron asked, his curiosity piqued.

"Did you know that the Litarian cloak, when used on such a small vessel, puts out a large amount of gamma radiation?"

"No, I didn't know that," Taron replied with interest.

Devlin turned his laptop around so that Taron could see it. "As soon as we found out he left and what he left in, I scanned the area surrounding the planet and came up with a gamma trail."

Taron smiled and said. "Dev, man you're a genius. Can we follow the trail to where he is?"

"No, unfortunately it disappears quickly. But I can tell you that he's headed in the general direction of Rhenari."

"And so is Stefan." Taron grinned. "Perfect. Maybe now's our chance to catch the son of a bitch."

* * * * *

Stefan took a moment to look around his office, trying to decide what he wanted to take and what he didn't. He had decided to keep the apartment, for he was sure he would be back here periodically. And everyone else in the family could use it as well, whenever they chose to.

For a moment sadness enveloped him, for this is where he had spent the majority of the last two years. Running his fingers along the top of the desk, he moved to stand behind it. He smiled. Fondly he remembered all the times he had fallen asleep in his chair while trying to work, only to be awakened by Taron yelling at him for working himself into a stupor.

All that was going to change. He had a reason to be home more. Krista. He was definitely looking forward to becoming an old married man like his brother. Reaching into his pocket, he pulled a ring out and smiled. The bright office lights made the lavender stone sparkle with blue flecks. The center stone was round, with one ring of white diamonds circling around it.

The color reminded him of the wedding and the lavender punch she dumped on his head. It was the first time he'd kissed her and, he was certain, the very minute he fell in love with her.

With a sigh, he put the ring back in his pocket. He would present it to her later, when he returned. Sitting in the chair, he leaned down and began pulling files from the bottom drawer. If he was going to get this done he might as well get started. He piled them on the desk and began to go through them one by one.

Taron strolled in and took the seat across from him. His usual spot. His shoulders slumped and Stefan glanced at him, his brows creasing in worry. "Nothing?"

"Not a damn thing."

"Word is spreading fast that I've resigned. I've already had five senators come in here and say their goodbyes." He sighed and dropped a file into an empty box. "I have a bad feeling, Taron."

Taron frowned. "About?"

"I don't know. But something has been gnawing at my gut all morning."

Taron nodded. "Finish getting your stuff together. We'll head back to Deago shortly. I'm beginning to think like you. We're wasting our time here."

*****

Krista strolled through downtown Deago, her mind not really on the window-shopping. It was focused more on Stefan and her love for him. Could she do this, be a countess? Would she disappoint him? Would she hate it?

She'd never been one for social gatherings and public appearances. She was a homebody. She liked watching movies and working in a garden. All afternoon she'd watched Kaylar. Stefan's mother was graceful, gracious. Everything Krista thought a royal should be. And everything she wasn't.

With a sigh, she sat on the edge of the center fountain. She loved Stefan so much. He had quickly become her whole life. Reaching down, she twirled her fingers in the water, watching the ripples move along the surface. She knew she shouldn't have done this. Falling in love with him had been such a huge mistake, but how could she now go on without him?

He was so good to her and so good for her. He made her more confident, brought out a side of her she didn't even know existed—especially in the bedroom. She'd never dreamed she could be so wild, so uninhibited. And it was all due to him.

"Ms. Sinclair?"

Krista looked up at the man standing above her, shielding her eyes from the midday sun. He wore a hat, the brim putting his face in shadow. A shiver ran down her spine as she stared at him.

"Yes?"

"I'm Vorhala. A friend of Stefan's."

"It's nice to meet you." She stood and tried to get a better look at the gentleman, but he shifted, keeping his face within the shadow of the brim. "Can I help you?"

"Actually, yes."

"How so?"

"I would like to show you something." He held his hand palm up. "Would you come with me?"

Krista hesitated. She didn't know who this man was or why he wanted her to go with him. Something wasn't quite right but she didn't know what. She'd left the house without telling anyone where she was going, only a note saying she needed time alone to think. Now she realized the folly of her actions. She hadn't believed the assassin would want her, but now she began to rethink the idea.

"I don't think that would be a good idea. I told my friend I would be right back and she's expecting me. Maybe another—"

Something hard poked her in the ribs and she glanced down. A gun? *Oh my God, what have I done*?

"You will come with me. Now."

Her heart raced like a runaway train. What the hell was she going to do and who was this man? "What if I don't? Are you going to shoot me right here?"

"Yes," he sneered, "I will. Make no mistake."

"Who are you?"

He pushed her along using the tip of the gun. "Let's just say you and I have a mutual acquaintance."

"Stefan?" He grunted and she licked her lips, thinking fast and hard for a way out of her situation. "Taking me won't help you find him."

"If I take you, I won't need to find him. He'll come to me."

Krista closed her eyes against the scream that wanted to rip from her chest. *Stefan, I'm so sorry.* Taking a deep breath for courage, she slung her purse as hard as she could, smacking him on the side of the head. While he was distracted, she took off down the street as fast as she could, refusing to even take the time to look over her shoulder to see where he was.

She should have. A hard yank to her hair brought her to an abrupt stop. She yelped, grabbing at the hand that held her and pulled her into an alleyway.

The man growled in her ear. "Stupid bitch. I can take you alive, or I can take you in pieces. It doesn't matter to me."

She cringed at the evil and anger in his voice. "You're making a mistake," she snapped. "He has no reason to come for me."

"I think otherwise," he snarled and slung her against the stucco wall of the building.

Her head cracked against the wall and pain shot through her neck. Her vision blurred and she slowly slid to the hard stone of the alley. *Why isn't anyone helping me*? she wondered as darkness closed in around her.

Chapter Thirteen

Stefan transported into his brother's den from the *Vultair,* anxious to see Krista. Nothing had gone right today. The assassin hadn't made the move they thought he would. Stefan was still in the dark and still a target. Where the hell to go now was a mystery. He was tired of hitting that damn brick wall.

Glancing around, he noticed the pensive frown on Mikayla's face. She bit at her nails and Stefan immediately went on edge. Mikayla never bit her nails. Turning his stare toward Sidious, his anxiety worsened at his brother's worried expression. Sidious wouldn't even look him in the eye.

After further study of the room he noticed his mother and father, both standing by the fireplace. His mother stepped forward and placed her hand on his arm in support. "Stefan, sweetheart, you should sit down."

"Why?" he demanded. His gaze whipped around the room again, immediately noticing the absence of Krista. "Where's Krista?"

His heart slammed in his chest. He knew now why they were all here. Why Mikayla was biting her nails.

"Carlone has her." Sidious stared at his desk, a muscle in his cheek working furiously. "We just heard from him."

"What?" Regret and anger slammed through him with a force he couldn't control, and he lunged for his brother. Sidious didn't budge, but Damon and Taron stepped forward, each grabbing an arm. "You son of a bitch! You were supposed to be watching her. You promised me she would be protected!"

Sidious appeared crestfallen. Guilt contorted his face. "Stefan I'm sorry…"

Mikayla stepped forward, coming between him and his brother, the man he most wanted to strangle right now with his bare hands. He strained against the two men who held him fast. "Calm down, Stefan," Damon snapped. "This isn't going to help matters."

"Stefan, listen." Mikayla placed her hands against his chest, her eyes pleading. "She left the house without telling anyone. She didn't believe she was in danger. She just wanted time to herself. To think. I found the note right before we heard from Carlone."

Stefan sighed. "I'm fine. Let me go."

Both men released their holds, but reluctantly. As soon as he was free, Stefan stepped forward and punched Sidious hard in the face. His head snapped to the left, but he remained upright.

"Damn it, Stefan," Damon yelled.

Sidious raised a hand, silencing him. "Let it go." His eyes bored into him, and Stefan waited for the retaliation but none came. "I deserved it, but hit me again and I will hit you back."

"Fair enough," Stefan snarled, his hands fisting at his sides. God, he wanted to hit him again, but he knew a brawl wouldn't do anything to get Krista back.

"All right, that's enough." Taron stepped between the two of them, a hand on each chest holding them back. "This won't solve anything and you know it. Did Carlone say anything other than that he had her?"

Sidious shook his head, sadness in his eyes. "No. He also didn't keep the channel open long enough for us to trace it."

"Son of a bitch." Stefan raked a hand through his hair and walked to the window. "So we're just supposed to sit here and do nothing?"

"He said he would be back in contact with us."

Stefan shook his head, tears burning the back of his eyes. The thought of losing Krista was more than he could bear.

He'd never loved anyone in his life like he did her. "I can't just sit here and wait."

"What are you going to do, Stefan?" His mother came up behind him and placed a hand on his shoulder, the other on his biceps. "Run around the galaxy blind? You have no idea where to even start."

"I have to do something."

"I know, sweetheart, but please think this through. Don't do anything stupid. I know you love her, and she loves you. The two of you are meant to be and we'll find her. I promise, we'll find her."

Stefan placed his hand over his mother's and squeezed. He hoped she was right. Going on without Krista was not something he wanted to contemplate.

* * * * *

Devlin stood at the window in his office, looking out over the floor of his bar. He'd had the window especially made so that he could see what was happening on the floor without anyone knowing it was there. He felt more in control of things when he could see what was happening.

Since losing Skylar, he'd made sure he knew everything that was going on around him. He refused to be caught unaware again. With a sigh, he thought about the beautiful woman he'd loved so much. She hadn't deserved what happened to her and if it hadn't been for Taron he'd have died right along with her. Sometimes he wished he had.

With a shake of his head, he brushed his thoughts aside. There was a time and place for thoughts of his beloved Sky. He still dreamed of her every night, still relived her death and his inability to save her. But right now he needed to focus. Taron and Stefan needed him and he wouldn't let them down.

As he watched the floor, he noticed a man come in and take a seat at the bar. There was something about him that looked familiar. When the man turned toward the hidden window Devlin noticed the scarring on the side of his neck and face. Burn scars. Narrowing his eyes, it dawned on him who he was. That was the man that Taron was looking for.

Turning away from the window, he walked over to his desk and opened a communications channel to Deago.

It didn't take Taron long to answer. "Hey Dev. What's up?"

"The man that you've been looking for is here," Devlin replied, getting right to the point.

"Carlone is there?"

"He's sitting at my bar as we speak. Do you want me to hold him here?"

"No," Taron said quickly. "He has Stefan's girlfriend. I need to know where he goes from there."

Devlin nodded. "I'll stay on him when he leaves here. Call me on the secure com when you arrive."

"Will do."

Closing the channel, Devlin left the office and went downstairs. He wanted to be able to stay as close to this man as he could. Silently, he held his hand up, telling his bouncers not to approach him. He took a seat in the corner of the room, keeping his eyes on Carlone. When Carlone left the bar, Devlin wouldn't be far behind.

* * * * *

Carlone sat at the bar waiting for the bartender to get his order. He'd ordered four bottles of Veenori Keenar, a drink similar to Earth whiskey, only a lot more potent. He had dropped the woman off at the shack he had in the foothills of the mountains to the north of the city. Locking her in one of the back rooms, he made certain that she couldn't get away.

She still hadn't come to before he left. That was fine. He wasn't in any hurry. Stefan had no idea where he was and he planned on taking his sweet time before telling him. Maybe even have a little fun with his woman before he arrived. That thought made him smile. It had been along time since he'd had a good fuck and the beautiful blonde was exactly what the doctor ordered.

Carlone had every intention of making that son of a bitch senator pay for what he had done. Stefan had taken everything away from him. Now he would take everything away from Stefan, starting with the woman.

* * * * *

Mikayla stood on the veranda staring out toward the lake, her arms wrapped around her stomach. Sidious hated seeing her like that. He knew she was worried about her friend and he'd have given anything to help her.

Walking up behind her, he slid his arms around her waist, pulling her against him. He placed a kiss on the top of her head and inhaled her jasmine scent. Sidious could well imagine what Stefan was going through. If he loved Krista anywhere near as much as he loved Mikayla, his brother would be dying inside.

Mikayla leaned into him and he tightened his hold. "How's Stefan holding up?" she asked.

"As well as can be expected."

"What do you think the chances are that she's still alive?"

Sidious sighed. He wouldn't lie to her. "I don't know. I can only hope Carlone hasn't done anything to her yet."

Her lips began to tremble. He turned her to face him and wiped a tear from her cheek. "I'll do everything I can, baby. I promise."

She nodded. "I know."

"Sidious, let's go."

Sidious turned to see Taron and Stefan in the doorway. "Go where?"

"We just heard from Devlin." Stefan checked the charge on his gun and placed it in the back of his pants. "Carlone is on Veenori."

"Any sign of Krista?" Mikayla asked.

Taron shook his head. "No. He just saw Carlone, but he's going to tail him and we're meeting him two miles west of the Veenori mines. It should be far enough outside the city to not attract attention."

Damon came outside as well, a weapon in his hands. All three men frowned. "Where do you think you're going?" Sidious demanded.

"With you."

Sidious stepped forward and shook his head. "No."

"Excuse me?"

"Someone needs to stay here."

"He's right, Dad," Stefan agreed.

"So leave the old man behind, is that it?" Damon snapped.

Taron snorted. "That's not it and you know it."

"Dad, please. We need to think of the women. The three of us can handle this. Four if you count Devlin."

Damon relented with a sigh. "You're right." His troubled gaze met Sidious'. "If he has any brains at all, he'll be prepared for you."

Sidious nodded in agreement. "I know."

Damon stepped closer, lowering his voice. "Watch out for your brother. He's not thinking clearly."

Sidious placed his hand on his father's shoulder. Damon had always counted on him and Taron to watch out for Stefan. Despite the fact Stefan was the oldest, he was also the one out of all of them that would run off half-cocked and do something without thinking it through. "I'll take care of him."

Turning to Mikayla, Sidious took her hand in his. She didn't beg him not to go, just squeezed his fingers and smiled her support. "Please be careful."

He grinned. "I'm always careful."

Leaning down, he placed a soft kiss on her lips. "I love you," he whispered.

"I love you."

With one final kiss to her forehead, he nodded to Taron and the three transported to the *Vultair*.

* * * * *

Krista felt the pounding in her head before anything else. Raising her hands, she realized immediately that they were tied together. *What in the world*, she thought as she slowly opened her eyes and looked at her bound hands. Then, in a flash, it all came back to her.

The scared man that came to her on Deago, the threat against Stefan and then being dragged in the alley and thrown against the wall. After that she didn't remember anything.

Sitting up on the bed, she looked around the small room. There was no window, only a single door and a bed. The walls were made out of rough wood, like an old country cabin would be. The floors were rough wood as well, with no carpet or rug to soften them.

Walking over to the door, she wiggled the handle and then let out a sigh when she realized it was locked. She should have known whoever took her wouldn't be stupid enough to leave the door open.

"Hello?" She beat against the door with her bound fists. "Let me out!"

When no one answered she leaned her forehead against the rough wood. "Is anyone out there?" Still no one answered.

She stood still and listened for any movement from the other side. Unfortunately she didn't hear a thing. Only the sound of her own heartbeat.

Making her way back to the bed, she placed her head in her hands. It still hurt terribly, and she squeezed her eyes closed to try and ease off the throbbing. She was terrified. Not just for herself but for Stefan as well.

Please don't let Stefan do something stupid.

Silently she waited for the man who had kidnapped her to make an appearance.

*****

Taron, Sidious and Stefan arrived on Veenori to meet with Devlin. They parked the small runabout ship they flew to the surface at the exact coordinates Devlin had given them.

After about thirty minutes, Stefan couldn't take the confinement of the ship anymore and decided to go outside to get some fresh air. As he paced back and forth along the length of the ship he kept an eye on the desert horizon for any sign of Devlin.

The heat on this planet was unbearable. The wind blew dry sand in his face and he swiped at it in aggravation. He certainly wasn't a patient man and the waiting was driving him nuts, as well as making him extremely short-tempered. He tried everything to keep from thinking about what might be happening to Krista. And he refused to even consider that she might already be dead.

If she were, he'd kill Carlone. There wouldn't be a planet anywhere he could hide. He'd find him and make him suffer the worst death imaginable. Raising his head, he noticed a speeder approaching in the distance. Looking through the binoculars he held in his hand, he verified it was who he thought it was. Devlin. He hit the side of the ship to alert the others and impatiently waited for the approaching speeder to come to a stop.

"Do you know where he is?" Stefan asked as soon as Devlin turned off the motor. The two others had gathered around as well, having come outside when they heard Stefan's knock.

"Stefan, listen to me. You have to relax."

"I can't relax, Devlin," Stefan replied angrily. "We have to get her back."

"We will get her back, but don't jump the gun and make the same mistake I did. Trust me on this."

With a sigh, Stefan relented. "You're right." He ran his hand through his hair, brushing it away from his face. He had forgotten until just then about Skylar. She had been the love of Devlin's life and for years Dev blamed himself for her death. He always said if he had thought things through better and not acted out of anger she might still be here.

Devlin turned to Taron. "He's in a small, run-down cabin to the north of the city, not far from the mines. I set a monitoring transmitter so we'll know if he leaves it."

"Did you see a woman with him?" Stefan asked.

"I haven't actually seen her, but I was able to get close enough to scan the cabin and there is a female inside. It could be her."

It has to be, Stefan thought trying desperately to keep his composure.

"How does the area surrounding the cabin look, Dev?" Sidious asked.

"It's in the center of a clearing. Sneaking up on him is out of the question."

"What about the body cloak I fixed for Sidious during the rebellion?" Taron asked, getting everyone's attention. "I still have the one that Sidious used when he set the bombs on board the *Destroyer*. I could replicate them and have everyone fitted in less than two hours. There are side effects, though, that kick in after about thirty minutes. But we'll be invisible to Carlone."

Devlin shrugged as he stood from the speeder. "I'll try most anything once."

"Stefan?" Sidious asked, looking at his brother.

"I'll do whatever it takes to get Krista back. You know that," he replied as he stared intently at his brother.

"All right. Let's get back to the *Vultair* and get this started. We'll work out the details while we're waiting on Taron."

* * * * *

Kaylar stood at the side of Hayden's bed, watching him sleep. Fondly, she remembered her own sons when they were that age. Hayden looked so much like his father but even at his young age they could already tell he had his mother's temperament.

Damon walked in and put his hands on his wife's shoulders. "Everything is going to be fine, Kaylar."

"The boys are good at what they do, I know," she sighed. "But I still can't help but worry about them. Any number of things can happen."

"I know," he said as he kissed the top of her head.

Kaylar turned to face her husband. "How's Mikayla holding up?"

"She's okay. Right now she's trying to take her mind off things by working in the garden. She said she and Krista were talking about planting more flowers down by the pool, so she went there to see if she could get started."

"She's not alone, is she?"

"No, Kain went with her to help with the digging and the heavy lifting. Why don't you go down and help her as well? I'll keep an eye on the boy. Being outside might help to take your mind off things."

"You're probably right." Turning, she smiled slightly in thank you and gave him a quick kiss before leaving to head to the pool.

* * * * *

Transporting down just inside the line of trees that surrounded the cabin a good fifty feet away, the men talked quietly amongst themselves.

"There's only one way into the cabin," Devlin said as they studied the scanner.

"That means there's also only one way out," Taron added.

"Well, only one way that we know of," Stefan said.

Sidious nodded. "You have a point. Maybe a couple of us should stay outside and make sure we don't see him exit the cabin some other way."

Devlin took his gun out of its holster and checked the ammunition. "Taron and I will stay outside, one on either side, while you two go inside."

"Speaking of going inside, how are we doing this? Are we remaining cloaked or are we just barging in?" Sidious asked.

"We should probably go in cloaked and try to position ourselves to our best advantage before we turn these things off," Stefan said. "I want to do whatever would be best for Kris. If we barge in we might inadvertently put her in danger."

Sidious raised an eyebrow. "Glad to see you're a little calmer and thinking like yourself again."

"Yeah well, can't guarantee I'll stay that way."

"All right, let's get this over with." Taron raised his wrist to hit the control button.

"Wait." Devlin put his hand up and stopped him. "How are we going to keep from running into each other?"

Taron smiled. "Push the button and you'll see."

All of them pushed their buttons at the same time and looked at each other. A red glow outlined their bodies, making them visible to each other.

"Interesting," Devlin said with a slight smile.

"I took a few minutes and interconnected them so that we are all on the same wavelength. They do this whenever they cloak multiple ships so they can see each other when they're cloaked," Taron explained. "We also have a phase shift attached. With that we should be able to walk straight through the door as opposed to opening it."

Stefan put his hand on Taron's shoulder and propelled him forward. "We've got thirty minutes before the side effects kick in. How about we get going?"

* * * * *

Krista sat silently at the table, watching the man sitting across from her eat his dinner. He had set a plate of food in front of her as well but she was afraid to eat it for fear he'd drugged it somehow. "Why am I here?"

"I told you why you are here," he replied as he stared angrily at her.

"What do you want with Stefan?"

"That's none of your concern," he replied nastily.

She narrowed her eyes at him. "I think it is."

He caught her by surprise when he reached across the table and slapped her hard. Her head snapped to the side and lightning flashed behind her eyes. The sting took her breath and she blinked rapidly, trying to stay conscious. She refused to show fear and stared at him angrily.

"You'll watch your tone with me," he said as he sat back down in his chair.

"If you're going to kill me I think I deserve to know why," she snapped.

"This is why!" he snapped angrily as he pointed to the scars on the side of this face. "I was a prominent general. I was Rigora's right-hand man. I could have had anything I wanted but Stefan took all of that away."

"How did he take that away?" she asked. He wasn't making any sense to her. *He's insane.*

"Stefan was in charge of the rebels. Stefan is the one that organized them, the one that led them, the one that is solely responsible for these," he said, pointing to the scars again. "I got these trying to escape from the ship that Stefan blew up."

Looking at him strangely she started, "There were—"

"Shut up!" he shouted and once again slapped her.

She bit her lip, trying not to cry out. Blood filled her mouth and she gagged. He grabbed her chin and turned her face toward his. Krista winced and tried to ignore the pain his grip caused.

"Stefan will come looking for you and when he does I'll catch him and then force him to watch as I do to you what he did to me." With a nasty smile he added, "Then I'll kill both of you."

Letting go of her chin, he sat back down in the chair and continued eating. She knew she should keep her mouth shut and not antagonize him, but for some reason she couldn't resist. "What makes you think that he won't kill you?"

He jumped from his chair and make a lunge for Krista. She screamed as he grabbed her and pinned her against the wall with his hand at her throat. Her feet dangled several inches off the floor. She was terrified but looked him dead in the eyes, refusing to show any more fear. She would not give him that satisfaction.

Her feet kicked against the wall as she fought the blackness that threatened to consume her. *Oh God, he's not going to wait, he's going to kill me now.*

Slowly unconsciousness overtook her, and she slid silently to the floor.

Chapter Fourteen

ꕥ

Stefan heard Krista scream and his chest tightened in fear. He stepped through the front door of the cabin, his heart in this throat. Where was she? Immediately, Sidious' hand was on his shoulder, holding him back, reminding him to stay calm—to find her before he flew off the handle.

His brother was right and he was thankful he was there. Glancing around the room, he found her lying on the floor against the wall. Bile crept up his throat as he rushed to her side, silently praying she was still alive. Placing his hand on her throat, he found her pulse and breathed a sigh of relief.

Anger immediately took its place. Her lip was bleeding and swollen, her eyes already turning black, a sure sign Carlone had hit her.

I'll kill him.

Standing, he glanced around the small room, spotting the swine in a chair, eating his dinner as though nothing had happened. His brother was closer but damn it, he wanted Carlone. He wanted to wrap his hands around his throat and strangle the very life from him.

Raising his wrist, he ignored his brother's warning and turned off the cloak. Carlone's eyes locked with his and widened before quickly he reached for his gun on the counter. Stefan was too quick for him.

"You son of a bitch!" Stefan roared.

He lunged for Carlone and smashed his jaw with his fist, feeling it shatter beneath his knuckles. When Carlone fell to the floor Stefan sat on him and continued to pummel him, over and over. He had never been so angry or had such a desire to kill someone as he did at that moment.

"Stefan that's enough," his brother yelled, but he ignored him and continued to beat Carlone senseless, unable to control the rage that held him in its grip.

"I said that's enough, damn it."

Sidious grabbed him by the shirt collar and pulled him off Carlone. Stefan tried to catch his breath and go back after him, the need to kill him rushing through his blood. "Stefan, stop."

Sidious jerked him around to face Krista. She sat against the wall, trying to wipe the blood from her lips. She looked exhausted and frightened. Her lower lip trembled and his gut clenched. "Go to her. Let me handle Carlone."

Stefan nodded and made his way toward her. She stood and launched herself into his arms, holding tightly around his neck. "Oh, God. You're okay," she whispered. "I love you so much. I'm so sorry I didn't listen to you and stay at the house."

He held her close, never wanting to let her go. "It's okay. It's okay. It's over. I'll never let you out of my sight again." Framing her face in his hands, he studied her. "Are you all right? He didn't..."

She quickly shook her head. "No. He didn't touch me, other than to smack me. But that was my fault. I should have kept my mouth shut."

He gave her a slight shake. "It was not your fault. Don't ever think that."

She nodded, swallowing down a lump. Now that it was all over she felt an overwhelming desire to cry. She was so relieved that he was okay and the assassin wouldn't get the chance to kill Stefan as he'd intended. Instead, he lay motionless on the floor, his face a bloody, swollen mess.

Over Stefan's shoulder, her gaze took in the scene. Sidious's voice was low as he talked quietly to Tilarian security, giving them their location. The whole while, his gaze never left Carlone's body. Another man, tall and dark stood in the door removing a band from his wrist before tossing it to the table.

Taron strolled in as well and tossed a pair of cuffs to Sidious. While Sidious's attention was on catching the cuffs, she saw Carlone inch his hand toward something lying under the table.

"Stefan," she whispered and Stefan turned to see what upset her before shoving her behind him.

Sidious moved with lightening reflexes and pointed his gun directly at Carlone's chest. Carlone froze, his gaze watching Sidious in fear.

"Go for it, you vigic. I dare you," Sidious snarled.

Krista was surprised at the menace and anger etched in Sidious's face. Gone was the teasing, fun loving Sidious and in his place was the Captain Marcone that was so feared during the prime minister's reign. She swallowed and wondered how Mikayla had had the nerve to stand up to that man when she'd first been captured. Silently Krista hoped she was never the recipient of that menacing look.

"You should have been hanged for treason," Carlone rasped and spit toward Sidious.

"And you should have died in the rebellion," Sidious snarled back and cocked the weapon in his hand. "Give me a reason to rectify that mistake, Carlone."

"Sidious," Stefan cautioned in a soft voice.

Sidious kept his gaze on Carlone as he held out the cuffs to Taron. "Tie this son of a bitch up, Taron before I shoot him."

Once Carlone was secured, Sidious turned back to Stefan and tossed a small metal object toward his brother.

"Get her home, Stefan. Take my personal ship, the *Triton*. It's in the docking bay of the *Vultair*. The rest of us will handle this."

Stefan took Krista's hand and pulled her from the cabin. On the way out she stopped to hug both Taron and Sidious. The other man she didn't know, but he smiled at her gently and touched her cheek. He was gorgeous, with black hair and a muscular build similar to Sidious and Taron, and just as tall.

"*Lekala tuinas vohla,*" he whispered.

Krista frowned. "What does that mean?"

He grinned, making his sapphire eyes crinkle at the corners. They were beautiful eyes, but so full of sadness. "Stefan is a lucky man."

She smiled in return and glanced at Stefan, next to her. "No. I'm the lucky one."

* * * * *

Sidious leaned against the doorjamb of his son's room and listened to Mikayla softly singing a lullaby. Hayden must be having trouble sleeping. Whenever he was upset Mikayla would softly sing to him and it would always calm him down. Her voice had the same effect on her husband as well. He loved hearing her sing.

Mikayla continued to softly hum as she walked over to the set of French doors on the other side of the room and opened them to let in some of the cool night air. Sidious had installed screens across the openings so that they could open the doors without fear that Hayden would get outside. Walking over to the crib, Sidious leaned down and spoke softly to his son.

When Mikayla turned back to her son's bed she jumped slightly when she saw the figure leaning over the side, but immediately relaxed. She recognized her husband's form. She would know it anywhere. Walking up beside him, she silently placed her hand on his arm to get his attention.

Turning to look at her, he smiled. "Hey, sweetheart. Was he giving you trouble?"

"He's used to you telling him goodnight as I put him in the bed. You weren't here and I think that upset him."

Sidious smiled slightly and softly touched Hayden's head. "Good night, little man," he whispered.

Then, taking his wife's hand, he led her from the room and down the hall to theirs. "I noticed the *Triton* isn't in the bay. Did Stefan not get here?"

"They were here earlier but Stefan wanted to take Krista someplace where they could be alone."

"How was she?" Sidious asked.

"She may have nightmares for a while, but she'll be fine. I think she was actually more worried about Stefan than herself."

She sat on the edge of the bed and watched her husband undo his ponytail and remove his shirt. The sight of him with his long hair down and his bare chest never failed to make her heart flutter.

As he undid the last button and pulled the shirt from his pants to slide it off his shoulders, he sensed her staring at him. Looking at her through his lashes, he smiled. "You keep looking at me like that and you'll find yourself flat on your back."

Bringing her eyes back to his, she gave him a teasing smile. "Is that a threat?"

"No," he replied as he walked over to her. Leaning forward, he pushed her to her back on the mattress and braced his hands on either side of her shoulders. "That's a promise."

She placed her palm against the side of his face. "I'm so glad you're back."

"Was there ever any doubt?" he teased as he rolled to his side and grabbed her hand, bringing it to his lips to kiss her palm.

Moving to her side to face him, she only smiled slightly in response. She would never admit to him that she had indeed doubted. She had been terrified that something would happen to him. He wasn't immortal, after all.

Bracing himself on his elbow, he tipped her chin up with his finger. "It's over and everything is fine," he said and then added huskily, "So come here and give me a proper welcome home."

She softly touched her lips to his. The feel of his hands on her body never failed to send her senses reeling. She shivered as his fingers worked her robe loose and slid it down her arms. "I love you," she sighed against his lips.

"I love you too, baby," he said as he softly brushed a stray hair away from her face. "Now come here and show me how much."

* * * * *

Krista watched Stefan hover over her like a child. He'd brought them to the old rebel camp yesterday and had been treating her with kid gloves ever since. She loved the fact he'd taken such good care of her, used the *medabri* to fix her cheeks and lip, but enough was enough.

"Stefan, please. You're driving me crazy."

He set a cup of coffee on the table and took the chair next to her. "I just want to make sure you're fine."

She smiled and placed her hand over his. "I am fine. Do I need to prove it to you?"

He returned her smile and brought her fingers to his lips, placing a soft kiss to the backs of them. "I know you're fine," he said with a sigh against her knuckles. "I've just never been more scared in my life. If I'd lost you I don't know what I would have done."

"But you didn't lose me. I'm right here."

Standing, she moved to sit on his lap. Wrapping her arms around his neck, she placed a soft kiss below his ear and reveled in the tremor she felt run through him. "See," she whispered, "I'm safe and sound."

He smiled and settled his arms around her waist, pulling her closer. His lips were soft and warm on her temple, and she leaned into him more, wanting to get as close as she could.

"I have something for you," he whispered and held something just under her chin.

With a gasp, she sat up and stared at the ring clasped in his fingers. It was beautiful. Not large, but dainty and absolutely perfect. In the center was a round lavender stone she recognized as a Rhenari *bortac*. Around it was a circle of blue Earth diamonds. "Oh, Stefan. I love it!"

"Lavender always reminds me of you and the day I fell held over heels in love."

She sniffed back her tears with a smile and placed her hand over her mouth.

"Marry me, Kris. Be my countess."

A single tear slipped down her cheek, and she wiped it away and nodded her head. "Of course I will."

He slipped it on her finger, then kissed her. Softly, gently and full of promise for the future.

*****

Two weeks later Krista was back to normal and extremely nervous about her and Stefan's wedding. Mikayla's mother Amy had arrived just in time and was thrilled that the young girl she considered her second daughter was officially going to be part of the family.

"Have we taken care of everything?" Krista asked Mikayla as they stood before the dressing mirror in Mikayla's room, putting the final touches on Krista's hair.

She had chosen a simple off-the-shoulder dress of ivory satin that looked perfect on her. Her shoes had been dyed to match and the toes of them just poked out under the hem of the long skirt.

"We've taken care of everything," Mikayla said with a smile. "Relax."

"I don't know why I'm so nervous," Krista said with a sigh as she fingered the string of pearls that Amy had given her to wear.

"All brides are nervous, dear," Amy said as she handed her a bouquet of flowers made of twenty ivory rosebuds with two lavender *seflans,* flowers from Daego that were very similar to carnations.

"Where did this come from?" Krista asked. She hadn't ordered flowers, there hadn't been enough time. She had decided instead she would cut some from the garden and carry them.

"They're from Stefan. He said there's a note attached."

Krista pulled the note from the flowers and quickly read it, then smiled.

"What does it say?" Mikayla asked.

"Are you ready?" Damon asked as he stuck his head in the door, interrupting Krista. She handed the note to Mikayla with a smile.

"Yeah," Krista said and nodded her head. She had been waiting for this day for twenty-seven years.

Damon walked Krista down the garden pathway to Stefan, who was waiting under the rose archway lit only by the light of the two full moons. The air smelled of the jasmine and roses that Mikayla had imported from Earth. The flowers as well as the lake just beyond the edge of the garden created a perfect backdrop for the ceremony. It was absolutely beautiful and there wasn't a florist anywhere that could have recreated such a scene.

Placing her hand in Stefan's, Damon leaned down to kiss her on the cheek before taking his place by his wife behind the couple.

It was a very small ceremony, with only the immediate family and closest friends present, Devlin included. That was the way they both wanted it. Krista had come to realize that she and Stefan were more alike than she'd initially thought.

Although their backgrounds were different, they still basically wanted the same things out of life.

She smiled at him as he slid the gold band with three lavender stones on her finger. The band matched the engagement ring perfectly. Bringing her hand up to his, he kissed her ring finger just as the regent said, "I now pronounce you man and wife, Count and Countess Marcone."

Krista's eyes widened slightly when she heard the regent refer to her as Countess Marcone. That was the first time anyone had called her that and her insecurities rose to the surface.

Stefan saw her expression and gave her hand a squeeze. "You'll be fine," he whispered and leaned down to kiss her.

Laying his forehead to hers, he smiled. "I love you, Kris."

"I love you," she whispered back just before they were bombarded with well wishes and hugs from everyone.

The End

CROSSING THE LINE

Prologue

Planet Tilarus – Legana Sector

ꟼ

"Why do I feel as though I'm about to be cornered?" Taron Sinnar asked dryly and raised an eyebrow at the four faces staring at him.

"Come in, Taron. Please." Senate Magistrate Carvic waved to a chair in front of the huge mahogany desk that dominated Stefan's office at the Tilarian Council Building.

Taron frowned as he stepped further into the room. It was highly unusual for the magistrate to be away from Rhenari and even more so for him to request an audience outside the Senate.

"Magistrate," Taron said with a nod as he took the seat across from him.

His two adopted brothers, Stefan and Sidious Marcone, stood on either side of Carvic. By the fireplace stood his adopted father, Count Damon Marcone, a worried frown creasing his brow.

"If this is about the young woman…" Taron began, trying to lighten the suddenly tense atmosphere with a joke.

Stefan cleared his throat, trying to hide the grin tugging at his lips. Sidious, on the other hand, narrowed his dark gray eyes.

"Be serious, Taron," Sidious snapped.

The two brothers had always been complete opposites. Sidious was serious and firm, where Stefan could find the humor in most any situation. Due to this, people always assumed Sidious was the older, but he was actually the younger. Even as a child Sidious had been the one in charge, the one taking care of himself and Stefan. Thirty-six years later, nothing had changed. Everyone did as Sidious requested, even Damon.

"If you want me to be serious, then perhaps you should tell me why I've been summoned here. 'Posthaste', I believe is what you said?"

"I'm terribly sorry about that," Carvic sighed. "I'm afraid it was necessary. We could not have had this conversation on Rhenari."

"Why not?" Taron asked, his curiosity now piqued.

"Let's just say there are too many ears on Rhenari," Sidious said dryly.

"*Let's just say* we get to the point," Taron snarled.

"I know that you've taken an extended leave from security," Carvic began, his expression one of a man who expected a not-so-pleasant outcome. "But I could really use your help."

And now he knew why. Taron sat back in the chair and frowned at Carvic. Somehow, he had a feeling he wasn't going to like this. "Help with what?"

Stefan sat on the edge of the desk and handed him a file. "Take a look at that," he said. Crossing his arms over his chest, Stefan waited for Taron to read through it.

Taron frowned as he studied the biography in front of him. Taron Karmase? There was a whole history within the file. Education, or lack thereof. A work history at numerous mining facilities and even a few months in lockup on Dellon Five. Karmase certainly had a colorful past.

The last page was an application, already filled out and approved, for a position as overseer in a mining operation. Then it hit him. They wanted him to go undercover, to portray Taron Karmase. "No." He slapped the file down on the desk.

Damon grunted from his position by the fire. "At least one of you has some sense."

"You're not helping," Sidious snapped.

"I told you I wasn't going to," Damon snapped back.

Taron stood and stepped between the two of them. "Enough."

Damon mumbled angrily and turned away. It wasn't normal for the man who had raised him to be so withdrawn and angry. "I know why I don't want to do this, but what's your problem with it?" Taron asked.

"I think someone else would be better suited."

"You and me both."

Stefan pushed his shoulder-length platinum hair off his face, his forearm muscles rippling as he clenched his fingers in frustration. With a pointed look at his father, he dropped his hand. "Damon is just being a dad. He finally has all his sons in one place and he wants to keep it that way."

Taron could tell by the furious look on Damon's face that was far from the truth. He'd known him all his life, considered him a father, so he knew the signs. Damon's normally gray eyes had darkened to black in anger. Worry lines creased his forehead and deepened the wrinkles around his eyes. His lips were clamped so tightly shut they were practically nonexistent.

Taron sighed heavily as he looked up to the ceiling. There was something they weren't telling him, he would bet his life on it. Otherwise Damon wouldn't be so dead set against it.

"You know I wouldn't ask this of you if it wasn't important." Stefan's voice broke through Taron's thoughts and he turned his gaze toward him. Stefan still leaned against the desk, his arms crossed, his ever-observant eyes watching. Probably searching for any sign Taron might be giving in. With a wave of his hand, Stefan continued, "Besides, you're the only one Devlin will work with."

"Devlin is in on this?" Taron asked in surprise. Devlin was a good man, but he usually chose to stay away from assignments that involved the newly formed senate.

"Yes." Stefan nodded. "He's your contact."

"But why me? Why can't you talk Devlin into working with someone else?" Taron asked.

"Because you have the most experience with this kind of undercover work," Stefan said in his most reasonable voice, which for the former Tilarian Senator was as close to begging as he would go.

"Plus with your build and...attitude, you would be perfect for the job," Sidious said with a shrug.

Taron rested his hands on his waist and scowled at Sidious. "What attitude?"

Sidious grinned at him. "That one."

"Go to hell," Taron growled.

"Taron, you would be perfect," Stefan began. "You're formidable when angry, you're arrogant. You're just the type of person who would strike fear in the people beneath him, and that's exactly what we need. Not to mention the fact you're familiar with Veenori—"

"Veenori?" Taron snapped. "Oh, hell no! I hate that damn planet."

Veenori was a wasteland, nothing but desert, rock and dirt. Temperatures reached well over a hundred degrees, even in the shade. Its twin suns beamed down twenty-four hour sunlight, making the place a living hell ninety percent of the time. No way were they going to talk him into this.

He pointed toward Sidious. "He's familiar with Veenori and just as formidable. The man can even scare the hell out of me sometimes."

Sidious snorted. "I also have a wife and two sons. No."

"Oh, so you dump it in my lap?" Taron snarled.

"Taron—" Stefan began.

"No!" Taron snapped. "I told both of you after that Carlone fiasco, I wanted out. I'm tired of chasing crazy loons all over the galaxy and being shot at. I just finished my house, damn it. I want to settle down with a sweet-tempered girl and have a house full of children."

"Oh, please." Stefan stood and walked to the chair by the fireplace. Sitting down, he grinned at Taron. "I know you. If you really want to settle down with a sweet-tempered girl, I'm Vorhallas."

"Hello, Vorhallas," Taron snarled. "Nice to meet you. Find someone else."

"We need you, Taron. *You.* You're the only one who can do this. The only one we trust to get this done," Sidious said in a quiet voice.

Taron rolled his eyes and turned to gaze out the window behind the desk. It was a beautiful day. The blue sky and surrounding greenery were reflected in the glass of the Tilarian buildings. Puffy white clouds rolled by as the breeze rustled the leaves.

Damon's small runner was secured on the landing pad just outside Stefan's office. The warm sunlight reflected off the metal, making it sparkle. Early spring on Tilarus was his favorite time of year. He had been looking forward to getting settled in his house, actually shopping for furniture. And he hated shopping.

We need you. That's all it took and they knew it.

"What exactly is it you want me to do?" he asked, his gaze still out the window.

"Go undercover at the Veenori Mines," Sidious said.

God, I hate Veenori. His teeth ground together in frustration. Of all places, why that one? "What am I looking for?"

"You're aware that the rebels want a dictator back in control?" Carvic asked as Taron turned from the window.

Taron snorted as he sat down. *Rebels.* Just four years ago, he'd been a captain in the rebel armada. Then they had been against the dictator, trying to free the people. Now there was a group of rebels that wanted the old oppressive government back. Why was beyond him. Serving under a dictatorship was nothing more than slavery, bowing to the whim of one man.

"Yes," Taron said with a nod. "I've also heard they've been shipping weapons and supplies. Supposedly gearing up for some kind of major battle against the government buildings on Rhenari."

"We believe someone in the Senate is behind it."

"A senator?" Taron frowned at the magistrate.

"If not a senator, then someone close, an assistant possibly," Stefan said as he handed him a glass of Earth brandy.

The drink was one of Sidious' favorites and he paid a fortune to have it shipped here. Lifting the glass, Taron gulped half the liquor at once. It burned going down and he grimaced.

"So how is going undercover at the mines going to track them down?" Taron asked as he continued to sip at his drink.

"The weapons are being shipped through there. There's someone in the mines acting as a middleman," Sidious said as he walked around the desk to sit in the chair next to Taron. "They hide the weapons in with the mineral shipments. Get close to the people involved. Do whatever is necessary to get inside. We believe the people in the mines will lead you to whoever is in charge."

Taron rubbed tiredly at his forehead. "How did you get this information?"

"A young man in the wrong place at the wrong time," Stefan said quietly.

"Is he still with us?" Taron asked. He would hate to think someone innocent was hurt over all this.

Stefan nodded. "He's well hidden and, for the moment, believed to be dead."

"Family?" Taron asked.

"One sister, Alyssa Carington, who we haven't been able to locate," Sidious replied. "Her brother told us he sent her some information as well so we're trying to find her before they do. We'll load your minicomputer with her image so if by chance she shows up there, you'll recognize her."

Taron sighed. "When do you want me to start?"

"Day after tomorrow." Carvic rose from his chair and indicated Taron should follow him. "That will give us a day and a half to get you ready for your role."

Taron followed the magistrate from the study, a heavy weight tugging at his chest. He had a bad feeling about this assignment. Something was going to happen—something he definitely wouldn't like.

The bang of the study door as it slammed vibrated through the hall and he turned to stare at it. Damon, no doubt. His adopted father's aversion to this job only added to his unease. The magistrate placed a wrinkled hand on his shoulder, silently indicating he should continue moving.

Taron turned his gaze to Carvic and smiled slightly. "Lead the way, Your Grace."

* * * * *

Damon stood for a moment staring at the closed door. Taron had been like a member of his family since the day he was born. His mother had been a close friend of his wife's. He loved him as much as he loved his own sons.

Taron had had such a sorrowful childhood. His father ran out on them when he was eight and his mother died less than a year later. He'd blamed his mother's death on his father. As far as Damon knew, he continued to even into adulthood. He was convinced if his father hadn't left she would still be alive. Damon wondered if that wasn't true as well. A lot of Taron's mother's problems had stemmed from a broken heart.

After Taron's mother's death, Damon and his wife had adopted him, giving him all the advantages they gave their own children. But Taron had chosen to keep his own name, refusing the title of "lord" that went with being the younger son of a count. He did it for his mother, to remain close to her. The thought of Taron taking on this assignment tore at his heart, especially knowing what they did.

He turned angry eyes toward Stefan, the brother closest to Taron. "Why didn't you tell him?"

"We don't know for certain," Sidious said as he slumped in the chair behind the desk.

"Even if it's a remote possibility, he has the right to know."

"No!" Sidious' thunderous voice echoed off the walls as he slapped the desk. "I'm not telling him. I'm not going to get him all upset over something that may not be true."

"What if it is?"

Both the men were silent as they pondered his question. Damon had been against the idea from the start, but he was the outsider. Both Sidious and Stefan worked for the senate. Stefan had been a senator and instrumental in the rebuilding of the government until he'd met his wife Krista and decided to resign.

Sidious worked organizing special assignments such as these. In this case, Sidious was in charge and there was nothing Damon could do, but damn it, he wasn't about to sit back and not let them know what he thought.

"How can you send him on this assignment, knowing what he may uncover?" Damon snarled.

Stefan stood and paced, a sure sign he was agitated. "We've discussed this. We agreed it would be better if he didn't know going in. If he knew, his mind would be on that and not on the assignment."

Damon sighed and turned to leave the room, frustration eating a hole in his heart. If what they suspected turned out to be true, Taron would be furious he had been left in the dark, and rightly so. "You're making a mistake. One I hope Taron can forgive you for."

"So, do I," Stefan replied with a sigh.

Chapter One

Vordak's Bar and Gaming Hall, Veenori

ꟗ

"Where the hell did I go wrong?" Alyssa Carington asked herself as she stood just off the stage behind the curtain.

Her body shivered despite the heat. She was dressed in nothing but a black leather collar around her neck, a matching leather strap attached to it so she could be led around like an animal.

This wasn't her plan. She wasn't supposed to be a slinoy, Veenori's version of a sex slave. She should have been sent to the mines. That was where her brother Anthony had been working as a transport pilot when he'd been murdered.

A week before she'd been informed of his death, she'd received a package from him full of photos, a list of names and a short note telling her to keep the packet of evidence somewhere safe. She hadn't been able to make heads or tails out of the scribbled notes and names, but one name kept appearing over and over. Vingosa.

She'd hidden the packet in a safe deposit box and given the key to a good friend who happened to be a criminal attorney. She handed over the key with strict instructions that if she wasn't back in six months, open the box and investigate the contents. She then headed to Veenori to begin her search.

Her plan had been to lose money gambling then be sent to the mines to work off her debt. There she hoped to be able to find the man she believed to be responsible for her brother's death, Vingosa. But somehow everything had gone wrong. When she'd asked why she wasn't being sent to the mines, they'd laughed at her, saying women were not welcome there.

She'd done her research, knew that to be a lie and confronted the owner of the gaming hall. Vordak had sneered and told her she was too frail to withstand the mines and that he'd stand a better chance of getting his money back by selling her as a slinoy.

So now here she stood, naked as the day she was born, a collar around her neck, waiting to be sent on stage and displayed before the mass of horny aliens that packed the hall. Reaching up, she fingered the gold figure eight charm that hung from the leather. It was where the leash was attached and while Vordak wasn't looking she tried to feel for a way to undo the strap of leather but, with a sigh of disgust, realized she couldn't figure it out.

Vordak had told her if she behaved and pleased her master, she should work off what her buyer paid for her in about a year. Oh, God. A year as someone's sex slave. She liked sex, but this was not her idea of a turn-on.

"Come forward, slave," Vordak ordered and tugged at her leash.

She cringed and fought the pull of the leather strap, grabbing it with her hands. Vordak turned to glare at her and grasped her fingers in a harsh grip, removing them. Moving behind her, he clasped her wrists and bound them at the small of her back with a set of leather cuffs. The movement caused her breasts to jut forward and she closed her eyes against the desire to fall apart as the locks clicked into place, sealing her fate.

How was she going to go through with this? What if the man who bought her was abusive? Or ended up killing her? She was terrified and tried her best to swallow the bile that tried to choke her. She couldn't do this.

Vordak shoved and she stumbled out onto the stage. Cheers erupted from the crowd and she swallowed a sob of mortification as Vordak pulled at her leash and tugged her to the edge of the stage. Her body trembled in fear and anger as Vordak pointed out her various attributes to the packed room.

"The next on the list, gentleman, is Alyssa. A spicy little vixen from the planet Earth. You'll notice the high, firm breasts..." Vordak smoothed his hand over her nipples and she flinched, shooting him a scowl.

"Don't touch me," she snarled.

Vordak grinned nastily. "Full of spunk, she is," he yelled and the crowd murmured its approval.

"Twelve hundred veenok," someone from the front shouted.

"Fourteen hundred," someone else shouted, and Alyssa wanted to sink to the floor. *Please let it at least be someone I can stand to look at.*

* * * * *

Taron stood at the back of the room with Rhia, Devlin's sister and assistant. Her stunning flame-red hair and light gray eyes were second only to her beautiful face. She was every man's desire here on Veenori, but Devlin was protective and had made it quite clear Rhia was off limits.

Even though the two were not blood-related, she'd been under Devlin's protection since the day their orphan freighter crashed here years ago, when Devlin was twelve and Rhia four. The same man who took in Devlin had also agreed to take Rhia on the condition that the small child be Devlin's responsibility.

Devlin had agreed and kept the child, raising her as his sister. Once she'd grown, he'd tried, with Taron's and Stefan's help, to get Rhia to move to Tilarus where she would be safer, but she'd refused, saying Veenori was the only home she knew and she would not leave it.

"I think the blonde you bought earlier is my favorite," Taron said with a grin.

"Don't like the brunette?" Rhia asked, her eyes sparkling with barely suppressed humor. "She certainly liked you."

Taron chuckled. "Really? I hadn't noticed."

"Kind of hard to not notice, don't you think? How many times did she grab your cock?"

"At least three," Taron said dryly. "I believe she's done this before."

"That will be one less that I have to explain the rules of being a slave then." Nodding her head toward the stage, she asked, "What do you think of that one?"

Taron turned and stared at the stage. "Wow," he growled.

She was one hot number. Long legs that he could well imagine wrapping around his waist as he fucked her smooth pussy. A firm, flat stomach with a diamond bellybutton ring that made his eyebrow quirk in interest and high, handful-sized breasts that begged to be suckled. Moving up toward her face, he couldn't help but admire her full lips, upturned nose and the silky black hair that curled softly around her shoulders.

He imagined holding a firm grip on her thick locks as he fucked her from behind…until he met her almond-shaped gray eyes. *Fuck.* He knew those eyes.

Alyssa Carington. What the hell is she doing here?

"Damn it," he snapped.

"Taron?" Rhia asked. "What's wrong?"

"We have a problem," he mumbled. "Call Devlin and tell him the woman he's been looking for is here."

"What?" she gaped and turned back toward the stage. "That's Anthony's sister? What the hell is she doing up there?"

"I don't know."

"Taron, you have to buy her."

"Me?" he snapped. "What about you?"

"I've already bought my limit. Vordak won't let me buy another one."

Taron groaned. "What the hell am I supposed to do with a slinoy?"

"Whatever you want," she said with a grin.

"We're talking about Anthony's sister, Rhia. We told him we'd protect her, not fuck her."

Rhia shrugged. "It's either you or one of them." She waved her hand, indicating the mass of salivating men moving closer to the stage.

Damn it all to hell.

A slinoy was the last thing he needed—especially one who looked like that.

Vordak eyed the crowd with narrowed golden slits. "Come now, gentleman. She owes thirty-five hundred veenok. I can't let her go for a penny less." Moving her closer to the edge of the stage, he spread her legs, running his hand between her thighs.

Alyssa flinched, but didn't take her gaze off the back wall. She stood proud, her head held high, but a telltale blush covered her beautiful face.

Bringing his hand to his face, Vordak inhaled her scent. "Ah, she smells lovely. Clean, tight and unbroken. Surely someone will pay what she's worth."

Taking a deep breath, Taron shouted a bid. "Sixty-five hundred veenok."

* * * * *

Alyssa gasped at the sudden jump in amount and searched the crowd for the man who possessed such a deep timbre.

"That's almost twice what you owe, slinoy. Someone must like the idea of sinking between your thighs."

Alyssa glared at Vordak, then again searched the crowd. She had no idea who'd yelled out the amount. The darkened hall was full of aliens, it could have been any one of them.

There were tall blue men with horns, short men with fangs and long hairy ears. She shuddered at the image of having to please one of them.

Then there were the lizard-like Veenori natives with their golden eyes and long, flicking tongues. There were a few humanoids, some could have even been from Earth. It was hard to tell, for some alien races were almost indistinguishable from Earthlings.

Her gaze caught a movement in the crowd, and she stared as someone stepped forward. Her heart stopped. *Oh, God. Is this the man?* His whiskey-colored gaze raked over her, heating her flesh, and she swallowed a strong sense of dread. It had been a while since a man had looked at her like that. He looked as though he could eat her alive, and the very idea sent a wave of heat up her body.

He was huge. His height and wide shoulders dwarfed the men standing next to him, giving him a stunning air of authority she doubted even the bravest of men would question.

Her gaze moved upward, catching the dim light of the room as it reflected off his tan, bald head. Normally she loved bald men, there was just something sexy about them. But how was she supposed to feel about this man? Or any man who bought her? She swallowed as she watched him stroll closer, his eyes taking in her heaving breasts then moving lower. Refusing to cower, she met his stare head-on when it finally moved back to her face.

He was confident, almost arrogant. She could tell by the way he practically swaggered forward, his whole body exuding confidence. Oh boy did he exude it. It practically oozed from every pore.

"Overseer Karmase," Vordak said, his voice holding just a hint of fear.

"Vordak," he answered back and tiny tingles ran down her spine.

His deep voice rumbled low in his chest and she felt the vibration in her own, making her skin prickle. She'd never had this kind of reaction to a man and it stunned her. She was unprepared for what had happened to her. She had no idea how a slinoy should behave or what happened to them once they were bought. The idea of her being bought by such a prime specimen of a man sent her body into immediate arousal mode and it pissed her off.

Vordak turned back to the crowd. "The bid is sixty-five hundred veenok. Do I hear sixty-nine?"

The tall giant's gaze spanned the room, his stance and expression daring anyone to bid. No one spoke, no one looked at him directly and who could blame them? If it were possible to kill someone with a look, he could do it. Who was this man?

"Looks like you win her, Karmase."

Vordak handed her leash to the man he'd called Karmase and quickly moved on to the next woman. Alyssa followed, trying to recall where it was she'd heard the name before.

Karmase? The mines, she realized with a start, her heart hammering in her chest at her luck.

She'd researched the mines before arriving here and Karmase was the new overseer. Things couldn't have worked out any better. Well…it would have been better if she wasn't going in as a damn sex slave.

Her new owner stopped at the table and tugged Alyssa to his side. The heat from his skin flowed into her naked body and she unconsciously moved closer.

"Karmase," the cashier grumbled. "How are you paying for her?"

Karmase dropped his currency chip on the table and it clanged against the glass, bouncing twice before settling just at the edge of the electronic books. She looked up, her gaze scanning the room and the people moving around them. Men and women alike openly admired her naked body as they passed by. Some even stopped to boldly ogle her, giving her the creeps. She tried her best to ignore them, to somehow forget she was naked, but she couldn't.

She scowled, wishing she could remove her shackles and cover herself against the multitude of prying eyes. "Would you at least be kind enough to give me a cover? I'm cold."

Karmase snorted. "How can you be cold? It's a hundred and twelve degrees."

"Then I'm embarrassed," she growled.

Karmase glanced down at the man watching them, then turned narrowed eyes at her. "Quiet, slave," he snapped.

Sticking her chin out, she met his stare with equal anger. He was so tall she had to crane her neck to meet him head-on. Her efforts were useless though. Her anger only seemed to amuse him, as well as those around them.

The man at the table chuckled, his golden eyes dilating then snapping back to normal as he stared at her breasts. "I think your slave needs a lesson in manners. I have a whip, if you need use of it."

"I'll handle it," Karmase growled and a shiver of fear ran down Alyssa's back.

A whip? Please let him be joking.

Once the money exchanged hands, Karmase led her from the table and back toward the crowd. Cold clammy hands slid along her skin as men passed them, making her feel ill. "Can we please get out of here?" she asked.

Karmase's amber gaze flicked to her, a hint of amusement twinkling in its depths. "Anxious to begin pleasing me, slave?"

She snorted. "In your dreams." She was loath to admit it but the thought of pleasing someone who looked like him was more of a turn-on than she'd expected, especially in a place like this.

"You have a lot to learn about being a slinoy, woman," he growled close to her ear.

"I'm new to this, so I'm winging it. Okay?"

"I'll give you one thing," he said, his voice dripping with barely controlled laughter. "You've got balls."

"Please," she whispered. "Just get me out of here and into some clothes and I'll be the perfect slave."

Karmase chuckled. "I doubt you will ever be the perfect slave." His intense whiskey eyes stared down into hers and her heart lodged in her throat. "And that makes you worth every veenok I paid for you."

"Like your women feisty?" she asked snidely.

"No." His lips twitched and she wasn't sure if he were teasing or not. "I like breaking them."

Alyssa swallowed a sudden lump of dread. What the hell was she in for?

Taron almost regretted his comment as he watched fear cloud her eyes. He would never hurt her, or any woman for that matter. But if this was going to work, he needed her to be a true and obedient slave.

Now that he'd bought her, he was stuck with her. And keeping her obedient was the only way to protect her as well as himself.

Grasping her leash, he led her toward the entrance. Men stared and more than once he heard her grumble to herself, he was sure cursing him to oblivion, but as she was his slave, he could not show her any kind of consideration. She would have to walk naked behind him for now.

Just thinking about that body of hers in his bed, lying next to him, there to do his bidding, made his cock harden painfully beneath his coarse pants. "I can't think like that," he mumbled.

"What did you say?" Alyssa asked.

Taron came to a stop and rolled his eyes toward the stars in exasperation. She needed training. "Do not speak to me, slave, unless you are spoken to."

"Well, I thought you were speaking to me."

With a sigh, Taron spun to face her. Narrowing his eyes, he stepped closer. His nostrils flared as he inhaled her flowery scent mixed with the smoky smell of the bar. Hell, even her scent aroused him, and a muscle twitched in his cheek as he fought hard to keep his reaction to her neutral. She was under his protection and he wouldn't cross that line of protector. He'd promised her brother he'd keep her safe and he'd keep his word. Even if it drove him insane.

To her credit she didn't back away, but raised her chin, meeting his glare head-on. She was going to be the death of him, he had no doubt. "Don't push it, Alyssa, or I swear, I'll put you over my knee right here and beat your ass until you can't sit for a week," he growled quietly.

Her eyes widened then narrowed into gray slits that sparked fire from their depths. She was absolutely breathtaking and it would take every ounce of his control to keep his hands to himself—especially if he had to spank her. "Say 'yes, Master, I understand'," he growled.

Her full red lips dropped open in shock, and if not for the nosy eyes around them, he would have found her comical. "Don't," he snapped, "even think about saying something smart. Repeat what I said, Alyssa."

She clamped her mouth closed, her jaw working in anger. He could tell she was gritting her teeth and her spunk amazed him.

"Now!" he bellowed, making her jump.

"Fine," she hissed through her teeth. "Yes, Master, I understand."

He nodded and began to once again move toward the door. "That you're an ass," she said with menace behind him, just loud enough for him to hear.

Chapter Two

ꕥ

Alyssa could not believe what she'd just done. If looks could kill, she'd most definitely be a dead woman. Was she out of her mind? One of these days her smart-ass mouth was going to get her into loads of trouble, and she had a sneaking suspicion that day had arrived.

"I'll take her with me and explain things to her," a woman said as she stepped between her and Taron, taking her leash within her grasp.

"I think that's a good idea," Taron growled, then shot her another murderous glare before turning on his heels and leaving the building.

The woman turned and for a second Alyssa was speechless. She was absolutely beautiful with long flame-red hair that hung halfway down her back. Her eyes were the color of ocean ice—stunning and intelligent with just a hint of coldness. She was tough, she could tell by the set of her shoulders and the way she carried herself. If she were a man, Alyssa would consider her to be arrogant. But there was something else in her gaze—compassion.

"You can not," the woman began softly, her voice holding just a hint of accent similar to a French accent, "antagonize him." She nodded toward a couple on the other side of the room. "Do you see them?"

Alyssa looked. A woman just as nude as she knelt before the man holding her leash, her head bowed just slightly. She never appeared to look him in the eye, never spoke to him. She just obeyed like a damn pet. Alyssa scowled.

"That is how you must behave in public. In private, you may behave however Taron wishes you to."

"Taron?" Alyssa asked. Interesting name.

"Yes. Taron Karmase, the man who bought you. But you must refer to him as 'Master'. Unless he specifies otherwise."

"I don't think I can do this," Alyssa mumbled. "It goes against everything that I am. I'm not a slave."

A tiny grin pulled at the woman's lips. "Honey, as of right now, you are. Come on. Let's get you ready."

With one final glance at the woman bowed before her master's feet, Alyssa followed the woman out of the building and into the hot Veenorian sunlight.

* * * * *

"I heard," Devlin drawled in amusement as Taron stomped down the hallway toward his office on the top level of Devlin's bar. He was still furious.

"Don't start with me," Taron growled as he pushed past Devlin's massive frame to enter the immaculate office.

"What?" Devlin asked, barely containing his laughter. "All I said was 'I heard'."

Taron began to pace in front of the massive cherrywood desk that dominated the room. There were very few trees here, so Devlin had had to have the desk shipped in from Tilarus. He preferred wood to the otherwise steel and stucco construction that covered the mostly barren planet and would pay whatever price necessary to get it.

"What the hell was I thinking?" Taron snapped.

"I don't know. What were you thinking?"

Taron stopped pacing to glare at him, then resumed his traveling.

"Where is she?" Devlin asked as he shut the door then settled into the leather seat behind his desk.

"She's with Rhia. Your sister had to step in to keep me from putting her over my knee." Devlin raised an eyebrow but said nothing. "How the hell am I supposed to do my job and keep her from driving me insane?"

"Looks like you'll have to figure it out."

Taron rolled his eyes and ran his hand over his head. "What do we tell Tony?"

Devlin shrugged. "The truth."

"The truth?" Taron gaped at him. "We don't even know what that is. What the hell is she doing here? How did she end up on that stage being sold as a slinoy?"

"I'm willing to wager she's here to find her brother's killer."

"Fuck. That's all we need."

"Maybe we should tell her that he's still alive."

"No. Telling her that would mean telling her who I am and why I'm here. That would put her in unnecessary danger. The less she knows the better."

Devlin nodded. "I'll go along with whatever you think is best."

Taron didn't know what he thought was best at the moment. One thing he knew for certain—having her in his bed was going to make an already hellish assignment even more so. His cock was already aching for her body, but all his hands wanted to do was strangle her.

* * * * *

Alyssa sat before a mirror, watching Rhia fix her hair into a mass of ringlet curls. "You have stunning eyes, Alyssa." Rhia smiled at her in the reflection.

"Thank you. My brother has some just like them. We both got them from our father." She swallowed back a sob. "Or I guess I should say he had some just like them."

"He's no longer with you?"

"No," she whispered. "He was murdered."

"I'm sorry to hear that."

Alyssa watched Rhia curl her hair, wondering why Rhia was here. She wasn't a Veenorian, that much was certain, but she wasn't from Earth either. "Where are you from?" Alyssa asked. When Rhia glanced at her questioningly, Alyssa shrugged. "You just don't seem like you belong."

"I don't," she said with a grin. "I wasn't born here. Devlin Armonde, the man who owns this bar and gambling hall, and I were on an orphan freighter destined for Rhenari. The freighter crashed here and we were the only two to survive. Devlin was twelve and knew where he came from. I was four and did not. Devlin had been kind to me the first day on the ship, so I attached myself to him, going wherever he did. He took it all in stride, taking care of me. When we crashed, he continued to do it. He basically raised me." She stared at Alyssa for a moment in surprise. "I'm sorry. I didn't mean to tell you my life story."

"It's okay." Alyssa smiled slightly. "It's interesting. You really don't know where you came from?"

Rhia returned her attention to Alyssa's hair. "No. I still don't know. All I had was a necklace." She raised her hand to finger to gold charm around her neck that resembled a puzzle piece. "It's the only link to who I am, but so far we haven't been able to find anything out about it."

"Maybe one day you will." For some reason she felt a kinship with this woman. Rhia may turn out to be the only friend she would have in this godforsaken place.

Rhia quickly turned all business. "We need to discuss the rules, Alyssa."

Alyssa sighed. "Of course, the rules."

"Taron is a good man. A little rough around the edges, a little frightening when he's in a foul mood, which lately seems to be quite often, but he would never physically harm you."

"Why would you tell me that? Shouldn't I be afraid of him?"

Rhia smiled. "Yes, you should, and when in public you should act like you are. Never speak until spoken to, never look him directly in the eyes unless he tells you to, and for God's sake, never talk back to him."

"Why? What would he do if I did?"

"Let's just say you don't ever want to be in a position to find out. Alyssa, please. Don't challenge his authority in public and force him to make an example of you. Taron has hundreds of men below him and he can't afford for them to see him challenged by a woman. Do you understand?"

Alyssa nodded. "I think so."

"Good," Rhia said with a smile. "Now let's get you something to wear."

Once dressed, Alyssa stared at herself in the full-length mirror. She wasn't much better off. The top was like a bra, pushing her beasts together, although she had to admit the deep blue color went well with her skin tone. The bottom portion was nothing but a gold band around her waist with a flimsy piece of deep blue material to cover her front and one to cover her back. Her legs remained exposed. "You can't be serious."

She eyed Rhia in the reflection of the glass. She would much prefer her outfit, rust-colored pants and matching sleeveless jacket. The material was thin, allowing for the extremely hot temperatures here on the small planet. "Why can't I have an outfit like yours?"

Rhia chuckled. "Because, dear, you are a slinoy, so you must dress like one. Later Taron may dress you as he sees fit but for now, you dress your station.

"Peachy," Alyssa whined, making Rhia laugh.

"Relax, Alyssa. If you please him he will give you pleasure beyond anything you could imagine."

Alyssa studied her and for a fleeting second jealousy ran through her. "Do you know this firsthand?"

"No," Rhia said with a knowing grin. "But I've heard the other women talking about him. He's an attentive lover." Rhia stepped closer to whisper in her ear. "And quite large."

Alyssa gulped. Just how large?

"Come on." Rhia reattached the leash and led her from the room. "It's time to return you to your master."

As she followed Rhia down the long maze of hallways, she took a moment to study her surroundings. It was cool in the building, very few windows graced the outside walls. Since Veenori had twenty-four hour sunlight, she was sure it helped to keep the heat at bay.

The walls were made of clay and concrete, which trapped the cool air and helped to keep the interior temperatures down. Even the floors were concrete or slate, depending on the wealth of the owner. It was obvious Devlin had wealth for all the floors of his buildings were slate.

At the end of the hall, Rhia knocked at a set of massive double doors made of what appeared to be mahogany. Seeing the wood surprised her, for all the other doors had been metal. "Enter," someone shouted from within.

Alyssa's heart began to pound as Rhia opened the door and pulled her inside. Her gaze moved across burgundy walls and dark, wood furniture. For him to have had wooden furniture shipped here meant he was wealthy indeed.

"Alyssa," Rhia began. "You know Taron, but this is Devlin."

Her mouth practically dropped open as she stared at the man sitting behind the desk. He was breathtaking with shoulder-length, unruly black waves and eyes the color of sapphires that stared back at her in interest. His shoulders were massive and stretched the material of his shirt to almost bursting. Her gaze strayed to Taron and she gulped at the pure lust that shone in his eyes.

Where the hell were men like this on Earth?

"Damn, Taron," Devlin drawled. "You must share."

For a split second she imagined being sandwiched between the two intergalactic hunks and her nipples hardened beneath the material of her bra.

Taron's gaze dropped to her breasts and he grinned devilishly. "Something tells me you like the idea."

"Don't be ridiculous," she snapped.

Rhia's hand met Alyssa's ass with a stinging slap, making her gasp in surprise.

"We discussed this, Alyssa. He didn't give you permission to speak."

"It's all right, Rhia," Taron drawled. "Although I liked seeing you spank her. Give her another, just for good measure."

Again Rhia's hand smacked her, this time landing across the other butt cheek. Alyssa was prepared this time and refused to make a sound, despite the little shots of pleasure that shook her to the core. Refusing to examine her surprising arousal, she met Taron's gaze without flinching. Devlin's chuckle caught her attention and she turned her glare to him.

"She's going to be a handful. I have no doubt." He turned to Taron and smiled. "I envy you. It's been a long time since I've had the privilege of breaking in such a stunning beauty."

"Devlin," Rhia cautioned from behind her.

"I'm not a horse to be broken, damn it. I'm a woman."

Taron snorted. "I think that's rather obvious, Alyssa."

"*Neeca vortune ali van moran timot*," Devlin spoke quietly to Taron, who shook his head.

"*Neevok*," Taron responded.

Okay, that Veenori word she knew. It was "no". But the others Devlin had said too quickly for her to catch.

"Don't do that," she snapped and they stared at her with amusement.

"Do what, slave?" Taron chuckled.

"Speak another language in front of me. It's rude."

"I can speak whatever I wish. Would you like to know what we were talking about?"

"Yes," she hissed with a sneer.

"Fine." He grinned and a sick feeling tightened her stomach. "Devlin wants to bend you over the desk and fuck your ass."

Alyssa gaped angrily at him. He was joking, surely.

"Taron, stop that," Rhia yelled. "That's not what he said and you know it. Stop trying to terrify the girl."

Rolling his eyes, Taron moved to rest his hip on the edge of Devlin's desk. "We never have any fun with you around," he drawled. "Devlin, make your sister go play somewhere else."

Devlin laughed, a deep rumbling sound that sent shivers down her back. He and Taron sounded a lot alike when they laughed and the thought was unsettling. It was bad enough she was attracted to Taron. God forbid they both tried to seduce her. When the hell did she turn into such a damn slut?

"I think not. When you get going the two of you are entirely too entertaining."

"Can we please just go?' Alyssa asked.

Taron grinned knowingly and she gritted her teeth against the desire to smack that smug look off his face.

"I'll talk to you later, Devlin. I think I better get my slave back to my quarters before she commences having a fit."

"I don't have fits," she snapped.

Taron came to a stop directly in front of her. She tilted her head back, trying to look him in the eyes. A tough feat, considering she only came to his collarbone. Taking a deep breath, she tried to calm her fluttering heart. If he'd keep his mouth shut he wouldn't be too bad to look at. Who was she kidding? She could stare at him all day. He was magnificent.

"It's time I found out if you're worth all that money I paid," he murmured against her lips. His warm breath fanned across her mouth and her nostrils flared, inhaling the scent of *kinok,* a Veenori alcohol. Her whole body tingled and she fought the overwhelming desire to lean into him and cover his full, kissable lips with hers.

"Come, slave," he said and tugged at her leash, forcing her to follow him.

* * * * *

Rhia stepped behind Devlin and smacked the back of his head with her hand. He laughed, then reached up to rub it. "Ouch. You're getting good at blocking me, little sister," he drawled. "That one caught me by surprise."

She walked around his desk and smiled. Devlin was Dorian, an empath from the planet Thallion, and could sense her emotions, which sometimes made it extremely difficult to keep secrets from him. "You deserve a whole lot more. Both of you do."

"What?" he asked innocently, but Rhia knew better. There wasn't a damn thing about the man who'd raised her that was innocent.

"You know what." She glared at him before turning to leave the room. "Like you're going to share Anthony's sister."

Devlin's chuckle followed her out the door and she clucked her tongue in frustration. *Men.*

Chapter Three

ꝏ

Alyssa followed Taron down the hall and into the main floor of the bar, her leash dangling between them. They'd entered through the back entrance earlier so she'd missed the main salon. It was huge and her steps slowed as her gaze took in the crowded tables.

At the center of each table were women and men dancing for the patrons around them, their bodies glistening with glitter and jewels as they undulated around the poles coming up through the center of the tables. No one paid them any attention as they made their way through the mass of people. Close to the door, a woman dancing on the table before them caught her eye.

The soft, muted lights reflected off her sparkling body, making the tiny jewels glisten like diamonds. Jeweled clamps dangled from her nipples and jingled like tiny bells as she swayed and undulated around the pole. For some reason, Alyssa couldn't take her eyes off her. The dancer's fingers moved lower to touch her shaved pussy and the men around her table all grunted their approval.

Taron moved behind her and the heat of his body seeped into hers. Darting her gaze to the next table, she stared as a male dancer surrounded by women gripped his cock and stroked it. The women sighed and licked their lips as his cock grew in size. Slowly he worked his way around the table, allowing each woman seated there to swipe her tongue around the head of his shaft.

Alyssa's body burned as she watched the erotic images surrounding her. She'd never seen anything like it and couldn't for the life of her look away. Taron's fingers slid beneath the split in her skirt and brushed along her slit. She closed her eyes with a moan, mortified that he would feel what this place had done to her. What his softly spoken words earlier had done.

She tried her best to remain compliant, tried to remember what Rhia had told her. *Never challenge him in public,* but she couldn't let him do this to her here. She'd never had sex in front of people and the very idea made her tense.

"Relax, Alyssa," he purred in her ear. "I won't fuck you here. Just watch them."

She swallowed and kept her gaze on the man and woman before her, both now pleasuring themselves on separate tables a good twenty feet away from each other, his hands stroked his cock, hers plunged and fingered her clit as the dancers twirled around the pole.

Taron's fingers continued to gently stroke her wet pussy, fueling her already out of control passion. Why was he doing this? Did he want to humiliate her? But as her gaze moved around the room, she realized no one paid them any attention. No one noticed what Taron was doing.

Moving her gaze back to the man dancing on the table, she softly gasped as Taron separated her folds and slid two fingers deep within her aching walls. He stepped closer, supporting her back against his chest. "Watch them, Lyssa," he whispered as he wrapped his other arm around her waist.

She opened her heavy-lidded eyes and watched the couple. They were more than a few feet apart, but they seemed to move in unison. "They're Dorian," Taron purred. "Because they are both Dorian, they can mentally link themselves, but they must do it together. She can feel his cock thrusting inside her and he can feel her pussy clenching his cock."

He increased the rhythm of his fingers, plunging them deeper, harder. "Imagine it's my cock thrusting inside you now, Lyssa." His deep, sexy voice washed over her, sending her to heights beyond anything she'd felt before. "Pretend I'm fucking you, burying myself deep inside your hot pussy."

Panting now, her gaze remained glued to the man's cock as he pumped it hard and fast. His balls tightened and pulled upward, his breathing harsh and labored. Taron's thumb shifted to circle her clit and she moaned, her knees weakening in desire and need. God, what the hell was he doing to her?

Alyssa's hips rocked against his hand and she exploded, falling back against Taron's chest, her walls clenching and unclenching around his thick fingers. Taron's soft voice whispered soothingly in her ear and her body began to slowly relax. In front of her the dancers were still moving, still working their bodies toward fulfillment.

Just as the female dancer screamed her release, the male dancer spilled his seed with a shout, then allowed each woman to take turns licking him, cleaning his cock with their tongues. It was the most erotic thing she'd ever witnessed or felt and for a fleeting second she forgot to be embarrassed.

Taron's breath brushed across her neck as he spoke softly, sending little shivers down her spine. "You're definitely worth the amount I paid for you."

* * * * *

Taron settled Alyssa in his speeder and turned to walk around the back. Lifting his hand, he inhaled her honeylike scent and his cock tightened painfully. He didn't have a clue what he'd been thinking, but when he'd seen her reaction to the sharing suggestion earlier and then again as she watched the couple dance, he hadn't been able to stop himself.

She was beautiful, stunning and so fucking hot he had wanted to lift that skirt and fuck her right then and there. She was his slave. It would be within his rights, but the last thing he needed to do was demonstrate how little control he had around his slinoy. What he was doing was dangerous enough. Add this to the mix and he was screwed.

"Where are we going now?" she asked as she eyed him warily.

She'd been suspiciously quiet since the bar, and he took a moment to study her. "Did I say you could speak?" he asked.

She grumbled something under her breath and turned away from him to glare across the desert wasteland. It would take her a while to get used to these rules, he was sure. As he watched her, he frowned. What the hell was he supposed to do with her? He knew what he wanted to do—use her as the slave she was. But he'd promised Anthony he'd take care of her and taking care of her didn't include fucking.

But damn, after that little impromptu session in the bar, all he could think about was sinking his cock into that delectable body of hers. Damn she was hot. Taking a deep breath, he tried to turn his mind from fucking her and answered the question she'd asked. "We're headed to my quarters at the mine." After a brief pause, he added, "You may ask questions if you wish."

"Aren't you the generous one," she sneered and Taron turned away to hide a grin.

"I can be very generous, slave." He glanced back at her and ran his finger along her jawline. She flinched and narrowed her eyes in apprehension. "When I'm pleased. And your reaction to my touch earlier pleased me very much."

She scowled and moved her angry gaze to the dash of his speeder. "I would prefer to forget that ever happened."

Taron chuckled despite himself. "Are you always such a *vigic*?"

"What's a *vigic*?"

"What you Earthlings would call someone who's surly all the time."

She gave him a tight-lipped grin. "If I was would you release me and let me work off my debt in the mine instead?"

Taron snorted. "No."

With a sigh, she crossed her arms over her chest and sulked.

Taron leaned closer and traced the shell of her ear with his tongue. She jerked away as though startled but Taron grabbed her arm and held her close. "We have people watching," he whispered. "Behave yourself."

She tilted her head and snapped at him, "Do you enjoy toying with me in front of an audience?"

"I enjoy making you squirm. I have to wonder, though. Why would you want to spend more than twelve hours a day at hard labor when you could spend twelve hours a day being pleasured by me?"

"What makes you think you pleasure me?"

A slow smile spread across Taron's face as he gently licked the side of her neck, making her shiver. "I think that orgasm you had in the bar says it all, *ni pahti*." For a second his use of that particular endearment made him pause. It meant "my angel". Brushing the thought aside, he slowly slid his hand up the inside of her leg. The muscles bunched and twitched beneath his touch as he moved closer to her smooth, hot pussy. "Do you need a reminder of just how well I can please you?"

His hand cupped her and he smiled as her warm juices coated his palm. She gulped in a sudden intake of breath then bit down on her lip. "Don't do this here," she whispered in a strained voice. "They're watching."

With a gentle touch, he separated her folds and softly stroked her swollen clit. She gasped, her hips wiggling in the seat. Through his lashes, he glanced up and noticed that indeed several men had their eyes locked on his slinoy and the quick rise and fall of her breasts.

The color of her cheeks deepened to the most adorable shade of red and he applied a little more pressure to the hard bud beneath his finger. Her blush deepened along with her breathing. "You will find, slave, that I do what I want, where I want," he whispered in her ear. "That includes pleasing you. Come for me, Lyssa. Let me feel your pussy quake against my hand."

Shifting slightly, he pushed two fingers deep within her folds. She was slick with her juices and hot as lava. Closing his eyes, he imagined his cock buried inside her tight walls. "That's it, Lyssa," he purred as her walls clenched his fingers, pulling them deeper.

He increased his thrusts, his thumb circling her now engorged clit. She whimpered and bit down on her lip. He increased his rhythm, fucking her harder. "Don't fight it, Lyssa. Let it go. Show them how pretty you are when you come, how hot."

Her mouth dropped open and her head fell back against the seat. Closing her eyes tight, she let out a mewling sound that almost drove him over the edge. The walls of her pussy spasmed around his fingers over and over, milking them as they would his cock.

Once her throbs subsided, he removed his hand and slid his fingers into his mouth to lick her juices. Her eyes opened to stare angrily into his. "I hate you," she snarled.

He smiled as he licked the last of her essence from his knuckle. "Give it a week, *ni pahti*. By then you'll really hate me."

* * * * *

Alyssa stared in awe as the small speeder descended into a deep hole in the ground. All around them were steel structures and landing pads built into the side of the rock. As they fell lower, the temperature dropped dramatically and she hugged herself to keep warm. Since the top had been removed, leaving the inside exposed like a convertible, there was no climate control within the ship.

Leaning her head over the side of the ship, she tried to tell how deep the hole went, but the bottom was covered in darkness. "How far does this go?" she asked.

"Five dectons, or three miles. My quarters, or I guess now our quarters, are halfway down, in the residential levels."

"What's above the residential level?"

"Docking stations, offices, supply bunkers."

"And the mine itself is below them?"

"Yes."

She darted her gaze quickly from one landing pad to another, trying to get a glimpse of everything. It was amazing. Steel walls jutted out from the rock. Some of the windows were lit, their soft yellow lights casting a little brightness in an otherwise dark and damp environment. Lower they descended, into what could only be the bowels of hell.

The faraway sound of machinery could be heard over the engine noise and white smoke drifted up from the dark bottom. Taron moved the ship closer to the side and came to a stop on a small pad. He pushed a button on the dash and the metal wall slid open, allowing her a view of the apartment within.

"Your own personal parking space. Aren't you special." she said with a frown.

Taron shook his head in amusement. "I think we should go back to the rule of don't speak unless you're spoken to."

"Fine," she snapped and turned her nose up. She ignored him as she stepped out of the speeder, holding her leash within her hand so as not to trip on it. Her gaze moved upward, trying to gauge how far down they were. A wave of dizziness swept through her and she wobbled, almost falling onto the cold concrete beneath her bare feet.

Taron's arms snaked around her and held her close to his warm chest. "I've got you. Be careful," he said as he gazed down into her face, his eyes full of concern and just a hint of mischief and lust. "It's a long way down if you fall over the edge of the platform."

The heat of his body seeped into her cold one, filling her with warmth. She raised her hands to rest against his chest and felt the hard muscles twitch beneath her fingers. He was so big he dwarfed her when she stood this close to him, which unnerved her greatly. She didn't like feeling this vulnerable or this out of control.

She swallowed a sudden lump of desire. "I'm fine now. You can let me go."

His hands moved lower to cup her bottom as a sensuous grin tugged at his lips. Oh, God. What was he up to now? She couldn't take another lesson on just how much control he had over her body.

"I don't think I'm quite ready to yet," he purred and pulled her flush against him. His hard cock pressed into her stomach and she gasped at his size and the pure, hot lust that suddenly gripped her. Even through his clothes she could tell he was huge. Much bigger than anyone she'd been with in the past.

"Feels to me like you're ready for something," she murmured then clamped her eyes shut in aggravation. *What made me say that?*

Taron chuckled and released his hold on her. She staggered back from him, unsure if she was happy with the release or not. She definitely missed the warmth of his flesh as the cool air brushed across her heated skin.

"Come on inside. It's much cooler down here than on the surface and I'm sure you'll need to get warm. You're starting to shiver."

She followed him into the suite of rooms and jumped when the wall slid back into place behind them. The interior was much different then she expected—steel walls, thick-shaded windows that overlooked the landing pad outside and tile floors that felt cold against her bare feet, adding to the cool temperature. The furniture was all metal and glass. "Is the whole planet like this?"

"Like what?" Taron asked from the room to her left.

Following the sound of his voice, she stepped into the bedroom. He stood by the closet, thoughtfully studying the clothes that hung there. For a second she let her gaze wander down his wide, strong back and firm hips and thighs. The man was a mountain and would surely crush her during sex.

Raising her gaze, she found him staring at her over his shoulder. "Like what?" he asked again.

"Oh, sorry. Desert. Is the whole planet like a desert?"

"For the most part. There's a small grove of trees to the north of the mine. Even has a wooden cabin, if you can believe that. Trees don't grow here easily, so they're protected. No one can cut them down."

"How do they survive?" she asked as she searched the room for a place to sit. She really didn't want to sit on the bed and give him any ideas.

"There's an underground spring that feeds the trees, keeps them alive. The only place it flows to the surface is a few miles west of the city. There are a few trees there as well, but they're small. The heat and constant sunlight stunts their growth."

"Oh," she breathed then finally decided to just remain standing.

"Here. Put this on," he said as he handed her a wool shirt and reached out to unhook the leash attached to her collar. "It'll help keep you warm until I can get you something else to wear. Sexy as that outfit you're wearing is, I can't have you traipsing around the mine in it. The men are sometimes hard enough to control as it is."

"Thank you." She wrapped the thick material around her shoulders then slipped her arms through the sleeves. It swallowed her whole, but it at least helped to ward off the chill.

"Are you hungry?" Taron asked.

"Yes. I don't think I've eaten in several hours."

Taron nodded then headed for the door. "I have to work for a while, but I'll have my assistant bring you something. When he gets here do not speak to him, understand?"

"What if he speaks to me first?" she asked.

"He won't."

With that, he stepped out into the hallway, the door clicking shut behind him. Running over, she quickly grabbed the handle and gave it a turn, hoping he'd left the door unlocked. With a growl of aggravation, she realized he hadn't forgotten and slapped her palm against the thick metal.

"Nice try," Taron drawled through the metal. The amusement in his voice was obvious and she scowled at him through the door, silently cursing him to hell.

Chapter Four

ഇ

Taron jumped off the elevator ledge before it came to a stop on the first floor of the mineshaft, toward the bottom of the hole. A dusting of pebbles rained down on his head and he brushed them away with his fingers. "Neelok," he shouted.

"Yes, Overseer?"

Taron frowned at the tall man before him, his long, spindly legs bent at awkward angles as he tried to stay low and keep his narrow head from scraping the ceiling. "Get someone down here to fix that," he nodded to the constant shower of dust and tiny pebbles that fell from the roof of the cavern, "before the damn thing gets any bigger."

"Yes, sir." Neelok nodded then headed off to find someone.

"Karmase."

Taron rolled his eyes heavenward at Jonah's voice, then turned to stare at the intruder questioningly.

Jonah was from Taron's homeworld of Tilarus, and Taron tensed whenever he was around him. The man hadn't given any indication so far that he recognized him, but Taron was careful nonetheless. He was glad he'd thought to lose his Tilarian accent before coming here, adopting the Norgosen accent of his father.

"What is it, Jonah?" he asked.

"The shipment bound for Hilarac is ready for your approval."

Taron nodded and took the small computer Jonah handed him. As quickly as possible he scanned the minerals to be shipped then checked the weights. Right away he noticed they didn't match up. Foran Five was a dust and should weigh no more than a few thousand pounds. He narrowed his eyes at Jonah. "Since when does a full shipment of Foran Five weigh over two tons?"

"What?" Jonah stared at him in surprise then grabbed the manifest from his hand to see for himself. "There must be a mistake."

No, Taron thought to himself, *there's a shipment of weapons mixed in with the minerals*.

He didn't believe Jonah was behind it, but he had a sneaking suspicion Master Chief Morlak was. His only dilemma was, how did he find out who Morlak worked for?

"There's no mistake," Morlak purred from behind Taron.

Taron stiffened and turned to glare at Morlak. "Care to explain the discrepancy?"

Morlak took the computer from Taron and nodded to Jonah. "You may go," Morlak said. Once Jonah had headed back down the shaft, Morlak turned his attention back to Taron. "An additional shipment of un-ground mineral rock that was accidentally left off the manifest. I'll take care of it."

"You do that," Taron replied softly.

Morlak studied the list then glanced at Taron with his gold, lizard-like eyes. "I understand you bought a slinoy, Karmase. Paid a hefty sum for her from what I hear."

"So?"

"Where did you get such a large amount of money? I know you don't make that much here."

"Maybe it's none of your business."

Morlak's lips lifted into a sideways grin. "I like you, Karmase. You have balls."

"I'm thrilled," Taron murmured.

Taron had made sure since he'd been here that the men knew about his bloody past and time spent at Dellon Five. His well-constructed reputation could be the one thing that got him in.

"Perhaps you and I should get together. Discuss a way for you to line your pockets even more," Morlak suggested.

"I'm listening," Taron purred as he crossed his arms over his chest.

"I'll let you know when. For now, I'll take care of this." He waved the computer and turned to jump on the elevator, which had begun the slow climb back to the top level. Taron watched him go and wondered if maybe he'd finally found a way inside.

* * * * *

Taron opened the door to his quarters with caution. He expected to be pummeled by his stubborn little slave, and when he stepped in and wasn't greeted with something being thrown at him in her attempt to leave, he quickly scanned the room looking for her.

He caught a glimpse of her small ankle dangling off the edge of the mattress and he moved further into the bedroom for a closer look. She was sound asleep, stretched out across his bed. For a moment he just watched her, letting his gaze wander aimlessly across her exposed flesh.

In her sleep, she'd knocked the covers off, leaving most everything but her hips visible to his hungry gaze. Never in his life had he seen a more fascinating woman. Or a more beautiful one. Her eyes were especially stunning and extremely expressive. Everything she felt could be seen there, shining in their bright, intelligent depths.

Walking closer, he brushed a stray lock from her forehead. Long black lashes graced her cheeks and fluttered in her sleep. She was dreaming. He smiled and softly trailed his fingertip along her eyebrow, smoothing out the strip of black.

She moaned and rolled to her back. His gaze moved immediately to her ample breasts. They were perfect—full and firm, and the rose-tinted nipples perked upward, begging to be suckled. He moved his fingers down her neck and chest, all the while watching her face for any sign she was waking. With the barest of touches, he circled her nipple with the tip of his finger. It beaded into a hard bud and he gently pinched it, making her moan in her sleep.

His cock hardened instantly beneath the coarse material of his slacks. He knew he shouldn't. This woman was Anthony's sister and Anthony trusted him to look out for her. But another side of him—the lust-filled side—wanted desperately to fuck her.

What was it about her he just couldn't seem to resist? With an inward growl he moved back to the living area, putting some distance between him and the temptation she offered. He plopped down into a chair and rubbed at his temples, trying to ease the pounding that had started behind his eyes.

He hoped the conversation he'd had with Morlak would lead somewhere. Alyssa rolled to her side, giving him a perfect view of her delectable backside. He ran his hand down his face with a sigh. The first order of business was to get the woman some decent clothes before she drove him insane with desire.

"This is ridiculous," he murmured. "It's my damn bed and it's big enough for both of us."

Standing, he walked back into the bedroom and removed his clothes then climbed into bed beside her. Her body curled instinctively against his and he wrapped his arm around her, holding her close. She was soft and warm and her body fit perfectly within his embrace. The rightness of it all startled him.

He'd never had a woman feel like this in his arms, like she belonged, and he wasn't sure what to make of it. This was going to be a long assignment.

"Too long," he whispered toward the ceiling.

*****

Alyssa awoke with a start and sat upright in the bed, her fingers grasping the sheet beneath her chin. At first she couldn't remember where she was but then it all came back to her—every mortifying touch of his hand. She closed her eyes with a groan and brushed her hair from her eyes.

Where was the jerk anyway, she wondered and glanced around, looking for him. She stopped cold the second her eyes landed on his gorgeous, rock-hard form in the bed next to her. His skin was bronze and stretched tight over massive muscles that flexed when he shifted. In surprise, she realized there wasn't a scrap of hair on him anywhere. So apparently his being bald wasn't by choice.

With deliberate slowness, she lowered her gaze past his firm pecs, his washboard abs, his thick... She swallowed a lump at the sight of his thick cock. The thing was huge and she couldn't imagine being able to take all of it. Was he actually going to fuck her with that?

"Stop staring at me like that, Alyssa," Taron drawled with a just a hint of amusement. "The damn thing is hard enough."

Oh, God. It can get harder? Biting down on her lower lip, she turned her back to him so he hopefully wouldn't see her trying not to giggle.

"Come back to bed. It's too early to get up," he grumbled.

She glanced back at him over her shoulder. He had one arm thrown over his eyes, the other resting on his hard stomach. God, he looked good. "I'm wide awake now," she said with a shrug.

With a speed that shocked her, Taron grabbed her arm and pulled her back to the bed. She landed on the mattress with a squeal, then gasped as he swiftly rolled and settled over top of her, pinning her small body beneath his larger one. His hard shaft pressed into her thigh and she stared up at him in shock, her heart beating frantically in her chest. The move didn't scare her. Quite the opposite. It turned her on.

"I never said anything about sleeping," he whispered against her lips.

Blood rushed through her ears and down to her pussy with alarming swiftness as the smoldering heat of his whiskey stare bored into hers. She felt hot, and thoroughly thrown for a loop as his mouth slowly lowered, coming to a stop just inches away from hers.

"I don't have time for you, *ni pahti,*" he murmured, his lips brushing softly across hers as he spoke. "You're a distraction I can't afford."

"Then why did you buy me?" she whispered back, her lips opening in silent invitation for his kiss. He smelled of mornings and hot male and she inhaled deeply, pulling his essence into her. Welcoming the heat of his flesh.

He grinned then licked at her bottom lip, making her shiver. "You were just too tempting to pass up." His smile faded and his gaze sobered, turning her insides to molten fire. "Too beautiful for the other men to ruin and abuse."

"So you saved me?"

"And damned myself, it seems," he murmured just before his lips claimed hers in a deep, all-consuming kiss.

She moaned as his tongue slid into her mouth, taking complete and utter possession. His kiss was wild, deep and incredibly erotic. His tongue delved and licked, his teeth nipped. He put his whole mouth into the kiss, leaving her hungry for more.

Suddenly Taron stiffened and pulled away from her, his labored breaths fanning across her lips. At first she didn't understand what was wrong, why he scowled so angrily. Then she heard it—the knock at the door.

"Son of a bitch," he growled and rolled off her, stomping across the floor. Throwing open the door, he snapped, "What the fuck do you want?"

Alyssa watched in awe as the young man cowered before his furious glare. "I'm sorry, sir. But you requested this be brought to you first thing this morning."

With a shaking hand, he passed a small silver box to Taron, who snatched it from him with a growl then slammed the door.

"You know, you probably gave that poor boy a heart attack," she scolded as she sat up and covered herself with the blanket. Her hands shook as she brushed her hair from her eyes. She still couldn't believe what they'd almost done. But wasn't that what she was here for? To appease his basic needs and desires?

His gaze flicked to her momentarily, then shifted back to the box he held in his palm. "He's not a boy, Alyssa. He's older than both of us put together."

"And how old is that?" she asked.

"Well, I'm thirty-four and you're twenty-six, so that makes him sixty or better," he said as he made his way across the floor to his desk.

She lost her train of thought as what he'd said sank in. "How do you know how old I am?"

He stopped mid-stride but didn't look at her before continuing across the room. Wrapping the sheet around her body, she climbed from the bed and stomped to glare at him across his desk. "Well?" she snapped.

Slowly, he took his seat before meeting her questioning gaze. "I guessed."

"Bullshit," she snapped.

Taron remained quiet as his eyes slowly slid down the length of her body, heating her flesh and sending a sudden wave of desire to the pit of her stomach. He wasn't going to sway her that easily, damn it.

"Taron," she started, then licked her lips.

"You look delectable in that sheet, Lyssa. But I think I'd rather you take it off."

"That reminds me," she said, tightening the sheet around her breasts. "When do I get some clothes?"

"Who said you were getting clothes?" he asked, his eyebrow arching adorably.

"You did, last night. You might be comfortable naked," she snapped, trying to keep her gaze from flicking to his massive cock, which still stood fully erect. "But I'm not. I'd prefer some clothing."

"Haven't you figured out yet, Alyssa, that you're a slave and you get what I choose to give you, when I choose to give it to you? What you prefer is irrelevant."

She took a deep breath and counted to ten. "Please. You can't keep me here in the nude until you tire of me."

"I most certainly can. I paid for you, remember? You are at my beck and call. Whatever I want you to do you are required to do and if that means living here naked, then you live here naked."

"As much as I love the idea of being your beck-and-call girl, I refuse to be forced to run around here naked," she snapped angrily.

"You refuse?" he asked as he slowly stood from the chair, his eyes narrowing dangerously. "You're treading awfully close to trouble, slave. You better calm down before you say something you'll regret."

"Why? What are you going to do? Spank me?" she snarled. "I dare you." The second the words left her lips she regretted them. Why did she always have to lose her temper and spout off at the mouth? Why couldn't she think before she spoke? "I…um…I didn't mean that," she stammered.

"Too late," he growled and lunged for her, his fingers wrapping around her upper arm.

"You wouldn't dare," she hissed. "I'm a grown woman, not a child. You can't be serious." She tried to pull her arm free of his grasp as he tugged her to the bed. He looked furious and completely serious and her struggles increased, in earnest.

Sitting on the side of the bed, he ripped the sheet from her body before throwing her across his lap on her stomach, her ass high in the air. She bit down on her lip, determined to not make a sound as the first stinging slap landed across her buttock. "I can't believe you're doing this," she growled.

"You'll learn to control your temper, Alyssa, or you'll get more of these," he purred, then slapped her ass again with his palm.

She stiffened, but not from pain. It was something else that shook her to the core. Desire. Every time his hand met her flesh, her whole body tingled, sending shock waves of lust to settle between her legs. This wasn't right. How could a spanking make her want him?

The slaps stopped and his palm softly massaged her muscles. "Your ass is now the most adorable shade of red," he purred and slid his fingers between her butt cheeks and down her cleft to her pussy.

Tremors of molten desire made her groan and she buried her face against his thigh.

This can't be happening. Please, tell me this isn't happening.

"I can't believe you actually spanked me," she growled. "You should be shot, hanged, left to die a slow death."

Taron chuckled and smoothed a fingertip along her sensitive slit. "I think you protest too much, slave. You're awfully wet for someone who didn't enjoy it."

"And you're awfully like a tyrant who gets his kicks out of..." He pushed two fingers deep into her aching pussy and she gasped, clamping her mouth closed against the desire to scream her pleasure.

Of their own accord, her hips lifted to meet his gentle thrusts. Her juices coated his fingers then slipped lower to soak the side of his leg. He leaned down and softly bit her shoulder. His mouth was hot against her flesh and shivers of unanswered need moved along her limbs. "I want more than just my fingers inside you this time, Lyssa. I want to feel your pussy come around my cock."

She whimpered, remembering the thickness of his cock, and more wetness pooled from her center. Could she take him? She wasn't sure but at the moment, more than anything, she wanted to try.

Removing his fingers, he grabbed her arms and turned her so his mouth could claim hers in a deeply erotic kiss. His lips moved over hers with a skill that left her breathless. She wrapped her arms around his neck and deepened the kiss, her tongue battling his for control. The arm around her shoulders held her close while his other hand massaged her breasts and rolled her nipple between his thumb and forefinger.

"Taron," she sighed. "Hurry before we're interrupted again."

With a soft chuckle, he lifted her then turned to lay her on the bed. Spreading her thighs wider with his, he positioned the head of his shaft at her opening. She moaned and bucked her hips against him, silently begging him to take her, to appease the terrible ache that was eating her alive.

"Damn," he sighed into her kiss. "Easy, Alyssa. I don't want to hurt you. You're so fucking small."

"Please," she whispered, and it was all the encouragement Taron needed.

Slowly, he slid his cock inside her. Inch by excruciating inch he plunged deeper, retreating then pushing back in. She gasped as his thick cock stretched her, filled her so completely it took her breath away. Aggravated with his patience, she wrapped her legs around his hips and pulled him deeper inside her. With a growl he thrust hard, burying himself balls-deep.

She screamed, throwing her head back against the bed and lifting her hips higher, forcing his cock even deeper. "Oh, God," she groaned as he began to move. Slowly at first, then harder, nearly splitting her in two.

"*Shetah*, you feel good," he growled as he gently nibbled the sensitive spot behind her ear. "Too good."

"Taron," she gasped as the first waves of her release began to work their way through her body. The insides of her thighs tightened and trembled as the waves increased in intensity.

Taron slowed his thrusts, grinding his hips in circles against her clit as he plunged deeper. Every muscle in her body tensed as she tried to hold back, to fight it off. But it was no use. Her body wanted it, needed it too much.

"Oh, God, yes," she screamed and bucked against him harder. "Harder, Taron."

Rising up on his hands, Taron thrust harder, his balls slapping against her ass. She began to scoot across the bed and threw her hands over her head to grip the mattress and push herself back. The movement forced her into him and forced his cock even deeper, bringing her closer to orgasm.

She held her breath, trying to delay it. He felt so good inside her she didn't want him to stop.

"Look at me, Alyssa," he said and she opened her eyes, meeting his hot stare.

"Don't hold it back," he ordered as he began to move his hips in tantalizing circles against her sensitive clit. The movement sent a shock wave of sensation up her vagina. "Come with me, *ni pahti*."

She closed her eyes again and let herself go. With a loud groan, she shattered into a million pieces, her pussy spasming around Taron's invading cock.

With a shout of his own, Taron stiffened above her, his body shivering in the throes of his own release.

Chapter Five

ꟸ

Alyssa paced the floor of Taron's suite, thoroughly bored out of her mind. She had to find something to do before she went crazy. Taron had left this morning right after he'd finished with her. He didn't say a word but as he dressed he kept stopping to glance at her with this odd expression—like he didn't know what to make of her.

Well, she didn't know what to make of him either. He made her body feel things she never dreamed it could. And God knows he was gorgeous. Beyond gorgeous. The man was a god. He was also an arrogant ass. It infuriated her, the way he led her around by the leash and made her call him "master". Although he didn't push the use of master when they were alone, which made her pause in her pacing.

Shaking her head, she continued walking from one end of the room the other, her arms swinging back and forth. She needed to keep her mind on why she was here. Vingosa. She needed to find Vingosa. With a sigh, she glanced at the locked door. She certainly wasn't going to find him in here. She needed to find a way out of this room and into the mine. Unless…

Thinking, she strolled over to Taron's desk and stared at the small, square computer. What she assumed to be a password prompt blinked on the screen.

"Damn, I wish I'd thought to learn Veenorian," she mumbled to herself as she leaned closer to study the letters.

The door opened and she jerked upright, meeting Taron's suspicious gaze. "What are you doing?" he asked.

"Nothing," she replied, and inwardly cringed when her voice cracked.

"Nothing, huh? You look awfully guilty for someone who's doing nothing. Did my assistant bring you dinner?" he asked.

"Yes. He came about an hour ago. Did you bring me some clothes?" she asked and hugged his shirt around her more tightly.

He shook his head in amusement. "You have a one-track mind."

"It's kind of hard to not think about it when you're cold," she snarled. "*Master.*"

"Then turn up the environmental controls," he answered back. "*Slave.*"

She chewed on her lower lip and moved her gaze away from him. Just looking at him reminded her of earlier and the way his hands had played her flesh like an instrument, making it sing in pleasure. "I can't. The panel is in Veenorian and I can't read it."

Taron set his handheld computer on the table and motioned for her to join him at the panel. "Come here."

She walked over and stood next to him. "This symbol," he said as he pointed to a small triangle with a squiggly line through it, "is the on switch." He pushed it and the panel lit up, causing other symbols to become visible. He pointed out each one, showing her how to raise and lower the temperature.

Each symbol, she realized, was a complete word, not just a letter. This would be a difficult language to learn. "Is there some way I can learn more of this language?"

He studied her for a moment, thoughtfully, and her stomach knotted. Could he read her mind? Did he know she was up to something? "I'll teach you."

That surprised her and she stared at him in shock. "You will?"

"Yeah," he snorted. "What? Didn't think I knew how to read?"

"Well—" she began but Taron held up a hand, stopping her.

"Never mind. Don't answer that."

A knock sounded at the door and they both turned to frown at it. "Who's that?" she asked quietly.

"Probably Morlak. He said he would be by here later."

"Who's Morlak?" she asked.

"He's the master chief."

"So he's your boss?" Alyssa asked. Taron didn't seem like the type to take orders and she couldn't imagine him under anyone. *Except maybe me*, she thought with a wicked grin.

He noticed her smile and his brow wrinkled into a stern expression. "No. He controls the ships and the pilots." He stepped closer, his brow creasing into a frown as he leaned down to meet her eye to eye. "This isn't a game and it's important you do as I say. Understand?"

She swallowed her trepidation at the dangerously serious tone his voice held.

"When I open that door, I need you to remember your place. I know it will be hard for you, but be submissive."

She opened her mouth to speak but he scowled, putting his finger over her lips. "I mean it, Lyssa. So help me if you do anything stupid..."

"Okay, I get it," she hissed. "I'll be submissive."

He studied her for a moment as though he didn't quite believe her, then moved to the door. He glanced her way and she nodded, then moved to take a submissive stance, eyes downcast, hands clasped before her. The door opened and she watched Taron through her lashes.

"Morlak," Taron said.

"Taron," Morlak replied as he stepped into the room.

He was tall and thin with green-tinged skin and gold eyes that darted to her in interest. He walked toward her and she inwardly cringed. His eyes dilated then quickly shrank back to normal as they roamed over her body, sending goose bumps along her flesh. The man gave her the creeps and she darted a nervous glance toward Taron, who shook his head ever-so slightly.

Morlak brushed his cold, clammy fingers along her neck and she tried not to noticeably flinch. It didn't work. Morlak scowled down at her, making her heart pound in fear. Would Taron let this man abuse her?

"She's lovely. No doubt worth the amount you paid for her," Morlak said as his hand moved to pull open her shirt and expose her breasts, and she stiffened before moving back a step. "Still unbroken, I see. She hasn't learned yet that anyone can touch her."

Close to panic, she shot Taron a frightened gaze, silently praying he would do something. The possessive scowl on his face startled her and she watched, mesmerized, as he moved forward and grabbed her elbow. "Only at the owner's discretion. Go to the other room, slave," he ordered.

"Yes, Master," she whispered, but mouthed a silent thank you as she walked past.

Taron scowled at Morlak. Fury had punched him in the gut when he saw the Veenorian put his hands on Alyssa. He didn't want anyone touching her and the realization startled him. She'd been on his mind all day, ever since this morning when he'd lost his control and fucked her. He had no business doing that. She was Anthony's sister and they'd promised him they'd find her and take care of the girl. But now that he'd had her once, he wasn't so sure he could keep from having her again.

"I'm sure you didn't come here to get a closer look at my slave, Morlak. What do you want?"

Morlak grinned, sending a shot of apprehension down the back of Taron's neck. He didn't like this man. Taron's gut told him to watch his back around him. "Like I said, Karmase.

I like you. Come with me to Devlin's. I'd like to speak with you about a little side project I have for you."

Taron nodded. "I'll meet you there."

"Good." Morlak grinned and left the room, quietly shutting the door behind him.

With a sigh, Taron turned to see Alyssa step from the bedroom, her eyes watching him expectantly. His lips quirked, fighting a grin. "Please tell me you're not going to read me the riot act about how I never take you anywhere."

She scowled adorably and his gut tightened. What the hell kind of effect did she have on him? Whatever it was, he didn't have time for it, nor did he like it. He sighed and ran his hand over his head.

He punched the panel next to the door and the outside wall slid open. Cool air rushed into the room and he watched Alyssa hug the shirt around her more tightly. Tomorrow he would have Rhia take her shopping. As much as he liked looking at her body and loved teasing her, she needed some clothes. "Don't open the door while I'm gone," he ordered.

"I think that's a given since I don't know how to unlock the damn thing."

Taron frowned, then nodded. "You don't want to go out there, Alyssa. Trust me on this."

Alyssa remained silent as she watched him walk out to his speeder, parked on the extended dock. Part of her wanted to run after him, beg him to take her too. She hated being cooped up here alone and would give anything to have someone to talk to. She just didn't know if she should *want* to talk to him.

His ship lifted from the pad, spun around, then whizzed quickly toward the light at the top of the hole. She walked cautiously toward the end of the landing pad and peeked over the edge. Her head swam with dizziness and she immediately stepped back. She should have known better.

Placing a hand against her forehead, she watched a small ship levitate a few feet away. Two men leered at her and she shivered as nasty grins spread their lips. Fast as a shot she turned and ran back into the suite, anxious to close the wall and put a safety buffer between her and the men outside.

* * * * *

The metal door opened and Alyssa pretended to be asleep in the large bed. She could hear Taron moving around, his footfalls soft on the floor. She'd lain awake most of the night thinking about yesterday morning. Wow, she hadn't had sex like that ever. The man was incredible. Would he have his way with her again? And did she want him to? She wasn't sure. Part of her did and the other part wanted to hate him.

His large palm slapped across her ass, the thin blanket doing nothing to soften the sting. She'd been so wrapped up in her thoughts she hadn't heard him approach. "Ow," she snapped and jerked her head around to glare at him. "What was that for?"

"Because I felt like it," he replied with a devilish grin.

"Are you always such an ass?"

"No," he drawled. "Most days I'm worse."

"I can believe that." She moved to a sitting position, careful to keep the sheet over her breasts.

He came to a stop by the bed and leaned down, bringing his nose close to hers. His breath smelled of Veenori ale and she crinkled her nose in distaste. "Are you drunk?"

He snorted. "Not likely. I haven't been drunk since I was fifteen. Be nice, slave, or I won't take you out today."

Her heart hammered in excitement. "You mean I get out of this room?"

"It's only been a day," he choked in amusement.

"One day with you is like a lifetime," she replied dryly.

She hated being such a bitch, but it just came out. Her attraction to him concerned her, confused her. She should be thinking about finding her brother's killer, not ways to get Taron in the sack.

He stood straight and placed his palm over his heart. A purely dreadful look of mortification crossed his features. "You wound me," he gasped.

She bit back a giggle. "You're going to wound me with the lousy overacting."

He frowned down at her, but deep down Alyssa knew he was all bluster. For some reason he seemed to be in a good mood this morning. "I think I'm way too lenient on you."

"Considering you keep me here naked and at your disposal, I don't think you're lenient enough."

"So you think I should let you wander the mines? Do whatever you want?"

She shrugged and glanced up at him. "Is there a reason I shouldn't?"

"Lots of them."

"Like what?" she asked.

"I'll show you a big one later. For right now, put your clothes on. We're heading to Devlin's bar."

He turned and headed back to the living room and she couldn't help but admire his tight ass and wide back. "Isn't it a little early for drinking?"

Her skin prickled with intense heat as he shot her a smoldering look over his shoulder. "Would you prefer we stay here? I'd be more than happy to repeat yesterday morning."

Whiskey-colored eyes sparkled with the most intensely seductive look she'd ever seen and for a split second she almost wished he would. But her common sense took over and she quickly stood, wrapping the blanket around her more tightly. "I'll be ready in a couple of minutes."

"My loss," he drawled in a deep, sexy timbre and every inch of her flesh tingled in awareness.

God help her, the man was sexy.

* * * * *

Alyssa followed along behind Taron as they headed into Devlin's office. Well, not really followed along. More like was led like a dog. She hated that leash and would give anything to be able to shred it. Taron, on the other hand, seemed to enjoy leading her around. Either that or he just pretended to because he knew she hated it.

"Coming in," Taron shouted after knocking on the large wooden door. "Hope you're decent."

"When has my not being decent ever stopped you?" Devlin asked dryly.

Devlin sat at the desk, his sister Rhia behind him. Rhia sent her a friendly smile of welcome. Alyssa returned her smile then turned her glance toward Devlin. His eyes raked over her with interest and just a hint of amusement. He was gorgeous, and she would bet her life just as arrogant as Taron. But there was a deep sadness in his eyes and she wondered what had caused it.

"You know, now that I think about it, when you're not decent is probably the best time to come in here. I seem to recall an incident with the Begonite twins that was quite memorable."

Alyssa frowned at him, her gut clenching with something she didn't want to acknowledge.

"I remember that day," Rhia said with a chuckle. "I think it's one of the only times I've actually seen the twins thoroughly satisfied."

"Of course they were," Taron answered with a wide grin. "After all they did spend the evening with me and Devlin."

"Is this what you brought me here for?" Alyssa snapped. "To listen to the two of you brag about how good you are with women? If so, I think I'd rather head back to the room, thank you."

"What's the matter, slave?" Taron took a seat across from Devlin's desk and rested one ankle on his knee. "Jealous?"

She huffed and crossed her arms over her chest. "Not likely."

Taron turned to Devlin and the two of them shared a smile. "My slave's not a very good liar."

"I see that," Devlin purred, his amused gaze shooting to hers.

The two of them were unbelievable. Where did they get off insisting she was jealous? Why would she be?

"I think the two of you are having way too much fun," Rhia scolded.

"I actually came here for you, Rhia," Taron said. "Would you be so kind as to take my slave shopping?"

"What did you have in mind?" Rhia asked.

Taron studied Alyssa for a second before turning back to Rhia. "Something a little less distracting would be nice."

Rhia laughed and the sound was light and tinkling, like bells. "I think we can find something."

"Good," Taron sighed and handed her leash to Rhia. "She's all yours."

Taron watched Alyssa leave the room, letting his gaze wander down her slim back and firm, rounded hips. He shifted slightly in his seat, trying to relieve some of the pressure that had built up in his cock.

"You've already fucked her, haven't you?" Devlin asked.

With a sigh, Taron brushed his palm across his head. "Is it that obvious?"

"Just to me. I'm an empath, remember?"

Taron cringed. "I keep forgetting that."

Devlin chuckled.

"Did you get in touch with Stefan?" Taron asked.

"He was in negotiations with a couple of Tilarian traders. I told his assistant it wasn't urgent and that he could contact me when he's finished."

Taron nodded in acknowledgment.

"I noticed you with Morlak last night."

"That was an interesting evening," Taron sighed. "I think he's testing me."

"Testing you how?"

"He wants me to deliver a small package to the planet Haven. Not for the mine but for him personally. I think it's just to see if I can be trusted. He apparently found in my file I can fly intergalactic ships."

Devlin frowned. "I don't think I like this."

"What am I supposed to do, Devlin? Turn him down? This is why I'm here. If I do this for him then maybe he'll feel as though he can trust me and I can find out who's behind all this."

"Will you take Alyssa?"

"Do I have a choice? I can't leave her here alone."

"Have you ever been to Haven?" Devlin asked.

"Once, several years ago. It's virtually ice. Very pretty but damn cold."

Devlin's computer beeped, indicating an incoming message. "It's Stefan," Devlin said as he hit the button to open communication channels. "Hello, Count Marcone. What can I do for you?"

"You called me, if I'm correct," Stefan answered with a grin.

"We have some news for you," Devlin said, returning Stefan's grin.

"Good, I hope."

"We've found Alyssa."

Stefan smiled. "That is good news. Where is she? I'll go get her."

"No need," Devlin purred. "She's here as Taron's slinoy."

There was a moment of silence then a thundering, "What?" Taron cringed. "Is he out of his damn mind?"

Taron stood and walked around Devlin, coming in view of the computer screen. "I didn't have a choice. It was either I buy her or someone else would."

"What the hell was she doing there?"

Devlin sighed. "We're thinking she came here to try to infiltrate the mine in the hopes of finding her brother's killer."

"Does she know who Taron is?" Stefan asked.

"No," Taron replied firmly. "I'm afraid if she knows what I'm doing here it will put her in unnecessary danger. For now she believes I'm just an employee at the mines who happens to be her slinoy master."

Stefan dropped down in his seat and brushed his long white hair off his face. "Anthony is going to be furious."

"At me or her?" Taron snorted, trying to find a little humor.

"My guess would be all of us, since we didn't find her before she got in this mess."

"I don't envy you. I know how I would feel if Rhia were in this situation. Especially knowing Taron as I do."

Taron smacked the back of his head, making him chuckle. Stefan laughed as well. "If you weren't a member of the family before, Dev, you are now." With that, he leaned forward and put his finger on the disconnect button. "I'll let you know how Anthony takes the news."

"There's more," Taron said, stopping him.

"What?" Stefan asked.

"I'm making a run to Haven for Morlak. I think it's a test of sorts."

Stefan nodded. "I'll assign someone to trail you."

"No." Taron shook his head firmly. "What if they're seen?"

Letting out a tired sigh, Stefan pinched the bridge of his nose. "At least let Devlin inject a tracking chip. That way we can keep track of your vitals and location. It will make it easier to find you if you're ever injured."

"I'll agree to that," Taron replied with a nod.

Chapter Six

ഇ

Rhia pulled Alyssa into a room toward the back of the second floor. Inside it was a table and chairs with a single computer, behind it a large silver box. "What is this?" Alyssa asked. "I thought we were going shopping."

"We are," Rhia said with a smile. "We buy the clothes over the computer, then the replicator will produce them."

"Interesting."

"Let's see." Rhia sat before the computer and lightly touched the screen, making it come to life. "Taron said something less distracting."

"And preferably something a little warmer."

"Is it cold in the mines?" Rhia asked.

Alyssa nodded. "Yes. Which surprises me, considering the rest of the planet is so hot."

"You're deep in the ground," Rhia said with a grin. Her ice blue eyes sparkled with mischief. "But I'm sure Taron can keep you warm."

Rolling her eyes, Alyssa turned away and ran her fingers over the silver of the replicator box.

"Is it so bad being his slinoy, Alyssa?" Rhia asked quietly.

"Honestly?" She took a deep breath. "No. He's infuriating, impossible, arrogant."

"And?" Rhia encouraged.

"And…incredible in bed. There, I said it."

Rhia's tinkling laugh filled the room, floating around them. A high-pitched beep sounded and Alyssa jumped, her gaze searching the room for the cause. "What is that?"

"It's my brother," Rhia said with a sigh. She hit the button on a small box next to the computer. "Yes?"

"Pick up the earset, my love," Devlin's voice came through the small speaker. With a sigh, Rhia picked up a tiny black device and placed it in her ear, keeping Alyssa from hearing what was said on his end.

"It's in. What do you need?" There was a moment of silence, then Rhia raised an eyebrow in surprise. "Where?" she asked. "Haven? All right. I'll take care of it."

With a huff of surprise, Rhia disconnected from Devlin. "Looks like you're going on a trip."

"A trip?" Alyssa asked. "Where?"

"You and Taron are going to Haven, so you'll need something really warm."

Alyssa stared at her in shock. She'd heard of Haven. It was a cold planet far in the Outer Rim, completely covered in snow and ice. The sun hardly ever shone there through the thick haze of gray clouds. "Why are we going to Haven?"

"I don't know," Rhia said with a shrug. "I'm sure he'll tell you later. For now," she wiggled her eyebrows devilishly, "let's see how much of Taron's money we can spend in an hour."

A tiny smile lifted the corner of Alyssa's lips. She liked Rhia and she definitely liked the way her mind worked. "If there's one thing I know how to do, Rhia, it's spend money." She pulled up a chair and sat next to Rhia. "Point me to the expensive stuff."

With a laugh, Rhia again brought the screen to life.

"While we're doing this," Alyssa began. "Can I ask you something?"

"Sure."

"Is there a dictionary for translating English to Veenorian?"

Rhia frowned at her. "A dictionary? Do you mean a translator? What for?"

Alyssa turned away from Rhia's intense stare. She'd never been good at lying. "For working environmental controls and possibly doing something on the computer. I noticed he had one in his office. I'm bored there all alone and thought there might be something I could do to keep me busy on Taron's computer."

"Taron's computer links with the mine mainframe. I doubt there's anything you can do on there."

Rhia turned back to the computer, ending that particular conversation. "What do you think of this?" Rhia asked, pointing at an outfit on the screen.

* * * * *

Taron dropped the box of clothes on his bed with an overexaggerated sigh. Alyssa grinned and let her gaze roam over his wide shoulders. Tingling warmth spread through her stomach as she remembered how it had felt to be beneath him.

"How much clothing did you buy?" He glanced at her over his shoulder and she turned away quickly, looking for the wool shirt she'd had on earlier. The last thing she wanted was for him to see the desire in her eyes and she busied herself with pushing her arms through the sleeves. "Just enough to do me for a while. Are you going to tell me why I can't go out into the mine?" she asked.

"I think it would be better if I showed you. Take the shirt back off."

She frowned. "I have to go out there like this?" Holding the shirt open, she scowled. She still wore the skimpy slave costume, which left very little to the imagination.

His eyes traveled down her chest and stomach then slowly back up again, heating her flesh. "You are a slave, Alyssa. Accept it."

With a sigh, she removed the shirt and tossed it to the bed. "Fine."

Taking the leash that was still attached to her collar in a firm grip, he led her from his suite. Alyssa was amazed as they walked down the dark cavern hallways. Steel support beams held the walls upright every eight feet or so. Her bare feet were cold against the stone floor and twice she winced as pebbles pierced the tender soles of her feet.

After what seemed like forever they came to a wider and more traveled hallway. Men leered at her and she tried her best to ignore them. She kept her head partially bowed and her eyes as downcast as possible. But sometimes it was hard to not look around.

Turning to the right, Taron led her down another corridor then down three flights of stairs. The corridor emptied onto a balcony that overlooked a massive great room.

Alyssa scooted to the edge and glanced over the waist-high stone wall. Below them were several men, pacing and laughing. Her eyes narrowed to get a closer look. They were nude? "Why don't they have clothes on?" she asked.

"You'll see," he said and nodded his head toward a set of double doors opening at the far side of the room.

Women sauntered in, also nude, and the men began to rush them, grabbing them roughly. There appeared to be one woman for every two men and Alyssa had to blink twice as she stared at the beginning stages of the orgy. Men struggled with one another as they fought over positions and control. Women were slammed against walls, thrown to the floor as the men used every possible orifice of their bodies to slake their lust.

The women didn't seem to mind and their moans filled the cabin below, becoming louder as the intensity picked up tempo. Her heart raced as she watched them and blood pounded through her ears. Why was he showing her this? The whole scene was insane. They were like animals, rutting and growling as they used and abused one woman after another.

They were insatiable and she grimaced at the sight of one woman satisfying three men—one in her pussy, one in her ass and one in her mouth.

"What's going on?" she asked.

"This is why I don't want you in the mines alone, Alyssa. These men are hard to control. They bring women in to satisfy their lusts once a week, but if you were within their midst unprotected, this is what you would be doing all day, not mining. They would abuse you, rape you, and I don't want that to happen. Those women are here because they want to be. They enjoy it. I don't think you would."

"No," she gulped. No woman wanted to be mauled. But those women were definitely enjoying it. They moaned and screamed as the men fucked them over and over. After a while the men would change partners, each experiencing several of the women before they were done.

Taron came up behind her and slid his palms down her arms. His warm touch sent tingles down her back. His hands came around her ribs and moved up to cup her breasts. She gasped as his palms squeezed them. "It's very arousing, isn't it?" he whispered in her ear. "Watching them rut like animals."

Alyssa swallowed and tried to close her eyes to the orgy below them. She had no idea how long they'd been watching. It seemed like forever but in reality probably wasn't more than thirty minutes. An hour at the most.

Even though she'd blocked the view, she could still hear it, the women moaning, the men grunting as they fucked one woman then another. The sound was more arousing than the image and part of that disgusted her. How could such a thing turn her on? But it did. And Taron knew it.

Taron's hand moved lower and slid behind the piece of cloth that hid her smooth labia. His fingers brushed along her slit, making her knees weaken. Her knuckles turned white as she tightly gripped the edge of the stone wall, trying to keep herself upright.

His touch was like fire as he separated her nether lips and circled her throbbing clit. She moaned, her head falling back onto his chest. The heat of his body seeped into hers, warming already overheating flesh. Her moans mingled with the sounds from below and she felt as though she and Taron were a part of it, centered in the midst of all the sex.

Taron moved to her front. Lifting her leg, he placed one of her feet on the edge of the wall next to his hip. She watched as he lowered to his haunches and placed his face between her legs. One flick of his tongue across her clit and she was lost, gripping his shoulders for dear life. Two thick fingers slid into her depths and she groaned and moved her hips in time with his thrusts.

Every muscle tingled and she gulped for air as her release hovered just out of reach. Without warning, Taron stood. "No," she gasped, "don't stop."

He kissed her hard, his tongue fucking her mouth in a way that made her melt, desperate for more. She could taste herself in his kiss and the realization only fueled her hunger.

"Undo my pants, Alyssa," he growled against her lips as he leaned back, resting his hips against the wall. "Release my cock so I can fuck you."

Her shaking hands moved quickly to do as he asked. With the pop of the final button his thick cock sprang free and she gripped it with her fingers, slowly sliding them up and down his steely length. Taron groaned and pushed her hand away before gripping her hips and lifting her to settle her pussy at the tip of his straining shaft.

She wrapped her arms around his neck and held tight as he used the wall to support his hips and impaled her hard. She screamed in pleasure as his massive cock invaded her aching pussy, pushing deep and stretching her tight walls. He felt so good and she ground her hips in a circular motion, rubbing her clit against his lower stomach. She moaned at the sensation the friction caused and began to grind faster.

Taron grabbed a handful of her hair and tugged, pulling her face back so he could claim her mouth in another all-consuming kiss. She couldn't get enough of him and returned his kiss with equal hunger. She'd never had sex like this. Had never even been sure passion like this existed. Sex had always been nice. But this…this went beyond nice and bordered on ecstasy.

Taron's lips nipped at her neck, his teeth gently biting as one hand shifted its grip on her ass. The tip of his finger slowly circled her anus and she started, her eyes shifting to his in question. A small smile touched his lips as he slowly slid his finger into the tight hole, his eyes closely watching hers.

She gasped at the unusual invasion, but soon relaxed as the finger added pressure to her vaginal wall from the other side, intensifying her pleasure. She felt full and so consumed. With a sigh, she leaned forward and bit the side of Taron's neck. He groaned and increased his thrusts, bringing her closer to orgasm.

Her stomach tightened, the insides of her thighs quaked as her release hit, pounding through her like a tidal wave. Tingles spread through her limbs to settle in her stomach and she screamed as pulse after incredible pulse gripped her pussy.

With a shout, Taron stiffened, his hot seed filling her throbbing channel.

Breathing harshly, she opened her eyes and caught Taron's gaze as he watched her in surprise. "You make me forget myself, slave," he whispered as he leaned back against the waist-high wall.

"Seems you do the same thing to me," she sighed.

One corner of his lips quirked and his eyes darkened, sparkling with humor and desire. He brushed her hair back, gently combing his fingers through her tresses. "Promise me you'll stay away from the mines, Lyssa."

The sound of the shortened name on his lips made her heart flutter. She'd heard him call her that before and she liked it when he used the nickname. She didn't want to lie and tell him she wouldn't go, because she did intend to go. So instead, she just nodded her head, hoping he wouldn't push her to actually say the words out loud.

"Good," he whispered and placed a soft kiss on the end of her nose. "We have a trip to get ready for. We leave tonight."

She sighed in relief and tried to untangle her legs from around his waist. He gripped her thighs, holding her still. "Did I say you could get down?" he purred and ground his hips against her, sending shots of pleasure up her spine. His lips captured hers in a kiss that was surprisingly gentle. She whimpered as his tongue slid into her mouth and leisurely explored.

The sounds of sex still rose from below and she felt herself getting wet again, coating his cock, which was still buried inside her. Shifting her hips, she tried to tell him without speaking that she wanted him once more.

He broke the kiss and slapped at her ass with his palm. It didn't hurt, but the sound was loud, echoing off the rock walls around them. His gaze held a tenderness that surprised her and sent a shot of warmth to her chest. "Save a little energy for later, *ni pahti*. I promise, I'll give you all you want," he whispered.

Her face heated in sudden embarrassment. She'd all but begged for it again. What was he doing to her? "You started it," she grumbled.

"Yes, I did. And I promise I'll finish it." With a wicked grin, he nipped at her lower lip before setting her down so that she could follow him back to the suite on shaky legs.

*****

Alyssa sat in the passenger side of the ship, watching out the window as they flew low over the light blue landscape of Haven. Space travel amazed her. She'd thought they would be traveling in some huge thing with quarters and multiple decks, but Taron had told her since Haven was within a day's travel, they could take a much smaller ship. The transport gate had been able to get them within a few hours of the planet. The shipment he was delivering was of a personal nature and very small, so a cargo hold had not been needed either.

Truth be told, she actually liked the close quarters and had enjoyed being able to see everything around them. Unlike other times she traveled through space, where she'd been stuffed into overcrowded indoor compartments. No windows, no view of the outside. But this, she thought with a sigh as she took in the swiftly passing landscape below them, this was amazing.

It looked so barren below but at the same time, so beautiful. Dark gray waters rippled between large glaciers and intermittent stretches of barren land. The sky was overcast, hovering somewhere between light and dusk. Light blue snow fell to the ground, sometimes flowing sideways when the wind picked up.

She huddled within her light gray, brushed-leather coat. Rhia had actually picked it out, saying it matched her eyes perfectly. It fit her pretty well too, with the tapered waist, large flowing skirt and jeweled buttons. Fur lined the collar, sleeves and bottom hem of the coat, brushing around her light-gray ankle boots when she walked.

They'd even bought a matching fur muff and hat, which she was extremely grateful for at the moment. The cold of the planet seeped into the small ship despite the environmental controls. Taron insisted it was her imagination, but she was cold nonetheless and kept herself bundled within the soft leather.

Reaching up, she fingered the gold charm that hung from her collar. It was in the shape of a figure eight, or infinity loop if she wanted to see it as something a little more romantic. She growled inwardly. Romance was the last thing she should be thinking about. Taron had bought her to use as a sex slave, nothing more. At least he'd left the leash behind. That had to be the most humiliating thing she'd had to endure so far.

Out of the corner of her eye she watched Taron fly the ship, his brow creased in a frown. "Why are we here, again?" she asked. "I don't think you told me."

He glanced at her, then back to the skyline. "I needed to drop something off for Morlak, then pick something up in return."

"That's it?"

"For the most part. We'll spend the night then head back tomorrow."

She started to ask another question, but stopped when a voice came over the ship's speaker. "Approaching craft, identify yourself."

"This is Taron Karmase. I'm here to meet with Major Janik. He's expecting me."

A moment of silence then another voice spoke. "Proceed to hangar bay six on the southern perimeter. Once past the outer marker, please release controls to the bay. They will guide you in."

"Understood."

They rounded a rather large mountain and Taron nodded toward something on the horizon. She looked as well, then gasped as the mountaintop castle became more visible. "Wow," she sighed. "That thing is huge." It stretched for what looked like miles, its deep gray stone walls blending into the rock of the mountain it sat upon.

Taron chuckled. "That *thing* is Belock City. There are eight of these manmade castles, each one a different city."

A castle that was a city—interesting.

She sat in silence as Taron let go of the controls, allowing the bay to fly the ship into the massive hangar. Numerous ships of varying sizes sat, secured, down the sides, leaving the center open for arriving and departing spacecraft. As the engines powered down, three men approached from the left and waited for her and Taron to step out.

"Taron Karmase?" the man asked.

His heavy beard hid most of his face, leaving only a hawklike nose and green eyes that studied them in hesitation, as though he wasn't sure he trusted them. His body was cloaked by a long black robe and a matching turban covered his head, leaving dark brown tendrils peeking out from underneath. Two men dressed as he was stood silent behind him, their eyes ever watchful. Alyssa had found out from Taron on the ride here that the people of Haven kept to themselves, not often allowing strangers within their home.

"Yes," Taron answered and placed a hand on Alyssa's elbow, pulling her close.

"I'm Major Janik. I understand you have a package for me from Morlak."

"I do. It's in the ship." Taron stepped back to the ship to pull the box from behind his seat.

Janik's stare made her nervous and she was anxious for Taron to return to her side. She felt safer when he was near. Taron handed the box to Janik, but the major didn't pay much attention to Taron. He kept his gaze on Alyssa as he reached out to touch the link that hung from her collar—the link where the leash attached and marked her as a sex slave.

"She's a slinoy." Janik said in surprise. "It's been a while since I've seen one of these collars. The Senate has outlawed slinoys on most of the planets within their jurisdiction. I don't think I've seen a slinoy quite this lovely before. What would it take to get her off your hands? Name your price."

"She's not for sale," Taron replied firmly and wrapped his arm around her back, pulling her close. "I'm afraid I've become quite fond of her."

Alyssa's heart soared and she tried desperately to remind herself that it was just for show. He was only trying to protect her and keep her safe.

Janik smiled slightly. "I understand. My last mate started out as a slinoy. She died just a year after we were officially joined." His eyes took on a faraway look as he shifted the box in his hands.

Alyssa felt bad for him. *He must miss his mate a great deal.* The idea that he'd actually married his slinoy surprised her. She'd heard of slinoys falling for their masters. Hell, it looked like she might be one of them. Out of the corner of her eye, she glanced toward Taron and studied his profile as he spoke.

"I'm sorry for your loss," he said and Janik nodded in thanks.

"Well," he said with a sigh. "I have a suite reserved for you in the north tower. My assistant will show you the way. In the morning I'll have Morlak's package brought to you before you leave. Enjoy your stay."

He bowed and the two silent men behind him bowed as well. Taron bowed and tugged at her sleeve, indicating she should bow also. Janik smiled at her again before turning to leave with one of his assistants. The other remained behind to escort them to their room.

"Interesting man," she whispered as she and Taron followed their escort to the suite. Her heels clicked on the hard stone floor as they made their way through the bay and toward the long hallway at the far end.

"Yes. Interesting. He certainly found you so, as well," Taron whispered back in hushed tones.

"Jealous?" she teased, but immediately regretted it. Even if he was he would probably never admit it. And why would he be? It's not as if he was in love with her.

"I don't get jealous."

"No?" she asked.

He turned to her and grinned suggestively. "No. I keep a woman so satisfied she has no desire to search out someone else."

She snorted and the man in front of them glanced over his shoulder in amusement. "You're so unbelievably arrogant. I'm amazed your head even fits through a door."

Taron's deep laugh echoed down the long corridor. The stone walls and richly colored tapestries reminded her of old England, where kings and knights ruled the land. Just ahead of them was a small cart that would take them to the north side of the castle.

He leaned in and grasped her elbow. She could feel the heat of his touch through the leather of her coat and without thinking leaned toward him. "You know I'm right," he whispered.

She glanced up at him and smiled devilishly. "Maybe. Perhaps later you'll refresh my memory."

"It's a definite, *ni pahti*," he murmured, returning her smile.

Chapter Seven

ஐ

Stefan strolled through the walled garden of his Tilarian Estate, trying to decide how he would break the news to Anthony. He would be furious his sister was on Veenori and would insist on getting her off. Devlin didn't think that would be a good idea. How would Taron explain letting a slinoy he paid a fortune for go just a few days later?

Rounding the corner, he spotted his wife Krista leaning over to pick a flower in bloom. She lifted it to her nose and smiled. The light spring breeze ruffled her blonde hair and she raised a small hand to brush it from her face.

Walking up behind her, he placed a hand on her very pregnant stomach. Their children were due to arrive in two months, and he couldn't wait to hold them in his arms. His and Krista's babies. He couldn't believe they were actually having twins.

"How are you feeling, *kisary*?" he whispered, his hand softly rubbing her protruding stomach.

"Like a fat cow," she grumbled.

He chuckled. "But you're a very beautiful fat cow," he teased, making her giggle.

"You're terrible. But I love you," she said and leaned back against his chest.

"I love you," he whispered back. A child kicked at his hand and he grinned, placing a soft kiss on her temple. "I believe our son is jealous. He always kicks at me when I touch you."

"How do you know it's not your daughter? There is one of each in there, you know."

Stefan's smile spread as he gently rubbed his hand in a soothing circle. "A boy and a girl. More than likely it's not me they're kicking at but each other."

Krista snickered. "If the two of them are anything like you and Sidious, I don't doubt that."

"My mother will be ecstatic that someone is finally having a girl. You'll never see her, you know. My mother will run off with her."

"We should probably tell them soon. She keeps watching me and wondering why I'm so big." she sighed and ran her hand over her stomach.

"We will. I want to keep this to us for a while longer. Our little secret." He sighed and pulled her closer against his back.

"Is something bothering you?" she asked, her voice full of concern. "You feel tense."

He sighed and rested his chin on the top of her head. "I heard from Devlin earlier. They found Alyssa."

She turned and smiled up at him. "That's wonderful. Your brother says that Anthony has been beside himself worrying about her."

"Well, I'm afraid that what I have to tell him isn't going to help matters."

Stefan took her small hands in his and brought them to his lips, kissing the back of them. "Now you have me worried."

"She's fine. She got herself in a mess and ended up being sold as a slinoy on Veenori. Taron recognized her and bought her."

"You're kidding," she said, her eyes widening in surprise.

He shook his head. "Afraid not."

"You know," she said, her lips spreading into a grin, "from what Anthony has told me, Alyssa is exactly like Mikayla. Quick-tempered, smart-mouthed, kind of sassy."

"Kind of?" he teased with a grin. He loved his brother's wife, but she definitely had a temper to rival her husband's.

"Stop that." She poked at his chest with the tip of her finger, making him chuckle.

"So what's running through that mind of yours?" he asked.

"Taron is always giving Mikayla a hard time. I've told him more than once he'd end up with a woman just like her."

Stefan laughed and shook his head. "So let me get this straight. You think Taron is going to fall in love with Alyssa?"

"Well, you've seen her picture. She's beautiful."

"I didn't notice," he replied in mock seriousness.

"I know good and well you noticed, just like I noticed that Anthony is gorgeous. With that thick black hair and those light gray eyes. My!" She sighed and fanned herself with her hand.

Stefan narrowed his eyes at his wife. "Gorgeous, huh? I think you should stay here while I go to Daego and tell Anthony."

She batted her long golden lashes. "You would leave me, your pregnant wife, here all alone? Who would take care of me?" Her arms wrapped around his waist and his hands settled at the small of her back, holding her close.

"I think you're more concerned with who would raid the kitchen for you in the middle of the night when you have those strange cravings."

"That too," she pouted.

"Woman, you're insufferable." Stefan smiled down at her adorable upturned face. Her blue eyes sparkled with life and happiness but were soon clouded with worry.

"Do you think she'll be okay?" she asked.

"I have faith that Taron will take care of her. Unless, of course, she's like you and he's having to constantly pull her out of trouble."

Her adorable china-doll features scrunched into a pout as she poked her finger into his chest, making him grunt. "Watch it, husband. I'll set your mother on you."

That made Stefan laugh. "Like I'm afraid of that little scrap of a woman."

"You should be. I always thought you and Sidious got your tempers from your father until I saw her angry with one of the traders the other day for slapping his wife. The man was actually trembling by the time she got done with him."

"I can believe that," Stefan said with a grin, remembering one of the few times he'd seen his mother that angry. "But trust me, I get my temper from my father."

He pushed an errant curl behind her ear then let his finger trail down her cheek. He'd never imagined he could love someone as much as he did her. She was his life and seeing her pregnant with his children just made her all the more beautiful. "Do you feel up to going to Daego?"

Her eyes lit up. "You don't even need to ask. Just tell me when we're leaving."

His wife liked the peaceful planet of Daego much more than the hectic estate here on Tilarus. "We leave within the hour. I already have your maid packing a bag for you."

She bit at her lower lip and glanced toward his chest in a move he'd come to recognize as hesitance. "I have a request concerning Daego," she said quietly.

"What?" He lifted her chin with his finger, forcing her to look at him. Surely she knew by now he'd give her anything she wanted.

"I want to have the babies there. It's so much quieter at your brother's estate than here and not nearly as crazy. Here there's always someone running in and out, always a commotion…"

Stefan put his finger over her lips. "Of course we can. I think it's a great idea." A smile of relief crossed her features and his gut tightened in desire. He grinned and pulled her closer, pressing his hardening cock into her stomach. "I also think we should take the long way to Daego."

"I agree," she purred and brushed her lips across his.

* * * * *

Alyssa stood in the center of the large room and turned a circle, trying to admire everything. The room was completely done in white. White carpet, white fur bedcovers, white curtains. Even the fireplace in the center of the room was white marble. She took off her gloves and placed her hand against the stone. "It's warm," she said with a smile.

"Of course it is, silly. There's a fire in the grate," Taron answered with a grin.

She scrunched her nose at him and he laughed. She loved to hear him laugh. It was low and rich, rumbling from deep within his chest. Taron seemed like the type that never did anything halfway. He laughed fully, lived fully, even made love fully.

The more she learned about him, the more she liked him, and that bothered her. Eventually he'd get tired of her and set her free. She was an impulse buy. One he would soon regret, and she didn't want to be heartbroken when it happened. She was here to do a job, to find her brother's killer, and she needed to focus on that. If she could just get out of that damn room at the mines...

"Your dinner will arrive shortly," their escort said from the doorway. "If everything is in order, I'll have your bags brought down."

"Thank you," Taron replied with a slight bow. The escort bowed in return then left the room, shutting the white double doors behind him.

"This place is amazing," she said and headed toward the open archway that led to an outdoor balcony. "Where do they get the firewood?"

"The moon," he replied, pointing to the sky, but with all the cloud cover, it couldn't be seen. "We flew past it on the way here."

She nodded, remembering the green-tinged planet. Her gaze took in the mountains below them, the blue snow falling around them and the water falling down the rocks just to the side of the terrace. She reached out to touch the water and felt a sharp tingle run up her arm. She jerked her hand back and gripped it with her other one. "What was that?"

Taron took her hand in his and rubbed her fingers. His grip was warm and firm, sending little shots of awareness through her chest. "The terrace is surrounded by a force field. It keeps the cold air out, but leaves the room open to the view."

"Is that what shocked me?"

"Yes." His lips lifted in a slight grin. "So you might not want to touch it again."

She frowned. "You could have warned me."

"Yeah, I could have," he said with a shrug. "But then I wouldn't have an excuse to touch you."

"You need an excuse?" she asked quietly, watching him through her lashes.

"I don't know, slave. Do I?" he whispered as he tugged at her hand, pulling her close to him.

Her heart fluttered in her chest at the sultry look in his eyes. They darkened to chocolate and smoldered with a heat she felt clear to her toes. "You are my Master. According to you, you can touch me whenever you wish."

"True. But tonight I only want to touch you if *you* wish it." His mouth hovered just above hers. His whispered words brushed across lips like a silken caress. "Do you wish it, Lyssa?"

She loved it when he called her that and opened her mouth to say, yes, she wished for him to touch her, but a knock at the door silenced her confession.

Taron sighed. "That would be either our bags or dinner."

"Hopefully both," she said with a slight smile. "I'm starving."

Taron turned and walked back inside. Her gaze followed him all the way to the doors—or at least his backside anyway. He opened them and smiled at her over his shoulder. "How hungry are you?" he teased and stepped aside, allowing the table to be wheeled into the room, the luggage coming in behind it.

Her eyes widened at the wide array of food on the table. Most she didn't recognize.

"Thank you," Taron said as the man bowed, then left the room.

"My God. There's enough here to feed six people." She picked up what looked like a blue grape and plopped it on her tongue. It was sour and she grimaced. "Uh," she groaned and waved her hand before her mouth, trying her best to finish chewing it. "What is this?"

Laughter rumbled through Taron's chest. "Something you probably won't eat again."

"Very funny," she grumbled around her chewing.

Her fingers worked loose the buttons of her coat and she shrugged, slipping it off her shoulders. The cool air of the room hit her bare arms and goose bumps worked along her flesh. Giving the coat one last look before laying it over the back of the overstuffed white chair, she brushed her hands down her wool slacks and sleeveless tunic. She might get cold and regret taking that off.

"I can move the table before the fire if you're still a little cold."

His deep voice startled her and she spun around to face him. "That would be nice."

They moved the small table before the fire and sat down. Taron quickly loaded a plate then handed it to her before filling one for himself. She eyed the food warily. "Is the rest of it as sour as the other thing?"

Taron chuckled. "No. I think you'll like the mollak, it's the brown stuff in the center."

"Where do they get this food?" she asked as she picked at it with her fork. "Somehow I don't think they grow it here."

"Actually, they do. They have artificial greenhouses below ground in the thermal caves."

She raised an eyebrow. "Really? Interesting."

As she chewed, she studied him. He didn't seem like the type to work in a mine. He appeared almost refined and he certainly knew a lot about other planets and their customs, which meant he traveled a lot. "Taron, where are you from?"

He finished chewing slowly as his gaze met hers. "My father was Norgosen."

"And your mother?"

"From Ricktorik."

"Wow. Isn't that a primitive planet? No technology allowed? How did they meet?"

Taron shrugged and Alyssa got the impression he was avoiding the subject. "Don't know. Never asked."

"Where are they now?" she asked, genuinely curious about him.

"Doing a report?" he asked with a quirk of his lips.

"No. I was just curious."

Taron sighed and set his fork down to reach for his glass. "My mother died several years ago, just a few months after my father ran out on us."

Inside, Alyssa cringed. God, no wonder he didn't want to talk about it. "I'm sorry. We can change the subject."

With a shrug, he resumed eating. "It was years ago. Long forgotten."

Alyssa didn't think so, but she didn't push him to talk any more about it. "What did you do after that? Have you been on your own?"

"Trying to find out if I have a wife?" he teased.

She jerked upright, staring at him in surprise. That wasn't why she'd asked. She hadn't even thought of him having a wife. "No. I just…I mean…" She sighed. "I just wanted to know a little more about you."

"Ah, I see."

Licking her lips, she stared at her plate. "Do you have a wife?" she asked with a frown. She would feel terrible if he did. She'd never been the "other woman" and didn't want to be.

"No. I am not now nor have I ever been married."

Relief seeped in her chest, but she quickly brushed it aside, convincing herself it was only because she didn't want to be the one he committed adultery with.

"After my mother died I was adopted by her best friend and her husband. I have two adopted brothers, who drive me crazy, two nephews who are the spitting image of their father and two beautiful sisters-in-law I would gladly give my life for. And of course I can't forget the twins on the way, which my brother doesn't know the rest of the family knows about."

Alyssa grinned. "He doesn't know they know she's pregnant or that she's having twins?"

He returned her grin. "That she's having twins. My adopted mother is a very astute woman. Can't keep anything from her."

She laughed and took a sip of the warm green liquid that filled her glass. It tasted like cinnamon and she licked her lips, capturing every drop. Warmth flooded through her as she raised the glass and took a second sip, again running the tip of her tongue around her lips.

Taron groaned softly. "Don't do that," he growled.

Glancing over at the pained expression on his face, she smiled innocently. "Do what?"

"I'm trying to eat and you're being seductive."

"Am I?" she teased. "I'm sorry. I was only enjoying the drink."

"Minx," he grumbled, making Alyssa giggle.

"What is this?" she asked before taking another sip.

"It's organas and very potent. You should probably eat something else before you drink any more."

She quickly set the glass back down on the table and dove into her food with relish. Suddenly she was very hungry. A couple of things had an odd taste she didn't care for, but for the most part the food was good, and she finished everything on her plate.

"Would you like some more?" Taron asked when she shoved her plate toward the center of the table.

Shaking her head, she reached for her drink to finish off the glass. "No, thank you. I'm full."

As she sipped her drink, Taron's gaze held hers captive. She wasn't sure if the tingling she felt was from the beverage or his stare. He had such gorgeous eyes, such kissable lips. She wanted to feel them against hers again. She wanted his tongue in her mouth, his cock in her pussy. Just thinking about how well he filled her made her wet with need.

His finger reached out and ran along the edge of her collar, his eyes thoughtful and sultry. Her breath quickened as his hot touch brushed along her flesh toward the back of her neck. With a quick flick he removed the collar and she stared at him in question, wondering what he was doing. Was he letting her go?

"Tonight we're not slave and master," he said quietly and dropped the collar on the table between them. "We're Taron and Alyssa."

She swallowed, her gaze glued to the smoldering question in his eyes. Licking her lips, she nodded and watched, breathless, as his hand moved to the back of her neck and pulled her to him, his lips hovering just a hairsbreadth from hers.

"Only if you wish it, Lyssa," he whispered.

"I wish it," she answered and moaned as he closed the distance and captured her lips in a kiss that sent her reeling.

Chapter Eight

ꙮ

Taron stood and pulled Alyssa up in front of him. He wanted her so badly his whole body ached with the desire to feel her beneath him. He should have never started this, but now that he had he couldn't seem to get enough. All he'd been able to think about since they'd arrived was sinking into her warm, tight body.

Grasping the hem of her tunic, he lifted it over her head and dropped it to the floor, letting it fall into a puddle of soft wool, completely forgotten. Her breasts stood firm and enticing, her nipples beading as the cold air of the room hit her flesh. He leaned down and blew softly across them, making the buds pucker even more. Her gasp was soft and mingled with the sound of popping wood burning in the fireplace.

Her tiny hands flew to the waistband of his pants and tugged. The buttons gave way, freeing his already engorged shaft, and her fingers quickly wrapped around him, sliding along his length. He groaned in pure pleasure mixed with agony as her grip tightened, her strokes quickening to create a shattering rhythm.

He pushed her hand away and stepped out of his pants, kicking them aside, then quickly removed his shirt as well. Alyssa stepped back, her hips swaying enticingly as she pushed her pants down her hips. Once she had them off, he lunged for her with a growl, both of them landing on the bed in a tangle of arms and legs.

Alyssa giggled, her arms snaking around his neck as he settled between her splayed thighs. His length rubbed along her slit while his lips brushed across hers. They parted in silent invitation, but he kept toying with her, teasing them both.

"I could fuck you right now," he whispered against her lips.

"Then why don't you?" she asked.

Her voice was breathy and needy as her hips moved with his. Her juices coated his cock, making it slick and warm. He knew she would feel like heaven as her walls encased his cock in a hot grip, but he had other plans for her.

"I want to taste you first," he murmured against her neck as his lips worked a path to her breasts. "I want to fuck you with my tongue. Feel the juices pour from the walls of your hot little pussy and down my throat."

His tongue licked a slow circle around her areola before engulfing the whole tip in his mouth. With a moan, she arched her back, pushing her breast more fully into his face, and he sucked harder. She squirmed beneath him, her soft whimpers echoing in his ears and driving him closer to the edge.

Shifting onto his knees, he continued down her stomach, leaving a path of goose bumps with every flick of his tongue against her flesh. With his teeth, he tugged at her bellybutton ring and she squirmed, lifting her hips slightly off the bed. Her skin was so soft, so smooth beneath his touch, and his fingers continued to explore every dip her curves created.

She was all feminine angles and valleys, her body designed for his. At first glance she was fragile, but first glances were deceiving. She was feisty and strong, her smart mouth entertaining and amusing. It wasn't just her body he couldn't get enough of, it was her personality—her spirit.

His palm moved to the inside of her thigh and pushed, spreading her legs wider. She complied, letting them fall open for him and giving him a perfect view of her pink, glistening pussy. He ran his hand over her smooth skin of her mound and smiled. "I like that you have no hair there."

She grunted an answer and her teeth bit down on her lower lip. Long lashes fluttered down over her eyes as he spread her labia and teased her clit with the tip of his tongue. She gasped and bucked her hips upward.

"No, no," he purred and placed a hand on her stomach, holding her down. "Be still."

"I don't think I can," she gasped, fighting against his hold.

"You will or you won't get what you want." His slid his tongue up her slit then circled her clit slowly. "And you want this, don't you, Alyssa?"

"Oh, God," she groaned, her hands fisting in the fur blanket beneath her. "Yes. I want it. I want you."

He closed his eyes, inhaling her sweet, musky scent. She smelled so good and tasted even better. "Then be still," he whispered. "Let me please you, *ni pahti*."

With a groan, he pushed his tongue deep within her depths, lapping up her cream like a man starving. Her hips moved slightly, the insides of her thighs quivered. He smiled, enjoying the fact that he was driving her to the edge. He brought her close, so close the walls of her pussy spasmed around his tongue, but he wouldn't let her come yet. He wanted to be inside her when she exploded.

Pulling away, he rose up and moved his hand beneath her hip, giving her a little push upward. "On your knees, Alyssa."

She rolled over and settled on her knees. She glanced at him over her shoulder, hunger and trust smoldering in the depths of her eyes. He liked it when she looked at him like that and his chest tightened with an answering hunger and something else—something deeper than just simple lust. Something he had no business feeling.

Closing his eyes, he tried to focus on the physical, not the emotional hold she had begun to have on him. With determination to keep it strictly about sex, he stared at her pussy and the rounded globes of her ass. Her juices glistened around her opening and he used two fingers to spread the cream along the cleft of her ass and around the tight rosebud opening of her anus.

She wiggled her hips and he inwardly groaned, wanting desperately to sink his cock into the tight bit of flesh. As gently as possible, he pushed one finger into the puckered hole then added another. She gasped and thrust back against him, taking his finger deeper. She would need a lot more preparation there than he was prepared to give her at the moment. Right now he needed to feel his cock in her pussy. Needed to be buried inside her balls-deep with an urgency that he'd never experienced before.

"Damn," he growled and then plunged his cock into her pussy, not able to hold back any longer.

His whole body trembled as he sank his rod deep. She was hot as lava and tight as a damn glove. Her walls gripped his cock and quivered along his length, making him grit his teeth to keep control. He kept his fingers in her ass, moving them in time with his cock as he pulled out then pushed back in, sheathing himself balls-deep over and over.

With a moan, she dropped her head to the mattress. Taron bent forward and wrapped her hair around his hand then tugged, pulling her head back up. He leaned down and groaned in her ear, his cock plunging in and out of her depths. She panted, her breaths coming in short spurts as she thrust back against him.

"I thought about doing this the first time I saw you on that stage," he ground out. "Fucking you from behind."

To emphasize his words he pushed deeper, slapping his balls against her pussy. She hissed, "Oh, yes."

"It's better than I imagined."

Removing his finger from her ass, he slid his hand around to her clit. With a soft touch, he circled the sensitive bud and she gasped, "Oh, God."

"Does that feel good?" he murmured.

"Yes," she sighed.

He applied a little more pressure and her pussy exploded around his hard rod. "So does your pussy," he groaned as she spasmed around him, milking his cock with hard convulsions.

She let out a scream as he rose up and thrust harder, burying himself deeper and deeper. Her hips pushed against him, taking everything he was giving her and unbelievably asking for more.

She was incredible. The way she responded, the way she felt. Everything about her was perfect. His balls tightened into hard rocks as he continued to pound her pussy until finally he couldn't hold back anymore. With a loud shout, he spilled his seed deep within her hungry channel. His muscles shook with the intensity of his release and he knew no other woman would ever get that kind of reaction from him. They were amazing together.

With a contented sigh, she pulled away from him and rolled to her back. He watched as she threw her hands over her head, her eyes closed, her lips spreading into a satisfied smile. The realization that he would love to see that smile forever startled him.

He frowned. *I'm not in love with her. I don't have time for that.* He closed his eyes and sighed. *She's a good fuck. That's all.*

But deep in his heart he knew that wasn't all there was to it. He just refused to acknowledge it. Her flesh was still flushed from her release and appeared golden against the white of the fur. Very slowly, he skimmed his fingers up her thigh and ribs, stopping to palm her breast and pinch her nipple. She moaned and arched into his caress, her eyes still closed.

"That feels nice," she whispered. He leaned down and flicked his tongue across the hard nub. She giggled and squirmed beneath his persistent mouth. "That feels good too. You keep that up I'm going to want you to fuck me again."

He smiled and moved to nibble on the sensitive spot behind her ear. "That's the general idea. I'm going to fuck you so much tonight you'll beg me to stop."

His fingers moved to toy with her already wet pussy. "Don't count on that," she purred and moved her hips in time with the thrust of his fingers. "You can fuck me all you want."

"Good," he whispered against her lips. "Because something tells me I may never get my fill of you."

* * * * *

Alyssa awoke sometime in the middle of the night, her body aching in places she hadn't even known existed. With a smile, she stretched against the soft, heated sheets. The warmth of Taron's body next to her caught her attention and she rolled over to stare at him. His chest rose and fell with the steady breath of sleep and she quietly watched him, thinking about all the things that had happened recently.

He was so handsome, with thick lashes lying across his cheeks, his lips full and enticing. Not to mention good in bed. Just thinking about some of the things he'd done made her pussy clench in renewed desire. My God. How could she want him again?

She was in deep trouble here. She'd begun to develop feelings for him and that wasn't a good thing. She needed to hate him so when it came time to leave it would be easier. But he was so hard to hate. He could be arrogant and infuriating but also gentle and funny. Sometimes she got a gut feeling he was hiding something. That there was more to him than he was telling her.

Letting her gaze roam over his muscular chest, she traced his light brown nipple with her fingertip then slipped lower to tug the blanket away, revealing his thick cock. She grinned mischievously as she ran her finger from the base of his fully erect shaft to the tip. Shifting position, she straddled his thighs and leaned down to run her tongue up his length. He moaned, but otherwise didn't stir.

Hmmm. Deep sleeper? Well, she'd wake him up.

Moving up further, she mimicked what he had done earlier and ran the tip of her tongue around his hardened nipple. Again he moaned and moved his head to the side, a muscle working in his cheek.

She wanted him. Wanted to feel his thick cock filling her, and she didn't want to wait until he woke up. Why waste such a tempting erection?

Positioning her pussy over the head of his cock, she sank down onto him, letting his full length stretch and fill her. She threw her head back with a sigh as his cock pushed to her womb, relieving her aching pussy. His hips bucked upward, lodging himself even deeper.

"Oh, fuck yeah," he whispered.

She moaned and rocked her hips in a circular motion, grinding against him. He felt so good, she couldn't get enough.

"This is a hell of a way to wake up," he mumbled as his hands traveled up to fondle her breasts.

In a surprising move, he cupped the back of her head and pulled her down for a deep kiss. He sucked and nipped at her tongue as it entered his mouth, sending little shots of pleasure up her spine. She moaned deep in her throat, loving the commanding way he took control of her mouth and body.

"Ride me, *ni pahti*," he whispered and pushed her upright. "Fuck my cock."

Arching her back, she reached behind her and gripped his thighs, digging her nails into his flesh. He groaned and bucked his hips upward, filling her beyond anything she'd ever imagined. When he slid his thumb between her legs to flick across her clit she lost it and erupted into a firestorm of extreme pleasure.

She screamed as every nerve cell erupted into a mass of molten sensation. Violent spasm after spasm clenched the walls of her vagina as every other muscle in her body quaked in release.

"Oh, God," she gasped as Taron pushed upward in the midst of his own shattering release, filling her vagina with hot semen.

With a sigh, she fell forward onto his chest and relaxed into a puddle. His arms lifted to circled her shoulders and hold her tight, his heat beating a frantic rhythm against her ear. He smelled of sex and hot male and she inhaled deeply, trying to commit the moment to memory. One she knew she would keep forever. Beneath her, she felt his heartbeat slow with hers and she snuggled closer, the warmth of his flesh soothing her tingling body.

They remained quiet, neither saying a word as they fell asleep in each other's arms, Taron's cock still buried inside her body.

* * * * *

"So this is where the party is," Stefan said with amusement as he stepped through the veranda doors and onto the patio.

His brother Sidious, sister-in-law Mikayla, father Damon and mother Kaylar, as well as Alyssa's brother Anthony were all gathered around the table, sipping corniga. The warm Daego sun had begun to set, casting a soft golden glow over everything, even the lake just beyond the terrace.

"Party's always at my house," Sidious mumbled and Mikayla shook her head in amusement, her dark brown curls bouncing around her shoulders.

"Don't mind him. He's in a mood," Mikayla said with a wave of her hand.

"A mood?" Stefan mouthed with a frown.

"It's one of her many Earth phrases," Sidious said with a sideways grin before grabbing his wife's hand and kissing her fingers.

Stefan noticed his father reach beside him and pick a leaf from Kaylar's hair. When she turned to see what he held in his hand, she blushed. Stefan inwardly grinned. His parents were still so much in love and he was thrilled he and his brother Sidious had found what they shared. Apparently, if his mother's red cheeks were any indications, they'd made love in the garden earlier. Again.

Krista walked outside and placed her hand on Stefan's arm. He reached around her back and pulled her close to his side. Her brow creased in a frown and her eyelids dropped heavily as she laid her head against his shoulder. She looked so tired. Maybe making love on the way here had been too much for her, especially after the hectic morning she'd had. A twinge of guilt gripped him. "You want to lie down, *kisary*?" he asked softly.

"Not yet."

Mikayla walked over and gave her friend a hug. "Oh, sweetie. You look wonderful. How do you feel?"

"Tired and bloated, but other than that, fabulous."

"Stefan, what were you thinking bringing her out here this late in her pregnancy?" Kaylar asked.

"She held a gun to my head, Mother. Told me if I didn't take her she'd keep my child in her belly forever."

"Now somehow I doubt that," Kayla said dryly.

Krista smiled and swatted at his arm. "I did make him, although I didn't threaten violence. The house on Tilarus was way too hectic. I needed the serenity of the lake."

"Well of course you did," Kaylar said as she pulled Krista away from Stefan and headed her toward the bedrooms on the upper floor. "I was the same way when I was pregnant with Stefan. I hated all those people in and out of that compound."

Stefan held his hands out and glared in exasperation at his mother. She always took over and acted as though he couldn't do a damn thing.

"Get used to it, Stefan," Sidious said quietly.

Stefan glanced back at the three men still sitting at the patio table. Damon nodded his head at what Kaylar was saying, making Stefan, Sidious and Anthony chuckle.

"Don't think I didn't see that, Damon," Kaylar snapped as she and Mikayla walked with Krista into the house.

Damon rolled his gaze toward the stars quickly becoming visible in the night sky. "I swear that woman has eyes in the back of her head."

"I have no doubt," Sidious said dryly. "I was always amazed, as a child, just how much she knew."

Stefan grinned, remembering things about his childhood as well, and moved to take the seat Mikayla had just left. His gaze strayed toward Anthony, who sat across from him. His black hair was cut short, his eyes the same gray as his sister's. He was a big man, almost as muscular as Sidious but not quite as tall. Obviously a man that could take care of himself, but how would he take the news of his sister?

"I heard from Taron earlier," Stefan began.

"And?" Damon demanded.

"He thinks he may have found a way in."

"Excellent," Sidious replied, but he didn't look relieved.

"He also said they've found Alyssa." Stefan kept his gaze on Anthony as he sat straight in his chair, his eyes wide and worried.

"Alyssa? Where is she?"

Stefan sent his brother a telling glance, silently communicating that there may be a problem. Anthony's gaze moved from one of them to the other. "What's going on?"

"Alyssa is on Veenori."

"What?" Anthony jumped to his feet and exploded, just as Stefan had known he would.

Stefan held a hand up. "She's fine, Anthony. Relax."

Damon placed a hand on his shoulder. "Sit back down, son."

"What is she doing on Veenori?" Anthony asked, his voice full of worry for his little sister, as he sank back in his chair. Damon remained behind him, apparently aware Stefan wasn't through.

"We're not sure," Stefan said.

"Well, go get her."

"We can't. Somehow, we're not sure if by accident or on purpose, she found herself being sold as a slinoy..."

"She what?"

"Taron bought her, she's fine. She'll remain with Taron until it's safe for him to send her here. He can't just let her go immediately after buying her."

"What the hell was she thinking?" Anthony demanded and Damon squeezed his shoulders in support.

"Taron is a good man," Damon said. "She'll be well taken care of."

Stefan glanced toward Sidious with a sigh. "There's more but I want to go check on Krista. Send Devlin a communiqué, he'll fill you in on everything else."

"I want to talk to her," Anthony demanded.

Stefan shook his head. "No. She doesn't know who Taron is yet. She needs to remain ignorant of all this for now. Taron won't take advantage of the situation, Anthony. Let him do his job and he'll get both of them out of there." Stefan said firmly.

Anthony drug his fingers through is thick black hair. "When she gets back here, I'm going to kill her."

* * * * *

Alyssa narrowed her eyes at Taron as he stood before her, dangling the collar from one thick finger. "I was hoping you would forget about that thing."

"Oh, come on, *ni pahti*. Don't you enjoy wearing this collar and being led around by a leash?"

She raised an eyebrow at him and he chuckled. The sexy sound rumbled from his chest, sending a little tremor down her spine.

"No. It just so happens that I don't. Couldn't we pretend we lost it?"

"No." He shook his head and moved behind her to clasp the collar around her neck. She reluctantly lifted her hair.

"I'm afraid not, Lyssa. This shows you're mine, although sometimes men don't pay attention to that."

"Then why bother with it?"

His hands squeezed her shoulders and she let got of her hair, letting it fall down her back. He leaned forward and buried his face in her hair behind her ear, inhaling deeply. "I love the smell of your hair."

Her insides melted at the deep timbre of his voice and she fell back against his chest. He sounded so sexy when he talked in that low, sultry voice. "I love the way you talk," she said with a grin.

His arms wrapped around her stomach, pulling her closer to his warmth. His fingers slid below her white tunic and cupped her breasts, giving them a gentle squeeze. "And I definitely love these," he purred.

She bit down on her lower lip, fighting the desire to rip his clothes off and fuck him again. She was insatiable where he was concerned. He removed his hands and she pouted at him over her shoulder. With a smile, he slapped his palm against her ass. The sting made her yelp and she reached around the rub at the burn. "You like doing that way too much."

"No," he said as he grabbed her wrist and tugged her into his arms, "I like doing *this* way too much."

His lips descended on hers before she could even blink in a kiss so commanding she had to grab his arms to remain upright. He tasted so good. The hint of sweetbreads they'd had for breakfast lingered on his tongue and she sucked at it, making him groan.

Flattening his palm against the small of her back, he pressed his hardening cock to her stomach. "See what I mean?" he whispered.

"I think I do," she whispered back and wiggled along his length.

"*Shorvick na bis torea,*" he growled and pushed her a few inches away from him. "Minx."

She laughed, and turned to grab her coat. "You just can't handle it," she teased.

Taron raised an eyebrow in amusement and her smile widened. She loved teasing him. Ever since they'd arrived here he'd seemed different. More at ease and relaxed than he always was at the mine. She slipped her arms through the sleeves, her heart sinking slightly.

Last night had been incredible. Actually, every night with him had been incredible, but here had been different. There had been something more between them, but she wasn't sure what it was—or if it was even mutual.

Her hands shook as she tried to button her coat, preparing to go back out into the cold of the hallway. Taron walked over and brushed her fingers aside, pushing the buttons through the holes himself. "Don't want to go back?"

"I'm not looking forward to being cooped up in your room alone, no."

A knock at the door interrupted whatever Taron was about to say. "Enter," Taron snapped at the closed door.

The same man who had escorted them there last night stepped into the room and bowed. "The package is in your ship, sir. She is fueled and waiting for you in the cargo bay."

Taron returned his bow then handed Alyssa her hat. Leaning close, he whispered, "I guess that means it's time to go."

A small smile curved her lips, but her chest ached. She was falling so in love with him and she had to stop.

Chapter Nine

ഇ

Alyssa watched Taron's assistant leave after setting her lunch on Taron's desk and waited for the click of the lock. It never came and her heart raced radically. Could she now get out, explore the mine a little and try to find out who this "Vingosa" was? Maybe this was her one chance.

With her heart in her throat, she stepped over to the door and turned the handle. It gave way and she smiled widely, almost jumping in glee. Dressed in the black velvet pants and deep blue sweater she and Rhia had bought the other day, she crept out into the hallway. Wary, she eyed both ends of the long corridor. When she didn't see anyone she stepped further out and headed toward the right—the same direction Taron had taken her in when they watched the orgy.

Part of her almost balked. Should she do this? She remembered what Taron had told her about the men and she reached up to finger the infinity loop that dangled from her collar. Despite her clothing, surely with the collar visible they would think twice about doing anything.

Straightening her shoulders, she headed quickly down the narrow walkway. At the end she turned left into a wider, more crowded hall. She had to find a file room or at the very least a computer in a language she could read. The men watched her in interest, their eyes roaming over her in a way that made her shiver, and not in a good way.

What was she thinking? She didn't have a clue what she was looking for. How was she going to get any information? Ask one of these men? One in particular licked his lips as he stared at her and she cringed, imagining that long tongue flicking into her mouth. No way.

She spun around, heading in the opposite direction and back to the safety of her room, but quickly realized she'd gone the wrong way. She was close to panic with no idea how to get back. Her hands shook and she fisted them at her stomach to try and hide some of her fear. This was not the time to panic.

Three men followed her, dogging her every step, and she realized with dread what it was Taron had tried to make her understand. She would have never survived working this mine. These men would have torn her apart. Is that what they planned now? Could she fight them off if she had to?

She rounded a corner and found herself on the upper level of a docking bay. It was huge, but mostly empty. Men bustled around, stacking boxes to the side to be loaded later when the ships returned. Running to the railing of the second floor landing, she frantically searched the lower level of the docking bay for any sign of Taron. Silently, she prayed that he was down there somewhere.

*****

Taron dropped the box onto Morlak's desk. The heavy package landed with a thump that echoed against the rock walls. "Here's your package."

"Thank you," Morlak replied, his lips quirking in a grin. "Did you open it?"

Taron raised an eyebrow. "Does it look opened?"

Morlak studied the package. "No."

"It's your box, Morlak. I couldn't care less what's in it. Now if you'll excuse me, I have work to do."

Taron turned to leave the room, but Morlak's voice stopped him. "Wait, Taron."

With a sigh, Taron turned to face him, wondering what he had in store for him this time. "What?"

"Come by level seven, docking bay C at midnight. I have something I want to show you."

Taron nodded then turned to leave the office. It looked like he was finally in, but later tonight would tell. He would have even less time to spend with Alyssa now. That thought brought him up short. What did it matter? It wasn't like she was his wife or something. She was his slinoy, and only temporarily. He needed to remember that.

With a determined stride, he made his way through the stone-lined halls and into the lower level of the main docking bay. At this time of day it was mainly empty, most of the ships having already left for the assigned drop stations. Something in his gut made him look up toward the second level and the balcony that ran the perimeter of the bay. What he saw there or, more importantly, *who* he saw there, turned his blood cold. Alyssa.

Behind her were three leering men, stalking her. Damn it! What the hell was she doing out here?

Stomping up the stairs, he scowled at the three men, sending them scurrying in opposite directions. Alyssa's eyes widened in relief then clouded in anxiety as he stalked toward her, his anger rising with every step. "What did I tell you, Alyssa?" he snapped.

"To not go through the mine alone. Okay. I know it was wrong, but I was bored out of my mind and…"

"To quote you, 'bullshit'."

He stood nose to nose with her, ready to tan her adorable hide. Just thinking about all the things that could have happened to her made his chest tighten in fear. Fear of losing her. That thought made him even angrier. He didn't need to have feelings for her. This situation was hairy enough without bringing a woman and love into it.

"Taron, look—" she began, but Taron held up his hand, stopping her.

Grabbing her wrist, he tugged her forward then threw her over his shoulder. She squealed and slapped at his back. "What are you doing?" she demanded.

"Taking you back and making sure you don't do this again."

* * * * *

Alyssa tried to draw more air in, but her position over Taron's shoulder prevented it. Her face heated from the rush of blood to her head as she hung upside down over his back. He carried her as though she weighed nothing, practically running up the stairs toward his rooms.

He had been furious with her, and rightly so. She could have been hurt, or worse. She pushed against his back, trying to bring her head more upright. "Taron, please. I can't breathe like this."

He ignored her and she blew out a breath, forcing her bangs from her eyes. *Damn man.* His door opened and she breathed a sigh of relief, thinking he would just set her down and leave again. But apparently Taron had other plans.

Setting her on her feet, he grabbed the hem of her sweater and pulled it over her head before she even knew what was happening. "Hey," she snapped through the thick yarn as it flew over her face. "What are you doing?"

"Making sure you stay put this time."

She snatched the sweater from his hands and held it before her breasts. Her ribs were sore from her ride over his shoulder and she winced at her jerky movements. Taron walked over to the top drawer of his dresser and pulled out a pair of handcuffs. Alyssa's eyes widened in shock. "You wouldn't dare."

"Guess again," he snarled and shoved her back onto the bed.

He grabbed one of her wrists in a firm grip and she fought against him, definitely not liking the idea of being tied up. "Taron, this isn't funny," she yelled, her voice rising in panic.

"Neither was your little stunt." With that, the lock clicked into place around her wrist.

Before he could attach it to the post she rolled away from him to the other side of the bed, but he was too fast for her. He quickly jerked her back, slipping the other end of the cuff around the metal bedpost. "Damn it, Taron," she snapped. "You can't do this."

"Wanna bet?" he snapped, then quickly moved to do the other one.

She kicked at him with her feet, desperately trying to stop him. She didn't like the idea of being bound. It infuriated her that he would go this far. This was worse than when he'd spanked her.

Her kicks had no effect on him and she growled in aggravation as the latch slid into place, locking her hands to the bed above her head. "You can't leave me here like this, damn it," she snapped, tugging desperately against the bindings.

With a murderous scowl, she growled and kicked at his leg with her foot.

"Careful or I'll tie your feet up too, slave."

His chest heaved, the muscles stretching his shirt across his wide chest. The brown of his eyes sparked fire as he stared down at her in anger. She'd never seen him so furious, but instead of scaring her the sight intrigued her. He was so gorgeous, even scowling at her in a murderous rage, and her body heated with the idea that she was helpless against him. He could do whatever he wanted to her and even as angry as she was she would welcome his ravishment.

With a determined set to his chin, he leaned forward and undid her pants, sliding them down her hips. They fell to the floor silently, leaving her naked and vulnerable to his heated gaze. "You'll learn to do as I say, Alyssa. One way or another."

She narrowed her eyes at him and curled her lip. "Go to hell."

He snorted and turned to leave the room. "Already been there." He smiled cockily at her over his shoulder. "They spit me back out."

"You are such an arrogant ass," she shouted as he shut the door. She growled and kicked her feet, her hands tugging at the handcuffs. "I can't believe the prick actually tied me up!" She huffed out a breath and glared at the closed door. "And fucking left me here."

* * * * *

Taron strolled into the old, deserted landing bay later that night, cautious, but trying not to appear so. He didn't trust Morlak. To not look at everything as some sort of trap would be a mistake. Glancing around the room, he noticed Morlak and two other men he didn't recognize opening the lid of a metal crate.

"Morlak," Taron yelled. His voice bounced off the rock walls and echoed back to him, indicating just how large this empty hangar was.

Morlak spun around to face him. "You made it. Excellent. Come." He raised a hand, waving Taron over.

Slowly, Taron made his way over to the three men, his gaze wandering to the open crate. Inside were numerous guns. Some that shot bullets, some lazers, but all of them obviously expensive and new. Morlak watched him in interest, apparently trying to gauge his reaction.

"Interesting cargo, Morlak," Taron said as he reached down to pick up a gun. He turned it over in his hand, looking for any sign of who might have made it. The metal was good quality, the sites top-of-the-line, but there were no markings to indicate the manufacturer.

"How would you like to be wealthy?" Morlak asked, a small grin tugging at his lips.

"I'm already wealthy," Taron replied and dropped the gun back into the crate. It wasn't a lie. Taron Sinnar was very wealthy.

"Okay," Morlak drawled. "How would you like to be even wealthier?"

"I'm always open to making more currency."

"Good," Morlak said with a smile. "And I'm always open to bringing in new blood, so to speak. You can handle yourself. I think you would be perfect for our little circle."

"Circle of gun runners?" Taron purred.

Morlak sneered. "Yes. Do you want to know who they're for? Why we're hiding them?"

Of course he did, but it would be stupid to actually admit it. Taron shrugged. "None of my business. So long as I get paid, I couldn't care less where it comes from."

Morlak's grin widened. "I think you'll fit in just fine, Karmase."

* * * * *

Taron stalled outside the door of his quarters. It was well past midnight and he was sure Alyssa would be asleep by now. Well, pretty sure. She had been damn pissed earlier, but then so had he. He needed to find out how she got out and make sure it didn't happen again.

His cock tightened as he thought about how good she'd looked lying there, her hands bound above her head, thrusting her breasts out. They'd heaved with her labored, angry breathing and her eyes had sparked with fire and passion. Even her skin had flushed from head to toe. She was magnificent angry and had been extremely hard to resist.

Even as mad as he'd been, he'd wanted her. Hell, he still wanted her. Glancing at the ceiling, he cursed fate. Why here and why the hell now? He knew now how Sidious must have felt when he met Mikayla, and why he'd fought his feelings for her for so long. Sidious had been undercover, just like he was now. The last thing Sidious had needed was a woman. It was the last thing he needed, but he was beginning to realize it was the one thing he wanted more than anything.

Taron was always teasing Mikayla about her smart mouth. More than once Krista had told him he'd end up with someone just like her. He'd always thought she was wrong. He wanted a sweet-tempered girl. Someone nice. Easy. But after spending time with Alyssa, easy was the last thing he wanted. He wanted wild, hot and complicated. He wanted Alyssa—smart mouth and all.

"Krista will never let me live this down," Taron mumbled with a sigh. "I've fallen in love with a hot-tempered wildcat."

Opening the door, he looked toward the bedroom where Alyssa lay, spread-eagle. Her eyes were closed, her head to the side. She looked so peaceful lying there, and so fucking tempting. Shutting the door, he removed his shirt and slung it across the back of a chair on his way to the bedroom.

For not the first time in his life he wondered if any of his father would come out in him after he married. Would he run off and leave his wife and child like his father had? No, he told himself with determination. He would never do anything like that. Ever. He wasn't like his father and never would be. Or at least that's what he continually tried to tell himself.

His finger brushed a strand of hair from her cheek. Beautiful, long, black lashes fluttered across her flesh and he grinned. "Wake up, slave," he whispered.

Her eyes fluttered again. Was she ignoring him, pretending to be asleep? Feeling mischievous, he ran his hand up the inside of thigh, straight for the heat emanating from her pussy. Her eyes popped open and she kicked at him with her foot. He caught it mid kick, before it actually made contact with his chest, and smiled wickedly. "You're not still mad at me, surely," he purred, enjoying the way her eyes sparkled in anger.

"Yes, I'm still mad at you, you prick," she snarled and tried to free her leg from his grasp. "Let me go, damn it."

"You're not exactly in a position to be making demands."

"You tied me up and left me here!"

"You deliberately defied an order," he countered.

"An order?" she snapped, and with a huff, kicked her foot loose from his hold. "You are such a fucking jerk."

"That's not what you said last night," he said with a grin.

He held her weary gaze as he moved to the foot of the bed and snatched both her ankles, holding them against the mattress. She squealed and squirmed, fighting his grip.

"Admit it, slave. This turns you on more than you want it to."

Her movements stopped and she gaped at him, her gray eyes wide with surprise. "No," she snapped, "this doesn't turn me on. You don't turn me on."

It was an outright lie and he knew it. He hadn't missed the smoldering desire she tried desperately to hide behind the anger. "Did you think about me?" he asked as he slowly slid his fingers up her legs, making sure to hold them down so she couldn't kick him again. "Did you imagine me having my way with you while you remained tied to the bed, helpless and completely at my mercy?"

The gray of her eyes deepened and a muscle jerked in her cheek. Oh, she was definitely fighting it.

"No," she cried indignantly. "I definitely did not. I dreamed of strangling you."

"Really?" he purred as his palms pressed her thighs outward, giving him a perfect view of the juices coating her pussy. "Is that what made you so wet?" he asked as he dipped his head toward her labia.

"Don't you dare," she snarled.

His tongue slowly licked up her slit and she groaned, biting down hard on her lip. "I hate you," she groaned.

"Do you really hate me?" he whispered against the skin just above her pussy. His tongue flicked out to tickle her bellybutton and her hips squirmed beneath him. "Say it isn't so, *ni pahti*," he teased.

"I'll say no such thing," she growled and he fought hard to keep from chuckling.

Her skin was soft beneath his touch as he skimmed his fingers up her ribs and around her nipples. His tongue joined in the play, teasing the tight buds. Her breathing became more erratic as he covered the tip of her breast with his mouth, his teeth nipping at her engorged nipple.

"Damn you, Taron," she hissed then arched her back, pushing her breasts further into his mouth.

Alyssa tugged at her bindings, her fingers clenched and unclenched in frustration and desire. For what seemed like hours she'd lain there wondering what he'd do to her when he returned. She'd dreamed up all kinds of pleasurable things, but this was definitely more intense than anything she could have imagined. His lips were so tender as they worked a path up her neck to nip at her ear. She gasped as his teeth sank into the sensitive flesh just below it.

She wanted to feel his soft skin, feel the hard muscles bunch beneath her touch. She loved exploring his body, the hard angles and deep planes. Everything about him was magnificent.

It was hard to keep her eyes open. She felt drugged with passion and lust. She needed him. Needed to feel his thick cock plunging inside her over and over until she screamed. He rose above her, his knees on either side of her shoulders, and unfastened his slacks. She watched in utter fascination as his hard shaft sprang free, tempting her beyond reason. She wanted to touch him but her hands were still bound and she tugged at the cuffs in aggravation. If she couldn't touch him, she could at least taste him.

"I want to taste you, Taron. I want to feel the length of your cock against my tongue."

Taron's eyes widened then narrowed, the brown glowing like amber as he stared at her hungrily. Her words must have surprised him. She licked her lips seductively, hopefully startling and enticing him further. "Put your cock in my mouth, Taron," she whispered.

Slowly Taron lowered himself and traced her lips with the tip of his shaft. She stuck her tongue out, licking at the pre-cum. Taron groaned and a muscle in his cheek flexed, indicating just how close to losing control he was. She opened her lips and he eased his length inside, inch by inch. Her mouth sucked at him, enjoying his musky, salty taste.

He moved his cock in and out, fucking her mouth. His hand kept a firm grip at the base to keep it from going too deep and choking her. She sucked hard, her eyes glued to his. Her teeth scraped across the head and he closed his eyes, groaning softly.

"I like that," he sighed. "I like the feel of your mouth on my cock, Alyssa."

She liked the feel of it in her mouth. More than she thought she would. Pulling him deeper, her lips nudged at his hand, trying to move it out of the way. She wanted more of him. All of him. In answer to her persistence he slid his hand back, pushing his cock further in her mouth. She relaxed her throat, swallowing as much of him as she could.

He hissed, the muscles in his jaw working frantically. Her cheeks hollowed out as she sucked harder, determined to make him spill his seed down her throat. But suddenly he pulled away. She gasped, staring at him in surprise. He stood over her, his hand slowly pumping his cock.

"Damn it, woman. You have one hell of a mouth."

"Put it back," she sighed, her words even shocking herself.

"No." He shook his head and positioned himself between her legs, the head of his shaft teasing the wet opening to her vagina. "I want to fuck your pussy, Alyssa. Now," he growled.

Before she could even utter a word of agreement, he thrust into her hard and deep, his cock practically splitting her in two. She screamed, her hands pulling at the cuffs, her legs lifting to wrap around his back. He felt so good. So huge. Her release was almost instant and she shattered, her pussy pulsing and clenching around his cock. He groaned and slowed his thrusts, prolonging her pleasure, and the sensations racing through her intensified.

"Taron," she screamed as another, stronger, orgasm hit, searing her flesh.

He continued to plunge into her, continued to demand more from her body. All that she could give him. With a groan, he slid from her pussy and unfastened the cuffs. Turning her, he helped her settle on her knees. She glanced at him over her shoulder in question, but he just grinned before sliding two fingers into her pussy. She moaned and rocked back against him, taking his fingers even deeper.

He removed his fingers and slid them along the cleft of her ass. Gently, he circled the tight hole of her anus. She started, wondering what he was up to. With one finger, then two, he pushed past the tight ring of resistance and she gasped at the unusual sensation.

"Am I hurting you?" he asked as he slowly stretched her, moving his fingers in and out.

"No," she sighed, intrigued with the burning need that had begun to develop there.

His other hand slid along her slit, toying with her clit in unrelenting circles. She groaned, moving her hips in time with the simultaneous movements of both his hands until she thought she would burst with need and lust. "Taron, please," she groaned. "I need you."

"Where, Alyssa?" he asked as he added a third finger to her ass. "Where do you need me?"

"There," she gulped. "I want you to fuck my ass."

She couldn't believe she was actually saying it, much less begging for it. She'd always insisted that spot was exit only, but she had to have him there. She had to feel his cock sinking into the one place she'd denied every other man.

With his thumbs, he spread her ass cheeks then pushed the tip of his shaft into the tight ring. She gasped at the fullness, the pain that bordered on pleasure. He stopped, allowing her to become comfortable with his invasion. When she didn't pull away from him he eased himself in further. It felt as though he was splitting her in two and she panted, trying to relax her body to accept all of him. He eased out, then pushed in again slowly, going much deeper this time.

She groaned and shoved against him, her body becoming more comfortable with the thick intrusion of his shaft. His cock was slick with her juices and easily plunged in balls-deep. His growl vibrated through her ear as he fucked her ass, gently at first, then harder—deeper.

His hand returned to her clit and flicked across the swollen bud. She moaned, her hand joining his at the juncture of her thighs.

"Oh, yes, *ni pahti*," he whispered in her ear. "Make yourself come for me."

He moved his hand, allowing her free rein to pleasure herself while he continued to pummel her ass. She could hardly breathe the pleasure was so intense. The first waves of her orgasm hit and she increased the pressure to the tiny nub. Her legs shook with the strain of holding back until finally she let loose, her screams echoing through the room.

Taron thrust harder, his cock plunging deeper. Her walls spasmed around him and he groaned, his own release just out of reach. Her anal muscles contracted around his cock, milking the very life from him it seemed, and he shouted as the first oncoming wave shook his muscles. With one final thrust, he spilled his seed deep in her ass along with what felt like his soul. His vision blurred and emotion unlike anything he'd felt before overwhelmed him, shaking him to the core.

He pulled free of her and turned her to her back. Softly he placed little kisses against her brow and cheeks, her sighs blowing across his lips on her breath.

"I can't believe what you do to me," she whispered.

"What do I do to you, *ni pahti*?"

She closed her eyes. "You make me feel alive."

A small smile touched his lips as he watched her fall asleep.

"May Norlicka have mercy on my soul, for you, Alyssa, are the very air I breathe," he whispered. With a sigh, he lay next to her and pulled her into the safety of his arms, where he wanted to keep her forever. "I just hope we both make it out of this alive to enjoy a life together."

Chapter Ten

ᘓ

Alyssa awoke with a start at the sound of the outer wall sliding open. Glancing to her side, she realized Taron wasn't there and quickly grabbed the robe he'd placed at the foot of the bed. Was he leaving?

"Taron?" she called as she slipped her arms through the sleeves.

"Well." Rhia's voice carried through the open wall and Alyssa ran into the other room, staring in surprise at the tall woman. Her flame red hair was drawn back in a braid that hung down the middle of her back. The frost blue outfit matched her eyes almost perfectly. "I'm not Taron," she said. "But he did send me to rescue you."

Rhia's face lit up with a smile and Alyssa grinned back. "What are you doing here?"

"Exactly what I said. There's not a whole lot to do here, tourism-wise, but surely we can find something."

"Where's Taron?"

Rhia shrugged, adjusting the thin spaghetti strap on her shoulder. "Working, I suppose. He sent a message earlier and asked if I would take you away from here for a while."

Alyssa pursed her lips. "He's just worried I'll try and run off again."

Rhia raised an eyebrow and stepped further into the room. "You what?"

"I went out into the mine yesterday. He caught me and had a fit."

"Alyssa. You can't go out there by yourself. Those men would show you no mercy."

"I know that," Alyssa sighed, not sure she should tell Rhia the truth. "Now."

Rhia seemed close to Taron. If she told Rhia why she was really here, would she tell Taron? And if she told Taron, would Taron help her? Or was Taron involved? No. She couldn't think that way. She refused to even consider that he might be involved in her brother's murder.

"Well good. Just remember it." Rhia smiled devilishly. "Don't just stand there. Put on one of those outfits I bought you and I'll show you around town. You won't need the leash, but leave the collar on."

She liked the idea of that and ran quickly back to the bedroom to change. Thank God she wouldn't need the leash. Taron actually hadn't used it much lately, although he occasionally threatened to. He knew she hated it and was grateful he didn't force her to wear it. The collar was bad enough.

Choosing a pair of thin slacks and a sleeveless top in a soft yellow, she threw on a pair of sandals and glanced at her reflection in the mirror. Her skin had a glow that hadn't been there before, her eyes more sparkle.

She hated to admit it, but she was in love with him. She knew she could never tell him. What kind of future could they have? Living here was out of the question. Raising children here was even more out of the question. She would make the best of what she had and when their time was up she would move on. She had no other choice.

Grabbing the pearl clip they'd purchased as well, she piled her hair on her head and secured it with the jeweled ornament. As she tugged a few tendrils around her ears, she smiled, remembering how Taron liked to comb his fingers through her hair as she fell asleep in his arms. She would really miss that when they parted ways. Her smile faded.

"Stop it," she mumbled to herself and turned away from the mirror. "I'm ready," she called out to Rhia and went to follow her to the tiny ship parked on the landing ledge.

"You can fly one of these?" Alyssa asked in admiration.

"If you live here, you have to learn how. It's not that hard."

"Devlin teach you?" she asked as they climbed into the small speeder.

"He tried once," Rhia giggled at the memory. "After that one time, he let someone else do it. Only time I think I've ever seen my brother turn green."

Laughter bubbled up in Alyssa's chest and she covered her mouth. Devlin was such a large, intimidating man, she couldn't imagine anything turning him green.

The speeder lifted from the pad and shot out of the hole with a soft whoosh. The sunlight beamed down on them, heating their skin through the glass windows. In the distance, barren mountains dotted the landscape but provided little to no relief from the sun. Only the caves a short distance south of the city provided a cool reprieve. Eventually these mines would also be deserted, just like the others, their veins depleted of resources and minerals.

They remained silent as the ship quickly approached the city. The roads had remained dirt since the vehicles floated above the surface. There was no need for paved roads. Three-story buildings dotted the landscape for miles, their beige stucco walls blending into the dry ground. Slate roofs ranged in color from light gray to black, depending on the age of the building. Covered sidewalks helped to shield pedestrians from the hot sun.

Rhia parked the speeder on the roof of Devlin's bar and hopped out. Alyssa followed her down the narrow stairs and into the cool confines of the bar. "Where are we headed?" Alyssa asked.

"We're picking up our escort," Rhia threw over her shoulder. "Devlin refuses to allow me out in town without one."

"Around here that's probably a smart thing," Alyssa mumbled, remembering her own experience at exploring unescorted. "Rhia, do you know who Vingosa is?"

Rhia came to a stop and stared at her with a startled expression. "Vingosa? Vingosa who?"

Alyssa shrugged. "Don't know. Just Vingosa."

A strange cloud passed over Rhia's eyes, but before Alyssa could decipher it she turned away from her. "I don't think I recognize the name."

A frown creased her brow as she watched Rhia continue down the hallway and a second set of stairs. She was lying, but why?

Once on the lower level, Rhia smiled at the tall Veenorian at the end of the bar. "We're ready, Misha," Rhia said.

Misha stood and Alyssa couldn't help but gape at his unusual appearance. His long legs stretched, forcing him to his full nine-foot height. His green-tinged skin and lizard-like eyes made her shiver.

"Good. Let's do this quickly," he replied sternly.

"Relax, Misha. We'll be done when we're done."

"Walking through town with you, Mistress Rhia, is anything but relaxing. Your brother should be accompanying you. Less happens when he does."

Rhia snorted. "There hasn't been anything happening in quite a while, Misha."

"Okay, wait," Alyssa said, placing one hand on her hip and waving her other. "What exactly happens when you go to town?"

"Nothing," Rhia said with a shake of her head.

Misha growled. "Nothing my ass. Every time I take this woman to town some newcomer who doesn't know who she is tries to take her."

She stared at Rhia in shock. "Why on earth do you stay here?"

"It's not as bad as he makes it out to be. Besides, Devlin won't leave and I can't leave Devlin. He's the only family I know."

Alyssa smiled slightly at the stubborn redhead. "I can certainly understand that. I would never leave my family either."

"Now that that's settled," Rhia said with a smile, "let's go."

Trying to keep up with Rhia as they made their way through Veenori City was an experience in itself. The woman had long legs and took long strides Alyssa had to skip to keep up with. Misha remained close behind, his eyes ever watchful. At one point Devlin joined them, escorting the two women to Viclak's—an upper-crust diner and bar toward the middle of town—for drinks.

Devlin sat across from Alyssa at the small tile table. He leaned back and crossed his ankle over his knee, his full lips morphing into a sexy grin. "How's slinoy life treating you, Alyssa? You look well."

His muscular arm slid along the back of the chair beside him, forcing the top of his shirt to open wider and show off a smooth, tan chest. She couldn't stop from admiring the gorgeous hunk. Heaven help the woman he decided to seduce. She wouldn't stand a chance. Her gaze met his sapphire one and he winked knowingly, causing the heat of a blush to move up her cheeks.

Rhia sat next to her and Alyssa didn't miss the movement under the table as she kicked her brother. "Behave yourself," Rhia growled.

"What'd I do?" he asked innocently.

A sad smile tugged at Alyssa's lips, memories of her own relationship with Anthony tugging at her chest. Devlin and Rhia were obviously very close and it made her miss her own brother even more so. If only she hadn't made such a mess out of things here. She'd made zero progress and wasn't sure she ever would. An investigator she was not.

"Siblings are such a pain in the ass, aren't they, Alyssa?" Devlin teased.

"Rhia's not a pain."

Alyssa reached up to take the drink the waiter handed her and set it on the table. The glass was frosted and cold, a wonderful contradiction to the stifling heat of the planet.

"You don't know her like I do," Devlin said with a grin. "I can remember when she was younger, always giving her nannies trouble, always under my feet."

"I was not always under your feet," Rhia pouted.

"Please, Ri," Devlin purred while rolling his eyes, "you were always under my feet, following me everywhere, imitating me and mocking me."

Alyssa grinned at the image of a young Devlin and an even younger Rhia dogging his heels. "The two of you are funny."

She took a sip of her drink, letting the cold fluid cool her parched throat. Devlin studied her as though trying to read her mind and she squirmed, unsure why his steady stare made her so uncomfortable. It was as though he knew all her little secrets.

"Where's Taron?" Devlin asked out of the clear blue and she blinked in surprise.

"I don't know. The mine, I guess," Alyssa said with a shrug.

"He said he'd be by the bar later to pick Alyssa up," Rhia offered.

Devlin nodded, his eyes still studying hers. She licked her lips and looked down at the table, trying her best to avoid his probing gaze. When she glanced back at him, his lips quirked into a small grin. "I told Misha he could go and I would escort you back to the bar. Did you get the translator I needed?" Devlin asked as he turned his attention back to Rhia.

"Yes," she replied with a nod. "It's being delivered later this afternoon."

"Good."

Someone shouted Devlin's name and he glanced toward another table, raising his hand in acknowledgment. "I'll be right back. You two stay right here where I can see you."

"Yes, brother dear," Rhia drawled and Alyssa giggled at Devlin's exasperated expression and rolling eyes.

"He's so gorgeous," Alyssa sighed, her gaze straying to his wide shoulders and tight ass as he walked away.

"Yeah. And he knows it."

"What man who looks like that doesn't?"

Rhia laughed. "True." She looked to Alyssa and smiled apologetically. "You'll have to forgive his probing earlier."

"Probing?"

"Devlin is Dorian. He can sense emotions."

"He's an empath?" Alyssa's eyes widened in surprise.

"Yes, to some degree. The closer he is to someone emotionally, the stronger the connection. But he asked you about Taron to try and get an emotional response."

Alyssa narrowed her eyes. "Why?"

Rhia shrugged with a sigh. "Who knows? Maybe he's just being protective of Taron."

Lifting the glass to take a drink, Alyssa snorted. "Protecting him from me? What does he think I'll do to him?"

"Break his heart," Rhia offered with a grin.

The drink lodged in her throat and she coughed, trying to catch her breath. "I think it's the other way around, Rhia. I think I'm the one in danger of getting her heart broken."

"So you care for him then?" Rhia asked softly.

Of course she did, but was it the sex? Or something else? Something much stronger. "I don't know," she sighed. "I feel something, I'm just not sure what."

Rhia put her hand over hers, offering a show of silent support. "Don't overthink it, Alyssa. Just let it happen."

"It's not that simple. I can't live here."

A small smile touched Rhia's lips as she gave her hand a gentle squeeze. "Who says you have to? Don't make assumptions, hon. Remember what I said. Just let it happen."

Just let it happen? Who was she kidding? It had already happened. Now she just had to figure out what to do about it.

* * * * *

Back at the bar, Alyssa silently watched the men and women saunter in. Scantily clad barmaids scurried around the room taking drink orders and warding off wandering hands. Some didn't and stopped mid-stride to enjoy a grope and feel from one of the patrons.

Several nude table dancers performed, shaking their assets for the interested table crowd. She couldn't help but stare at the same man she'd seen that first night. The night Taron had made her come in front of everyone. But as her eyes roamed around the room, she realized no one probably paid her any attention. They were too busy watching everything else.

Rhia had kept her sequestered behind the bar with strict instructions that she wasn't to leave the spot. She would be safe there. But the second she saw Taron walk through the door her heart jumped. He looked incredible. The thin material of his black sleeveless tank stretched tight across his wide chest, his trim waist was outlined by the form-fitting tan cotton pants.

She gulped in air, shocked at the ever-present stirring of lust within her stomach. It was always this way, even when she was mad at him. He had a power over her she couldn't even begin to understand, nor did she really want to. If she looked at it too closely, she'd have to admit her feelings ran deeper than just lust and she couldn't do that.

His whiskey gaze met hers, sinking her heart into a frantic rhythm. It burned with desire and possession that sent shivers down her spine. Suddenly she wanted desperately to be near him, to feel his protective embrace around her. Without thinking it through, she ran from behind the bar and headed toward Taron.

Before she even got halfway, someone grabbed her from behind, his hot, smelly breath against her cheek making her cringe. Why couldn't she listen and do what she was told?

"Let me go," she snapped. "I don't belong to you."

"I don't care," he snarled, his arms tightening their hold. "You look too good to pass up."

"She's Karmase's slave," someone warned from beside them.

"Good. I've always wanted a reason to kick the bastard's ass. She's as good a one as any."

Alyssa's stomach flipped in fear for Taron. Her frightened eyes met Taron's gaze across the crowded room and she flinched at the raw anger reflected in their depths. Her gut told her Taron didn't have anything to worry about, but the man holding her did.

Taron stomped toward them, his gaze hot, fury and possessiveness shooting from the amber orbs. Her breath caught at the impressive sight.

"Let her go, Negosh. She doesn't belong to you."

"Fuck you," he drawled. "She's in my arms. She's mine. You shouldn't have left her here alone, Karmase."

Taron grabbed the man's wrist and squeezed, hard. The distinct sound of a bone cracking made Alyssa flinch. Negosh groaned then hissed in fury.

From the side, Devlin grabbed her hand and pulled her from Negosh's relaxed grip. She kept her eyes on the two men as Devlin tugged her several feet away, safe from the fight she could sense unfolding.

Taron drew back his hand and hit Negosh with his fist square in the nose. Negosh staggered back, his hand rising to try and stop the flow of blood gushing from his now-broken nose. "You son of a bitch," he snapped. "I claim her, Karmase. What are you willing to do to win her back?"

Taron snorted. "Whatever you want, Negosh. Name it. Winner takes Alyssa."

"No," she gasped and tried to break free of Devlin's hold.

"Stop it, Alyssa," Devlin hissed, his fingers tightening around her wrist. "Remember your place."

"But he can't do this," she cried.

"Would you rather go with Negosh?"

She instantly stopped struggling, her worried gaze never leaving the two men. Of course she didn't want to go with Negosh.

"I challenge you to a race, Karmase. Cycles."

"Where and when, Negosh?" Taron snarled.

"Here and now."

Devlin whistled and Taron turned to look at him with a questioning expression. "Use mine," Devlin said as he tossed something into the air. The small silver object flew across the room and landed in Taron's outstretched hand.

Taron nodded and turned to head outside with Negosh. Alyssa finally broke free of Devlin and took off after Taron into the hot Veenori sunlight.

Word had already spread and a crowd quickly gathered along the main strip. The cycles were brought around and Alyssa swallowed down a lump of pure fear. Did he know how to ride one of those?

"Negosh is good," someone to her left whispered close to her ear. "He's never been beaten. Looks like you'll belong to him now."

She curled her lip at the tall man. "We'll see, won't we?"

Moving away from them, she ignored Rhia's shout for her to come back and stomped toward Taron. He crouched on his haunches, studying the cycle, his thick fingers making quick adjustments to the wires sticking out of the side.

"Are you out of your mind?" she snapped.

He ignored her, his gaze remaining on the monstrous-looking machine he would be riding.

"Taron, you can't do this." She followed behind him as he moved from one side of the cycle to the other. It didn't seem to her that he was even paying attention. Instead he knelt down and began to fiddle with the plugs and wires located just below the seat. "Taron," she said again, trying to get his attention.

He stopped what he was doing and stood to his full height. "Why can't I do this?" he asked with a little aggravation as he looked down at her.

"From what I understand this man has never lost a race." She tried to make him see reason.

"He's never raced me." Taron shrugged his shoulders arrogantly.

She slapped her thigh in exasperation. "You have to be the most arrogant man I think I have ever met. Arrogance will not win this race for you!"

"No." He smiled. "Skill will."

Rolling her eyes, Alyssa wondered why she was even out here trying to stop him. Let him kill himself. Surely Devlin would see she didn't end up with…what's his name.

"You know…" Taron moved closer, pinning her against the side of the cycle, and she glanced up in question at his face. What the hell was he doing? "I have to wonder what it is that's motivated you to come out here and try to stop me. Could it be concern, possibly?"

"Don't flatter yourself." She narrowed her eyes and tried to look for an escape route. She refused to admit anything to him. Especially here.

"The race is about to start. How about a kiss for luck?" He touched the side of her face and softly ran his thumb along her bottom lip.

"How about not?" she replied, trying to ignore what his closeness and the look in his whiskey-colored eyes was doing to her.

"Come on, Lyssa." The corner of his mouth twitched as though fighting a smile. He tipped her chin up with his finger, bringing her mouth closer to his. His breath fanned across her lips as he whispered, "We fuck too well together for you to not feel anything for me."

"This has nothing to do with that, damn it."

"No?" he said with an infuriating grin that told her he didn't believe a word she'd said.

"I just came out here to try and talk some sense into you, but I see now that it was useless—"

Before she could finish her thought he covered her mouth with his. She hated when he did this, for no matter how hard she tried to play indifferent she always melted beneath his skilled kisses. There was just something about the way he kissed and the way he made her feel that made him so hard to resist.

With a slight whimper, Alyssa opened her lips beneath his and welcomed the onslaught of his tongue and the passionate kiss that followed.

Chapter Eleven

ꙮ

Taron's arms snaked around the small of her back and molded her body closer to his. She smelled of jerrywine, a small red flower indigenous to Tilarus, and he inhaled deeper. Rhia must have gotten this scent for her. He loved that smell and when it mixed with Alyssa's own sweet scent, it was heavenly.

With a moan, he nipped at her tongue, sucking it further into his mouth. Her taste was so incredibly erotic. The voices behind him faded as he continued to plunder her sweet lips. He couldn't get enough. Her tiny hands fisted in his shirt, her nails scraping at the skin of his chest, and his cock hardened instantly. Damn, he had to get control of himself or he'd take her right here, crowd be damned.

"Race starts in two senahs," Devlin shouted.

Taron lifted his head and stared at Alyssa's shocked expression. Her eyes were wide with anxiety, desire, and… He grinned. Anger.

"You insufferable, arrogant…" she fumed, her lips pursing as she tried to think of something else equally as bad to call him.

He wrapped his arms tighter around her and pressed his hard cock into the soft flesh of her stomach. "Ah, I love it when you talk dirty."

"Ugh!" She growled and shoved hard at his chest.

He let her go and watched in amusement as she stomped back toward Rhia, who stood under the shade of the sidewalk overhang.

"Man your cycles," Devlin shouted as he took his place before them.

He raised his hand high in the air and waited for the two of them to take their positions. Taron hit the switch, starting the engine. The cycle purred beneath him as he straddled the seat, his hands gripping the handles in front of him. The sun beat down on his head as he studied the horizon in the distance.

"Three kilometers. First one to Porlacy Falls and back is the winner and retains possession of the slinoy Alyssa." Devlin eyed both men. "Are you ready?"

Taron and Negosh both nodded.

"Go!" Devlin shouted, then dropped his arm.

Taron revved the engine and braced himself against the sudden thrust of the cycle as it took off toward the falls, Negosh close behind.

* * * * *

Alyssa watched him go with a sinking heart. Why did her last words to him have to be so harsh? What if he didn't make it back?

"Stop worrying." She blinked and noticed Devlin studying her, his brow creased in a frown. "He'll be fine."

"So you can tell the future as well as read my emotions?" she snapped. Immediately, she regretted her remark. "I'm sorry. You didn't deserve that."

Devlin shrugged. "I know he will be fine because I know he's a good driver. Don't forget, I've known Taron for a long time. Now," he said with grin, "come and watch the race from the roof. They'll be returning shortly."

Alyssa and Rhia followed Devlin to the flat roof of the bar. Several others came as well and they all lined the edge, watching the horizon for any sign of the two cycles. The heat came off the ground in waves, making the skyline appear fuzzy. She squinted, trying to focus in on the two riders in the distance, but it was no use. They were too far away.

A lump formed in her throat as she felt Rhia place her hand on her shoulder. Rhia seemed to know exactly what she was going through, even though half the time Alyssa didn't. How had things become so complicated? She had come here to find her brother's killer and she'd ended up falling in love. With a mine overseer of all things. Boy, wouldn't her mother be proud.

She rolled her eyes toward the hot sun and wrapped her arms around her stomach, trying to squelch the nervous nausea. Taking a deep breath, she concentrated on the two riders in the distance as their shadows loomed closer. From here she couldn't tell who was ahead, but it looked close. Too close.

"Please," she whispered as the two became more visible.

A cloud of dust surrounded them as their cycles stirred the ground beneath the vehicles. Her heart hammered in her chest as Taron's figure became clearer. He was ahead, but not by much. She clenched her fingers into fists as the two approached, making their way down the main street of the city. A black line had been drawn on the ground, marking the finish.

Time seemed to stand still for Alyssa and when Taron passed over the line first she closed her eyes in relief. Rhia hugged her from behind as the crowd below them erupted in cheers for the winner. "See. Everything worked out just fine."

Alyssa nodded and watched Taron continue to speed down the street. The cycles were going so fast it would take him several more feet to slow down. With a relieved sigh, she turned to stare in surprise at Devlin. His hand was held out, collecting money from grumbling men and women who walked by.

"Thank you," he said with a grin. "Always a pleasure."

"I can't believe you bet," Rhia said.

"Why wouldn't I? The man's a sure thing."

"You could have told me that," Alyssa grumbled.

"I believe I did," he answered with a grin. "Maybe you were just too worried about him to notice."

With one last smile, he took Rhia's arm and escorted her downstairs with the rest of the spectators, leaving Alyssa alone on the roof with her jumbled thoughts. The crowd below had dispersed, heading back into the cool buildings and away from the killer daylight. Shielding her eyes, she stared toward the blue sky. She missed home so much, but the thought of never seeing Taron again tore at her heart.

I hate it here, but I love him. I must be out of my mind.

"The race made for an interesting day, didn't it?"

Alyssa spun around with a start and gasped. Taron stood just a few feet away, his clothes and skin covered in dust. She smiled then raced toward him, throwing herself into his arms. He grunted then laughed. "You're going to be a mess. I'm filthy."

"I don't care," she mumbled against his neck. "Just please don't do this anymore."

"Ah, *ni pahti,*" he sighed, "I would gladly do it again for you."

Slowly she pulled back and stared into his eyes. They sparkled with humor and love. She swallowed against the growing warmth that began to spread through her chest. Licking her lips, she shook her head. "We have to be out of our minds. This could never work."

"You have to have a little faith, Alyssa," he whispered before claiming her lips in a deep, sweet kiss.

Her whole body melted against his as she fell into the kiss, meeting his passion with a rising passion of her own. He never failed to do this to her. Make her crazy with need and passion. He made her feel alive and whole. But this was nuts. Could this really work and did she really want it to?

"Taron," she sighed, "We need to talk."

"Later, *ni pahti,*" he purred and moved his fingers to undo the buttons of her top, revealing her aching breasts. His thumb brushed across her nipple and she moaned, arching her back and thrusting her breasts toward his touch. "Much later," he whispered before leaning down to capture the pert bud in his mouth.

* * * * *

"Senator Marshe." Stefan stared at the tall man in surprise. "What are you doing here?"

The man grinned sheepishly. "I'm terribly sorry, Your Grace, but I needed to speak with you and your office said you were here."

Stefan frowned, both at the title and the fact his office would give his whereabouts without clearing it with him first. "It's fine, Marshe. Please come in." He stepped back and opened the front door to Sidious' lake house, allowing the senator to step inside. "And it's Stefan. We forgo formalities here."

"Of course…Stefan. Lovely home," Marshe said as his faded green eyes took in the massive mahogany entry.

"Thank you. Sidious' wife did most of the decorating."

"Antiques from Earth?" Marshe asked as he studied a table in the center of the foyer, running his finger along the edge.

"Yes. She's from there and it helped her feel a little more at home."

A frown creased the senator's brow. "Your brother spoils his wife."

"Yes," Stefan drawled, his unease growing. He'd never really trusted the Snorlakin politician. He'd taken the place of one of last year's assassinated senators and the whole situation had left Stefan with a bad taste in his mouth. There was something about his election that hadn't set right with him. But he wasn't sure what. "When you love your wife, like Sidious loves his, you give her whatever will make her happy. I probably have my brother beat when it comes to spoiling his wife."

A tight smile touched Marshe's face. "I've found over the years that developing feelings for a woman can only lead to trouble. I married for an heir, then sent her away. Much easier that way."

"Yes, well. That's just one of the things you and I differ on. Which makes me wonder why you're here."

Marshe turned to stare at him, his brow raised in amusement. "Where are your brothers?" he asked.

"One of them is here," Sidious drawled from the far side of the entry.

Marshe turned to him with a weary smile. "Sidious."

"Lord Marcone," Damon practically growled from his position beside Sidious.

"I see. Lord Marcone." Marshe bowed slightly toward Sidious. As he straightened a wicked grin spread his lips. "Why is it Taron...that is the adopted son's name isn't it...why is it he doesn't go by 'lord' as well? Where is he, by the way?"

"Out," Stefan said as he crossed his arm over his chest, leaning against the back of the main door. "And why he chooses to not use the title is really not any of your business."

"Will he be back soon?"

"What do you need with Taron, Senator Marshe?" Sidious asked.

"I understand he's part of the investigation into the weapons smuggling. I had some questions I wished to ask him."

"Who told you he was part of that investigation?" Stefan pried.

"Well, no one." He shrugged and brushed at a piece of imaginary lint on his blue jacket. "I just assumed."

"You assumed wrong," Damon volunteered.

Marshe sighed dramatically. "I know the three of us have had our problems in the past, but can't we put that behind us and work together toward the conclusion to this situation?"

"You may have your people fooled, Marshe, but not me." Damon strolled to the front door and gently pushed Stefan to the side so he could open the door. "I'm sorry you wasted a trip. Taron isn't here. He's out shopping for furniture for his home that is under construction on Tilarus. Perhaps you can catch up to him on his next trip to the capitol building on Rhenari."

Marshe frowned, his green eyes flashing fire. "I'm part of the Galactic Senate, Marcone. I have a right to know what's happening."

Damon pursed his lips, seemingly not the least bit concerned with Marshe's growing temper. "You are in my home, Marshe. You are asking questions about my son. You have a right to know only what I say you do. Like I said," his voice lowered, his gray eyes darkened to black as he stared hard at the senator, "you may have fooled your people, but I don't trust you. I know you're up to something and I'll find out what, sooner or later. Now," he waved his arm toward the open door, "have a safe trip back."

Stefan turned to Sidious to hide his grin from Marshe.

"Fine." Marshe thrust his chin out in defiance. "I can find information elsewhere."

Damon slammed the door shut just as Marshe strolled through it.

"What the hell was that all about and how did he know there's an investigation?" Sidious demanded.

"Good question," Damon sighed. "I don't like this. Marshe is fishing for information. There's no other reason for him to be here." He turned to Stefan with a worried expression. "I've always thought he was up to something, but I'm not sure about this. If he's involved, he's not in it alone. He's not smart enough for that."

"But who's he working with?" Sidious murmured.

"What about Taron's father, Vingosa?" Damon asked.

"We still haven't been able to find anything on him. If the man in the picture Anthony has *is* Vingosa, then he's very good at keeping himself hidden," Stefan said as he brushed his hair from his face in aggravation. "It's like looking for a damn ghost."

"You have to find him, preferably before he finds Taron," Damon snarled, then stomped off toward the back of the house, his mouth set in an angry line. "I don't want Vingosa to get another shot at killing Taron."

Stefan sighed. "Tell me again why we sent Taron?"

"Because he's the best?" Sidious replied with a raised eyebrow.

"I'm beginning to think we may have made a mistake. I have a bad feeling about this."

"You and me both," Sidious sighed, then turned to head back to his study.

Chapter Twelve

ꟸ

Alyssa moaned into Taron's kiss, molding her body tighter to his. The hot sun beat down, heating the top of her head and her shoulders. Taron's flesh scorched the rest of her, fueling her desire and need for his touch.

His large hands moved lower, gripping her ass and lifting her. She wrapped her legs around his waist, grinding her already throbbing pussy along his growing length. Warm, firm lips devoured hers, making her giddy and wild. She held tight to his neck as he walked her toward the small runner parked a few feet away.

"Ever been taken against the side of a ship?" he asked with a grin as he pinned her against the cool outer shell of the ship beneath the shade of one of its wings. The covering was designed to remain cool, even in some of the hottest temperatures.

"No. But I have a feeling I'm about to be."

"Hell yeah, you are," he growled. "You drive me crazy, slave. Do you know that?"

"And yet you risked your life for me," she purred and wiggled her pussy against him as he tugged her shirt down her arms.

He groaned and held her hips still. "Stop squirming, minx, and get those pants off. I want you," he whispered against her lips.

She smiled and lowered her legs, but made no move to remove her pants. Instead, she worked the fastenings loose on his and tugged them down his hips. His massive cock sprang free and she encircled him with her fingers, squeezing just under the engorged purple head. He moaned and jerked his hips toward her. His gaze smoldered as she dropped to her knees and licked her tongue across the tiny slit, wiping away the drop of escaping pre-cum.

"You're killing me, Alyssa."

"I like your taste," she murmured and licked at him again. He closed his eyes and a muscle jerked in his cheek.

"I like the feel of your mouth on me," he growled and dug his fingers into her hair, tugging her closer. "Take me in your mouth, *ni pahti*."

Her lips opened, taking his thick cock into her mouth. She loved the feel of him beneath her tongue. All salty and musky. All man. Her fingers massaged his balls, testing their weight and size within her grasp as her tongue wrapped around his length, teasing him with light strokes.

A noise caught her attention and she opened her eyes, then jumped away from Taron with a start. Devlin stood a few feet away, watching them with an interested gaze, his sapphire eyes almost neon in desire. She swallowed at the sudden wave of lust that screamed through her. She'd never been with two men, but the thought of these two gorgeous men smothering her with sexual attention sent a shock wave of desire to her belly.

Taron turned as well and smiled at his friend. "Enjoying the show?"

"Immensely. Is she as good as it looks like she is?"

"Better," Taron drawled and gripped the base of his shaft in his fist.

A shiver traveled down Alyssa's spine as she met Devlin's sultry stare. He wanted in on their little party and it made her pussy clench in hunger. What would it be like to be with both of them? She'd bet her life it would be incredible.

"Did you return my cycle in one piece?" Devlin asked with a devilish grin.

Taron snorted. "Nah, man. I wrecked it."

Laughter rumbled through Devlin's chest and Alyssa wondered what Devlin would look like without a shirt. She licked at her lips, then glanced at Taron. Both men watched her expectantly, as though waiting for her to say something. She may never have another opportunity to do this, experience sex with two men, and she made a quick decision to jump at the chance.

Leaning close to Taron, she whispered in his ear, "Have you and Devlin ever shared?"

He raised an eyebrow in interest. "Hey, Dev," Taron drawled with his sexy timbre, "she wants to know if we've ever shared."

"More than once," Devlin replied as he stepped closer and ran his fingers softly up her arm. "Are you saying that's what you want, Alyssa? To be fucked by both of us?"

"It's an intriguing idea," she admitted. "If Taron's willing to share me."

"Just this once," he whispered and pinned Devlin with a hard stare.

Devlin chuckled. "Once is all we need."

Removing his shirt, Taron turned her to stand in front of him, her back to his chest. "Once is all we need for what?" she asked, her voice squeaking with nerves.

"It's all we need to show you an afternoon you'll not soon forget," Taron murmured in her ear, and she shivered in anticipation.

"But not here," Devlin said as he reached into the ship and pulled out a small, square device. "The falls?" he asked, facing Taron.

"The falls are good," Taron answered and the two of them sandwiched her between them.

"Wait. What are we doing?" she asked, her voice rising an octave in her nervousness.

"We're going to transport to the falls," Taron replied.

"I've never done that," she squeaked, not sure she liked the idea of being transported.

"It'll be over in a flash, I promise," Devlin said, then placed a soft kiss on her temple.

Devlin raised the device then hit the small red button in the center with his thumb. She gasped as sharp tingles spread through her body. The area around them blurred and she screamed as the tingles intensified, bordering on pain.

"Relax," Taron whispered in her ear. "It hurts if you tense up."

But it was too late. She was already tense and the tingles only made her muscles contract more. Closing her eyes tightly, she tried to ignore it and leaned back against Taron while her fingers grabbed hold of Devlin's shirt, bunching the soft fabric within her tight grasp.

Finally the tingles faded and she breathed a sigh of relief as her muscles relaxed.

"Open your eyes, Alyssa," Devlin whispered.

She opened them to stare at the oasis around her. It was beautiful. Three cliff faces surrounded them, with water pouring from the top of one face creating a small pool at the bottom. It was a pure crystal blue and so clear she could see all the way to the sandy floor. Trees grew around the edge, creating shade and a welcome reprieve from the hot sun.

"This is amazing," she sighed. "Is this where you raced to?"

"Yes. Other than under the grove of trees a little to the north, this is the only water on the planet. It goes miles below the surface, circles around and comes back out here. But I think we can forgo the geography lesson for now, don't you?" Taron asked as his hands reached around and cupped her breasts, giving them a gentle squeeze.

She moaned and arched her back, pushing her breasts further into his hands. With growing excitement, she watched as Devlin removed his clothes, his sapphire eyes holding hers hostage with their smoldering intensity. Her heart beat a frantic rhythm as sudden nervousness hit her like ice water. Had she lost her mind? But as more of Devlin's incredible body came into view, those nerves were replaced by lust. White-hot lust that had juices pouring from her pussy.

The same black hair that hung around his shoulders sprinkled his chest and her fingers itched to sift through it. His muscles were almost as big as Taron's and she swallowed at the image of being squished between two such massive specimens. Three puckered scars on his chest were the only things disrupting the incredible beauty of his hard body. In the back of her mind, she told herself to ask Taron about those scars later. Right now she didn't think she could speak as Devlin dropped his slacks to the ground, freeing a cock that was almost identical to Taron's.

His shaft was long and thick, standing clear to his navel. The black hair on his chest pointed downward like an upside-down arrow toward his impressive erection. She swallowed at the idea of both of these massive cocks thrusting into her at once. Her nipples beaded and she licked at dry lips, watching mesmerized as Devlin walked toward them.

Taron's hands continued to massage her aching breasts, his lips softly biting at her neck. "If you don't want to do this, Lyssa, just say so and I'll send him away."

"No," she sighed. "I want to try this."

Devlin stopped before her and every nerve under her flesh tingled. Taron lifted a breast, offering it to Devlin, and he leaned down, flicking his tongue across her hardened nipple. She gasped, sagging back against Taron. His arm wrapped protectively around her stomach, holding her upright.

Two sets of hands moved along her skin, setting her on fire so hot she thought she would spontaneously combust. She closed her eyes, relaxing and falling headlong into the wild and erotic moment as they slid her pants down her legs, tossing them toward the edge of the water. Her pussy ached, screamed to be fucked, and she squirmed, spreading her legs in silent invitation for one or both of them to touch her there.

Taron's fingers slid along her slit from behind, making her shudder in pleasure, seeking a more firm touch. Devlin added his from the front, gently circling her sensitive clit. Her mouth dropped open as she gasped for air and Devlin covered her mouth with his, his tongue seeking hers. She moaned into his kiss. His lips were firm against hers, his taste erotic and hot. He kissed differently than Taron. Each man had his own way, his own style, and each made her melt into a wanton puddle.

Her fingers moved to sift through the hair on Devlin's chest. It felt soft and the muscles beneath it hard, creating an interesting contrast for her exploring hands. Her thumbs brushed across his nipples and he shuddered, his lips forming a smile against hers. "Taron's a lucky man," he whispered.

"I have a feeling I'm the lucky one," she sighed as Taron sucked on the sensitive spot behind her ear. Every muscle in her body quivered in lust and need that demanded fulfillment.

Devlin turned her to face Taron so that he could take his turn at kissing her. His lips moved across hers with a possessiveness that stole her breath, making her weak. Devlin's lips burned a trail across her shoulders, his hands moving down her back to smooth over her ass.

Through the fog that was surrounding her brain, she realized they were moving her sideways toward a flat rock. Devlin sat, then they turned her to face him, Taron's palm gently pushing her to her knees. She settled between Devlin's legs and eyed his hard, thick shaft standing straight between his thighs with interest. Her fingers slid up the muscled limbs, brushing at the coarse hair that covered the tan flesh.

The muscles quivered and bunched beneath her touch and she moved closer, wrapping her fingers around his massive shaft. His breath hitched and his beautiful sapphire eyes closed as she slowly worked her hand up and down his long length.

Taron moved to his knees behind her, his hands wickedly spreading her juices along the cleft of her ass. Leaning down, she licked her tongue across the head of Devlin's cock just as Taron slid one thick finger deep into her sopping pussy. She moaned against Devlin and he jerked his hips upward. The tip of his shaft nudged at the back of her throat and she sucked harder, thrusting her hips back against Taron's hand.

"Damn, Alyssa," Devlin groaned. "She keeps this up I'll explode quicker than I want to."

"She's a hot little piece of work," Taron said, then slapped at her ass with his palm.

She gasped at the sharp sting, then resumed sucking Devlin's cock. Taron added another finger to her pussy then pulled them out to circle the tight hole of her anus. She squirmed against him, wanting to feel his fingers thrusting there like they had in her pussy. "You want it here, *ni pahti*?" Taron purred.

Her head bobbed a yes, her lips unwilling to let go of the delectable cock filling her mouth. Taron sank two fingers into her ass and she shoved her hips back, pushing them deeper, the pleasure quickly overriding the slight bite of pain.

"She's fucking killing me," Devlin growled, then shifted, pulling his cock from her mouth.

Burying his hand in her hair, he pulled her up and captured her lips in a kiss that sent her senses reeling. They were driving her crazy, sending her over an edge she never dreamed she'd face. Taron grabbed her arm and tugged her away from Devlin to kiss her himself. She squealed into his mouth, her body so turned on and hot she could hardly breathe.

Slowly, he pushed her back until she landed on Devlin's lap, her back against his chest. She squirmed, rubbing her ass along his length. Devlin groaned and gripped her hips, holding her still. Her breath came out as pants as she watched Taron spread her legs, resting them on either side of Devlin, who then spread his, pushing her thighs out wider. She gasped as air hit her aching mound, her pussy clenching in desperation.

"Fuck her, Devlin. Get your cock wet," Taron murmured as his tongue licked at her swollen clit.

"Yes," she gasped as Devlin lifted her hips and set her down on the head of his shaft. Gently he pushed upward, filling her to the womb, and she screamed, "Oh, yes."

Taron's warm, wicked tongue continued to flick at her clit, licking the juices that coated Devlin's cock and continued to flow from her vagina. She wiggled her hips, forcing Devlin even deeper as her nails dug into his thighs, creating half-moons on his flesh. His groan vibrated against her back as his hand reached around to squeeze her breasts. "Damn, your pussy feels good, Alyssa. So hot and wet."

"Oh, God," she moaned as Taron increased the pressure against her clit. "Taron, please."

"Please what, *ni pahti*?" he asked, his words blowing across her pussy. "Do you want both of us to fuck you?"

"Yes," she groaned.

Devlin lifted her and repositioned the head of his rod at her ass. Gently, he pushed in, his cock slick with her juices. "Oh, fuck, she's tight," he groaned.

Taking a deep breath, she pushed against him, forcing his cock balls-deep into her ass. She threw her head back and bit down on her lower lip. The first initial invasion was always the worst, but she knew once her body became accustomed, he would feel incredible.

"Look at me, Alyssa," Taron commanded.

She opened her eyes and met his hungry gaze. The amber depths shone bright with possession and love. She smiled, then ran her tongue along her bottom lip. Taron moved closer, positioning the head of his shaft at her drenched labia.

"You are so beautiful," he whispered just as he pushed his cock deep into her pussy.

The invasion startled her and she screamed, her lungs almost bursting from the pressure and filling pleasure of two men buried inside her. It was the most incredible feeling. Gently, they both began to move in unison, their cocks sliding out then pushing in together, their thrusts timed perfectly. Every part of her body screamed in pleasure so intense she thought she'd die.

Taron watched Alyssa's facial expressions as he and Devlin pleasured her, looking for any sign of discomfort. What he saw made his heart burst. Her eyes shone with passion, lust—and love. Something he didn't expect to see and it touched him in ways he never imagined. He had no doubt he loved her and wanted to spend the rest of his life with her. But how angry would she be when she found out he wasn't who she thought he was?

"Taron," she sighed. "Oh, God. I'm so close."

"I know, *ni pahti*," he whispered against her lips. "And it feels so good. I can feel your pussy squeeze me. I can feel your throbs milking my cock."

"And your ass, Alyssa," Devlin purred from behind her, "it's so tight and hot. It feels so good."

"Come for us, Alyssa," Taron ordered. "Let it go."

She gasped, her lips dropping open in shock as her body erupted around him. Her pussy spasmed and convulsed around his cock and he groaned, trying to keep his own release at bay.

"Fuck, Taron," Devlin bit out. "I'm gonna come."

With a groan, he pushed upward and Taron followed, timing his release with Devlin's and spilling his seed deep into her pulsing channel. Every time he made love to her he felt as though he was losing a little more of himself. But in reality, he wasn't. He was becoming closer to Alyssa, more a part of her. The woman he'd come to love more than his own life.

"Oh my God," she whispered.

Taron watched her as she laid her head back against Devlin's chest and closed her eyes in rapture. Her face and chest were flushed, her lips swollen from their kisses. She'd never looked more beautiful. His gaze flicked to Devlin, who watched him with humor and just a bit of sadness. Taron was sure he was missing Skylar and remembering the one time they'd shared her.

"Tell her, you ass," Devlin whispered.

Taron turned quickly to Alyssa. Had she heard him? If she had, she wasn't showing any indication. Moving his eyes back to Devlin, he mouthed, "Later".

Devlin's lips lifted into an amused grin. "I think our little vixen could use a bath."

"In the falls?" she asked, her eyes still closed.

"If that's what you want," Taron said then placed a soft kiss on her nose. "While here at the falls, we're your slaves. Whatever you wish is our desire."

"Really?" she purred, her lips spreading into a mischievous grin that sent his heart racing.

"I think we're in trouble," Devlin replied with a chuckle.

Chapter Thirteen

ꟗ

"Well?" Vingosa asked Senator Marshe as he stepped into his Rhenari apartment just below the senate chambers on the one-hundred-and-sixty-fifth floor of the capitol building. "What did you find out?"

Senator Marshe stopped and stared at Vingosa in anger. He slammed the door then moved over to the window to shade the glass. "What the hell are you doing here, Vingosa? You know we can't be seen together."

"Relax, Marshe. No one saw me come in here."

Marshe huffed in agitation. "You can't know that for sure. Do you have any idea how much surveillance they have in this damn place?"

"Yes, Marshe. I know exactly how much is here. What did you find out about the investigation?"

Marshe sighed and moved to the black-and-glass bar that flanked the far wall. Grabbing a bottle of Earth whiskey, he pulled down two glasses. "Nothing. Damon doesn't trust me and won't tell me a damn thing."

"Where's my son, Taron?"

"Out shopping, according to Damon. Furniture for his new home, supposedly."

Vingosa snorted, his deep brown eyes narrowing in humor. "Somehow I doubt that. He's working, but where?"

"I couldn't get any info out of Damon. There's nothing in the senate mainframe, either. If he's undercover somewhere, it's an outside job. For all we know he could be on Veenori now."

Vingosa pinned Marshe with a dangerous stare and Marshe swallowed.

"Maybe, but even if he is he has no idea we're behind this." Vingosa strolled to the couch and sat, stretching one arm along the back.

"Are you sure about that? We were never able to find the information Anthony had on you. He could have sent it to Stefan."

"He sent it to his sister," Vingosa said, sipping at his whiskey.

"Who, may I remind you, we haven't been able to find." Marshe downed half his glass at once, wincing at the burn. "I'd be willing to bet the Marcones have her."

"They don't have her. She's on Veenori."

Marshe slammed the glass down on the counter. "She's where? And why wasn't I told?"

"She was sold as a slinoy to one of the overseers. Apparently she tried to infiltrate the mine and find her brother's killer. Little does she know she's looking in the wrong spot."

A small smile touched Vingosa's lips and Marshe inwardly shuddered at the evil that emanated from his gaze. This was one man he never wanted to be on the bad side of. "You find this amusing?"

"Yes. In a way. As long as she's there, she's no longer our problem. Besides, it'll be easy enough to take care of her when we blow the place."

"Blow the place?" Marshe asked in confusion.

"Yes. It's time to move on. It's too risky to stay there."

"But why blow it up?"

"Too many people there know too much. If we pull out and they no longer get paid, they'll be more inclined to talk. We take care of the problem before that happens. Mines cave in all the time," Vingosa said with a shrug, "easy enough, and no one asks questions."

Marshe swallowed his bile but kept his mouth shut. The last thing he wanted was to be left in the mine with everyone else they wanted to silence. But how long before Vingosa wanted to silence him?

* * * * *

Alyssa dove under the water, letting the cool liquid slide over her skin in soothing waves. It felt so good and she smiled as she burst through the surface. She brushed her hair back from her forehead and sighed. "I love it here."

"You look incredible. Like a water sprite," Taron said with a grin.

"I was thinking more along the lines of an Argonian water maid," Devlin added.

Taron nodded. "Oh, yeah."

"What the hell is a water maid?" she asked. Bending her knees, she sank below the water so that it rested just above her breasts. Taron and Devlin sat on the edge of the pool, their legs dangling in the water, their cocks hanging enticingly between their muscular thighs.

"It's similar to an Earth mermaid." Taron nodded toward her chest. "I don't know why you bother. We can still see them."

She glanced down at her breasts, just below the surface of the clear water, then shot them a sexy smile. "Maybe I'm trying to tease you," she purred.

"Maybe you need to be spanked," Taron purred back.

Devlin's lips formed a devilish grin that sent shivers of delight down her spine. "Now that would be a sight I'd love to see."

Taron nudged Devlin's shoulder. "You can help me. She enjoys being spanked, don't you, Lyssa?"

Alyssa's eyes narrowed at the two of them. Memories of the last time Taron spanked her ran through her mind and her nipples hardened in response. Okay. Maybe she did like being spanked. And just maybe the idea of being spanked by both of them at the same time was intriguing. So intriguing her body was already burning with renewed desire.

"The two of you wouldn't dare," she snapped, hoping to goad them into it.

Devlin raised his eyebrow at Taron. "Did she just challenge us?"

"I believe she did," Taron drawled in amusement.

"She's your slinoy." Devlin smirked as he waved his hand toward her. "You going to let her get away with that?"

"Absolutely not."

Alyssa began to back away, fighting the smile that tugged at her lips. This was going to be fun.

Both men jumped into the water and began to slowly stalk her toward the falls. The refreshing spray fell across her shoulders, cooling her exposed skin. With a squeal, she dove under the water and swam toward where the falls emptied into the pool.

A hand tugged at her ankle, pulling her back. She halfheartedly struggled against the hold before giving in completely. She and Taron broke through the surface at the bottom of the falls. She gulped for air, her hands shoving her wet hair from her face.

"You should know by now, slave. You can't challenge me and get away with it."

"What are you going to do, Master?" she purred playfully.

Devlin molded his body to her back, his hard cock pressing into her spine. She gasped and wiggled against him. Devlin groaned, his fingers biting into the flesh of her hip. "I think this woman definitely needs to be spanked."

She grinned and licked at Taron's lips. "Think you're man enough?"

Devlin's chest rumbled with his deep chuckle as Taron's eyes widened in surprise. "I think I've already shown you just how man enough I am, slave. But if you need a reminder, so be it."

With a growl, he bent and lifted her over his shoulder. She squealed, her legs kicking at the air as he trudged from the pool to the soft ground at the edge. His hand landed on her backside with a stinging slap and her whole body trembled in anticipation. The warm Veenori air hit her damp flesh, making her shiver despite the heat.

He set her on the ground then turned her to face Devlin. "On your knees, slave," he ordered.

Instantly she dropped to her knees, which put her eye level with Devlin's impressive erection. She smiled wickedly and reached out to run her finger down his length. His cock jerked and her grin widened. She loved the control she had over them. With a grin of his own, Devlin dropped to his knees as well.

"Bend forward," Taron ordered as his palm gently pushed between her shoulder blades.

She liked this side of him—the bossy, arrogant master, and every muscle in her body tensed with lust. Leaning forward, she rested a palm against the hard ground and with the other she massaged Devlin's firm balls, preparing to take him in her mouth. Taron went to his knees behind her, his hand softly rubbing across her hip. When the first slap hit she flinched but then sighed as a wave of pleasure surged through her veins. Her tongue flicked across the head of Devlin's cock, making him groan just as Taron slapped her other hip, heating her flesh.

Wrapping her hand around the base of Devlin's cock, she sucked him farther into her mouth. Behind her, Taron slid two fingers into her dripping pussy and she shoved her hips back, taking his fingers deeper. He went back and forth between fucking her with his fingers and slapping at her hips, and the combination nearly sent her over the edge.

Never in her life had she imagined she'd enjoy this kind of stuff. Spanking, ménage a trois, bondage. She'd loved it all and wanted to experience it over and over, but only with Taron. With him she knew she could explore her wild side without any shame or reservation.

Taron's fingers spread her juices along her labia , then moved to circle her engorged clit with gentle strokes. She moaned and moved with him, her teeth nipping at Devlin's cock.

"That's so hot, Alyssa," Taron groaned against her back as his lips nibbled along her spine. "Your sweet mouth engulfing Devlin's cock."

She moaned an answer, too far gone to say much of anything else. Devlin's fingers buried themselves in her hair, holding her head in place as he fucked her mouth. Her jaws ached from wrapping around his massive girth, but she didn't want to stop. She wanted to feel his cum spurting into her mouth and down her throat.

Taron rose up behind her and slid the length of his cock along her slit, teasing her. She groaned and moved her hips with him, desperate for the feel of his shaft thrusting into her, filling her to the womb. The fingers of her free hand dug into the dirt and she used the leverage to shove her hips into Taron's.

Finally, with a powerful thrust, he gave her what she wanted and plunged balls-deep into her tight passage. He growled deep in his chest and immediately began to move, pulling almost out then pushing back in hard. His balls slapped against her pussy as he fucked her over and over.

She sucked harder at Devlin's cock the closer she got to climax. Every muscle in her body quaked with the pleasure of her oncoming release. She clenched her muscles, clamping down on Taron's cock. The sound of his primal groan sent her soaring and convulsing as her body erupted into rapture. Just when she thought she couldn't take any more, Taron moved his hand around to toy with her clit.

She let go of Devlin's cock to scream as another, more powerful, orgasm gripped her. Determined to give them the same pleasure, she returned to Devlin's cock and sucked hard as her pussy continued to pulse and contract around Taron's cock. Their moans rose in unison and she inwardly smiled as they both found release at the same time—Taron filling her pussy while Devlin filled her throat. Her tongue lapped at his salty taste, getting every drop that escaped her mouth and slid down his cock.

"Damn," Devlin sighed. "I need to fucking sit down."

Alyssa giggled, pleased with herself and how well she'd done.

"The hell with sitting. I need a nap," Taron said.

Glancing over her shoulder, she grinned at Taron. Very slowly, she pulled away from him then pushed back, taking his still-hard cock deep into her body. She moaned and closed her eyes against the tingling sensation that spread down her legs.

"You're going to kill me, slave," Taron drawled. "Or is that what you had in mind all along? To fuck me to death?"

Alyssa laughed. "Somehow I doubt that anyone could fuck you to death."

"One more swim, then we need to head back," Devlin said, breaking the mood. "I have a bar to run."

"Rhia can take care of it," Taron said as he pulled from Alyssa's body and helped her to stand on shaky legs.

"I know she can, I just don't like for her to."

"Why on earth not?" Alyssa asked in exasperation.

Devlin shrugged, a tiny grin pulling at the corner of his lips. "I know she's capable. But I've been protecting her for so long it's hard to stop. I still see her as the tiny four-year-old who wouldn't let go of my leg all those years ago."

"You did a fabulous job with her. You should find a woman and get married. You would make an excellent father," Alyssa said with a smile, and she meant it. Devlin would make a great dad, there was just something about him that seemed fatherly. Maybe it was because of Rhia, or maybe it was just the way he was.

A sadness fell across Devlin's eyes and her smile faded. Had she said something wrong? She hadn't meant to upset him.

"I think my time for that has passed," Devlin said quietly.

"No it hasn't, Dev," Taron argued. "Skylar wasn't the only one for you. There's someone else out there."

"Maybe," he said as he stood and headed toward the water. "Are you swimming or not?"

Devlin didn't wait for an answer but dove straight under the water. Alyssa watched his lithe body skim along the bottom. "Who's Skylar?" she asked.

"A woman Devlin was deeply in love with. She was killed a few years ago. It happened right in front of him and he couldn't do anything to stop it."

"Oh, God," she sighed. No wonder he'd looked so sad. "I shouldn't have brought up having children and getting married."

"It's okay. He needs a good kick in the butt as far as I'm concerned."

"He must have really loved her."

"He did. And boy did he fight it."

Alyssa grinned and turned to stare at him. "Why did he fight it?"

"Well, Devlin is a big man," he said as he stared at her pointedly.

She shrugged with a frown. "Yeah, so?"

"So...Skylar was very small and delicate. Devlin's done some pretty nasty things in his life and for a long time he thought she was too good for him. As well as too small. But Skylar was pretty determined herself and one night she got Devlin a little buzzed and seduced him."

Laughter bubbled up in her chest. "She what? She got him drunk?"

"Yeah, well. He was almost drunk before she got there. I was in the office with him when she arrived. She sent me packing and made Devlin stay behind. I think Devlin kept drinking, thinking that if he got drunk enough he wouldn't be able to perform and there would be no danger. But it apparently didn't work out that way. According to Skylar, he had no problems performing and she loved every minute of it."

Alyssa covered her mouth with her hand to try and stifle the laughter. "Oh, gosh. I can't imagine Devlin drunk—or smitten, for that matter."

"He was. And when she was killed he tried to save her. That's where the scars came from. He took three rounds in the chest. One nicked his heart, another collapsed his lung. He almost died. It took Rhia demanding he not leave her to bring him back. But when he did, he wasn't whole. Part of his soul died with Skylar."

"That's terrible," Alyssa sighed as her gaze strayed to Devlin at the far side of the pool.

"Come on," Taron said as he pushed her toward the water. "Let's go swimming before he figures out we're talking about him and bites our heads off."

Chapter Fourteen

ꙮ

Taron stood at the side of the docking bay, breaking down guns then burying them among the minerals they'd mined earlier in the week. Off to the side, Morlak spoke softly to the other men. All night he'd been making his way around the room, acting the lord of the manor. Taron clenched his fist to keep from running over there and knocking the crap out of him.

He had to keep reminding himself that he needed to stay on Morlak's good side. He needed to know who was in charge, and the sooner the better. He wanted out of here.

As he worked, his mind wandered to Alyssa. She'd fallen asleep when they'd returned, as soon as her head hit the pillow. It was no wonder. He and Devlin had worked her pretty hard. Taron grinned as he remembered how well she'd responded to them. How beautiful she'd looked pleasing them.

"You look awfully pleased with yourself."

Taron stood straight and stared at Morlak with a narrowed gaze. He needed to keep his mind on his work. Morlak should have never been able to sneak up on him like that. "Just thinking about all the money I'm going to make."

Morlak chuckled. "I have some good news. You're finally going to meet the man in charge."

The gun in Taron's hand almost fell to the floor. Could he be this lucky? He raised an eyebrow. "Really?"

"Yes. He has special instructions for us and he specifically requested just you and I be here."

Taron raised an eyebrow. "Why just you and I?"

"Normally it's just me and I pass on the information, but I told them you would be taking over. I've had enough of mine life."

A frown creased Taron's brow. Apparently Morlak hadn't been doing this long enough to know you didn't just walk away. He was now a liability to them. He had a bad feeling in the pit of his stomach over this one.

"Think you can handle being in charge, Karmase?" Morlak asked, his lips twitching in a slight grin.

Taron snorted, making Morlak laugh. "I thought so. Be here bright and early. They like to meet while everyone is preoccupied with the running of the mine."

"I'll be here."

Hell yeah, I'll be here, and with any luck I'll finally find out who's behind this.

* * * * *

Slipping into his room as quietly as possible, Taron threw his shirt on the back of the chair and strolled softly into the bedroom. Alyssa was still asleep, her hair fanning out on the pillow beneath her. The blankets had been kicked free of her legs and he smiled, admiring the firm, tan thighs. She got hot at night and almost always kicked the covers free.

He quickly removed the rest of his clothes and climbed into bed beside her. She instinctively moved closer and snuggled next to him. "You're back," she whispered sleepily.

"Yes. Come here, *ni pahti*," he murmured and moved his arm so she could lay her head on his chest.

"I never got to tell you earlier what I wanted to tell you," she sighed as she shifted, trying to find a comfortable position.

"What did you want to tell me?" He sifted his fingers through her soft hair, then brought a strand to his nose, inhaling her flowery scent.

"I wanted to tell you why I was here."

"I know why you are here. You want to find your brother's killer."

Alyssa sat up with a start, her eyes wide in shock. "What? How did you know that?"

Sitting up, Taron placed a finger over her lips. "I know a lot of things. But we can't talk about this here. Tomorrow we'll go to Devlin's and I'll tell you everything. Okay?"

She eyed him warily before nodding her head.

"Good. Now let's lie back down and get some sleep."

"I can't sleep now," she sighed in exasperation as Taron fell to his back on the mattress.

He chuckled then grabbed her hand, pulling her down onto his chest. "Fine. Then instead of sleeping, I can make use of you in other ways."

Quick as a shot he rolled her to her back, pinning her beneath him. She squealed then glared up at him, her eyes spitting fire. "You're awfully presumptuous."

"No, I just know I'll eventually get what I want." He wiggled his eyebrows and the corner of her lips twitched, fighting a grin.

"And what might that be?"

He raised his eyebrow and pressed his hardening cock into her thigh. "Do you really need to ask?"

"Yes. And I really need you to tell me."

He smiled wickedly. "All right. I want your legs wrapped around my waist. I want your lips begging me to fuck you. I want you, Alyssa."

"Then what are you waiting for?" she murmured and pulled his lips down to hers.

*****

With a tired sigh, Stefan stared at his cup of coffee. The house was quiet, everyone asleep for the night, but sleep eluded him. He was too worried about his brother.

"I see you can't sleep either."

Glancing up, he noticed his father standing in the doorway of the kitchen. Damon looked just as haggard as Stefan felt. His shirt lay open, showing off a chest that was still as muscular as it had been thirty years ago, a waist that was just a trim. Even his hair was still long and thick. His father had aged well and Stefan hoped he would be just as lucky.

"No," Stefan sighed. "Want to join me for coffee?"

"Might as well. I'm not going to sleep anyway. I can't stop thinking about Marshe and Vingosa. We've got to find a way to connect them to all this. Otherwise we have nothing."

"I agree."

Damon sat down at the small table, his cup clanging against the tile as he set it before him. Sidious strolled through the door a second later. He stopped and stared at them in surprise, then snorted. "We're pathetic."

"Yeah and if we don't get some sleep we'll be useless," Stefan sighed.

Sidious leaned against the doorframe and crossed his arms over his chest. "Somehow I don't think coffee is going to help that situation."

"What would you suggest then, brother?" Stefan asked in amusement.

"Lots of strong alcohol and a good rousing fuck."

Damon choked on his coffee, making Stefan smile. "Well that's out for me. This pregnancy is wearing Krista out."

"Don't look to me to pick up the slack," Sidious replied dryly.

"I wouldn't touch your ass with a dirty stick, much less my cock," Stefan threw back, making Damon squeeze his temples, his shoulders shaking in silent laughter.

"Find something funny, Dad?" Stefan asked.

Damon raised his face and shook his head, his eyes still crinkling in amusement. "I was actually thinking about Sidious' suggestion of a rousing fuck. It's been a couple of days since—"

"Dad," Stefan grimaced and held up his hand. "Please spare me."

"What? You don't think your mother and I have sex?"

"You and Mom have sex?" Sidious gasped playfully.

Damon snorted. "Like you haven't walked in on us more than once."

"Oh, yeah. I remember. The image gave me nightmares for months."

Stefan chuckled and Damon narrowed his eyes at Sidious. "Very funny. You know your mother was right. The two of you are rotten."

"No man wants to think about his father doing to his mother what I do to... Well, you get the idea." Stefan raised his cup to take a sip of coffee.

"What's your problem? If your mother and I didn't have sex, then where did we get you?"

"I prefer to believe I was left on your doorstep by fairies," Stefan replied dryly, making Sidious chuckle.

"Immaculate conception," Sidious snickered. "I am, after all, the know-all, see-all of this family."

Stefan snorted. "You're the one that's most full of shit."

Damon shook his head, his eyes rolling toward the ceiling in amusement. "The two of you will never change."

A shrill beep filled the kitchen and Stefan glanced down at his pocket. "I forgot it was in there," he mumbled as he reached in to pull out his communicator. On the screen was a message to check his computer. "Looks like we may have some information."

"On what?" Sidious asked as he set his cup down on the table, his expression one of interest and dread.

"I'm not sure yet. It just says to check the computer."

"Well, then." Damon's chair legs scraped across the tile as he stood. "Let's check the computer."

The three of them made their way down the stretch of hall toward Sidious' study. Stefan immediately took the seat behind the desk, using his brother's computer to link to his own on Tilarus. It took the computer a few seconds to interface and he tapped his finger on the edge of the desk in impatience.

"Finally," he mumbled the second his password prompt showed up on the screen. Entering the six-letter code, he watched as the file downloaded.

"What is it, Stefan?" Damon asked as he stopped in his pacing.

Stefan frowned at the file as it opened. "It's from the men we had following Marshe."

Using a special lens, the photographers had been able to capture the images even through the tinting of the apartment glass. It was very clear who the two men in the apartment were and his heart lodged in his throat. It was exactly as they'd feared. Marsh was working with Vingosa, and they were pretty sure Vingosa was behind the arms deal.

Sidious came around behind Stefan. With one hand on the back of the chair, he leaned over to get closer. "Son of a bitch," he mumbled. "Is that who I think it is?"

"Looks like it." Stefan adjusted the picture, trying to zoom in on the man sitting down.

"Can we adjust the audio? Maybe we can hear what they're saying."

Stefan opened the audio portion and adjusted the sound, filtering out background and ship noise from outside. The man's voices came through loud and clear.

"She was sold as a slinoy to one of the overseers. Apparently, she tried to infiltrate the mine and find her brother's killer. Little does she know she's looking in the wrong spot."

"You find this amusing?"

"Yes. In a way," Vingosa replied. "As long as she's there, she's no longer our problem. Besides, it'll be easy enough to take care of her when we blow the place."

"Blow the place?" Marshe asked.

"Yes. It's time to move on. It's too risky to stay there."

"But why blow it up?"

"Too many people there know too much. If we pull out and they no longer get paid, they'll be more inclined to talk. We take care of the problem before that happens. Mines cave in all the time," Vingosa said with a shrug, "easy enough, and no one asks questions."

"This isn't good," Stefan sighed.

"If Vingosa sees Taron, he's a dead man. Get him the hell out of there, Stefan. Now!" Damon demanded in anger. "We have what we need. He doesn't need to be there anymore."

"I'll go," Sidious volunteered. "You need to stay here with Krista."

"What about the bomb?" Stefan asked.

"Surely between Devlin and I one of us can figure out how to diffuse it."

"It's been a long time since you've worked with bombs, Sidious. Are you sure about this?" Stefan asked, worry for his brother choking him.

"What choice do we have?"

Damon ran his hand through his hair, brushing it back from his forehead. "I'm going with you. Taron isn't going to take this well."

"Get your things together," Sidious said to his father as he headed out of the study as well. "Taron left the *Vultair* in orbit, we'll take her."

"You might want to take Anthony also. He'll want to be there for his sister."

Damon nodded and turned to leave. Stefan remained in the office, opening a channel to Devlin. He needed to let him know Sidious was on the way. At least now they had what they needed and could make arrangements to have Marshe and Vingosa picked up. The only other obstacle was getting everyone in the mines out alive.

* * * * *

Alyssa followed Rhia into Devlin's office early the next morning. She was anxious to know what Taron wanted to tell her but he'd had to stay at the mine that morning and finish up some things. He'd made her leave with Rhia, promising to meet her back at the bar shortly.

Ever since the night before, a feeling of dread had settled over her, although why she wasn't sure. Maybe it had been Taron's comment. Or maybe it was something else.

Coming through the door, she stopped dead in her tracks at the sight of the two tall, blond men standing beside Devlin's desk. They were gorgeous, and practically identical. Each had long platinum hair, with shoulders to die for and eyes the color of storm clouds. Both had trim waists and firm thighs and both stood with a commanding air that screamed authority.

On closer inspection, one was definitely older than the other, by a good thirty years. Were they father and son? They certainly looked enough alike.

Turning to the younger, she took a closer look. She knew him. "You're Lord Sidious Marcone. You were a captain in the militia that tried to invade Earth several years ago," she said and pointed at Sidious. "You're the man who fed the president all that secret information and the informant I've heard so much about."

A small grin tugged at his lips. "Guilty as charged." He nodded toward the older man. "This is my father, Damon."

She smiled at the older man as he bowed in her direction, his eyes sparkling with mischief. "It's good to see you're well, Alyssa. And Rhia," Damon stepped forward and kissed the grinning redhead on the cheek, "you look as gorgeous as ever. When are you going to take us up on our offer and move to Tilarus?"

"When you become available," she teased, making Damon laugh.

"I don't think that will happen anytime soon."

"How is Kaylar?" Rhia asked.

"She's well and waiting impatiently for Stefan's wife to finally have her twins."

Twins? Alyssa glanced at Damon, then back to Sidious.

"Alyssa, where's Taron? We thought he would be with you." Damon asked, suddenly turning serious.

"He was supposed to be, but he contacted Rhia at the last minute to come and get me. He had some things he needed to take care of before he came here," Alyssa said.

"We need to find him," Sidious murmured to Devlin.

Devlin nodded, then opened the screen to his computer. "Easy enough with the chip implant."

Chip implant? "Wait. What's going on?" Alyssa demanded. "What do you want with Taron?"

"It's a long story but we need to talk to him," Damon said.

"You're the family he spoke of." Her heart hammered in her chest as realization dawned. Taron had said his brother's wife was about to have twins. Surely not. Why would the son of a Tilarian count, even the adopted son, work at a mine? "Taron isn't who he says he is, is he?"

"No," Rhia whispered as she placed her hand on Alyssa's arm for support.

Alyssa didn't know whether to laugh or cry. He'd lied to her, but then she'd lied to him as well. Or not really lied, but only omitted stuff. But this... Taron was the son of a Tilarian monarch? What was he doing here? None of it made any sense.

With a shake of her head, she backed out of the room. "Alyssa," Rhia called out, but Alyssa held up her hand.

"I just need to be alone, please."

Without a backward glance, she left, heading to the roof for some air and alone time to think. As she walked out the bright sunlight made her squint and the heat scorched the top of her head and shoulders, but she ignored it. She needed the time alone to get her thoughts in order and try to make some sense of it all.

Shading her eyes, she stared toward the horizon and the dark mountains in the distance. What now? Who was Taron really and had she been a complete fool all this time? He was the youngest son of a count, which meant he carried the title of lord, just like Sidious. That alone made him so far out of her league that it wasn't even funny.

What a sick turn of events. Thank God she'd never told him she loved him. A warm blast blew her hair and she shielded her face against the hot air. A small speeder hovered just off the edge of the roof and she scowled at the pilot as he turned sideways to face her. She wasn't in the mood for another horny jerk thinking he could have his way with her. The man grinned nastily, sending a shiver of fear down her spine.

He was bald, just like Taron, and broad in the shoulders, with tanned skin that had seen years of sunlight. She couldn't tell his height for he was sitting but she would bet he was tall. His gaze raked over her and she cringed in distaste. There was something about him, something familiar about his eyes...

"So you're Alyssa," he purred in the same Norgosen accent Taron used. "You've been a real bitch to track down."

She frowned and began to back away from the edge and the hovering craft. "Excuse me?" The more she looked at him, the more she realized why he seemed familiar.

"Where do you think you're going?" he asked as he raised a small gun and pointed it directly at her.

She gasped, glancing around for somewhere to hide. Could she make a run for it? Just as she turned, a sharp prick hit her upper arm. She raised her hand to pull the dart free, then wobbled as a strong wave of dizziness overtook her and she fell to the tile roof in an unconscious heap.

* * * * *

Vingosa loaded the woman onto the speeder and, with a final glance to the roof, headed off in the direction of his ship, parked just outside the city. As they flew away, he studied her. Her black hair shielded her face, but it did nothing to hide the sexy body beneath the slave outfit.

"My son has good taste in women," he murmured as he brushed a stray lock from her brow. "It's a shame he isn't going to get any more time with you."

All the money he'd spent on informants had finally paid off. The day before he'd found out Taron's whereabouts. Right here on Veenori. And the topper had been finding out Taron had been the one to buy Alyssa. She'd come in handy later this morning when he confronted him.

Won't Taron be in for a surprise, he thought, his lips spreading into a nasty grin.

He couldn't wait to see the look on his face. It was time he finally got his annoying son off his back.

* * * * *

Taron strolled into the deserted docking bay, his gaze seeking out Morlak. He found him quickly, his beady eyes searching the horizon through the open bay door. Taron frowned as a sense of unease settled on his shoulders.

The loud sound of thrusters being thrown into reverse vibrated through the cavern. Taron watched a small ship fly into the bay then frowned at the markings on the side that indicated it was a diplomat's ship. Well, they'd thought it was someone in the senate. Looks like they were right. But who was it? And would they recognize him?

The side door opened with a swoosh and four men stepped out, each carrying a gun. Taron's features drew up into a scowl as he recognized the tall man making his way down the gangplank behind the four armed men.

Senator Marshe.

The weakling senator wasn't smart enough for this, there had to be others involved, and Taron's gaze continually strayed to the ship, searching for anyone else he might recognize. Slowly, he moved to the shadows, hoping Marshe wouldn't recognize him right away. At least until he had a strategy. Unfortunately, he was outnumbered four to one. He doubted he'd get any help from Morlak. If anything, Morlak would probably go against him.

His thumb rubbed across the back of his hand, feeling the hard implant just beneath the surface. Was there a way he could contact Devlin with the chip? Without hurting himself, of course?

"Hiding, Taron Karmase?" Marshe stepped past the four armed men and sneered in his direction. *Damn.* "Or should I say, Taron Sinnar?"

Taron shrugged. "Interesting seeing you here, Marshe. I know you're not smart enough to put something like this together. Who are you working for?"

"Taron Sinnar?" Morlak croaked. "I swear, Marshe, I had no idea."

Marshe snorted but Taron's gaze strayed to the man stepping from the ship and the woman he was shoving before him. *Oh God. Alyssa.* His heart contracted in his chest at the sight of her slightly disoriented steps, the long silver blade at her throat. Her frightened eyes met his and his gut clenched. How the hell was he going to get her out of this?

"Well, well, well," the man hiding behind Alyssa sneered. "If it isn't my son, the adopted lord of Tilarus."

Chapter Fifteen

ꟸ

Alyssa gasped, both at what the man had said as well as at the anguish and gut-wrenching fury contorting Taron's face.

"Vingosa," Taron growled through clenched teeth. "Why don't you stop being a coward and step out from behind the woman so I can wring your neck? I should have known you were fucking behind all this."

Vingosa snorted. "Is that any way to talk to your father?"

"You're not my father!" Taron snapped, the fury in his voice making Alyssa flinch. "You haven't been my father since the day you fucking walked out on us."

"You're his spitting image," Morlak whispered.

Taron glared at him and Morlak backed away, moving to stand flush with the rock wall behind him, his scaly face red in fear and anger.

"Let her go, Vingosa. This is between you and me. She has nothing to do with this," Taron demanded.

"She can identify me, Taron. I'm not a fool. I'm the reason she came here. I think it's only fitting she die by my hand, don't you? Just like her brother."

"Anthony isn't dead, Vingosa. So even if you kill us, there's still a witness who can put you away."

Alyssa gasped, her heart racing in her chest. Anthony was still alive? Was he telling the truth or was he just goading Vingosa?

"You're lying," Vingosa snarled.

"Am I?" Taron sneered. "You sure about that?"

Taron took a step forward and the tip of the steel blade bit into the flesh of her neck. She gasped at the sharp pain then held her breath, waiting to see what would happen. Taron paled, his eyes glued to the trail of warm blood that slid down her neck.

"No closer, Taron. Or I swear I'll slit her throat."

"What do you want?" Taron sneered, his hands fisting at his sides.

"Anthony's whereabouts."

"No," Alyssa whispered. "Taron, no."

"Why should I give you anything? We're dead anyway." Taron crossed his arms over his chest and glared menacingly at Vingosa.

"It will mean the difference between a slow death or a quick one."

"Fuck you," Taron snarled.

"Suit yourself." Vingosa shrugged and shoved Alyssa toward Taron.

She landed against his chest with an *oof*, then almost lost her balance as Taron grabbed her shoulders and forced her to the side. With a growl, he lunged toward Vingosa, but his father raised a gun and, in a move that shocked Alyssa, shot Taron just under the ribs.

"No," she screamed and ran toward him, catching him against her chest as he was thrown backward with a grunt.

She fell to the floor, Taron's heavy weight resting against her. Blood poured from his wound as she tried to maneuver from under him. He groaned and tried to sit up, but Alyssa shoved him back down and pressed her palm against the seeping wound.

"How could you?" she screamed. "He's your son."

"I'll find you, Vingosa. I swear it," Taron sneered angrily.

Vingosa laughed evilly and Alyssa stared at him in shock. *He's insane.*

"You won't make it out of here alive, *son*."

"What about me?" Morlak asked.

"What about you?" Vingosa sneered.

"I've been loyal to you. I've done everything you asked, and now you're just going to kill me?"

Vingosa pursed his lips in thought. "Looks that way, doesn't it?"

Pain sliced through Taron's stomach and lungs as he tried to stay conscious. His chip should notify Devlin that he'd been hurt and where he was, but how long would it take them to find him? He didn't have much time. His gaze strayed to a pale and angry Morlak.

"What the hell did you expect from a man who would shoot his own son, Morlak?" Taron asked dryly.

"My own son has been trying to put me away," Vingosa yelled. "Set the bombs. Let's rid ourselves of this mess then get the hell out of here."

Through blurred vision, Taron watched as two men set the bombs into the rock wall while Vingosa and Marshe boarded the ship. Morlak went down on his knees next to him. "Those bombs will wipe out every inch of the mine. Nothing will survive," he murmured as the men boarded Vingosa's ship.

"Can you tell what kind they are?" Taron asked weakly. "Maybe I can talk you through defusing them."

Morlak shook his head, his eyes straying sadly toward the massive hole in Taron's stomach then back to his gaze. His look said it all. They didn't have time for that. His wound would kill him long before they were finished with the bombs.

In silence they watched as Vingosa's ship left the cargo bay. Once outside, it turned and fired at the rock over the outside opening, causing a cave-in. The ground shook and Alyssa squealed and moved her body to protect Taron's as rock rained down on them, covering them in dust. The exit was now blocked by large boulders and debris.

"Son of a bitch," Morlak growled as he stared at the damage, waving his hands to dispel the dust.

Taron tried to sit up again, but Alyssa pushed him back down. "Alyssa, damn it. Stop," he growled around the sharp pain. He was too weak to fight her. Too far gone.

"No. You have to stay there. The more you move around, the more blood you'll lose."

"I'm a dead man anyway, *ni pahti*. I've got to try and defuse those bombs."

Her eyes widened in fear and sadness as she shook her head. "Tell me how."

He smiled slightly and touched the side of her face with his hand. His blood-soaked fingers left black blotches on her cheeks and he pulled his hand away, staring at it with a frown.

"Please tell me you're different than people from Earth and that black blood on your hand is normal and you're not bleeding from your liver," she whispered, her voice shaking with unshed tears.

He squeezed his eyes closed and blew out a harsh, gurgling breath. No. Black blood meant he'd been hit in the liver. He tried to clear the fog, the ever-growing fatigue. He didn't know how much time they had left. "Listen to me, Lyssa. You've got to get out of here. Go with Morlak and warn the others."

She shook her head, tears streaming down her face. "No. I won't leave you."

Breathing had become difficult and a coldness had seeped into his bones. He was so tired, so weak. He raised a shaking finger and pointed toward the rock wall. He didn't have the strength to defuse anything. Their only chance was to make a run for it. "There's a secret passage just behind you in the rock. You and Morlak go through that passage and get to the other side as quick as you can. Understand?"

"No," she snapped stubbornly, her head shaking firmly.

"Alyssa, please," Taron sighed.

"No. Damn it, Taron. I'm not leaving without you. So just suck it up and help me get you standing."

Taron shook his head, his eyes drifting closed. Morlak grabbed her hand, holding it still over his chest and slowly beating heart. "Feel his heart, Alyssa. He wouldn't survive it."

She choked on a sob and slapped at his chest. "Damn you, Taron. How could you do this to me?"

"Do what, *ni pahti*?"

"Make me fall in love with you, then leave me," she cried.

His lips spread into a slow smile and warmth spread through his chest. He could die a happy man. Alyssa loved him. "I love you, Alyssa," he whispered and lifted her fingers to his lips to kiss them. Her hands were so warm in comparison to his.

She hiccupped and leaned down to place a soft kiss on his lips. She smelled of jerrywine and he smiled. Turning his gaze, he narrowed his eyes at Morlak. He didn't have a choice. He had to trust him. "Get her out of here, Morlak. Go to Devlin and testify against Vingosa. Make him pay for this."

Morlak nodded. "You can be sure of that, Taron. I'll see the *vigic* rot in hell. Mark my words. The son of a bitch isn't going to double-cross me and get away with it."

Taron's eyes slipped closed and he felt his body slip away and fall toward a deep sleep. "I'll always be with you, Lyssa," he sighed.

Alyssa watched the slow rise and fall of his chest dwindle to practically nothing and her heart felt as though it had been ripped from her chest. In just a few short weeks, he'd become her everything and now she'd lost him. Her shoulders shook with sobs as he slowly slipped away from her.

"We must go, Alyssa," Morlak pleaded as he tugged at her elbow, trying to force her to stand, but she fought against him. She couldn't leave Taron.

A loud rumble from outside made her jump, and she jerked her head up to look toward the now closed-off exit. Another rumble shook the cavern and she braced her hand against the ground, trying to steady herself. Her gaze flicked to Morlak's in fear. "Now what?"

He shook his head. "It sounds like a ship."

"Are they coming back?"

A loud explosion made her scream and she ducked her head against Taron's chest as debris and rock flew around them. Pebbles nicked her shoulders, making her flinch as the sharp shards pierced her flesh. Once the dust had settled, she and Morlak turned to stare at the small ship that hovered just a few feet above the ground before settling amidst the debris.

"Who the hell is that?" Morlak asked. "I don't recognize the ship. Do you?"

She shook her head with a frown, but let out a sigh of relief the second she saw Devlin as he stepped from the ship. "Devlin," she screamed and waved her hand through the dust. "We're here. Hurry, Taron's hurt."

Devlin ran toward her, Damon and Sidious directly behind him, their faces drawn with worry. "What happened?" Devlin demanded as he dropped to his knees next to them.

"He shot him."

"Who shot him?" Sidious demanded.

"His father, Vingosa," she whispered in anguish. "Please don't let him die."

"Sidious?" Damon asked as he knelt beside him. Sidious ran a medi-scanner slowly up Taron's body, his eyes studying the screen carefully.

"It's bad," Sidious whispered.

"What about the bombs?" Morlak asked while wringing his hands. "We don't know how much time is left."

"Where are they?" Sidious snapped.

Morlak raised his hand and pointed toward the bombs that had been embedded in the rock behind them. "There."

"*Shetah*," Sidious growled. "Dad, get Taron to the ship and put him in stasis while Devlin and I try to defuse these things." He stood and glanced toward Morlak. "Are these it?"

"That I know of," Morlak said with a nod.

Damon placed his hand on Taron's chest then glanced up at Alyssa. "Put your hand on his chest as well, sweetheart."

She swallowed a bit of fear and placed a shaking hand over Damon's. "Have you ever transported before?" he asked.

She nodded. "Once."

He returned her nod and hit the red button on his transport device. She tried to relax but pain laced through her anyway, making her moan. Damon's hand twisted to squeeze hers in support and her heart warmed toward the older man.

Once the transport was finished Damon lifted Taron in his arms easily—for a man of his age—and laid him on the metal table in the center of the brightly lit room. She couldn't take her gaze off Taron long enough to study her surroundings. Maybe once he was better. "Can they help him?" she asked.

Damon glanced at her through his lashes as he shot medicine into Taron's neck with an injector gun. "We're going to do everything we can, Alyssa. Right now I'm putting him in stasis. Sidious was trained as a medic when he was in the militia. When he returns from the caves he'll work on him."

"Stasis?" she asked, her hand softly rubbing the top of Taron's head, wiping away the black dust that had settled on his skin. "You're freezing his body?"

"In a way. He's in a coma. His body functions have all but ceased temporarily. It'll help keep him alive a little while longer, but we can't keep him in stasis for long. There's a time limit."

"What's the time limit?"

"Two hours."

Alyssa swallowed her sob, praying they could fix him before time ran out and he died.

"Lyssa?"

The whispered name coming from behind her made her freeze, her heart racing in her chest. Was she hearing things? Slowly, she turned and stared in shock at Anthony. Taron had said he was still alive, but she hadn't expected to see him standing in front of her. Shaking hands flew to her mouth and covered the choked sob that left her throat.

"Anthony?" she sobbed, then ran toward him, throwing herself into her older brother's outstretched arms. "Oh, God. You're really alive. How did it happen?"

"We'll talk about that later," he whispered as his arms tightened around her back.

The sobs broke in earnest and she cried against his shoulder. "I can't lose him, Tony. I just can't. I love him so much."

"I know," he whispered. "I know."

Anthony led her from the room and down the hall to another one. It had a large table with a massive row of windows that overlooked the planet below them. It was beige in color, like sand, and she knew without even having to ask it was Veenori.

Sitting down at the table, she stared blankly at the coffee Anthony set before her. She just wasn't interested. She wouldn't be until she heard how Taron was.

"Are you okay, Sis?"

She glanced up at her older brother and gave him a halfhearted smile. He appeared older than the last time she'd seen him, even his hair had a little more gray. There was a long, nasty scar across his throat that made her flinch. Had Vingosa tried to slit his throat? Had he done to her brother what he'd threatened to do to her? She reached out and traced it with the tip of her finger. "Vingosa did this?" she whispered.

"Yes," he said with a nod.

"How did you survive?"

"I was lucky. Stefan found me before I lost all of my blood. He apparently didn't go deep enough."

She noticed the scratchy sound to his normally deep voice and realized the cut had apparently gone deep enough to damage his vocal cords slightly. Anthony's gaze strayed to the shallow cut that ran across her neck. Standing, he walked to the replicator and asked for a damp cloth. Once it appeared, he returned to her side and wiped at her neck, removing the dried blood.

"Who did this to you?" he asked, a muscle in his cheek jerking.

"Vingosa. He's Taron's father," she whispered, her eyes once again filling with tears. "How could he shoot his own son, Anthony? What kind of man is he?"

Anthony sighed and tossed the cloth back to the table. "I don't know, Alyssa."

"You knew?"

"Yeah. Damon and Sidious told me on the way here. I know that Vingosa didn't raise Taron, but are you sure about him, Alyssa?" His worried gaze met hers. "How do you know Taron won't turn out just like him?"

She frowned. "He's not like him, Tony. Taron's a good man. He's kind and gentle and—"

"And he took advantage of his position as your slinoy master," Anthony snarled. "Didn't he?"

"He didn't do anything I didn't want him to do," she snapped.

Anthony stood and strolled to the window, his gaze staring thoughtfully toward the stars. For several minutes he didn't say anything, just stared ahead. She knew her brother well enough to know he needed time, so she wouldn't push him. He'd say something when he was ready.

Finally, when she was about to scream and rail at the too-silent room, he spoke. "I trust your judgment, Alyssa. If you love him he can't be all that bad, I suppose."

He threw her a grin over his shoulder and she smiled back at him, her shoulders sagging in relief. She would have hated it if Anthony really and truly disliked Taron. But if he didn't survive it was all a moot point anyway. Just thinking about living her life without him made tears well up in her eyes.

The door opened, allowing Damon inside, and he dropped into a chair next to Alyssa. His lips were clenched tight, his eyes narrowed and dark in fury. "I had to get out for a while. That shot really messed him up inside," he sighed. "Devlin said he'd come get us when they're done. What happened on the surface, Alyssa? How did Taron get shot and what the hell were you doing there?"

Alyssa recounted the events as best she could. When finished with her story, she glanced questioningly at Damon. "Did they defuse the bombs?"

"Yes and Morlak is onboard. Devlin has him locked in one of the rooms. He'll come in handy when we find Vingosa."

"If we find him," Anthony sighed.

"Not if…when," Damon said with a slight grin. "I didn't raise stupid children. The men Stefan hired to follow Senator Marshe put tracking devices on all his ships, as well as the one they knew to be Vingosa's. We're tracking them as we speak. It's only a matter of time before we find them. They think they've won. They'll be lax for a while." He raised his hands and rubbed at his forehead. "I just wish we'd gotten to Veenori a little sooner."

She placed her hand on his arm and gave him a reassuring squeeze. "He'll make it, I know he will."

Damon put his hand over hers and one corner of his mouth lifted in a wry smile.

With a sigh, he spoke. "I hate to ask this now, but where's the evidence your brother sent you?"

"Do you think you'll need it?"

"Yes. With what Anthony sent you and everything we have, it should be enough to keep Vingosa locked away for a very long time."

She nodded. "Good. It's in a safety deposit box on Earth."

"Once all this is over, we'll get it," Damon said.

"You're more than welcome to it. I would say I wish I'd never seen the stuff, but if I hadn't…" She turned to her brother with a trembling grin. "I wouldn't have met Taron."

Damon squeezed her hand and the warmth of his touch seeped into her cold fingers, and she rested her head on his broad shoulder. The three of them waited silently for news of Taron.

Chapter Sixteen

ꟃ

The door opened with another *whoosh* and they all turned to stare at a haggard Sidious. Damon stood, his worried gaze locked onto Sidious. "Well?" he demanded.

Sidious leaned against the side of the door. "He should be fine. He's still under so the lovar serum I gave him can work quicker."

"Good," Damon said with a sigh of relief.

Alyssa let out a breath she hadn't realized she was holding and almost sank to the floor. He would be all right. With a smile, she placed her hand over her heart and shifted to gaze at Anthony, behind her. His hand had rested on her shoulder, giving her his silent support, from the moment Sidious had walked into the room.

"What's lovar serum?" Alyssa asked.

"It's a medicine that will help his injuries heal and make his blood multiply three times faster than normal. He lost a lot of it," Sidious replied.

"Can I see him?"

"Yes. He's down the hall, third door on the left."

"Thanks," she whispered and placed her hand on his arm as she walked by.

Sidious turned back to his father and didn't miss the murderous rage in his eyes.

"I want Vingosa," Damon snarled.

"Not as much as I do. Devlin is communicating with the men we have following him. He's on Korlatis."

Damon's eyebrow rose. "That's on the Eastern Rim. How long will it take us to get there?"

Sidious sighed and pushed away from the frame. "Even with the use of the gate, it will take us about twenty hours, give or take."

"Then let's get going." Damon left the room and headed toward the bridge at a brisk pace. "Tell Devlin to have the men notify us if he leaves. I don't want that son of a bitch getting away this time."

* * * * *

Taron opened his eyes slowly and tried to focus his gaze on the dark room. Shapes were fuzzy and he blinked twice, trying to clear his vision. *Where am I*? he wondered with a frown. *Whatever the hell I drank last night sure did a number on me.*

His mouth was parched and he licked his lips with a grimace before trying to sit up. The second he did he regretted it as pain sliced through his abdomen. He fell back to the bed with a growl as images ran through his mind of the last twenty-four hours.

He'd been shot, by his own father of all people. He shouldn't be surprised. Vingosa had made it clear since as far back as he could remember that he'd never wanted a child.

With a sigh, he took another look around the room. His vision was getting better and he was able to make out a couple of pieces around him. The antique sailing ship on the dresser caught his eye and he realized immediately where he was. He was on the *Vultair,* in his own quarters.

How the hell did I get here?

It had to have been Devlin, but was Alyssa okay as well? Bracing himself, he tried one more time to sit up. Pain again sliced through his stomach and he gritted his teeth, determined to not lie in the bed another minute. He had to find out where Alyssa was.

Finally upright, he slung his legs over the side and took a deep breath. His hand shook slightly as he inspected the light pink scar across his midsection. It was healing quickly, but he knew from experience the pain would remain for at least a day longer.

"What are you doing?"

Taron glanced over his shoulder and caught Alyssa glaring at him. He relaxed in relief. "I was wondering where you were. Are you all right?" he asked.

"Much better than you," she snapped as she made her way over to his side. "You shouldn't be up. Sidious said you should stay in bed at least another three hours."

Taron snorted. "Sidious isn't here. Besides, he's known to be extremely overprotective."

She crossed her arms over her chest and narrowed her eyes adorably. His Alyssa was quite the spitfire and he loved it. She would certainly never be dull.

"All it takes is for me to push that button on your end table to have him running in here, Damon right behind him, and you know it. Is that what you want?"

Taron cringed. "Damon is here too?" he groaned.

"Yep. As well as Devlin, Rhia and Anthony."

"Oh God," Taron sighed as he remembered the trouble he'd had keeping Devlin in his recovery bed. He was sure it was payback time. His life would be hell for the next week.

"It's not that bad is it?" Alyssa sent him an amused grin. Amazingly, just looking at her sent his blood pounding through his ears.

"You have no idea," he groaned, making her giggle. He glanced up at her with a cheeky grin. "Did I hear you say in the mine that you were in love with me?"

Her cheeks turned red instantly and she stammered. "I um…I don't remember."

"You're a lousy liar, Alyssa. You always were. Just admit it."

"Okay," she drawled playfully. "I'm a lousy liar, I admit it."

Taron laughed and tugged at her hand, pulling her down on her knees before him. "That's not what I wanted you to admit, minx, and you know it."

Her beautiful features morphed into a scowl. "You are such an ass."

"Come on," he whispered against her lips. "Admit it."

She placed her small hand against his cheek, warming his cold flesh. He'd apparently lost a lot of blood, but the warmth shining in her eyes was all the heat he would need.

"I'm in love with you," she sighed, then her lips quirked into a tiny smile.

He smiled and placed his forehead against hers. "I love you too, my feisty little slave."

The soft sound of the door opening made Alyssa pull away from him, her cheeks blushing adorably.

"Not even fully recovered and already he's trying to seduce a woman," Sidious snickered.

Taron sighed and sat upright, sending his brother a halfhearted scowl. "You're one to talk."

Damon, Anthony, Rhia and Devlin strolled in behind Sidious. "How are you feeling, Taron?" Damon asked, his expression one of fatherly worry. *This* man was his father, not Vingosa.

"Like I've been shot," Taron joked. "And I'm cold."

Alyssa wrapped a soft Tilarian fur blanket around his shoulders. He smiled at her over his shoulder. "Thank you, Lyssa." He didn't miss the slight frown Anthony sent his way at the use of her shortened name. Alyssa had told him some time ago that Anthony had been the one to start that. He'd have to talk to him later and let him know he loved his sister and would never do anything to hurt her.

"You lost a lot of blood." Sidious sat in the chair flanking the fireplace. It was a silly thing to have on a ship, but something he'd wanted. For almost six years during the rebellion this ship had been his home and he'd wanted it to be as much like home as possible. He'd included a holographic image inducer that made it look like an actual fire burned within the grate. The thing even produced heat. "Your body is still trying to recoup its losses."

"I wish it would hurry the hell up," Taron growled.

"You also took a massive hit to the liver. The bullet pretty much obliterated it. The lovar serum should help it to regrow but it will take time, so stay away from Sidious' brandy stash until he gives you the okay," Damon ordered.

"Yes, Dad," Taron drawled, but the sudden spark of surprise in Damon's gaze caught him off guard. Surely Damon knew how he felt about him. Didn't he?

"I hope you know this is payback time," Devlin said with a grin. "It's time I repaid you for all that crap I took from you when I was injured."

Taron cringed. "I knew that would come back and bite me in the ass one day." He glanced around at the smiling men and Rhia. As much as he enjoyed the ribbing, he wanted some answers. "Where's Vingosa?"

"We're on our way to get him now," Sidious said, his expression turning serious. "We should be arriving at Korlatis within a couple of hours."

"Good. I want to be the one who arrests him."

"Taron," Damon cautioned, "you're not well enough for that..."

"I don't care," he snapped. "The son of a bitch is mine, Damon."

Damon nodded but said nothing more. Taron was sure the battle wasn't over yet.

*****

"Taron?" Sidious asked quietly. "Are you sure you want to do this?"

Taron narrowed his eyes at Sidious, who raised his hands in surrender. "All right. Just asking."

Closing the last button on his shirt, he turned to grab a small gun from Devlin. Most of the pain had subsided, but some still remained, making it hard for him to move with ease. He refused to let a little bit of discomfort keep him from seeing this through. He'd been after Vingosa for years and he was now finally in his grasp. He wasn't about to let him go.

With one final check of the gun's charge level, he placed it in the holder at his ribs. Raising his head, he met Alyssa's worried gray gaze. She hadn't told him not to go. She'd supported his need to do this himself, despite the anxiety evident in her eyes.

Walking over, he cupped her cheek and brushed his thumb along her soft skin. "Be here when I get back?" he asked with a grin.

A gentle smile softened her features as she leaned into his touch. "Of course, I will," she whispered.

"I love you," he mouthed silently.

"I love you," she mouthed back and moved out of the way so he could activate the transport device.

He planned on transporting directly into Vingosa's apartment. According to the scans he was alone. Armed militia soldiers waited for the word to apprehend his father, but Taron wanted time alone with him first. He had some things to say to the son of a bitch. With one final glance toward Alyssa, he winked then nodded toward Devlin to activate the transport.

Alyssa watched Taron disappear with a heavy heart. He still wasn't healed. What if there was a fight or Vingosa tried to shoot him again? Out of the corner of her eye she noticed a commotion and turned to see what was going on.

Damon stood where Taron had been, checking the bullets in his gun. He preferred the ones that actually shot rounds as opposed to the phaser-type gun that Taron used, which shot a laser capable of burning a hole through someone's midsection.

"Have the soldiers meet me at the back entrance," Damon commanded Sidious.

"Taron will have your head," Sidious said with a slight grin.

"I don't care. I'll be damned if I'll sit back and let that *vigic* try to kill him again. Besides," he added with a sigh, "I don't want Taron to have to live with killing his own father. You know as well as I do Vingosa isn't going to go willingly."

Sidious nodded and activated the transport. Damon faded into a fog then disappeared completely.

Anthony moved behind her and wrapped his arms around her shoulders. She leaned into his warm and comforting embrace, silently praying Taron would make it back in one piece.

"He'll be fine, Lyssa," Anthony whispered. "From what I hear, he's a tough guy."

"I know," she sighed, and deep in her heart she prayed she was right.

* * * * *

Taron transported to the living quarters of Vingosa's apartment and immediately tensed, his gaze scanning the small room. The bamboo poles and thatched roof were typical for the tropical planet of Korlatis. The green waters of Milokis Lake lapped against the deck surrounding the small cabin nestled on the shore. Warm, flower-scented breezes blew through the open glass doors and ruffled the curtains that flanked the entrance.

His gaze narrowed at the cozy, rustic home. It looked more like a romantic hideaway he would take Alyssa to than a place his father would inhabit. The bamboo and linen furniture didn't suit Vingosa's more opulent taste, but then maybe that's why he'd chosen it. The place and atmosphere were so out of the norm for him it would be the last place anyone would look.

A loud bang sounded from behind him and he spun around, searching for the cause. A set of French doors stood partially open. Through the slit he could see his father throwing things into a small case, his movements unhurried, as though he didn't have a care in the world.

Inside, Taron seethed. What had his mother seen in this man? On top of that, how could a man shoot his own child? But then, wasn't he about to do something just as monstrous? He was perfectly willing to shoot Vingosa. Did that make him just as bad or did the situation warrant his actions? After all, Vingosa was a criminal. One of the most highly sought after in the galaxy.

Taking a deep breath, he decided it didn't matter. Vingosa would do his time and if he wouldn't go willingly he'd go in a box. He put his hands against the doors and silently pushed them wide.

"Surprise," Taron drawled, and felt immense satisfaction as his father stiffened before turning to face him. "Bet you didn't expect to see me again, did you, *Dad*?"

Vingosa's lip curled into a nasty sneer. "You're like a damn cat. Aren't you down to your last life yet?"

Nausea rolled Taron's stomach but he refused to let this man get to him. "Not yet, but it's not for your lack of trying."

"I'll have to work on my aim."

"You'll have plenty of time for that during your stay on Dellon Five."

Vingosa's eyes narrowed and glowed amber with anger and just a hint of fear. "I refuse. You'll have to kill me first." His lips spread into a nasty grin as he turned to drop the lid off the box. The loud bang of metal hitting metal reverberated through the room like the final nail in a coffin. "If you can do it."

"Oh, have no doubt, Vingosa. I'll do it," Taron snarled.

"You're too much like your mother. You don't have the stomach to actually kill your father."

"Like you have the stomach to kill your son?"

"I do what I have to do to survive. It's something your mother couldn't do. She had morals. A conscience."

Taron stared at the older man with murder in his eyes. He refused to think of him as his father. He was just a sick man who needed to be put in his place. "My mother was a good woman, which makes me wonder what the hell she ever saw in you."

Vingosa smiled at him over his shoulder and a shiver of apprehension snaked down Taron's spine. "Maybe I was just that good in bed."

Taron raised his gun and pointed it at Vingosa's chest. The need to shoot almost choked him in its intensity. "That's enough, Vingosa. Let's go."

Vingosa snorted and turned back to lift the box in his hands before turning to face him head-on. "I told you already. I'm not going to Dellon Five. You'll have to shoot me."

"Fine," he snarled and tightened his finger on the trigger.

Chapter Seventeen

ꟃ

Taron stiffened as a shot was fired from outside, shattering the glass of the French doors leading to the outside deck. The bullet lodged in Vingosa's knee, splattering blood and bone fragments along the light blue tile. He dropped to the floor with a yell, his hands grabbing his leg. The metal box landed on the tile with a clang, spilling its contents around Taron's feet.

In confusion, Taron searched the deck outside the glass doors, his gun still poised to fire at the intruder. A tall, broad figure stepped through the door, the sun behind him keeping his body in shadow, but Taron knew who it was.

"Damon, what the hell are you doing here?" Taron snapped.

Damon didn't answer. Instead he stepped toward Vingosa, who desperately tried to reach an antique bronze letter opener that dangled from the corner of his desk. The toe of Damon's boot pressed down on Vingosa's knee, making him scream in agony before stopping his pursuit of the weapon.

"I think he's ready for Dellon Five, gentleman," Damon said over his shoulder to the two men standing behind him. Turning, he grinned down at Vingosa. "You really didn't think you were getting off that easy, did you, Vingosa? There's no way I would let you miss out on the exquisite accommodations at Dellon. You'll have your very own underground cell with a view of the popular lava flows. Should keep your room a very comfortable temperature—just below hellish."

Vingosa snarled up at Damon, his eyes narrowed in anger and pain. "I'll get you, Damon. I swear it."

Damon harrumphed, then the corner of his mouth lifted into a slight grin. "Somehow I doubt it. But please, feel free to give it your best shot."

Taron watched in stunned silence as Damon pushed down on Vingosa's knee one final time, eliciting a growl of agony from the man practically writhing on the floor. Despite how angry he was, Taron cringed at the thought of how much anguish that pressure against the wound had caused. The two soldiers moved forward and bound Vingosa's hands behind his back then helped him to stand.

"Vingosa," Damon began, "you're under arrest for treason and numerous counts of attempted murder. Get him the hell out of here."

"Yes, sir," the soldier said before hitting a transport button and disappearing.

"You're letting them take him alone? Aren't you afraid he'll get away?" Taron asked as he squatted down to pick up a piece of paper by his foot.

"Sidious and Devlin are going with them. They'll make sure he's settled."

Taron nodded, his gaze scanning the page in his hand. It was a list of names and contact information, even monetary amounts listed by each name that Taron could only assume meant how much money they'd put toward the cause.

Unbelievable, Taron thought with a sigh.

"Taron," Damon spoke quietly.

Taron looked up at the man he'd considered a father in aggravation. "Why, Damon?"

With a sigh, Damon leaned back against the desk and crossed his arms. "I didn't want you to have to do it."

"I had the right. Look at everything he's done to me in the past. What he did to my mother!" Taron snapped.

"You would have regretted it later. Despite everything he's done, he's still your father."

"The hell I would have!" he argued, although deep down he knew Damon was right.

In anger, Taron turned and walked out onto the deck, his gaze scanning the light blue horizon. A small boat could be seen in the distance, its sail unfurled to catch the wind. He felt Damon's presence behind him, but Damon didn't speak, just did as he always did—let him know he was there for him if he needed him.

"What did my mother ever see in him?" he asked softly.

Damon placed a hand on his shoulder and gently squeezed. "Don't be angry with your mother, Taron. Love is blind. It's a fact of life. Look at me, for instance. I fell in love with a woman who was forbidden."

"But Kaylar isn't a criminal," Taron sighed.

"No. In my world she was something much worse. A commoner," Damon said with a grin, making Taron's lips twitch despite his anger. "Vingosa wasn't a criminal when your mother met him. And to his credit, he did try for a while to be the man your mother wanted him to be." Damon shrugged. "He just wasn't the father and husband type. There was always something evil about him, something wild."

"How do I know that wild side won't come out in me?"

"There's no chance of that. You may have his looks, but in every other way, every way that counts, you are your mother. You have her compassion and heart, Taron. Never doubt that."

Taron nodded, but kept his gaze on the horizon.

"Come on, son. Let's gather up all these papers then go home," Damon said quietly.

"Home," Taron sighed. It seemed like forever since he'd been home and he was anxious to get back.

"Mikayla and Stefan have a surprise for you."

Taron turned to his father with a raised eyebrow. "A surprise? A surprise is not always a good thing when it involves Stefan."

Damon laughed. "Trust me. This is a good one. They finished your house."

"Furniture and all?" he asked with hope.

"Furniture and all," Damon replied with a nod, his lips spreading into a grin.

"Hot damn, no shopping," Taron said, making Damon chuckle.

"So," Damon started as he bent at the waist to pick up several pieces of paper to be sorted through later, "will this house have a mistress?"

Taron's body relaxed and he smiled the first real smile in hours. Just thinking about Alyssa made him forget everything else. "I think so," he answered, his smile widening at the thought of being an old married man like the rest of the men in his family. And if he knew Alyssa, married life with her would be anything but dull.

*****

Alyssa stuck her head in the nursery door and smiled. Taron sat in the chair holding Krista's tiny baby, Jacquelyn, whom he had lovingly nicknamed Jack, much to her mother's chagrin. Krista had quickly given in, saying no one but Taron could call her daughter Jack.

Over the last few days she'd realized just how close this family was. How willing they were to open their hearts and homes to people they considered friends. Even Devlin and Rhia were treated like part of the family while they were here. Anthony fit in quite well also, and had even been offered a job on Tilarus as a pilot for the many monarchs who called the small planet home.

She would have it all—a man she loved as her husband and her brother close by. Anthony had warmed up to Taron and the two now acted like close friends, teasing each other mercilessly. It was such a relief that the two men she loved most in the world got along.

There had been a tense few moments at first, but Taron had pulled Anthony aside and spoken to him quietly. Neither had told her what was said, but whatever it was, it had done the trick. The ice had been broken and things had gone smoothly from then on.

As quietly as possible, Alyssa strolled over and knelt by the chair. It was so amazing how someone so tiny could turn someone so large into a puddle of cooing fluff. Taron was an amazing uncle. The second he'd walked into the door Sidious' oldest son had come screaming through the house and thrown himself into his uncle's outstretched arms. Most of his first day back had been spent playing with the boys, wresting and taking them for rides on his hovercycle.

The baby sneezed and scrunched her nose in the most adorable manner, making Alyssa smile and dream of having a baby of her own.

"She's beautiful, isn't she?" she whispered.

The tiny child wrapped her fist around Taron's large finger, her eyes drifting closed as she fell back asleep. Jack's brother Jonah was sleeping soundly in the bed close by. It figured the girl would be the hardheaded one and not want to go to sleep.

"Yeah," he whispered. "She's gonna be a looker. Krista and Stefan both seemed exhausted so I told them I'd handle this shift. It's been a rough couple of days for Krista."

"Stefan too." Alyssa rubbed her finger down the soft skin of the baby's arm. "He's been right there with her. They take turns, one taking Jonah while the other takes Jacquelyn, then they switch. Kaylar and Damon got them last night so Krista and Stefan could get some sleep."

Taron grinned. "I sent them down to the lake so they could relax."

"You just wanted to cuddle Jack," she teased.

"Well, that too." He sighed and placed a soft kiss on the baby's forehead. She drew in a deep breath and her lips quivered as though sucking at a bottle, making Taron smile. "I want lots of these, Lyssa."

"Girls?" she asked with a grin.

"Babies. I don't care which."

His expression sobered as he watched the sleeping baby and Alyssa placed a hand on his forearm, feeling the muscles twitch beneath her touch. She knew what was worrying him.

"You're not like him, Taron. You're like Damon and you're going to make a wonderful father, just like the man who raised you."

A small smile touched his lips as he looked down at her. "I had kept the name Sinnar even after Damon adopted me, for my mother. But now..." He sighed and rubbed his thumb across Jack's fist, soothing her. "I can remember as a child, even when Vingosa was around, Damon was more a father to me than Vingosa was. Damon was always there for me. Everything I learned, I learned from him." Jack sucked at her bottom lip, making Taron grin. "I've decided I'm taking the Marcone name and the title Damon offered to me at the adoption. Think you can tolerate being called Lady Alyssa?"

She glanced up at him, startled. *Lady* Alyssa? "I never gave it much thought. Will our children be titled as well?"

"No," Taron said with a shake of his head. "Only the children of counts are titled. The title of "Lord" will not pass down."

"So Jack will be Lady Jack and Jonah will be Lord Jonah, since their father is a count?"

"Yes. This one will be special, though. Twins are rare, and having a girl with the first pregnancy is even more so among the Tilarans." His deep brown gaze locked onto hers and the pounding of her heart increased. "But you haven't really answered my question."

She smiled and leaned up to kiss his cheek. "I'll be happy with whatever name or title you choose. I love *you*, Taron. Not your name."

He grinned back at her then stood, placing a sleeping Jack in her crib. Turning, he grabbed Alyssa's hand and pulled her into his arms. "You're in for a rough life, Lady Alyssa," he said with a smile.

"Rough, huh?" She wrapped her arms around his waist and tilted her head back to meet his loving gaze.

"Oh, yes. It's widely known that being spoiled by a Marcone man is very rough indeed."

"Oooh, I'm shaking in my shoes," she whispered.

"You will be," he murmured against her mouth, then licked at her lower lip.

She grinned and pressed her breasts against his chest. He moaned in response and nipped at her upper lip, making her giggle. "Maybe if you spanked me, then I might be scared."

Taron's full lips spread into a sexy smile as his hand skimmed lower and slapped at her ass. Not hard, but it still stung through the thin material of her slacks, making her shiver from head to toe. She backed away from him seductively and grabbed his hand, pulling him along with her to their room.

His gaze fell to her neck and he stopped, his fingers reaching out to finger the gold latch that hung from her slave collar. "What's this?" he asked.

She shrugged and could feel the heat of a blush moving up her cheeks. "It's become a sentimental thing, I think. I enjoyed being your slave most of the time."

He smiled tenderly and moved to brush the backs of his fingers along her cheek. "You have it all wrong, *ni pahti*. I've always been the slave to you."

Why an electronic book?

We live in the Information Age—an exciting time in the history of human civilization, in which technology rules supreme and continues to progress in leaps and bounds every minute of every day. For a multitude of reasons, more and more avid literary fans are opting to purchase e-books instead of paper books. The question from those not yet initiated into the world of electronic reading is simply: *Why?*

1. ***Price.*** An electronic title at Ellora's Cave Publishing and Cerridwen Press runs anywhere from 40% to 75% less than the cover price of the exact same title in paperback format. Why? Basic mathematics and cost. It is less expensive to publish an e-book (no paper and printing, no warehousing and shipping) than it is to publish a paperback, so the savings are passed along to the consumer.
2. ***Space.*** Running out of room in your house for your books? That is one worry you will never have with electronic books. For a low one-time cost, you can purchase a handheld device specifically designed for e-reading. Many e-readers have large, convenient screens for viewing. Better yet, hundreds of titles can be stored within your new library—on a single microchip. There are a variety of e-readers from different manufacturers. You can also read e-books on your PC or laptop computer. (Please note that Ellora's Cave does not endorse any specific brands.

You can check our websites at www.ellorascave.com or www.cerridwenpress.com for information we make available to new consumers.)

3. ***Mobility.*** Because your new e-library consists of only a microchip within a small, easily transportable e-reader, your entire cache of books can be taken with you wherever you go.
4. ***Personal Viewing Preferences.*** Are the words you are currently reading too small? Too large? Too... ANNOYING? Paperback books cannot be modified according to personal preferences, but e-books can.
5. ***Instant Gratification.*** Is it the middle of the night and all the bookstores near you are closed? Are you tired of waiting days, sometimes weeks, for bookstores to ship the novels you bought? Ellora's Cave Publishing sells instantaneous downloads twenty-four hours a day, seven days a week, every day of the year. Our webstore is never closed. Our e-book delivery system is 100% automated, meaning your order is filled as soon as you pay for it.

Those are a few of the top reasons why electronic books are replacing paperbacks for many avid readers.

As always, Ellora's Cave and Cerridwen Press welcome your questions and comments. We invite you to email us at Comments@ellorascave.com or write to us directly at Ellora's Cave Publishing Inc., 1056 Home Avenue, Akron, OH 44310-3502.

Cerridwen, the Celtic Goddess of wisdom, was the muse who brought inspiration to storytellers and those in the creative arts. Cerridwen Press encompasses the best and most innovative stories in all genres of today's fiction. Visit our site and discover the newest titles by talented authors who still get inspired - much like the ancient storytellers did, once upon a time.

Ellora's Cave
Romantica Publishing